Tor Books by Neal Asher
from Tom Doherty Associates

Gridlinked

The Skinner

THE SKINNER

Neal Asher

TOR®

A TOM DOHERTY ASSOCIATES BOOK
NEW YORK

THE SKINNER

Copyright © 2002 by Neal Asher

First published in Great Britain by Macmillian, an imprint of Pan Macmillian Ltd.

A Tor Book
Published by Tom Doherty Associates, LLC
175 Fifth Avenue
New York, NY 10010

www.tor.com

Tor® is a registered trademark of Tom Doherty Associates, LLC.

ISBN 0-765-35048-3
EAN 978-0765-35048-3

First edition: May 2004
First mass market edition: May 2005

Printed in the United States of America

0 9 8 7 6 5 4 3 2 1

For Caroline – now in a real book.

Acknowledgements

Thanks to all those excellent people whose names stretch through the alphabet from Aldiss to Zelazny, and who have kept me spellbound for most of my life. All their names are too numerous to list here, but they have been a continuous source of pleasure to me and a huge influence on what you find between these covers. Also my thanks to the wonderful people at Pan Macmillan for their hard and meticulous work.

1

In any living sea on any world there are always creatures whose fate is integral to the gastronomic delight of other . . . creatures. Boxies might more correctly be described as lunch-boxes, such was the purpose they served in the sea—and they knew it. Feeding upon occasional shoals of vicious plankton—which would make the experience of swimming for a human akin to bathing in ground glass—and the dispersing remains of those many other creatures which, at some point, always served as an entrée, the boxies swam at high speed and with a kind of nervous determination. Only by keeping moving like this could they reduce the frequency of leech attacks on their nerveless outer bodies. Only swift movement kept them from the sickle-legs of prill and the serrated claws of glisters, or from the mouths of larger leeches, which would swallow them down whole. However, a successful survival strategy for a species was not always so successful for all of its individuals: a boxy shoal increased with each addition of fry from each hatching of eggs laid on the stalks of sea-cane and decreased with each attack upon it by a hungry predator, and therefore old age was not a common cause of death in it.

The reif sipped at his clear drink through a glass straw and seemed to have his attention focused beyond his companion, at somewhere in the middle of the opposite wall. Erlin supposed he must be drinking one of the many chemical preservatives he used to prevent his flesh falling from his bones. The man who had just joined the reif sat with his back to Erlin, who now noticed that he had something on his shoulder. When this something took off to do a circuit of the room, she was fascinated. It was an insect as large as a severed thumb and the drone of its wings was loud in the subdued atmosphere of the shuttle lounge. The man was obviously indentured to a Hive mind, for the flying creature had to be a hornet from Earth—the eyes of a Hive mind. What the hell could bring a reif and such a man here, together? Erlin picked up her coffee and began walking across to them, till a thickening of the air and a vague feeling of disorientation made her pause.

From taking one step to another, Erlin realized that the safety field had tripped: a rough entry into atmosphere. But then, in her experience, things got steadily rougher from now on. She glanced to the windows that slanted out at forty-five degrees from the outer edge of the lounge. The shuttle was now circling above the honeycomb which was the Polity base on the island of Chel, and she observed how the sea surrounded the island in concentric rings of varying shades of green, as of split agate. The sea was calm down there, so what had tripped the safety field must be one of the many storms that ripped through the thick upper layers of cloud. Finally reaching their table, she turned her attention fully on the seated pair.

'Mind if I join you?' she asked.

There was little discernible reaction from the reif, but the man grinned at her and gestured to an empty seat. He wasn't bad-looking, Erlin thought, and his manner was pleasant, but he was not *the* man. *Her* man was somewhere down on the sea below. She placed her coffee on the table, then pulled out the seat, turned it, and sat astride it with her forearms resting across its back.

'I'm curious to know why a reification should want to come here, and why someone indentured to a Hive mind,' Erlin noticed the man frown, 'should come here also.' She looked with interest at each of them in turn, then glanced at the other passengers occupying the lander's lounge. It was clear that fear or disgust had cleared a wide space around the reif and his companion, and embarrassment had cast a pall over general conversation. Many of them were now trying very hard to appear not to be listening. Erlin shook her head as she focused her attention on the reif. He was no cause for disgust. He didn't stink, as reifs were popularly believed to, nor was he any cause for fear—some of the augmented types here in the lander could have torn him limb from limb. But to Erlin he was a source of almost painful interest. What purpose had driven this man to want to continue functioning after his own death?

'I am *not* indentured,' said the reif's companion, then took up his drink from the table before him and sipped.

Erlin turned to study him. 'What?' she asked

'I'm *not* indentured,' he repeated succinctly, putting down his drink.

'Oh, I see,' said Erlin, inspecting him.

He wore jeans tucked into the hard-wearing boots of an environment suit, and a loose cloth shirt, which was open at the neck to expose a Maori tiki charm. There was no visible sign of augmentation on him, but that did not mean he was without it. Below unruly blond hair, his features were handsome and hawkish, and Erlin thought it likely he'd had his face restructured in the past, but long in the past, because character now showed through and had softened the aseptic beauty of the cosmetic job. In his left ear, he wore a single diamond stud—which was probably his Hive link transponder.

'*Were* you indentured?' she asked him.

'Two years,' he replied. 'And those ended about twenty years ago.'

'Two years . . . that's the usual sentence for killing a hornet, isn't it?' said Erlin.

The man nodded and grinned, before reaching for his drink again. Erlin observed him for a moment longer, then curiosity drew her attention back to the man's companion.

The reification was clad in a utile monofilament overall of bland grey, and he had a smooth lozenge of metal hanging from a chain around his neck. He had obviously been a heavy-worlder when alive. Now his muscles were stringy on his thick skeleton, his hands bony claws, and what was visible of his face, under a half-helmet augmentation, was that of a grey mummy. Erlin next studied the aug: it was golden, had a cartouche inset into its surface, and had, extending from the inner side of it and curving round under the reif's one visible eye, an irrigator fashioned in the shape of a cobra with its hood spread. The reif's eye was blue, and it seemed to be the only part of him that was remotely alive.

Of course, she could see now what might have brought these two people together: the fear and disgust of the others here. Most people had yet to dispel their atavistic fear of large stinging insects, and most did not like to share the company of corpses, no matter how interesting the conversation might prove to be. More than anything else in any world, Erlin wanted something to maintain her interest. She wondered just what stories there might be here.

The reif dropped his glass straw back into his drink and, with slow precision, he leant back. As he turned his blue eye upon her now, Erlin imagined she could hear the creaking of his neck. There came a clicking gulp from deep in his throat, then he spoke in a surprisingly mild baritone, his words slightly out of sync with the movement of his mouth. But then, Erlin thought it unlikely that his vocal cords actually generated his voice.

'Many would seek immortality here,' he said, and deliberately tilted his head to peer at the circular blue scar on Erlin's forearm. It was an easy conversational gambit to turn attention away from himself. Erlin pretended no reaction to his words, but suddenly felt very hot and uncomfortable. The secret of Spatterjay had been out for many years, and immortality was a commodity in a buyer's market. Why did she feel guilty?

'Many would find it and wish they hadn't,' said Erlin. Just then, the hornet droned back from across the room and Erlin could not help but notice how the other passengers flinched away from it, then tried to appear as if they had not. There was much nervous laughter in its wake. As it settled again on the man's shoulder he merely glanced at it, then reached into the top pocket of his shirt and removed a small vial. From this he tipped a puddle of syrup on to the tabletop. The insect launched from his shoulder to the table, where it landed with a noticeable rattle, then it walked stiff-legged to the puddle to sip. Erlin saw that the creature's thorax was painted with luminous intricate lines, as of a circuit diagram.

They must mean something to someone—but not necessarily anyone human. On the table also lay a shoulder carry-case for hornets. Inside the case was another hornet, still as if sealed in clear liquid plastic.

After a brief silence the man said, 'There's a place, you know, where people live in the bodies of giant snails which float in the sky suspended from gas-filled shells.'

Erlin absorbed the comment with almost a feeling of delight. At the sound of the next clicking gulp, she turned back to the reification.

The reif said, 'On Tornos Nine, people live under the sea in giant mechanical lobsters. It's all for tourism, really. Every lobster contains its own hotel and restaurant. There are few private lobsters.'

The man laughed. Erlin switched her gaze between the two of them. She wondered if the reif would have smiled, if he could. She replied, 'On the ships here you have to wait for your mainsail to fly to you and take the mainmast. Through the mechanisms of the ship, it controls the fore and aft sails, and all you have to do is feed it. Every sail has the same name.'

The reif finally lifted the gaze of his one watery eye from its study of her scar.

'What name is that?' he asked.

'Windcatcher.'

'You have been here before,' he said. It wasn't a question.

'You know that.'

'So have I, a very long time ago.'

With a deprecatory grin the man said, 'I've never been here before.' He held out his hand. 'Janer.'

Erlin clasped the hand he offered.

'Erlin,' she said.

Janer nodded and smiled, and only reluctantly released her hand.

'You'll have to excuse me for a moment. I just want to see this.'

He stood and moved over to the slanting window, to watch as the shuttle finally came in to land. Erlin turned expectantly to the reif.

There was no clicking gulp this time before he spoke. 'Keech,' he said, and did not offer his hand, which, considering his condition, Erlin felt was only polite.

The hornet watched and listened.

'Land is at a premium here,' said Erlin as the three of them later walked down the shuttle ramp to a curved walkway running parallel to a parking area around the edge of the landing pad. She felt buoyant now, though that was probably due to the higher oxygen content in the air and the lower gravity she had felt immediately on stepping from the shuttle's gravplates. She scanned these distantly familiar surroundings. The sea made a continual sucking hiss underneath the huge floating structure upon which the gun-metal wing of the shuttle had settled, and the air was thick with the smells of cooling metal, decaying seaweed, and of virulent aquatic life.

'Just islands and atolls, no continents, and no island bigger than, say, the Galapagos islands on Earth,' said Janer.

'Yes,' said Erlin, 'and there are other similarities too, though you'll find the wildlife here somewhat . . . wilder.'

'Wilder?' Janer echoed.

Erlin grimaced. 'Well, it's not so bad on the islands,' she admitted.

'But bad in the sea?'

'Look at it this way: most Hoopers are sailors, but few of them can swim.'

'Right,' said Janer.

Rank upon rank of aircabs were parked here along the edge. Beyond them, the sea was heaving but not breaking, and underneath that surface Erlin knew the water would be writhing with leeches, hammer whelks and turbul, glisters and prill. And all of them would be hungry. She gazed up at the misty green sky and wondered at her foolishness in returning here, then she followed her two companions off the ramps, her obedient hover luggage trailing along behind.

Keech was intent on getting to the first cab before all the other passengers swarmed off the shuttle. When there came a hissing crack, followed by a stuttering as of an air compressor starting, Erlin noted how the reif snapped his head round and moved his hand to one of the many pockets of his overalls, and how Janer dropped into a semi-crouch. She studied them for a moment longer as they warily surveyed their surroundings, then they slowly relaxed.

'Over here,' she said, and led them to the rail along the seaward side of the parking area. Below this rail, the foamed-plascrete edge of the floating structure sloped steeply down into the sea. Erlin pointed to an object like a metre-long chrome mosquito that was walking along the plascrete, just above the waterline. She then pointed to a disturbance out in the water. Pieces of shell and gobbets of flesh were being pulled at and rabidly denuded by dark, unclearly seen, anguine shapes in the water.

'Autogun,' explained Keech. 'What did it hit?'

'Well, out there, probably a prill or a glister. Most of the large lethal molluscs here are not swimmers,' Erlin replied.

'Charming,' said Janer.

Keech stared for an interminable moment, but offered no further comment. Instead he turned and continued on towards the nearest aircab.

The vehicle was an old Skyrover Macrojet with a ridiculous and unnecessary airfoil attached, and its pilot was all Hooper in attitude and appearance.

'The three of yah?' he asked. He remained inside his cab as he cleaned his fingernails with a long narrow knife that Erlin recognized as a skinning knife, and she tried not to inspect too closely the memories *that* evoked.

The Hooper's skin was pale, and the circular scars on his arms and down the sides of his face were only just visible. She supposed that, like all Hoopers on the Polity base, he was on one of the Intertox family of drugs to keep the fibres of the Spatterjay virus in abeyance. Usually it was the bite of a leech that caused infection but, even though the virus could not survive for a long time outside of a body, no one was taking any chances. Polity scientists felt that, despite the so-far-discovered huge benefits of the virus, it might still be some kind of Trojan. Erlin herself had not been infected by the bite on her forearm. Like many other viruses, the Spatterjay virus could be transmitted by bodily fluids, and she knew precisely when she had contracted it.

'All three,' replied Keech to the Hooper.

The Hooper looked askance at him, then stabbed the knife into the dash of his vehicle. After a moment he transferred his attention to Janer, then to the hornets in the transparent box on Janer's shoulder.

'Can they get out?' he asked.

'Only if they want to,' said Janer.

'Look like nasty buggers.'

Erlin bit down on a burst of laughter. *That* from a Hooper on a world where just about every creature was a nasty bugger out for its plug of flesh.

'I assure you they are harmless unless forced to defend themselves,' said Janer.

The Hooper studied the hornets more closely. 'They got brains then?'

How's he going to explain the hive mind? Erlin wondered.

'They are the eyes of the hive,' said Janer.

'Oh, them . . . hornets, ain't they?'

'Yes.'

'OK, stick y' luggage in the back and climb in. Y'want the Dome?'

'Please,' said Erlin as she stood aside to allow Keech to take his hover trunk around to the back of the cab. As he moved past, she caught a slight whiff of corruption. He glanced round at her, and perhaps it was her imagination that she was able to read a look of apology in what small movement his face managed. After dumping his backpack on top of Keech's trunk, Janer went forward and quickly climbed into the front beside the driver. Erlin gazed around before stowing her own hover luggage. She was here now, and she would carry on through with her intention, though sometimes she felt simply like . . . stopping.

'Erlin Tazer Three Indomial,' said Keech as the aircab rose and boosted over the pontoons and floating pads of the shuttle port.

Janer glanced over his shoulder. 'I thought you looked familiar. You're the one who opened that particular box of . . . leeches.' He shrugged at his little joke.

The hornets, Erlin saw, scuttled about in their carry-case and moved tail to tail so as to take in every view.

Janer peered down at them in annoyance, then gazed ahead through the screen at the winged shapes that glided in the haze over the island, like embers in jade smoke. He went on, 'There was quite an uproar after your studies were published and, as I recollect, the Warden here had to limit runcible transmissions. Big rush to come and live for ever.'

'Big rush for an easier option, but there never is one of those,' said Erlin. 'Our technology can extend life indefinitely, but even now there are . . . drawbacks. The rush of people here was of those searching for something beyond life extension. They were searching for miracles.' She noted how Keech, at the word 'miracle', reached up to rest his skeletal fingers against the lozenge resting on his chest. Perhaps it had some religious significance.

'How does it operate here, then?' Janer asked.

'The bare facts?' Erlin asked, sensing the man had more than an intellectual interest in the subject. He nodded and she went on, 'The viral fibres bind every life form here . . . They're the leeches' way of maintaining their food supply. They are very efficient parasites, though it can be argued that what happens here is a perfect example of mutualism. Nothing dies unless severely injured, and I mean *severely*.'

'It is . . . logical,' said Keech.

Erlin had to agree.

'Surely the death of the prey is preferable?' said Janer, puzzled.

'No,' Erlin told him. 'Isn't it preferable for the leeches to be able to harvest their meat and keep the prey alive to be harvested again? Though they don't suck blood, the leeches are aptly named.'

'Why've you come back?' Janer asked.

'Just looking for someone: a Captain I knew. We have unfinished business.'

The Hooper turned and gave her a strange look but said

nothing. The Captains were the weirdest Hoopers of them all.

'Why are *you* here?' Erlin asked Keech. The reif did not react for a moment, then he slowly shook his head. Erlin waited a little longer, then returned her attention to Janer as he now turned to inspect her over the back of his seat. She knew that look.

'What about you?' she asked.

'I go where the mind directs. The ultimate tourist.' He grinned.

'No resentment?' she asked.

'Once—but only at the beginning.'

Erlin nodded. 'You said you'd served out your indenture twenty years ago?' She was curious: once people indentured to a Hive mind had served out their time, they were usually grateful to be rid of their little companions, particularly as those who made the mistake of killing a hornet usually possessed some deep-rooted aversion to the insects. Hive minds also had a reputation for sending their human servants into some really sticky situations.

'Why carry on?' she asked.

'Adventure. Money. In the last twenty years I've not often been bored, Erlin.'

She studied him more closely. He had originally struck her as being rather naive, perhaps not even out of his first century. She decided to reassess that judgement. Once, disease and accident had been the greatest killers of humankind; now the greatest killer was boredom, usually leading to the latter of the first two causes. Perhaps Janer was much older than she had first thought; perhaps he had the same problem as herself.

'Erlin?' said the Hooper abruptly, the content of the conversation apparently only just penetrating. 'Thought so . . . It's the skin.'

Erlin smiled to herself at a remembered conversation aboard a Hooper sailing vessel called the *Treader*. Peck, the 180-year-old mechanic, had been attacked by a leech and it had unscrewed a fist-sized lump of flesh from his leg—a lump of flesh he had, after beating the leech to pulp, subse-

quently screwed back into place. The wound had healed in
minutes.

'*Doesn't that strike you as a little odd?*' Erlin had asked
him.

'*Who you callin' odd? At least I ain't got skin the colour
of burnt sugar. Bleedin' Earthers, always callin' us odd.*'

Peck had been very odd after his second . . . accident, but
Erlin, even now, didn't like to think about that too much—
and wasn't even sure she believed it had really happened.

'Do you know Ambel?' Erlin asked the Hooper.

'Who don't?' was his reply.

With a complicated manipulation of the airfoils, he put
the aircab into a spiralling glide. The three passengers gazed
down at the long, partially artificial island below them.
Around the much larger central geodesic dome of the Polity
base clustered many smaller ones—as if the island had been
blowing bubbles in the sea. There were also a few smaller
ones at the centre of the island's widest stretch: transparent
spheres dropped into the deep dingle that grew there. Erlin
could just make out the groves of peartrunk trees speared
with the occasional tall yanwood, and she reflexively rubbed
at the scar on her forearm. A leech dropping from a
peartrunk tree had been her first close encounter with the appetite of Spatterjay life forms. Later, Ambel had saved her
from the persistent attentions of a creature innocuously
called a frog whelk. Without his intervention, it would have
taken her hand off. She gazed across the wide sea, remembering that other island where, if she could believe Ambel,
the body of something which had once been a man was living an independent existence. It would apparently live well
enough, but would have no intelligence. Ambel kept the
Skinner's head in a box.

'The gating facility was closed, down here,' said Keech.

'Heat pollution,' Erlin told him. 'The Warden had it
moved to Coram after an explosion in the hammer-whelk
population around the deepwater heat sinks.' She also remembered that Coram, the moon they had so recently quit,
by shuttle, had been named by the runcible AI—an artificial
intelligence which was also the planetary Warden. 'Coram'

was actually short for 'coram judice', which, it turned out, meant 'in the presence of the judge' in some ancient Earth language. It was a name she supposed indicative of Warden's opinion of itself.

'They had a gate here, then?' said Janer distractedly.

'It was established on-planet when the Polity arrived here. They had it here for about fifty solstan years before moving it. That was two hundred solstan years ago,' she replied.

In the roof of one of the largest dome, a hatch irised open and the Hooper brought his cab down through it. Earth light illuminated the inside, stark in contrast to the soft green light of Spatterjay. Forests and crops grew in neat patterns around a small city of processing plants and a single sprawling arcology like a giant plascrete fungus seemingly nailed to the ground by gleaming hotel towers. 'Dome-grown food' the Hoopers called what was produced in the fields here. It was what, if they did not have access to Intertox, stopped them becoming more like the Skinner.

With a cycling down drone of thrusters, the Hooper landed his aircab on a neatly mown lawn, near the edge of the arcology, and the three disembarked.

'How much?' Erlin asked, leaning to the open window.

The Hooper paused for a moment as he calculated how much he might get away with asking for. Erlin groped in the pocket of her jacket and pulled out a wad of New Carth shillings. The two notes she proffered he quickly took and, obviously pleased, he got out of his cab to unload their luggage. Janer appeared bemused and Keech, of course, had no expression at all. Erlin understood that the both of them hadn't realized they might need hard currency. She felt they had a lot to learn about this place, and was about to comment on this when Janer beat her to it.

'Perhaps we need a little guidance here,' he said, glancing at the reif. Keech showed no reaction to this either. Erlin was quick to reply; she had nothing to lose by being helpful.

'I have to do what I have to do here, but you're more than welcome to accompany me until you find your feet,' she said, turning to study them. Keech gave a brief nod in reply and

Janer grinned at her. Feeling slightly uncomfortable, she turned away from that grin.

'You know that Polity law does not apply outside the main dome,' she said.

'It should do,' said Keech.

'Sometimes,' added Janer.

Erlin continued, 'Try defining assault or murder to a Hooper. They just laugh at all our rules. The way it works here is that the older a Hooper is, the more authority he has. This by dint of the fact that he knows so much more than you and that if you disagree with him he could probably tear your arms off. Ambel, the man I've come here to find, is old. I once saw him tow a deep-sea-fishing ship with just a rowing boat. His boat was specially strengthened, and the oars made of ceramal composite.'

'How old *is* he?' asked Keech.

'Seven centuries, minimum. He said he came here just after the war, but I wonder about that. Some of the early Hoopers are reticent about their pasts, and the viral fibres were very advanced in him.'

'Yeah,' said Janer, grinning. 'I've heard plenty of stories like that.'

Not looking at him, Erlin went on, 'His skin is mottled with leech scars overlaid one on the other. He's so packed with fibre it's impossible to take blood samples from him. I frankly doubt he even has any blood inside him. If ever he's wounded, the wounds close just like that.' She held up her hand and snapped it shut into a fist.

'You believe him?' asked Janer.

'At first I didn't, but I was with him for a number of years and I eventually ceased to doubt.'

'Perhaps . . . Hoop is still alive?' said Keech.

Erlin thought about the head kept in a box on the *Treader* and refrained from comment.

'That's it then,' said the Hooper, standing next to their pile of luggage.

'Thank you,' said Erlin. She clicked her fingers and her hover trunk separated itself out from the pile of luggage and moved obediently to her side. It had surprised her that Janer used merely a backpack, but now she realized he must be a seasoned traveller and so only carried a few essentials. Keech, however, could not possibly have carried his trunk very far, it being the size of a sea-chest.

'Luck,' said the Hooper, climbing back into his cab.

'Wait.' Erlin turned back to him and he paused at the door. 'Do you know where I can find Ambel?'

'On the *Treader*.'

'Where is the *Treader*?'

The Hooper shrugged. 'Nort Sea and the Skinner's Islands. Sou' at the atolls. East in the Sargassum or West over the Blue Wells. Buggered if I know.'

It was not the answer Erlin would have liked but it was the kind she expected of a Hooper.

'Thanks for you help,' she said dryly.

'This Ambel,' said Janer as the cab rose into the air above them and tilted towards the hole in the Dome, 'something more than clinical interest?'

'You could say that,' said Erlin. 'We go this way now.'

She led them down paved walkways from the lawns, through neatly laid-out rose gardens, towards the looming metallic wall of the arcology. Daffodils bloomed in bunches, neatly circumnavigated by robot mowers that munched their way across the grass like iron beetles. Some of these flowers were old-Earth yellow, but the rest were blue and violet. Ahead, wide arcades and boulevards cut into the wall of the arcology, and here there were more gardens and lawns, from which sprang coconut and fishtail palms, fuchsia bushes and the occasional pineapple plant—this diversity of life, as Erlin well knew, genetically adapted to survive the odd conditions inside the Dome.

'I thought you said land was at a premium here,' said Janer, scanning about himself.

'It is,' Erlin replied. 'All of this,' she gestured ahead of them, 'is sitting on ten metres of foamed plascrete, which in turn is sitting on a thousand metres of seawater.'

'Ah,' said Janer then, 'busy little raft they have here.'

Amongst these gardens strolled all manner of people: seasoned travellers who lived only to use the runcibles and briefly see new worlds; altered humans—catadapts and ophids and the like; and Hoopers nervous in these garden surroundings, with the rolling gait of those more used to having a deck under their feet.

Erlin said, 'A lot of the people who come to see this world get no farther than this. Many come here not realizing that Polity law doesn't extend outside the Dome itself. They come here for the immortality you mentioned, and discover that they feel very mortal once they step out into the Hooper's world.'

'*You* did,' Keech reminded her.

'I like new worlds, new experiences. You gain nothing without risking something.'

'Trite,' said Keech. 'There should always be law.'

Erlin glanced at him as they moved into one of the boulevards, and then she gestured to a pyramidal metrotel entrance situated near the end of it.

'I'm staying here for tonight. Unless you have other plans, I suggest you stay here as well. Tomorrow, if you like, we can get equipped. It would be a good idea if you both bought some hard currency, as you won't get far here without it.'

'Which is preferred?' asked Keech.

'New Carth shillings or New yen. Don't bother with the Spatterjay skind—the exchange rate for it goes up every day.'

'How quaint,' said Janer.

Once they had entered the pyramidal metrotel Janer insisted on paying for all their rooms, by smart card at the automated check-in desk. Erlin reached down to her hover trunk and, into its miniconsole, punched one of the room codes the screen showed them—slaving the trunk to the hotel AI. For a moment she watched while it trundled off, then she checked her watch.

'Down here at about nine, then, solstan?' she suggested.

'Definitely,' replied Janer, and Keech gave his characteristic sharp nod.

Without further pause, Erlin headed for the room the hotel AI had allocated her.

'Don't forget that currency,' she said, glancing over her

shoulder. As she entered a lift, she wondered what had possessed her to take up with these two. Loneliness, maybe?
When she reached the entrance to her room, her trunk was
there ahead of her. She followed it in through the door, then
slumped on to the large bed provided. Tucking her hands behind her head, she stared at the ceiling and said, 'AI, I'd like
some information about reifications'.

'Can you be more specific than that?' the hotel AI asked
her.

'Well . . . didn't the practice originate from some sort of
religious sect?'

'It originated from the Cult of Anubis Arisen. It was their
conjecture that souls do not exist, and that there is nothing
more sacred than the body. They hung on to life for as long
as they possibly could then, when they died, had themselves
preserved and kept moving by use of the cyber technology
of the time.'

Erlin recalled the decidedly Egyptian design of Keech's
aug and eye irrigator. 'They were brain-dead though, and
Keech is sentient,' she said.

There came no reply then from the AI, as its privacy restraints had cut in. It could not discuss other hotel guests
with her.

'Reifs nowadays are often sentient—to all intents alive,'
she persisted.

'The cult of Anubis Arisen is still extant, and now has access to mind-recording and mimetic computers. Some of
those who have been technically dead can be repaired and
brought to life using some of the newer nano-technologies.'

'With those mind recordings and mimetics . . . are they
alive?'

'The contention of most is that they have become AI. The
lines become blurred and the arguments heated when reifs
with partial use of their organic brains are discussed. On the
whole, reifs are uncommon. Most physical damage to human beings can be repaired, and most humans with mind-
recorders choose memplantation in an android chassis.'

'How do you explain Keech then?'

The AI didn't.

* * *

Once alone in his room, Keech opened his trunk and removed a clean pair of monofilament overalls, which he laid
across his bed. Almost reverently, he removed his lozenge
pendant and placed it on top of them. Then, moving with
great care, he took off his used overalls and dropped them
on the floor, before turning to a mirror on the nearby wall
and inspecting his grey and golden reflection. As well as the
half-helmet augmentation over his face, an area from under
his armpit to his waist and then his groin was also enclosed
in golden metal. This metal was deeply intagliated with
Egyptian hieroglyphs. He stood perfectly still as he studied
them, until his irrigator sprayed his right eye. He did not
blink, but turned back to the trunk. Now he removed a
golden case made in the shape of a small sarcophagus,
closed the lid of the trunk, and placed the case upon it. In the
surface of this case was an indentation ideal for accommodating the lozenge he had placed on the bed. He ignored this,
though, and instead freed two nozzles, which came away
trailing coiled tails of clear tubing. These nozzles he
plugged into two sockets in the metal covering his side.
Through his aug, he sent the activation signal to this device
that really kept him from rotting away: his cleansing unit.

One of the coiled tubes turned dirty blue as the unit drew
preservative fluid from his vascular system, filtered out a
sludge of dead bacteria and rotifers, corrected certain chemical imbalances, then pumped the fluid back into him. The
fluid in the return pipe was liquid sapphire. After a few minutes, a row of red-lit hieroglyphs on the unit began, one at a
time, to flick to green. When the last glyph changed, the
tubes cleared of liquid and he detached them and returned
them to the unit itself. Next, he turned a disk on the unit and
withdrew a cylindrical container filled with the same blue
fluid. He turned to the mirror again and, using a swab that
detached from the head of the container, he wiped himself
from head to foot, at the last partially detaching his aug to
swab at the skin concealed underneath. The now exposed
left half of his face was ruin eaten back to bone, and set into
that bone was a ring of triangular copper-coloured contacts.

Keech stared for a moment at the wound that had killed him before snicking his aug back into place with a wet click, then reaching down to press some pads on the metal enclosing his side. This shell lifted with a slight hiss and he detached it completely and put it on top of his trunk. The side of his body now exposed was mostly transparent synthetic skin under which could be seen organs repaired with synthetics, a network of blue tubes spreading from the two nozzle orifices, and rib bones that had been burnt black. After a brief visual inspection, he swabbed this area down too. When he had finished, he replaced the metal shell, then returned to the bed to don the clean overalls and his lozenge pendant. After yet another inspection of himself in the mirror, there sounded that dry click from his throat, and he spoke.

'Hotel AI, I wish to take a sum of a thousand New Carth shillings from my account, in hard currency. Do you have this facility?'

'I do,' replied the hotel. 'There is an auto till in the wall to your left. You are aware that a thousand shillings may be much more than you will require here. The exchange rate against the Spatterjay skind is very high.'

'I am aware,' said Keech, 'but I may be here some time.' He took a smart card from his pocket and inserted it into the slot in the wall. A hatch immediately slid open and the auto till poked his card back out at him. Behind the hatch rested a stack of hundred-, fifty- and ten-shilling notes. There was also a cloth bag containing coins. He opened this and took out one transparent octagonal coin, which he brought up to his eye. In an approximation of surprise, he raised the brow of this eye. He hadn't seen one-shilling pieces in a very long time—centuries in fact.

Janer lay back on his bed with hands folded comfortably behind his head. He thought about Erlin and felt a vaguely pleasurable buzz at the prospect of getting to know her. She was classically and strangely beautiful, with her white hair, black skin, and blue eyes, yet Janer felt sure her appearance was not due to cosmetic alteration. These combined features were too much at odds with each other to be anyone's natural choice. In his experience cosmetic alteration fell into two camps: the extreme where people went all the way into something like catadaption or ophidaption, or the subtle one, where they just had some small alteration made to their appearance to make it more pleasing. More likely, he suspected, her appearance was the result of a past genetic alteration in her family line, as no doubt was her intelligence. This was how it was for most people now. He closed his eyes and summoned up an image of her to contemplate. This didn't last though, and his mind began to wander.

Nothing from the link at the moment—which meant that the Hive mind was preoccupied. That was good, as he didn't feel much like talking. There had been no communication from it for a number of hours now, but that was nothing unusual. The mind controlled a huge conjoined hive of something like a billion individuals, so it had plenty of other tasks on which to focus its attention. Janer considered how things had changed since the days of paper nests and maybe just a few hundred hornets.

Back then it had come as one shock in many when arrogant humanity had discovered it wasn't the only sentient race on Earth. It was just the loudest and most destructive. Dolphins and whales had always been candidates because of their aesthetic appeal and cute stories of rescued swimmers. Research in that area had soon cleared things up: dolphins couldn't tell the difference between a human swimmer and a sick fellow dolphin, and were substantially more stupid than the farm animal humans had been turning into bacon on a regular basis. As for whales, they had the intelligence of the average cow. When a hornet had first built its nest in a VR suit and lodged its protests on the Internet, it had taken a long time for anyone to believe what was happening. They were stinging things, creepy-crawlies, so how could they possibly be intelligent? At ten thousand years of age, the youngest Hive mind eventually showed them. The subsequent investigation had proven, beyond doubt, that groups of

nests thought as a single mind, not with the speed of
synapses, but with the speed of slow pheromonal transfer.
The nest in the VR suit had been linked, at that rate, to many
other nests. It had communicated using the anosmic recep-
tors inside the suit, and this had taken it many months. Now,
every hornet carried a micro-transmitter, and the speed of
Hive mind thought had become very fast indeed.

Of course, immediately after this revelation, there had
been a scramble to find more of the like, and all the other social insects of Earth were intensively studied. Disappointment after disappointment finally brought home the fact that
hornets, like humans, were a bit of an oddity. The only social
insects that came close to them were the wasps, but they
came in at the level of a chimpanzee as compared to a human. Bees, it turned out, did have Hive minds, but they were
alien beyond the interpretation of the most powerful computers; their communication was limited to the 'now'—the
concepts of past and future being beyond them. Ants had no
Hive minds at all.

Janer considered how he himself had been plunged into
this strange world: his payment—his service to this mind—
for killing a hornet that had tried to settle on his shoulder in
a crowded ringball stadium. It had been tired, that hornet,
searching for somewhere to land and take a rest, tempted by
the beaker of Coke Janer had been drinking. His reaction
had been instinctive; the phobic horror of insects had risen
up inside him and he had knocked the hornet to the ground
and stamped on it. The court judgement had come through
the following day, and not having the funds to pay a fine, he
had signed up for two years' indenture. Killing a hornet was
not precisely murder, as each creature was just one very
small part of the mind. There were stiff penalties, though.

Janer sat up, swung his legs off the bed, then stood and
moved over to the window of his room. The view was a
mildly interesting one, between tower blocks and across
crop fields and hydroponics houses, towards the wall of the
Dome. It wasn't the view he wanted, though. Now he wanted
to see *outside* the Dome, now he wanted something of more
interest. In his two years of being indentured, there had been

no shortage of that, and it was the main reason he had gone directly from indenture-ship to paid service for this particular Hive mind.

'What's out there?' he asked.

When there came no response from his Hive link, he shrugged and returned to his bed. He knew something about what lay beyond the Dome itself, and anything else there was to know he would find out soon enough.

2

The others, clustering like sheep on the small islet, fed by leaping into the sea and sinking through passing shoals of boxies, snapping up one or two of the creatures during the descent, but that was not enough for this particular whelk. Perhaps more intelligent and adventurous than its fellows, it had found an excellent feeding-ground some distance from the islet. Here opposing faces of rock walled a passage through an undersea ridge, and the whelk had learnt that at certain times this passage swarmed with shoals of boxies. It did not know anything about tides or how it was that, when the moon was not in the sky, the apex of the ridge broke the surface so it acted as a barrier to the eternal migration of the strange little fish. Nor did it understand that the passage was the only way through the ridge. All it did know was that if it waited for long enough on one of the rock faces, there would be a cornucopia of mobile dinners just about when it was beginning to feel hungry again. It also found that by leaping from face to face through passing shoals, it could gobble up many more boxies—before it reached the bottom—than by simply falling through a shoal. Of course there is no such thing as a free lunch—someone is keeping a tab. The whelk grew faster than its own shell, and soon its tender pink body was bulging out around the lid-like clypeus that had otherwise kept it safe. A

small leech, which had also discovered the bounty of the
passing boxy shoals, eventually dropped on to the dispeptic
whelk, wound around its shell and, extruding mouthparts like
the head of a rock drill, reamed in through tender flesh and
fed.

Ambel had nightmares of a sea of shifting leeches, and
dreams of a thousand years of better days. The wind from
Deep-sea bulged the sail, and the sail was content with the
lumps of rhinoworm it had eaten that evening. Dawn's green
light threw those lumps into silhouette, where they were being digested in the sail's transparent gut, and it brought Peck
hammering at Ambel's door.

'There's turbul coming under! Turbul coming under!'

Ambel sat upright and distinguished the distinctive thumping coming from the hull, as the shoal of turbul passed under
it, from the usual ratchet and clack of the ship's mechanisms.
In something of a daze, he gazed around his cabin and inspected the meagre requisites of his existence. His blunderbuss was secured with hide straps in one corner, next to the
cupboard containing powder, shot, and the extensive toolkit
for the weapon's maintenance. A narrow wardrobe contained
his plasmesh shirts, trousers, and reinforced boots—the only
clothing that satisfied his requirements of durability. Below
the oval brass-rimmed portal was a shelf on which he had
stuck a few ornaments with clam glue: an ancient piece of re-
entry screen polished like a gem, a miniature human skull of
faceted flint, and a cut slave collar. His gaze slid across his
desk strewn with maps held down with a satlink position-
finder fashioned in the shape of a preruncible calculator, and
came to rest on his sea-chest. So easy to accumulate so much
in the course of a long life. He stared long and hard at the
chest then gave a half-shrug as he tossed his covers back.

'Turbul!' shouted Peck again. 'Turbul!'

'One moment,' Ambel replied.

He put his feet over the side of his bunk, stood and walked
to the wardrobe to take out his neatly folded clothing. Back
at the bed, he dressed, then sat down and carefully pulled on

and laced up his boots. Standing once again, he walked to the door and carefully opened it. He had to do *everything* carefully, did Ambel. A moment's inattention could have him inadvertently ripping off someone's arm or putting his elbow through the ship's hull.

Peck was hopping from foot to foot in his excitement to get back to the lines. He had a piece of rhinoworm in one hand and bait-plug cutter in the other. Purple blood was dribbling from the meat and in his agitation he was spattering his long hide coat, canvas trousers, and the surrounding woodwork. Ambel gestured for him to get on. Peck eagerly nodded his bald head, a crazy look in his greenish eyes, and then he turned back to his fellow crewmen on the deck. Here there was much yelling and swearing, and there were many heavy wet creatures thrashing about. Ambel looked past Peck just as Pland hauled in a turbul the size of a canoe and leapt on top of it to stop it from flicking itself over the side again. The turbul was much the shape of a canoe, in fact. Its head was the head of a caiman, and all around its dark green body, bright blue fins seemed to have been scattered at random. Its tail was a whip ending in a fin that resembled a hatchet.

'Yahoo!' yelled Pland as the turbul bucked underneath him and tried to throw him off, then, 'Keep still, yer bugger.' He was indifferent to the wide gash the turbul had opened in his back with the lashing of its tail. Ambel stepped over and caught hold of the turbul's snapping jaws in one hand, then with his other hand reached over and flicked it firmly between the eyes with his forefinger. There was a dull thud as of an iron bar hitting a log. The turbul's eyes crossed and its body went limp.

'Thank you, Captain,' said Pland as he dismounted. 'Reckon you can pull this'n. He's a bit big for me.'

Ambel shrugged, took a firmer grip on the turbul's jaws with his right hand and put his left hand on the flesh behind its head. He pulled, and with a ripping sound the head pulled out of its socket with the spine following. As he continued to pull, the tail and fins drew into the turbul's body, finally to disappear. When Ambel repositioned his grip halfway down

the turbul's spine for one last heave, the creature's flesh
came off like an old sock, leaving him holding a straggly
mess of head, spine, a baggy sack of internal organs, and the
fins and tail—all still joined. He held this up in front of himself for a moment and gave it a couple of shakes. The eyes
uncrossed and the spine, fins and tail began to writhe. The
end of the tail whipped at Ambel's face but he easily caught
it.

'Naughty,' he said, then tossed the turbul over the side. In
the water the skeletal creature swam around for a moment
before sticking its head out above the surface and issuing a
noisy, snorting neighing. It then dived and swam onwards
with the rest of its shoal.

'Remember, lads, we only need enough for fifty pickle
barrels!' Ambel shouted to the rest of his crew as they hauled
in smaller turbul and pulled them similarly. One after another, stripped turbul swam away making those indignant
snorting noises. Soon the deck was scattered with slippery
tubes of meat sliding about on the acrid turbul chyme. While
baiting a gleaming hook Ambel contemplated how so very
slowly Polity technology was filtering into their lives. Ceramal hooks that never seemed to get blunt now, when he
could remember the days of carving them out of bone. At
least the bladder floats were still the same. Stepping back a
little so that he had room to cast his line out, he nearly
tripped over on a sliding turbul body.

'Anne! Barrels and vinegar!' he bellowed—but not too annoyed as he knew his crew tended to get distracted at moments like this.

Anne shot him an irritated look, reeled in her line and
hung it on a hook fixed to the rail, then called a few of the junior crew to join her. Hopping over turbul bodies, she led
them to the hatch leading to the rear hold, slid it aside then
swiftly climbed down. Two others followed her down into
the hold, and two remained on deck to swing across a winch
arm and feed the rope down.

'Reckon that's it,' said Pland, holding up his latest catch.
This turbul was long and thin, its body pocked with leech
holes. The thumping against the hull of the ship was abating

now and becoming difficult to distinguish from the clunking of the mast chains. Ambel pulled up his own latest catch, inspected it for a moment, then unhooked it and tossed it back.

'End of the main shoal now,' he said. 'Just the leech-hit.'

Peck reluctantly pulled in his own line and coiled it, then, from a locker below the rail where most of the ship's hunting gear was stored, he removed a long and lethally sharp panga. Ambel moved over to join the juniors and help them swing across the barrels Anne and the others had loaded into a cargo net. Once the net was on the deck, they rolled the empties to one side. Ambel then broke open a sealed barrel and the rich smell of spiced vinegar wafted out, almost drowning the acrid smell of turbul. Meanwhile, Peck had started cutting the turbul tubes into neat rings of flesh.

'Good run,' he said, sawing away enthusiastically.

'Good run,' agreed Ambel, taking up the lacework of rhinoworm steak, which was all that remained of their bait, and heading towards his cabin. Peck watched him go, his knuckles whitening around the handle of the panga. When he returned his attention to the turbul meat, he hacked at it savagely.

The Line, in this case, was a glassite strip set in the ground, running across under the arched exit from the Dome. Janer had a puzzled expression as he stood staring at this strip, his identification card held loosely in his hand.

'No real barrier here, nor any form of customs. All that was at the runcible installation on Coram,' said Keech.

'But what about the other side—the Spatterjay side?'

'The Hoopers don't give a shit about things like that,' said Erlin.

On the Polity side of the Line, a neatly slabbed path ran between fields of giant maize and plantations of pomegranate trees. Janer looked round at the trees, then down at the Line again. On the black earth of the Spatterjay side lay the burnt husks of this planet's equivalent of vermin: the stinking remains of some kind of bird, a spiral shell the size of a man's head, and some flat decaying remains the size of a man's leg, which had to be one of the famous leeches. Janer took this all in. He glanced up at the small laser mounted in the apex of the arch, then at the hornets in their carry-case on his shoulder.

'It's monitored,' said Erlin. 'I don't think an AI would like to end up indentured to a Hive mind, do you?'

'The mind has never viewed this world before,' said Janer. 'Its worry was not about its units crossing the Line now, with me, but about them returning across it, should the mind wish to send one back alone.'

'I would think the automatics could distinguish, but you can ask at the gate. There's sure to be one of the Warden's sub-minds in attendance.' Erlin gestured to the side of the arch as the three of them advanced. At the gate itself, Janer looked up in the air, as most people did instinctively when addressing a nonvisible AI.

'Warden, my Hive mind has expressed some reservations about your automatic bug-zapper. Will it distinguish between hornets and Spatterjay life forms?' he asked.

'Of course it will,' replied a somewhat irritated voice. 'Only humans make that mistake.'

Janer muttered something obscene and stepped out of the Polity. With her amusement barely concealed, Erlin followed him. Keech had no expression on his half face, even when the laser and attached eye swivelled to follow his progress.

Beyond the gate was a wide street lined with peak-roofed wooden buildings, many of which were shops and drinking dens. A market sprawled across the earth road, and Hoopers were enthusiastically hawking their wares to other Hoopers, and to the Polity citizens who had dared to come across the Line. Erlin gestured to a stall where wide green-glass terrariums contained the writhing and glistening shapes of leeches.

'You can buy the bite of a leech there for a few shillings. Cheap immortality you'd think, but a bit of a rip-off when all you have to do is walk into the dingle and stand under a peartrunk tree for a while.' She glanced round at Keech. 'I don't suppose it would work for you though.'

Keech clicked dryly for a moment before speaking. 'That is debatable,' he said.

'Would you try it?' asked Janer. He was giving the stall a strange look.

'To become immortal I would first have to become alive,' Keech replied.

Janer glanced round at him again and wondered what he meant by that, but of course the reif's face was unreadable. Erlin led them on.

'That's the place we want,' she said, pointing at the plate-glass window of a shop set between a bar and a cooper's establishment almost concealed behind the stacked barrels. Over the window of the middle shop was mounted a long barbed harpoon.

'Big fish they've got round here,' observed Janer.

'You could say that,' said Erlin, pausing at the shop entrance. As she pushed open the door, a dull bell clanked and two Hoopers inspecting something in a glass cabinet glanced up before turning back to each other and continuing their conversation.

'You can pay in stages, Armel,' said one. 'I'll trust y' on a ship oath.'

'I'll think 'bout it,' replied Armel, and with one last wistful glance at the case he hurried past the three newcomers and out of the shop. The shopkeeper rubbed his hands on his shirtfront before coming over to them. He grinned widely.

'Polity?' he asked.

'Yes,' said Erlin cautiously, 'but we've been here for some time.'

The man's grin lost some of its exuberance at this.

'How can I help?' he asked.

Janer surveyed the wares in the shop. In the glass case was a neat selection of projectile guns the like of which he had only ever seen in museums. Around the walls were also sharp-edged weapons of every description. There was enough armament here to equip a small medieval army.

'Stun guns and lasers,' said Erlin.

The shopkeeper's grin widened again and he gestured to the back of the shop.

'Are you sure we need this?' asked Janer.

'You saw that shell at the gate?' Erlin asked him.

'Yes . . . '

'It was the shell of a frog whelk. One of those sees you, it'll try to take a chunk out of you. It could take your hand off with one bite. Hoopers view them as amusing little pests. And there's much worse.'

From a locked cabinet the shopkeeper produced three hand weapons with belts and holsters.

'Y' can have lasers and stunners separate, but I got these,' he said.

Erlin picked up one of the weapons and inspected it dubiously. Keech stepped beside her and took up another weapon. He knocked back a slide control, opened the bottom of the handle and peered inside, then slammed it shut.

'QC laser with slow burn, wide burst . . . the lot,' he said. He glanced at Erlin. 'These'll do all you need.'

'QC?' Janer queried.

'Quantum cascade; standard solid-state,' Keech replied.

'What about stun?'

Keech tapped the stubby barrel set below—and off-centre of—the main mirrored barrel. 'Ionic burst—good for up to about five metres,' he said. 'And,' he studied the three weapons, '*I* will not be requiring one of these.'

Erlin eyed him thoughtfully for a moment before turning back to the shopkeeper.

'How much?'

'Two hundred shillings each.'

Janer thought he must have got it wrong: surely he meant two thousand shillings?

'You're a robber and a thief,' said Erlin. 'I'll give you two hundred for two of them.'

'*I'm* a thief! *I'm* a thief! One seventy-five each, with the belts and holsters.'

'Seventy-five each and I'll tell no one how you robbed us.'

'One hundred and fifty each, and for that I make no profit at all.'

'One hundred, and may the Old Captains forgive you.'

'I have a family! I have mouths to feed!'

'One hundred.'

The shopkeeper's expression was one of outrage, but that

expression swiftly disappeared when Erlin turned to leave. He caught hold of her arm and she turned back to him.

'One hundred and twenty-five and you must tell no one how you have robbed *me*,' he said.

'Agreed,' said Erlin with a smile.

Janer opened his wallet, but before he could remove any money, Keech laid one bony hand over it. 'You neglected to mention the required power cells. Does your price include them as well?' he asked.

'You are all thieves!' shouted the shopkeeper.

Keech stepped back and left the bargaining to Erlin.

With the door to his cabin firmly closed, Ambel sat on his bed and stared over at his sea-chest, the bait meat held in his right hand like a bloody hankerchief. He tilted his head as if listening to something, then shook it in annoyance, before abruptly rising and stepping across his cabin to stand before the chest itself. With his free hand he opened the lid and took out an oblong box a metre long and a third of that wide and deep. This he placed on his table then took a key for the lock from his top pocket. After unlocking the box, he returned the key to his pocket, then stepped back a bit before flipping up the lid. The thing inside did not leap out, though there were signs of movement.

It was blue and filled the box. It was a head. Once it had been a human head, but now it was so horribly enlarged, stretched out and distorted that it was difficult to recognize it as such. It was more like the head of some bastard offspring of a baboon and a warthog. Ambel stood and glowered at it as it shifted in its box, and one of its insane black eyes blinked open and returned his look. It was still alive, and he questioned the impulse that made him keep it so. That the historian, Olian Tay, had offered him a fortune for it, he now knew as incidental—he wasn't keeping it for her. Perhaps he kept it out of sadism. No one could be more deserving of punishment than this . . . individual. Ambel dropped the piece of bait meat in the box and slammed the lid shut. Next time he looked, he knew the meat would be gone, as the Skinner retained a tenacity for life. After wiping his hand,

Ambel locked the box then placed it back in his sea-chest before slamming and locking the lid of that. He left his cabin speedily, as one glad to be away from some unpleasant but necessary task. Peck was standing just outside, gazing at him strangely. He held the panga in his right hand and was spattered with purple blood and flecks of turbul meat. Even to Ambel he was a disquieting sight.

'Turbul all chopped, Peck?' Ambel asked.

The crewman took a moment to reply. 'How . . . is the bugger?' he asked.

'Alive,' said Ambel. 'Still alive.'

Peck nodded slowly. 'Can still hear 'im muttering,' he said.

'We'll always hear that,' said Ambel, reaching out and carefully slapping Peck on the shoulder. 'Let's get that turbul pickled and stowed, man.'

As Ambel walked past Peck, the crewman stared at the door to the cabin with his face screwed up in an expression that might have been remembered pain, might have been longing.

'How many barrels?' Ambel asked Anne as she lowered a full net down to the hive of activity in the hold.

'Twelve in all, with enough spare to do us for a week or so. Good run,' she added.

Ambel studied her face. The leech scars there had not detracted from her rugged attractiveness, and her long black hair showed not a speck of grey despite her many years. The virus affected different people in different ways. Some became wrinkled prunes with grizzled hair; some, like Anne, stayed at their peak; others lost all their hair and sometimes their teeth too. Ambel himself had been like Anne, long in the past. Over the numerous years since, he had, like many of the Old Captains, incrementally increased his muscular bulk. Now he had cropped white hair, a young-looking but wide face, and the overall appearance of someone who could snap deck timbers between his fingers—and it wasn't a deceptive appearance.

'We going after another run?' Boris asked from below.

'Nope, lad,' said Ambel. 'It's a night moon and we've still

got time to get to the sands. I don't want *all* our barrels filled with turbul. It only pulls down a few skind and the market'll be flooded.' He looked up. 'We go east,' he spoke loudly so the sail could hear him.

'Amberclams?' asked Pland, picking bait meat from under his fingernails with a skinning knife.

'Amberclams,' Ambel confirmed.

'That's a relief,' he said. 'I thought you were thinking of a hunt.'

Ambel grinned at him, then went below to help Boris and the juniors stow the barrels.

The voice from his Hive link had a hint of buzzing behind it but Janer reckoned that was just showmanship. Hornets did not communicate by buzzing, and Hive minds certainly did not. He suspected that this ersatz buzzing was the mind's idea of a joke.

'I would like you to travel with this Erlin. I find her interesting,' the mind told him.

It wasn't an instruction any more. The mind had ceased to issue instructions when his indenture had run out two decades back. The request, though, was backed by the promise of unlimited credit, travel and lack of boredom, and for Janer boredom could be a problem, as it was for so many Polity citizens now.

'I thought you wanted me to stick with the reif,' he whispered, conscious of the people all around him.

'The reification, I suspect, will go with her. If he does not, he will find her again in the future. His story and hers connect.'

'You haven't told me his story yet.'

'In good time, in good time. Let us watch this fight for the present.'

The two Hoopers facing each other in the dirt ring had stripped naked and oiled themselves from head to foot. The crowd was baying for blood, yet there seemed an insincerity about their shouting.

'You note that they strip off their clothing first,' said the mind.

'So?' said Janer.

'Their bodies repair themselves. Clothing has to be repaired.'

Janer absorbed that and nodded to himself. A passing tout assumed the nod was for him and he turned to Janer.

'Domby or Forlam? Shillings, yen, dollars—or skind if you have to. What bet?'

The man was short and powerfully built. He seemed to have none of those distinctive Hooper leech marks visible on him. Janer recognized his accent as off-world.

'What are the odds?'

'Domby's a three-fifty and Forlam a one-fifty, with an impressive list of recent wins. Thirteen to one on Domby for an E, and ten to one on Forlam for a pop. Either of them drops from a vaso, and you lose. The fight is two hours limited.'

'I'll put ten shillings on Domby for an E,' said Janer.

'Very good, sir.' The tout looked worried as he wrote out a betting slip and accepted Janer's ten-shilling note. Others in the crowd were eyeing Janer speculatively.

'That was a high bet here,' said the mind. *'Your average Hooper here would have to work half a year for such a sum.'*

'Really. If you know that much, perhaps you can tell me what Es, pops and vasos are,' said Janer.

'An E is an evisceration and a pop is a burst eye. A vaso is when one or both of the contestants collapse through loss of blood,' the mind replied succinctly.

'Oh, very nice. What are my chances of winning?'

'You heard the odds.'

Janer glowered at the two hornets in their case then returned his attention to the fight. Domby, whom Janer presumed to be the one showing the most leech scars, had stepped into the ring with a long curved dagger in each hand. Forlam then stepped in to face him. His weapons consisted of a stiletto and something that looked like an ice-axe. As soon as they were face to face, someone rang a dull-sounding bell. The volume of the shouting immediately increased as the opponents began to circle and feint. Domby was the first to get a hit. He opened Forlam's arm through to the bone, and blood jetted for a moment before abruptly ceasing to flow. Forlam backed away then leapt forward to jam his stiletto in Domby's stomach. In reply, Domby cut Forlam's ear so it was hanging by a thread. Forlam managed a low blow that cut Domby's scrotum in half. Five or six more blows followed before the two parted and circled again. Janer stood with his mouth open and a sick feeling in his gut as he watched Forlam shake his head in irritation and with his forearm press his ear back into place. When the Hooper moved his arm away, the ear remained in position again, if slightly askew. On the other side of this dusty arena, the crowd had parted round an off-worlder who was spewing vomit on to the dirt. Janer was a little harder than that. He'd seen some horrible things in his time, but this . . .

Domby and Forlam went at each other again. There was blood all over the ground. Not huge amounts, as all their wounds bled for only a short time. Janer noticed that the wound on Forlam's arm had nearly closed and that Domby's scrotum was back together.

'Illuminating, isn't it,' said a voice at his shoulder, which he first took to be the mind's until he turned to see Keech standing next to him. He was also glad to notice that those who had shown interest in him earlier when he had opened his wallet were now nowhere in evidence. The crowd had parted round Keech just as it had around the vomiter.

'That's one way of describing it,' said Janer. 'Erlin found her Captain yet?'

'He's not here, but she's still trying to find out where he went,' the reif said. He nodded towards the fight as another hideous wound was inflicted—and ignored. 'It takes little imagination to visualize the damage these people could do off-world, had they the inclination,' he said.

'But they don't,' said Janer.

'No, *most* of them don't.'

It took an hour for the fight to reach its climax. By that time, there were pools of blood everywhere in the dirt and Forlam was heading for a vaso. Janer did not see the move that ended the fight. Forlam had his back turned so Domby

was hidden. The roar of the crowd alerted him before Forlam turned, dropping his weapons as he tried to prevent his
intestines dropping out.

'I think I've won some money,' said Janer as the crowd began chanting 'Full! Full!'

'What does that mean?' Janer asked.

The Hive mind replied. *'It means full evisceration, though
I believe that to be a misnomer. According to the rules of this
kind of match there only has to be one clear loop of intestine,'* it said.

'What?' said Janer, not quite taking in what he was being
told.

Domby continued after Forlam, and Janer soon found out
precisely what the mind had meant. He came close to losing
the beer and sandwiches he had consumed a couple of hours
before. It wasn't so much the sight as the smell that did it.
When he finally felt sure he had his nausea under control,
the crowd was heading off in pursuit of various touts, and
Keech was watching him impassively.

'You'd better hurry if you want to collect your winnings,'
the reif suggested.

Janer nodded, looked around for the tout, whom he now
saw surrounded by a small group of winners, and clutching
his ticket he went over to collect. As he drew close, two
ugly-looking Hoopers suddenly stepped in front of him.
Both of them had knives like Domby's.

Janer halted then stepped back. 'OK. OK, I don't mind,'
he said. A hundred and forty shillings was not worth the risk
of suffering what had happened to Forlam. Nevertheless, the
two thugs kept coming at him. For half a second Janer considered running, then he swung a fist at the nearer of the
thugs. The man's head turned with the force of the blow, but
otherwise he seemed unaffected. He grinned at Janer as if to
indicate that the blow had now freed him of any restraints.

'Fuck,' said Janer. This was going to get nasty. He stepped
back slightly, spun on his heel and drove a thrust-kick
straight into the man's stomach. He might as well have
kicked a tree for all the effect it had. He backed off, trying
not to put too much weight on a knee that was already begin-

ning to ache. The thug was still grinning that same grin. Behind him, his companion just stood with his arms folded, and was smiling with nasty expectation.

'Can't we talk about this?' Janer suggested.

The thug slowly shook his head, and then abruptly moved in. Janer readied himself for the fight of his life. Suddenly there was a flash and a low thud. The leading thug staggered back and sat down. He peered with perplexity at the smoking hole in his stomach then glared past Janer. Janer glanced round as Keech stepped up beside him. He was holding in his skeletal hand a chromed gun similar in appearance to a Luger, only heavier, and with a longer barrel. He next shot the second thug, and put him on the ground too.

'I'll go for headshots if either of you tries to get up,' warned the reif. The first thug, who had been considering just that, sat back down again.

'Get your winnings,' said Keech. 'I hate people reneging on bets.'

Janer stared at Keech, then at the weapon the reif held. This was why he had not required one of the QC lasers; what he held was a JMCC military-issue pulse-gun. Janer now cast his eye over the two thugs. One of them was poking a finger into the hole in his body, to see how deep it went. The reality of Spatterjay was rapidly coming home to Janer. Perhaps it had not been such a good idea to put the weapon he had purchased earlier in his backpack.

He took out his slip and advanced on the tout, who stared at him for a moment then began to reach into his jacket. A hand, deeply cicatrised with leech scars, reached down and caught the tout's wrist.

'Now now,' said a pleasant voice.

Janer gaped at the owner of that hand. This Hooper was big, shaven-headed, and blue with leech scars. He wore hide trousers and a thin shirt. Even his muscles had muscles. Janer wondered if he would even notice a punch delivered by an off-worlder. This one looked as if bullets would bounce off his skin and knives would bend and break on him. There was a boulder-like solidity about him, and a stolid assurance.

'Captain Ron,' said someone in the crowd, and there was almost reverence in the voice.

'I think you should pay the man,' said Captain Ron.

'Yes, yes.' The tout dropped his moneybag in his eagerness to get the money out. He stooped and quickly retrieved it before counting out notes and change with shaking hands. Janer accepted the money while keeping half an eye on the Captain, who was gazing with ponderous insouciance back at the ring.

'You all right there, Forlam!' the Captain suddenly bellowed.

A groan came from that direction.

'Soon have you back together,' said the Captain. He gazed round at the crowd. 'Anyone found his fingers yet?'

'Got 'em, Captain,' someone yelled.

'Get 'im back to the ship then and tell Roach to thread 'im up.'

Janer just could not take in what he was hearing. He knew Hoopers were very hard to kill, but this was ridiculous. He glanced round to see Keech approaching, while the two Hoopers he had shot had moved off into the background. They seemed unperturbed by wounds that would have killed an off-worlder, but were now pensively watching Captain Ron. Janer guessed they were hoping the tout wouldn't call for them. It did not require much imagination to guess what the result of such an encounter would be.

'I'd like to buy you a drink,' Janer said abruptly.

With a vague smile, Captain Ron turned back to him.

'Now that could work out expensive,' he said.

There was laughter from the other Hoopers.

'Well, I've had a bit of luck today,' said Janer.

'All right,' said the Captain. 'I'll see you in the Baitman.' He cast a baleful look at the tout, then at his thugs, who ducked their heads and tried to appear unconcerned. 'And he better get there safely,' he said loudly. Then he sauntered off.

With Keech at his side, Janer surveyed the people around him. All he could find were friendly expressions. The two thugs had already gone. The tout was slinking away, as if hoping not to be noticed.

'Obviously not someone to mess with,' said Janer.

'You remember what Erlin said?' asked Keech.

'Remind me.'

'He, I would guess, is an Old Captain, and has authority by dint of the simple fact that he could tear your arms off.'

'Yes, I remember now.'

The Baitman was a ship Hoopers' drinking den, and no other off-worlders were present when Janer and Keech entered. Looks of vague curiosity were flung in their direction, before conversations resumed. Keech and Janer walked up to the bar, behind which sat a Hooper who seemed only skin and bone, with white curly hair. He was bending over a board on which chess pieces and small model ships were positioned. That he seemed to concentrate even harder on the board when they entered was obvious to Janer. He rapped on the bar with his knuckles. The barman glanced up at them with an albino's pink eyes.

'This place is for ship Hoopers,' he said, and returned his attention to the board.

Janer was at a loss for a moment, then he started to get angry. Before he could say anything, Keech spoke up.

'Then we are in the right place to meet Captain Ron for a drink,' said the reif.

The barman stood upright, and only then did Janer realize how tall he was.

'Ron invited you?' He was studying them carefully.

'I invited him, and he suggested here,' said Janer.

The barman's gaze flicked from Janer's face to the two hornets, in their box on his shoulder, then to the reif. He inspected Keech for a long while, with a puzzled expression, then clearly decided not to ask. He put two pewter mugs on the bar, uncorked a jug, and filled them both. Then, from a rack behind the bar, he took down a two-litre mug and filled it with the same liquid. The vessel had 'Ron's Mug' engraved on it. Janer picked up the mug in front of him and took a gulp.

'It is best to approach such things with caution,' said Keech, removing a glass straw from his top pocket and stooping to take a careful sip of his own drink.

'Ung,' Janer managed.

'Sea-cane rum,' added Keech.

'You can drink it?' Janer said, once he had his breath back.

'My stomach is atrophied but I have a filter system which can remove impurities from high-alcohol beverages. What is pumped round my veins is alcohol based,' replied Keech.

'Why do you always use a straw?'

Keech gestured towards his mouth. 'My lips, though having enough elasticity to mimic speech, do not have enough to form a seal.'

'You'd dribble,' said Janer.

Keech gave a measured nod.

Janer went on, his curiosity piqued, 'How do you speak, then?'

Keech tapped his half-helmet augmentation. 'It's generated from here. With what little movement my mouth does have, the illusion is completed,' he said.

Janer nodded, then took another, more cautious sip of his drink. He noted how the barman had not made a move on his chessboard since the commencement of their conversation. Understandable, as this had to be a fascinating interchange.

'What about taste?'

'A saporphone imbedded in the roof of my mouth transmits taste information to the mimetic computer in my aug and to what remains of my organic brain.'

'But you can't get drunk?' said Janer.

'No, I cannot, but I don't feel that to be a disadvantage. In most situations I find it advisable to keep a clear head.'

Keech imparted this information with clinical detachment. Janer studied the reif as he thought carefully about his explanation. Keech was partially alive, since he had *some* functioning organic brain. The part that was not functioning was made up for by a recording of his previous living mind being run as a program in his augmentation. Thus it came down to the fact that Keech was a corpse made motile mainly by AI-directed cyber systems.

'Why don't you implant in a Golem chassis?' Janer asked.

'This is *my* body,' said Keech, as if that was answer

enough, and returned his attention to his drink. As Janer watched him, the Hive mind took the opportunity to interject. *'The cult of Anubis Arisen believes physical life to be sacrosanct and that the life of the body is the only life. Perhaps Keech believes that too, though I doubt it.'*

Janer did not get a chance to ask the mind to explain *that* comment, as Captain Ron just then crashed into the Baitman like some stray piece of earth-moving equipment.

'Good sail to you!' said the Captain, stomping up to the bar and taking up his mug to drain it in one. He slammed the mug down on the bar so hard the timbers leapt. The barman waited for dust to settle before refilling the mug. As it was being refilled, Janer noted that it had a bloom on its metal surface identical to that left on ceramal after it has been case hardened. Obviously simple pewter would not prove suitably durable.

'That hits the spot,' said the Captain.

Janer looked on in awe, wondering about the durability of this man's intestine, before carefully taking another sip from his own mug.

'I have to thank you for your intervention back there,' he said, blinking water from his eyes.

'Don't like cheats.'

Janer gestured to Keech. 'You and him both,' he said.

Ron looked at the reif and nodded, his expression slightly puzzled. Keech, Janer supposed, would be a puzzle to most Polity citizens, let alone the denizens of an Out-Polity world like this.

Ron drained just half his mug this time and Janer dropped a ten-shilling note on the bar.

'Got anything smaller?' asked the barman.

'Just keep pouring,' said Janer. He felt drunk already, but warily slid his mug back on to the bar. 'In fact,' he said, 'drinks all round.'

'You told me to remind you if you ever did this again,' the Hive mind whispered to him.

'Shaddup,' said Janer and Captain Ron gave him a puzzled look. 'Sorry, not you.' He pointed at the hornets on his shoulder. 'Them.'

'Hornets,' said Ron. 'Insects don't do so well here.'

'Why's that?'

'The filaments clog up their air holes.'

Somebody laughed at this, and when Janer looked around he found that others in the Baitman had gathered behind them, and that the barman was pouring more drinks. He drank some more from his own mug and noticed subliminally that Keech had retreated into the background and was now carefully seating himself at one of the tables. The reif might appear fragile in this company, but Janer now knew how deceptive that appearance was.

'Not as clogged as your air holes, you old bastard.'

Janer glanced to one side to see Erlin standing at his shoulder.

'Erlin!' bellowed Ron. He reached past Janer and picked her up, but carefully. Janer noticed that the Hooper showed not a trace of effort. He might as well have been lifting an origami sculpture.

'Careful, Ron,' said Erlin. 'I'm only a ninety Hooper.'

'You've come back for Ambel?' said Ron, still holding her off the ground. After a moment, he realized what he was doing and carefully put her down.

'I have. We've unfinished business. Do you know where he is?'

'Last heard, he was out at the Sargassum.'

'Who's going out there?'

Ron grinned at her. 'The turbul's good out there this season,' he said.

Much of the rest of the evening was a blur to Janer. He remembered Keech joining in a conversation about Jay Hoop, the ancient piratical founder of Spatterjay after whom the planet was named, and he remembered later finding himself lying under a table. There was also a vague memory of being slung over Ron's shoulder, a long walk through darkness, then puking over a wooden rail into an oily sea. Then blackness.

3

In emerald depths the frog whelk, crippled by the leech that had wormed inside its shell to feed upon it, had lost all its survival instincts as it crawled painfully along the stony bottom, through forests of sea-cane and prill-peppered waters. Said instinct being the minimum requirement for plain existence in this savage sea, it did not last long, of course. Crawling into a what it thought was a flock of its fellows, it sank down like a weary pensioner and uncoiled its eye-stalks. Only when it observed the patterns of those shells surrounding it, and sensed the vibration thrumming through the seabed, did it realize its fatal mistake: the whelks surrounding it were hammer whelks. Panicking, it thrust down its foot and tried to leap away, but such was the damage done to it by the leech that all it managed to do was tip itself over. The hammer whelks closed in on this unexpected bounty extruding feet like brick-hammers to pound their victim's shell. Soon the water clouded with chyme, small fragments of flesh, nacreous glitters of shell and one slowly turning eye-stalk, like a discarded match—which was snapped up by a passing turbul.

Keech paid his hotel bill and, with his hover trunk in tow, he left the Dome and made his way into the Hooper town. As he walked, he saw Erlin walking ahead of him, also with her luggage in tow and Janer's stacked on top of it. Rather than catch up with her he turned down a side road and took a track leading out of the town into the dingle. Either side of the track, peartrunk trees quivered to the movement of small leeches in their branches, and frogmoles chirruped and burped from little pools in the centres of ground-growing

leaves as big as bedspreads. A stand of putrephallus plants
broadcast their presence before they came in sight, and
Keech turned off the anosmic receptor in his nose. Attracted
to the bright red tips of the stinking plants, a couple of baggy
lung birds flapped about and honked noisily. They looked to
Keech as if they were about to fly apart, like something ill-
made by an apprentice creator. They were sparsely covered
in long oily feathers between which feathers showed purplish septic-looking flesh. If these birds had the appearance
of anything recognizable, it was of half-plucked crows that
had been dead for a week or more. He moved on, down the
slope of the island via a path of crushed quartz spread over
black packed earth, and out beyond the edge of the dingle
and on to a strand of green sand scattered with drifts of mul-
ticoloured pebbles. There he ordered his trunk to settle and
open, and he began to remove its contents.

Keech's muscles did not work, in fact none of him
worked, except for half of his brain and one eye. Completely
stripped of his flesh, the AI Keech would still exist—a skeleton with motors at his joints and other pieces of hardware
affixed to his bones and, of course, the aug. The items of
Keech's survival therefore consisted of his cleansing unit
and two spare power cells for the cyber mechanisms that
kept him moving. Along with these items, he now removed a
black attaché case, a pack of clothing, and a small remote-
control. These had filled only a small portion of the trunk.
Keech closed the lid, stepped back, pointed the remote and
pressed a button.

The trunk rose half a metre from the ground and the lid
split in two along its length. These two halves, along with
the adjoining sides, folded down into cranked wings. The
front then folded itself down at forty-five degrees and from
its top extruded a curved screen. From under the seat, now
exposed in the centre of the trunk, a steering column and
control console whined forwards and up into position below
the screen. Keech stepped in to detach cylindrical thruster
motors from each side of the seat—revealing the AG motor
underneath—and to reattach them at the ends of the wings.
The back of the trunk tilted out to make a luggage compart-

ment and Keech put his belongings in this before mounting the hover scooter thus created. He would have smiled had he been able to. He pressed a touch-plate on the console and spoke.

'This is monitor Sable Keech registering AG transport on Out-Polity planet Spatterjay,' he said.

From the console a mild voice replied, 'According to my records, monitor Keech, you are dead.'

Keech paused for a moment—that was a very quick interception by the Warden.

'That is correct,' he said.

'Oh, I'm glad we've cleared that one up,' said the AI Warden on the distant moon of Spatterjay. 'But perhaps you can provide some further explanation?'

'My monitor status remains unchanged I take it?'

'It does.'

'Then I am not required to give an explanation.'

'No, you are not.'

'I'm a reification,' said Keech. 'I would have thought you'd already found all that out, if not when I first came through the runcible gate, then at least when I crossed the Line to come out here.'

'Yes, I see that now. I don't monitor all inward runcible traffic unless it comes with an attached record. The Dome gate was being run by one of my subminds at the time, and it did not see fit to inform me of your arrival. I must have words with it.'

Keech let ride the fact that he thought it unlikely that he had not come through with an attached record.

'I am clear to use AG transport, I take it?' he asked.

'You are, monitor Keech.'

'Thank you,' said Keech.

After running a diagnostic on the console, he thrust the column forward and, blasting up a cloud of sand, shot out over the sea.

With something of smugness in its attitude, the Warden observed the planet through a thousand pairs of artificial eyes. After a brief scan, it refined this fragment of its attention to

just one pair of eyes and the complex little mind that operated them. On an atoll on the opposite side of the planet
from the main human settlements, and where no human had
set foot, waves lapped gently at a beach of jade and rose-
quartz pebbles. Below the pellucid waters off this beach, the
stony bottom was alive with movement. Swarms of infant
hammer whelks shifted in a slow and intricate dance, their
shells glinting like coiled pearls, and leeches oozed between
them searching for softer prey. A disturbance where the bottom dropped into emerald depths had the whelks clamping
themselves safely to the stony bottom and the leeches turning as one to investigate.

Out of boiling foam rose the baroque shape of a seahorse
the length of a man's forearm, leeches hitting its iron-
coloured skin and falling away. It rose from the sea and,
seemingly balanced upon the surface with a coil of its tail, it
slowly revolved and took in its surroundings with topaz
eyes. Only someone with a very sophisticated underspace
detector could have heard the communication that followed,
and even then it would have taken a mind superior to that of
the Warden's to decode it.

'SM Thirteen, you were instructed to transmit yourself to
Dome Gate One for your assigned watch, and I see now that
this did not happen,' said the Warden.

'Sniper took that watch. He had some business to conduct
through the local server. And I have my so very important
studies to complete,' replied the Warden's thirteenth submind, from its odd drone body.

'Why then have I received no report from Sniper?'

In the pause that followed, the Warden considered then rejected the idea of subsuming Thirteen, of reintegrating the
little mind with itself in order to get at the truth. But the Warden had found from long experience that an amount of individualism in its subminds allowed them to originate insights
it never experienced by itself.

'Nothing of significance to report?' suggested SM13.

The Warden sensed agitation in the little mind and allowed it to stew for a few microseconds.

'The arrival of a dead monitor pursuing a seven-century vendetta I do consider to be worthy of note,' it said.

'Well that's not my fault,' said the seahorse drone. 'Take it up with Sniper. It wasn't my decision to employ an obsolete war drone, even if it was once a hero.'

The Warden did not answer this. It withdrew and did a brief search in the local server. That SM13 and the war drone Sniper both had accounts with the Norvabank evinced in it some surprise, though only some. The third account it found there, by tracking past transfers, gave it *more* than some surprise. It would have to watch this situation very closely; it might lead to questions about the rights of humans to exist on Spatterjay.

Janer woke with a sick feeling in his stomach and the apparent evidence that a small animal had expired messily in his mouth, probably squashed by the farrier who was making horseshoes in his head. He shoved the tangled blanket off, sat on the edge of his bunk, and tried to figure out where he was. The wooden room he lay in was moving, and loud snores came from the Hooper lying in the bunk opposite. Janer stood, swayed for a moment, and then abruptly sat down. His detox pills—one of his most important survival items—were in his backpack, but where the hell was that? His nausea abruptly increased its hold on him and he quickly stood and staggered to the door. Immediately outside the door there was a short corridor terminating at a ladder. He moved towards this and, for no immediately apparent reason, staggered into one wall, then back across the wooden flooring straight into a door. He shook his head. What the hell was that sound? From all around him came racketing and clacking sounds, creaks and groans. Upon reaching the ladder, he unsteadily climbed up it towards greenish light, then stumbled out of the deck hatch to a wooden rail, and retched into the sea below. As he did this he realized he had done so before, and remembered where he was: on board the ship.

'Good morning,' Erlin cheerfully called.

Janer got control of his retching—there wasn't much to come up anyway—and glanced round from the rail to where Erlin and Captain Ron stood, behind the helmsman, on the upper deck that formed the roof of the forecabin. He pushed back from the rail, lost his balance, and stepped back into the mainmast.

'Watch yer feet, asshole!'

The voice came from below him. He stared down at a large flat head on the deck itself, a mouth full of sickle teeth, and demonic red eyes that gazed at him impassively. He rubbed his face, then, running from this head, he tracked a long ribbed neck that rose up the mast behind him, to an expanse of veined pink skin spread out on the spars of the central mast, cutting out half the sky. This skin was braced with long thin support spines that issued spidery gripping claws at their joints. Ropes of muscle ran down these spines, also along the long heavy wing bones, and knotted into a huge keel of a chest, above which lumps of something unidentifiable were being digested in a transparent gut. The creature hung upside down like a bat, as it turned itself to the wind.

'Oh shit,' Janer said and quickly moved away from the mast and back to the rail. From here he could see how, whenever the creature moved, its movement was replicated in the fore and aft masts, which supported sails of a more commonplace fabric. The clacking sounds heard below the decks, he realized, derived from this motion.

'His name is Windcatcher,' the Hive mind told him. Janer blearily inspected the two hornets in their transparent box, as if searching for some sign of irony.

'Never let me do that again,' he said.

'That's what you said last time it happened. Unfortunately, I no longer have any control over your actions. Not that I had a great deal when you were indentured.' There was definite irony in the voice this time.

Janer returned his attention to Erlin and Ron, who were watching him with some amusement.

'Where's my backpack?' he called.

'Under your bunk,' Erlin replied.

Janer walked shakily to the hatch, pausing to let a woman

climb out, who grinned at him before moving off, carrying a bucket of something that looked like grease and smelt like something that should have been buried. He climbed back down the ladder, swallowing on a rush of saliva. Once in the cabin he went quickly to his bunk, pulled out his pack from underneath, found his detox pills, threw a couple of them into his mouth, and swallowed them dry. He then sat and waited for them to take effect.

The Hooper in the adjacent bunk snored and grunted, then, with muttered imprecations, turned over, allowing Janer a good look at his face. It was Forlam. Janer stood up and gazed at Forlam's right hand, which lay on top of the blanket. The last time he had seen it, that hand had been merely a stump with just the stub of a thumb sticking out of one side. Now the fingers had been reattached with rough-looking stitches, which also extended in a line up the Hooper's forearm to his elbow, closing a surgical cut Janer surmised had been made for the retrieval of severed tendons, for, as Janer knew from personal experience, tendons were like taut-stretched elastic, and severed in such a place, would have snapped back up inside Forlam's arm. Underneath these stitches, just as underneath those around Forlam's repositioned ear, were red lines of scar tissue, so it was apparent the needlework was no longer needed to hold the flesh together. Janer wondered if Forlam could eat yet, and it suddenly came home to him hard just where he was and the situation he was in.

Within a few minutes the sickness had receded enough for him to realize he badly needed to empty his bladder. Luckily he had noticed the lidded bucket underneath his bunk, and did not have to look far for relief. Afterwards, feeling somewhat better, he returned up to the deck.

'There's fresh water over there,' called Erlin, as Janer stood blearily surveying his surroundings. He went to the barrel by the back wall of the forecabin and gulped down a couple of ladlefuls. The water tasted coppery, and accelerated the effect of the detox in his stomach. Abruptly he felt buoyant, happy, and it occurred to him that the water might also be helping residual alcohol from his stomach into his bloodstream. He peered up at Erlin, who was leaning on the rail staring down at him.

'Where are we heading?' he asked, when at last he felt able to speak.

'The Sargassum,' she told him. 'Last known destination of the man I've come here for: Captain Ambel.'

'Oh.' Janer paused to gulp another ladleful of water and then gazed around the deck. 'Where's Keech?'

Erlin shrugged. 'Gone his own way, as far as I can gather. He wasn't in the hotel this morning, but left a message saying he had certain things to attend to, and that perhaps we would meet again some time. I'd say that's the last we've seen of him.'

'Shame, he was interesting,' said Janer, remembering something the mind had said. He dropped the ladle back into the barrel, scanned about again then went on, 'What's a sargassum?'

'Where the turbul gather to breed,' Captain Ron interrupted from behind Erlin.

Erlin eyed Janer sympathetically. 'It's an area of the sea where sea-cane and sea nettles grow thick enough to form into islands. Turbul are a kind of fish, and they deposit their nymphs on the underside of those islands. Ship Hoopers always head out there at this season to harvest the turbul,' she explained.

'Harvest?' Janer asked, vaguely recalling a previous conversation.

Erlin smiled, turned to say something to Ron, then made for the forecabin ladder, and climbed down to get nearer to Janer. She inspected him with amused sympathy then pointed towards the stern of the ship.

'Roach is hand-lining for boxies for our lunch. Come and see, and perhaps you'll begin to understand.'

Janer followed where she led, giving the sail's head a wide berth as he went. He saw now that not only did the creature control the movement of the fore and aft masts by some hidden linkage, but it also adjusted the fabric sails with cables gripped in some of its spider-claw hands. Janer swung his gaze along the full length of the ship, estimating it to be at least fifty metres long, with a beam of fifteen metres. There weren't many crew visible but, knowing nothing about sailing ships, he did not know how many might be required to navigate it, nor how many were *unnecessary* because of this weirdest of rigs.

Roach was a short raggety Hooper with a furtive look about him. He sat like a pile of dirty washing at the edge of the deck where there was no rail. He glanced up at Erlin and Janer, then hauled in the line he had trailing over the side of the ship. It came up with a boxy on the end, which he removed from the hook and tossed into the wooden bucket at his side. Boxy was an apt name for this fish, Janer thought. It had a purple and white cube-shaped body with eyes at the front and a tail sticking out the back.

With a gesture at the boxies already caught, Erlin asked Roach, 'You mind?' Roach looked sneaky for a moment as if estimating what he could get for one of the fish. He then glanced towards the Captain, thought for a moment, and made a noncommittal gesture. Erlin picked up one of the fish.

To Janer she said, 'Spatterjay life forms have evolved to survive being fed upon by the leeches—to have their flesh harvested by leeches.' She dug her finger in behind the boxy's eyes, hooked and pulled. The eyes, at the wide point of a small triangular head, the spine and sack of internal organs, and the tail, pulled from the surrounding cube of flesh like a cork coming out of a bottle.

'Look,' said Erlin, and threw the essential part of the boxy back into the sea. Janer watched it hit the surface of the water and lie there for a moment. He was just about to ask what she meant when the boxy wriggled, then wriggled again, and shot away into the emerald depths. 'They don't die,' she told him, and to his horror she took a bite out of the cube of flesh she held. 'Here, try some.'

Janer took the still-warm lump of flesh and stared at it. He glanced down at Roach, who was watching him with a ratty smirk, then he took a small bite and, gritting his teeth against his rebellious stomach, chewed and swallowed. The meat slid down and seemed to settle there with a sudden heat that dispelled his nausea. He was surprised at the effect and took another bite. After swallowing this too, he tried to identify the taste.

'Spicy . . . like curry . . . and bananas,' he said.

'It's loaded with vitamins, proteins and sugars—and the virus of course, but don't worry about that. The virus can't survive human digestion, just as it can't survive long exposure to the air. Your usual methods of contracting it are either through a leech bite or by sexual transmission.' Erlin seemed uncomfortable at mentioning the latter method. 'Are you on Intertox?'

Janer shrugged. 'I'll take my chances,' he said, then remembering part of a drunken conversation the night before he asked, 'Tell me, with food like this so easily available, why do they bring out here what they call "Dome-grown" food?'

Erlin smiled at a memory of her own, and Janer felt almost jealous of it. She said, 'Dome-grown foods are Earth foods and the varieties grown here contain many natural germicides—toxins even—that inhibit the growth of the viral fibres. Hoopers have possessed the facilities for growing them since the days of Jay Hoop himself, and lucky they did or they wouldn't have survived. They enjoyed more variety when the Polity finally arrived. Garlic is particularly good. Hoopers like garlic. They've grown it here for nearly a millennium.'

'You'd have thought they wouldn't *want* to inhibit the growth of those fibres.'

'Slow growth is better than fast—that way you don't go native,' Erlin replied.

Janer waited for an explanation but none was forthcoming. He finished off the boxy meat first, and was about to pursue the matter when he heard a pitiful squeaking and looked down. Roach had opened a cast-iron bait box and was now baiting his hook. The creature wriggling in his fingers, in its attempt to escape being impaled, had the appearance of a miniature trumpet with a wading bird's legs and webbed feet.

'Let's leave him to it,' said Erlin. 'It can be dangerous for an off-worlder to stand near a Hooper while he's fishing.'

'What do you mean?'

Erlin pointed at the bait box.

'One of those things could chew into you like a drill bit. They're difficult to remove once they get started.'

Janer nodded and stepped back. The little trumpet-things were leaping up and down in the box and, though they had no eyes, they seemed to be watching him. Roach showed no particular caution of the creature he held as he finally impaled it on a gleaming hook. As it let out a bubbling squeak, Janer saw the others in the bait box quit their squeaking and sink out of sight. He nodded to the crewman before following Erlin, but so intent was Roach on getting his line out, he did not notice.

Erlin went on, 'Besides, there's all the other things Roach might bring up on his line. There's frog whelks and hammer whelks down there, not to mention glisters and prill. And there's always leeches of course.'

Janer had no idea what most of these things were, and was not sure he wanted to find out just then.

As they came opposite the mast Erlin gestured at his belt. 'You're not carrying your weapon. I suggest you do,' she said.

Janer nodded, then his attention was caught by a shoal of somethings sliding past the ship, just below the surface. At first he thought they might be dolphins, then he realized they were huge leeches.

'Why do people want to stay here?' he asked. 'It seems a hellish place.'

Erlin was thoughtful for a moment before replying. 'For Hoopers it's what they're accustomed to. Only in recent years have they become aware that they can leave. They stay because of the benefits they see. If they live long enough, they'll end up like the Old Captains: practically unkillable, almost inured to pain, utterly at peace with themselves.'

'Seems they'd have to survive for a long time to attain that,' said Janer, still watching the leeches.

'Yes,' said Erlin. 'There's also the fact of the economy here—something that with our own benefits we tend to forget. A Hooper has to work for a very long time to be able to afford passage away from here.'

Janer turned to her, the words 'afford passage' registering in his blurry mind.

'I suppose this particular little jaunt is not for free?' he said.

Erlin smiled. 'No, I suggest you see Ron soon and negotiate a price.'

Janer looked up at the broad back of the big Captain. 'I don't suppose that negotiation need involve me calling him "a robber and a thief", should it? I don't fancy the idea of *him* getting annoyed with me.'

'Old Captains infrequently lose their tempers—too dangerous,' Erlin told him. 'You can call him what you like so long as you pay him. I'm sure you won't want to disembark just here.'

Janer once again studied the passing shoal of leeches. He searched for something more to say to keep the conversation going. 'Tell me,' he said, 'do the leeches die?'

'Yes and no. They're preyed upon too, and as easy to kill as anything else here, but they don't actually die of old age. When fertilized, they divide into segments, which then collapse into a large encystment, or egg. That egg will attach itself to the bottom of a sargassum, and out of it will eventually hatch thousands of cute baby leeches.'

'Nice. What about the males?'

'No males, really. The leeches are hermaphroditic . . . sort of.'

'Same immortality as all life.'

'Yes, it is that.' Erlin nodded, lost to her own thoughts. Janer saw that she had now gone away from him and, thinking of nothing else to ask, he quickly returned to his cabin for his gun, deciding right then that he would be very careful here. It was apparent to him that this was a place where recklessness could soon get you dead.

On the great monolith of stone surrounded by empty ocean, Sniper reached out with one triple-jointed arm, clasped the bishop in his precision claw, and moved it halfway across the board. Keeping one palp-eye on the game he turned his other to the three objects that lay on a sheet of slightly putrescent skin spread on the rock beside the board. One of these objects was an explosive slave collar with Prador glyphs etched into its dull grey surface. A brief ultrasound scan revealed the information that the film of planar explosive inside it was still active even after all this time. This meant that at the antiquities sale on Coram this item would fetch over a thousand New Carth shillings. The two other objects were even more interesting and of greater value, as slave collars had already been found in their hundreds over on the Skinner's Island. One of them, Sniper recognized as a very early nerve-inducer, despite the fact that most of its ceramal casing had corroded away. The other was a mass of corrosion which the war drone had identified, after scanning, as a projectile gun. This last item, despite its terrible condition, would fetch a mint, as it was likely a weapon carried by either Hoop himself or one of his comrades. Sniper hunkered down on his six crustacean legs and returned both eyes to the game as his opponent made a move.

'How much you want for them?' the war drone asked as he registered a possible danger to his queen in eight further moves.

Sniper's opponent lowered to the stone the foot-talon he had used to move his knight, and blinked at Sniper with demonic red eyes. The sail, with his pink-skinned wings wadded into an intricacy of folds and spines that bore some resemblance to a monk's habit and some to the excess of Elizabethan clothing, and with his long neck hooked like a question mark as he observed the board, grinned his crocodilian grin and exposed a kilo of ivory.

'Two thousand, and you fit the augmentation for me *here*,' he said.

Sniper, who had the appearance of giant crayfish fashioned of polished aluminium, tilted his armoured head in acknowledgement.

'There's the alignment program—I wrote it myself. And that, Cheater, will cost you,' said Sniper.

Windcheater turned his head and eyed Sniper suspiciously as the war drone made his next move.

'You didn't tell me about that,' the sail accused.

Sniper raised his head and stared at the sail. Below the war drone's angled-back antennae and cluster of sensory bristles, two mirrored tubes shifted apart, coming to point sideways now and leaving a matt square tube centred on the sail opposite. This was the nearest the drone could come to a grin, having in place of a mouth an antiphoton weapon—and the business ends of a rail-gun and a missile launcher.

'Musta slipped my mind,' Sniper said.

'Why do I need this alignment program?' Windcheater asked, his talons rattling his impatience and splintering up flakes of the stone.

'Your brain ain't exactly human-shaped. Put the aug on you now and the nanonic fibres'll turn your head to mush looking for the right connections.'

'How different is my brain, then?' Windcheater asked.

'Upside-down and halfway down your two spines. Your cerebrum is in a linked triad round your oblongata, and there's other things in there ain't even got a name yet.'

'*Better* than human?'

'In your case, just. Your friends . . . '

Sniper gestured with his heavy claw at the other sails gathered on the far side of the rock and gave a clattering shrug. Windcheater studied his fellows.

'Put it this way,' Sniper went on, 'even auged-up, any sail called Wind*catcher* ain't gonna win any chess matches.'

Sniper moved a heretofore-ignored pawn and emitted a satisfied hum.

Windcheater peered at the board and shook his head slowly. The way he exposed his teeth this time could not easily have been identified as a grin. 'I didn't see that,' he said.

'I guess not,' said the war drone as he settled to forty-five degrees on his back legs. With his precision claw, he reached under himself and with a metallic click detached a chromed object the shape of a broad bean, but five centimetres long.

He passed the object to his heavy claw and held it up between the two razor points.

'Got the alignment program loaded and ready to go. It'll take only a few minutes to link in, and about an hour for all the control programs to upload. After that hour you'll be able to direct-access your account through the local server, and to download information on just about anything you want . . . all unproscribed technologies, learning programs, you'll be able to buy things and have them delivered by remote drone, you'll be able to make investments, and you'll be able to communicate with just about anyone in the Polity.'

Windcheater's mouth was hanging open now and his bifurcated tongue was licking across his many teeth. One talon was rising up off the stone as if he wanted to grab the aug right now.

'I think that's more than enough in exchange for these few corroded objects,' Sniper finished.

Windcheater's mouth snapped shut and his red eyes narrowed. 'One and a half thousand,' the sail said.

'I'm being generous if I offer you five hundred,' replied Sniper.

'Twelve hundred, and remember that there's more where these came from.'

'Being as it's you, I'll go to six hundred.'

Windcheater rocked back on his talons and let out a frustrated hiss. 'I'm fairly certain I saw a sealed box of five Prador thrall units,' he said.

'Where?' Sniper enquired.

'The Skinner's Island—you know, that place the Warden has expressly forbidden you to visit.'

It was Sniper's turn to hiss. 'All right, I'll give you eight hundred, and I'm being more than generous.'

'Twelve hundred, I said.'

'Slightest pressure and this aug could pop like a boiled amber-clam.'

'Eleven hundred then.'

'Don't want me to make a mistake while fitting this, do you?' asked Sniper, giving his antiphoton grin.

'I'll go no lower than a thousand. I know you can get that for the collar alone,' said Windcheater.

'OK, you got me there,' said the war drone.

Sniper lowered his heavy claw, released the aug from it, catching it in his precision claw. He held the aug out and Windcheater bowed low with his head poised above the chessboard. Sniper pressed the device against the side of the sail's head. There was a brief snicking sound, and Windcheater jerked his head to one side.

'Feels sort of—'

The sail did not complete what he was about to say. His eyes crossed. He jerked back, fell on his rump, and sat there making strange hissing and grunting sounds, his foot talons clenched into fists. While Sniper observed this odd behaviour, his own two antenna abruptly flicked upright. 'Oh hell,' the war drone said, just managing to draw the putrescent skin over the three objects he and the sail had been bargaining for, before the Warden fully linked in and could gaze through the drone's eyes. The Warden's presence was huge, and Sniper frantically opened excess processing space so that it was not so invasive. Fortunately, the presence pulled short of complete invasion of the war drone's mind.

'I see that Windcheater has acquired an augmentation. I hope, for your sake, that it is properly aligned, as even your heroic record will not exempt you from reprogramming if you've scrambled his brain, Sniper,' said the Warden.

'I know what I'm doing,' said the war drone.

'Do you? I often wonder about that. You've been a free drone for five centuries now. That's a long time to have been out on your own.'

Sniper hissed. 'I work for you. I ain't gonna become one of your subminds.'

'Well, let's not replay old arguments. Let's instead look at the *fact* of your working for me. What you do on your own time is not my concern, unless it infringes on Polity law— you know, laws like those covering the trade in cultural artefacts and dubious technologies. But when you fail to report to me the arrival of Sable Keech here on Spatterjay, I do wonder if you're properly attending to your duties.'

'Sable Keech,' said Sniper. 'Oh.'

'Oh, indeed. I take it that you were not physically present at the gate, and had a submind of your own keeping watch there?'

'Well . . . yes.'

'Then I suggest that the next time you do something like that you give said submind more sophisticated programming. It should have informed you of Keech's arrival.'

'Of course, Warden,' said Sniper.

The Warden paused for a little while before continuing. Always there was this temptation to subsume the mind it was in contact with, as that way the information the mind contained would be instantly accessible. It also had a sneaking suspicion that Sniper was not being exactly straight about something. Yet the Warden could not subsume Sniper without the war drone's permission, him being a free individual.

The Warden went on, 'Now, when you have finished here I strongly suggest that you go and join SM13, as it will be needing assistance with its hammer whelk survey. That should keep you out of trouble at least for a little while. I will link through Windcheater's aug when it connects to the server, just to check that what is on the other side of it still has some sentience. Understand, Sniper, that we are no longer at war and you cannot break the law with impunity.'

Sniper's antennae dropped back to their back-slanted position, and the war drone let go one long and metallic raspberry. Windcheater's eyes uncrossed and his foot-talons unclenched.

'Why do you do it?' the sail asked. 'You don't really need the money.'

'I'm a war drone, not a bloody flying whelk counter,' said Sniper, and with a low grumbling sound he rose half a metre from the rock.

'I still don't understand,' said Windcheater.

'I'm bored,' said the war drone then, with a gesture of his heavy claw towards the covered artefacts, 'Keep them safe for me. I'll be back when I've finished counting fucking whelks.'

A blade of fusion flame stabbed from underneath and behind the war drone, and then he shot away into the sky.
Windcheater nodded once, then allowed his eyes to cross
and his foot-talons to clench once more. The other sails, all
of them called *Windcatcher*, looked on with the same blank
lack of understanding as ever.

Keech controlled the scooter with a simple program set up
in his aug, while he flipped up the control console's screen
and activated it. The aug program kept the vehicle gliding
five metres above the sea and heading south, and as such it
did not take up much processing space. Through another
part of his aug, Keech accessed the local server, downloaded a mapping program, and relayed it to the scooter's
computer. He could easily have read the map in his aug, but
sometimes he preferred a more hands-on approach. Perhaps
it was his age . . . In a moment, the screen indicated his
present position on a 500-kilometre-square grid-map.
Ahead of him was a cluster of islets the map obscurely
named the 'Pepper Shells', and east of him was an object
labelled 'The Big Flint'. He was speculating on whether or
not this meant Spatterjay had chalk beds—out of which
flint is propagated—when there was a sudden spray of water, a crashing noise, and the scooter slewed sideways
through the air.

Keech immediately took manual control and turned the
scooter to prevent it tipping over. As the scooter rapidly decelerated, he glanced sideways and wondered just for a moment if he was hallucinating. The head of a pink rhinoceros,
at the end of ten metres of wormish body that was being
dragged through the waves, had clamped its beaked mouth
on the scooter wing, just behind the port thruster. The
scooter's AG units whined as it tipped and Keech found himself looking into angry little blue eyes. He quickly pulled the
column in the opposite direction and boosted the starboard
motor. There was a growling rumble and more sea spray shot
in the air. The scooter rose, and tilted further. The rhinoworm's body came clear of the water, then the creature
abruptly let go and dropped back into the sea. Keech shut off

the motors and let the scooter regain its stability, then he slammed the motors on full as the head of the worm rose out of the sea again. The Pepper Shells were now off to his left. He turned the scooter towards them, chose one and headed for it as quickly as he could, now careful to keep the scooter more than ten metres above the sea's surface.

There were at least fifty islets, all no larger than fifty metres across. Keech slowed the scooter and eased it down too the centre of the largest of them. He saw that his landing area consisted of worn stone inset with quartz crystals of every shade imaginable. Scattered loosely on this surface were broken shells and fragments of pink and white chitin like broken porcelain. The scooter crunched on these as it settled. Keech dismounted and immediately inspected the vehicle's wing: there were scratches on the metal. But it was otherwise undamaged. But the rhinoworm had come close to tipping the scooter over before its beak slid off, and from the organic part of his brain Keech had felt a surge of emotion that felt very much like fear. He gazed back out to sea and recognized the sinuous wave of the worm approaching. It was persistent; he had to give it that. Movement close by then attracted his attention and he glanced down at the shore close by to see a mass of spiral shells shifting about. Abruptly one of these bounced into the air on a thick white foot like an anaemic tongue, and came in to land only a few metres away from him. From this shell rose two eyestalks. As one, from all those down on the beach, rose a small forest of similar eyestalks. He had never seen anything quite so ridiculous. But when the shell nearest to him tilted back to expose a large circular mouth full of more moving parts than a high-tech food processor, he quickly remounted his scooter and took off. As he passed over those on the shore, a couple of them leapt up in the air and bounced off the underside of his scooter. He raised it even higher above the sea as he sped for his destination. The creatures here would have found his flesh unpalatable, but that would be little comfort to him.

With the rhinoworm and those things which he supposed must be frog whelks a couple of kilometres safely behind

him, Keech eased the steering column to rest and shut off the
motors. The scooter drifted along twenty metres above the
waves while he again studied the map. Twelve kilometres to
go, and then he must go down again. He reached behind him
to get hold of his black attaché case, which he opened on his
lap. From the objects inside, he selected a short QC laser
carbine to complement the JMCC pulse-gun at his hip. He
also selected a tray with a touch-control panel on the side. In
this tray rested three innocuous two-centimetre-diameter
steel spheres. He then selected a program via the panel, and
ran it. The three spheres rose out of the tray and positioned
themselves around him. Satisfied, he studied the disassem-
bled weapon that remained in the case. The dealer on Coram
who had supplied this weapon to him, had taken a huge risk
for which he had been well recompensed, yet Keech felt he
would not be needing such armament unless wholesale war
broke out on Spatterjay. He closed the case and replaced it in
the luggage compartment before easing the steering column
forward. The spheres held their positions around him as he
proceeded.

Lumps of coral protruded from the sea, like wormcasts of
stone and gothic arches. The sea hissed and slurped between
them, and past the banks of greyish and mounded below.
Through his binoculars, Ambel studied a clump of sargassum that was slowly being broken up and sucked through
one of these channels. There didn't seem to be any *untoward*
movement on the clump, but it would be best to be sure. He
lowered his binoculars and glanced down at the main deck.
    'Peck, you'll keep watch with Gollow and Sild,' he called,
nodding towards the two juniors he had only recently hired,
while reminding himself to memorize the names of the other
recent additions. 'It'll be me, Anne and Pland on the rakes.'
He then turned to Boris, who was at the helm, scratching at
his moustache and pretending disappointment. 'You stay
here, Boris, and make sure there's nothing nasty waiting for
us when we come back.'
    'Aye, Captain,' answered Boris as he eased the helm over
and brought the *Treader* into a deep-water channel between

sandbanks. The sail, with its neck now curved in an 's' and its head about five metres above the deck, glanced back at Boris and at his nod turned its body out of the wind, turning the fore and aft masts with it. It pulled on cables to fold the fabric sails, before releasing the spars and drawing in its wings. The shadow it cast quickly receded from the deck as it closed up, then hauled itself upright to perch on the fixed central spar. The *Treader* slowed and at the bows two of the crew lifted the heavy triple anchor and heaved it over the side. Greased chain ratcheted off the windlass until it bottomed, clouding the water of the channel. They secured the windlass as the ship tugged against the chain and halted. Anne had meanwhile opened one of the rail lockers and removed two long-handled rakes, a riddle, and some hide sacks. These she tossed on to the sandy bank below, before jumping down herself. She was soon followed by Pland as, with a whoop, he too leapt from the rail.

'Give him another two hundred years and he might grow up,' muttered Boris.

Ambel nodded in agreement, then gestured to the deck cannon bolted to the stern rail of the forecabin. 'That loaded?' he asked. When Boris nodded, he went on. 'Let off a shot if you see anything nasty coming in. Preferably at it. We'll get back sharpish.' With that, he climbed down the ladder to the deck and shortly followed Anne over the rail and on to the sandbank. After Gollow and Sild, Peck was last over the rail, landing in a crouch from which he slowly straightened while pumping a shell into the chamber of his shotgun. He gazed about suspiciously, and then nodded approval at the two juniors as they drew pangas from their belt sheaths.

'Likely only be prill here,' observed Ambel. Peck concurred but did not seem particularly reassured. Ambel stooped to pick up the two rakes, and handed one of them to Anne. To Pland he said, 'You collect and sack 'em.' And with that, they set off.

Soon they had reached a lower level where streaks of yellow were smeared across the flat sand. This area was also pocked with little hollows, and as soon as Ambel planted one heavy boot on the edge of it, squirts of water were ejected from these hollows and there arose a crackling hiss.

'Plenty here,' he said. 'You got the bait, Anne?'

Anne handed him a small bag closed with a drawstring. He opened it well away from his face, but even so the smell was strong enough to make his eyes water. He reached inside the bag and tossed a handful of its contents into the air ahead of him. Dried and flaked fish meat snowed down across the sand, and as it settled it elicited further movement; further hollows rapidly appeared and the occasional orange-lipped mouth opened at the surface. Ambel and Anne stepped forward and began vigorous raking, drawing the long white-shelled clams from just below the surface, into heaps. Pland came in behind them, selecting only those the size of a hand to drop into the riddle. When this was full, he took it to a nearby pool, to clean the molluscs of sand before tipping them into a sack.

'Hey up! Look at this lad!' shouted Ambel, hooking out a larger clam with the edge of his rake. It was almost twice the size of the ones Pland was collecting. Ambel dropped his rake and grabbed the mollusc before it buried itself again. It fought him for a moment, then came up with a sucking hiss, waving its fringed foot in the air.

'This is the one for me,' Ambel said, stepping to the nearby pool to wash his trophy before holding it up for all to see. He drew his sheath knife and inserted the blade between its shells, twisted, then hinged the clam wide open. Inside he revealed a pint of quivering translucent amber flesh.

'Always best fresh, though I could do with some vinegar and pepper,' he said.

A quick slice round with his knife and he tipped the whole lot into his mouth before discarding the empty shells. He chewed at it for a moment, with orange juice running down his chin, then swallowed, pulled a face, and reached into his mouth with his fingers. He pulled something out, then swallowed the rest, before wiping his chin on his sleeve.

'I'll be buggered,' he said.

Pland and Anne moved up to see what he had found. Peck tramped over as well, with the two juniors trailing behind him as Ambel held up a small silver sphere for their inspection.

'Pearl in the first clam of the season. Our luck's in, lads!'

Anne and Pland nodded in agreement. Peck gave first the pearl then Ambel a suspicious look before summoning to the two juniors and moving away again.

Ambel pocketed the pearl and stooped to take up his rake. 'Come on, let's get these sacks full. I got a feeling this'll be our best voyage yet!'

'Tis good luck,' agreed Gollow.

Peck meanwhile grunted and muttered something foul. Ambel threw him a glance of annoyance before he got down to more raking. Peck had been sailing with him for a very long time, and knew him a lot better than most of the crewmen.

4

The unexpected bounty of the crippled frog whelk had given the hammer whelks much satisfaction and made them forget a cardinal rule of the seabed: heads down and eyes up. In their excitement they hammered away at the bottom and further stirred water clouded by their victim's vital fluids. The passing turbul which had snapped up a floating eye-stalk, ruminated on how tasty its snack had been, and turned back to see what more it might find. Soon joined by its own fellows—who quickly sensed the possibility of an easy meal—it descended on the spreading cloud. The whelks, unable to see any more than a few metres through the murked water, were still hammering away, when the first turbul went through with its mouth open. Its fellows came arrowing after it and soon the water was further clouded by juices and a rain of glittering broken shell, or the occasional intact shell sucked empty. The turbul—not often having the chance of coming upon hammer

whelks unawares—had forgotten the cardinal rule that ap-
plied to the piscine creatures of the sea: feed and run. But the
approaching glisters had not.

Encircling the island were ridges of reef shaped like the ripples from a stone cast into water. These reefs were navigable
and it was possible to get to the island by ship, but few
Hoopers bothered, or so Keech had been told. It was this
piece of information that had resulted in, partially, his decision to bring his own transport here to Spatterjay. He came
in over the reefs and circled the island. Eventually he saw a
wooden jetty and beyond it a track cut into the dingle. From
above, it was impossible to see where the track led, so he
brought his scooter down on the stony beach between dingle
and jetty. The track was too narrow for the scooter, so he dismounted and, with his carbine tucked under one arm and the
three guard spheres following him, he walked into the tree
shadows. Immediately, on either side of him, he could hear
things moving in the foliage, and at one point caught sight of
the glistening body of a leech the size of a man, heaving
past. Nothing attacked him though and he wondered if he
was being over-cautious.

The track eventually led to a clearing. The earth here was
completely bare of growth and Keech assumed it had been
poisoned; so verdant was the surrounding dingle. At the centre of the clearing stood a short stone tower with satellite
dishes mounted on a pylon on the roof. Also on the roof, he
could see the edge of an AGC of a very old design. In the
walls of the building were wide mirrored windows, and
along one side was a conservatory with sun lamps mounted
inside. The glare of the Earthlight seemed harsh and crystal
in contrast to the natural greenish light of Spatterjay's sun.
To one side of this conservatory was a single steel door with
an intercom set beside it. Keech headed across the poisoned
ground to the door. Only out here in the open could he see
the autogun on the roof tracking his progress. He ignored it.

The intercom buzzed and clicked then a woman's voice
babbled, 'What do you want? What do you want?'

'Information,' said Keech.

'An important commodity, but all the same something that can be acquired in great quantities from AIs, libraries, and even, dare I mention them, books,' replied the voice.

'You are considered the greatest authority on the history of Spatterjay.'

'Yes, yes, yesss and I know who you are, corpsey. Deactivate your balls and enter.' This the woman followed with a giggle before going on in more sober tones, 'My house won't let you in still armed, so be sure you are not, Sable Keech.'

Keech held up his hand, and through his aug transmitted an instruction. The guard spheres settled in his palm and he placed them on the ground. He put his other weapons down next to them and by the time he was standing again, the door was open. He entered a narrow hall and stood still while a scanning light traversed his body. There was a long pause, then the woman spoke again.

'My house is a fucking moron!' Another long pause. 'You may enter now.'

The scanning light flicked off and the door at the end of the hall opened. Keech walked through into a luxuriously furnished room that was walled with books. The woman sat at a desk against one wall with a computer screen switched on before her. She spun round on her chair and looked him up and down. He in turn inspected her.

She appeared young, but then that could be a matter of choice. She had long black hair in a plait down her back. Her figure under her toga was lush and running to fat. Her skin had Hooper leech marks on it and revealed somewhat more of a blue tinge than he had so far seen. He guessed she had not been eating enough Dome-grown foods to prevent the mutation the Spatterjay virus could cause. 'Going native' was the Hoopers' way of describing it, and they were most reticent about the result.

'Why is your house a moron?' Keech asked her.

The woman stared at him in open confusion, then after a moment seemed to recover her senses. She shook her head and stared down at the floor of polished quartz.

'It thinks all your metalwork is weaponry. Doesn't realize it's just to stop you falling apart.'

She grinned at her little joke.

'You're Olian Tay,' said Keech.

'Yes I am!' She leapt to her feet and suddenly had a manic look about her.

Keech watched her silently for a moment, before speaking slowly, enunciating every word. 'You need Dome-grown food. You are going native.'

Tay held her arms out in front of herself and inspected them. 'Pretty blue,' she said.

'Very pretty,' said Keech, then, 'I won't take up too much of your time. I just need information.'

Tay turned and dropped into her seat again. 'It's all here; the definitive history of Spatterjay.' She waved her hand at the screen. 'But you have to pay.'

'I'm a wealthy man,' said Keech. 'I've had money invested for a very long time.'

Tay shook her head. 'Money money money.'

She shook her head again then stared up into the corner of the ceiling.

'What do you want?' he asked.

'Hungh?'

'What do you want, I said?'

Tay's gaze suddenly fixed on him and her soberness returned. 'You're right. I need supplements.'

She stood and quickly strode across the room to a cabinet. She opened it and took out a bottle, uncorked it and drank deeply. Draining it completely, she dropped it on the floor, and then, as if forgetting that she was not alone, she dropped on to a sofa, lay back, and closed her eyes. The thick smell of garlic permeated the air.

Keech walked to her and stood over her. She opened her eyes and glared at him.

'Go away,' she said. 'Come back in an hour.'

'Will your house let me back in?'

'It will. It knows what you are now.'

'And what is that?'

'A cop who won't even let death stop him from making that last arrest.'

Keech nodded and gave an approximation of a smile. He turned away and headed for the exit, and before he reached it, Tay was already snoring. Taking up his weaponry outside the house, Keech checked off the time in his aug and decided to look around. His patience had been centuries long, and in some places was a matter of legend. Another hour or so would make little difference to his quest. Ten minutes brought him to Tay's museum of grotesqueries.

At first, Keech thought he was seeing some kind of storage tank half-swamped by dingle. The thing was cylindrical, about ten metres high and three times that in diameter. There were no openings visible to Keech in its dull blued-metal surface until he had walked almost past it. Then he saw an archway nearly concealed by plaits of brown vines which sprouted silvery-green leaves like hatchet blades. He checked the vines for any lurking leeches, turned on the auxiliary light on his laser carbine, and then ducked inside, the guard spheres following like mechanical blowflies. Inside he found he did not need the light on his carbine, as fluorescent light globes were activated by his presence. For a moment, though, he thought he might need the other functions of his carbine.

It stood four metres tall and looked like a man who had been stretched on the rack for a hundred years. It was blue, monstrous, spidery and impossibly thin. Its hands were insectile and its head was a nightmare. This model—for model it was—seemed like something out of Hindu demonology. Keech advanced until he was standing right below it, and there gazed down at a brass plaque set in the floor. The plaque said simply 'The Skinner'. Keech moved past this weird exhibit to examine the first of three rows of glass cases.

'Full Thrall Unit' read the first plaque, but did not well enough inform of this example of Tay's obvious taste for the grotesque. Inside the case was a seated human skeleton with its skull bowed forwards. The top of the skull had been neatly cut away to show a metal cylinder that had been driven in through the back of the skull. From this cylinder, metal spines, like bracing struts, connected all around inside the skull, and from the end a glassy tube curved down into the spine. The second display showed one of these cylindrical units completely disconnected and mounted on a wooden pedestal. Further along was a bowed skeleton with a cylinder of grey metal clinging to the back of the neck vertebrae with its jointed legs. The plaque here described this device as a 'Spider Thrall Unit'. A touch-plate set into the plastiglass of the case turned the whole case into a holographic display. Keech recognized ancient scenes from the Prador war—of humans killing the mindless human 'blanks' that were the Prador's slaves. He moved on to the next item, then the next. These were all familiar to him as he had been alive at the time of the war, and had been involved in police actions then. He had held a weapon like this one, he had tried to release people from slave collars like those, and he had witnessed people dying in precisely that way . . .

The next case contained items that were more esoteric. 'Ten-Week Viral Mutation' was etched into the plaque before a skeleton of a human that had made it halfway to becoming the monster he had seen on entering this place. 'Feeding Tongue' was a pink tubular object suspended in a jar of clear fluid. There was no other explanation. What else there was in the case he never discovered, for then something in the third row of cases immediately caught his avid attention.

'Jay Hoop' nicknamed 'Spatter'.

The man was tall, handsome and saturnine, with black cropped hair and eyes that were almost black. He was posing in an ancient environment suit, holding a short flack rifle that rested on one shoulder. The details of the model were perfect, down to the small hook-shaped scar below his right eye and the semi-precious stones sewn below the neck-ring of the suit. Keech studied the model long and hard, then moved on to the next in the row of eight cases. He was on his third circuit of the cases when Tay's irritated voice spoke from an intercom.

'Did you come here for information or to gawp? I'd have thought you knew their faces well enough by now.'

Keech nodded to himself then returned to exit the arch. As he ducked out, he was lost in thought until something thudded on his shoulder. The leech struck just as he slammed his hand on it and pulled it away. One of the guard spheres went through the leech in mid-air, cutting it in half and puffing out a spray of ichor. Stepping away from the arch, Keech triggered his carbine and with one flash turned the two writhing segments to smoking ash. After a moment, he reached up and touched his neck. His fingers came away wet with the balm that ran in his veins.

ETERNAL CUT—MINIMAL: SEALING, came the message from his aug through his visual cortex. Of course, he felt no pain, just an awareness of the damage done to him.

The sand banks and packetworm corals receded into the distance, but still the ship seemed surrounded by islands. Seated on the stool he had brought out on to the main deck, with his blunderbuss primed and loaded on his lap, Ambel watched a humped mass of sargassum drift close past the *Treader*. On this tangle of rotting stalks and gourd-like bladders, swarmed creatures like huge circular lice, and the clicking movement of their hard sharp legs could be clearly heard across the water. It was for these that Ambel had loaded his 'buss. Nasty-tempered creatures were prill; Hoopers had been known to lose their lives to them, a rare event in itself. The crew stood in readiness also. Peck had his pump-action shotgun out of its wrapping of oily rags and Anne had her automatic. Pland had only a large hammer, and a cauldron lid he used as a shield. His rifle had exploded the last time they'd had to fight off a swarm of prill, blowing a lump out of his forearm. He had been very annoyed as he'd liked that rifle. Boris, of course, was at the helm, but ready to leap across to the deck cannon. And the juniors, those of the crew who had recently joined the *Treader* and had yet to become able to afford any armament that was more effective, waited with pangas and pearwood clubs. The sail had rolled itself up to the highest spar and was watching proceedings with great, if pensive, interest.

As soon as the smell from the sargassum reached the crew, there was an immediate relaxing of the tension. The smell of rotting vegetation was strong, but not half so strong as the smell of putrefying flesh. The prill that had not already fed were in the process of devouring a large carcass lying tangled in the decaying weed. Ambel stood up to get a better look, and saw the body of a huge crustacean, something like a lobster, but with more fins and adaptations to ocean-going life. Its shell had the beautiful iridescence of mother-of-pearl.

'Glister,' said Peck, stating the obvious.

'That shell'd fetch a skind or two,' said Pland.

'Nearly as much as a pearl,' said Peck, giving Ambel a look.

'You want to go get it?' asked Anne.

Everybody laughed.

'All right lads, back to your stations,' said Ambel. He looked at the sail. 'You too.' The sail unfurled its wings and grasped the spars. The light wind belled it and it turned the rig of the ship in consonance with Boris's spinning of the helm, and the mast chains and cogs clunked below. Ambel went on, 'Peck and Pland on the harpoons and ropes. You take the nest, Anne. 'Nother couple of hours and we'll be out of this and heading for the feeding grounds, I reckon.' Ambel carefully eased down the hammer on his bus and lowered its butt to the deck. The weapon, which weighed half as much as a man, probably had more firepower than Boris's deck cannon. Anne moved to the sail's head as it came down to the deck. She stepped on to it, grasping the creature's neck in her right hand, and it lifted her towards the crow's nest.

'Feeding grounds, I'll be buggered,' said Boris, mimicking Peck's tone to perfection. As she rose past him, Anne laughed then holstered her automatic.

'Look at it this way,' said Ambel, addressing them all after hearing the comment. 'We get a good haul and we won't have to go out during all the ice season. It'll be sea-cane rum and Dome grub for a six-month.'

'More like crawling ashore a stripped fish,' muttered Peck.

Ambel looked at him. 'Skin feeling a bit loose is it, Peck?' he asked.

Peck swore at him, but the other senior crew laughed anew. Junior crew were puzzled by this exchange, so Ambel assumed they had yet to hear Peck's story. He smiled to himself. It was always like this before a hunt. The lads would thank him afterwards. When had things ever gone wrong, he tried to ask himself without irony.

The *Treader* continued on its course, its sail turning to catch the best of the wind and muttering about feeding times, and the yellow and brown islands of sargassum slowly sliding behind it.

Skin feeling a bit loose, thought Peck, and the thought made him itch. He scratched himself whilst gazing back from the rail towards Ambel, as the Captain ducked into his cabin to put away his blunderbuss. *He* didn't know, in fact none of them knew what it was like. He glanced at the fabric foresail and saw that it had snagged part of the way down its slide.

'That needs sorting,' he said to the junior who was helping him, and indicated the jammed sail. The woman nodded to him and headed for the mast, taking up a hammer from one of the tool lockers as she went. She quickly climbed the mast and hammered at the slide mechanism until the lower spar dropped into place, pulling the sail taut. Peck lowered his gaze to the cabin again and felt the overpowering need to reveal what had been hidden, something that the Skinner had been about to reveal to him.

Come.

He could feel the call in the marrow of his bones and in the heart of everything he was. What would it be like to be . . . like that? What secrets were hidden?

'Those harpoons won't sharpen 'emselves, Peck,' said Pland, in the process of coiling up one of the harpoon lines as he strolled past. Peck glanced at his fellow crewman and wondered if he felt it too.

'Pland, do you—'

'Peck! Those harpoons won't sharpen themselves!' bellowed Ambel as he stepped out of the forecabin.

Pland grinned at Peck and went to untangle another line. Peck squatted by the rail where the harpoons were racked.

'Buggering leech hunt,' he muttered to himself. The hold was nearly full of barrels of pickling turbul meat, and they had four full barrels of amberclams which would spoil if they weren't back in port within the week. But Ambel always wanted that bit extra before the bergs started sliding down from the north. Admittedly, they often did well, and because of this were often in the chair at the Baitman. Their 'luck' had even once enabled them to afford a laser, but with the rocky exchange rate of the skind, they had been unable to afford replacement power packs for it, so had swapped it for a deck cannon. *Luck.* Peck snorted—how many times had he seen Ambel do that pearl trick? Anne and Pland had only been with the Captain for the last thirty years, so they were not yet wise to his ways. Still grumbling, Peck reached into the pocket of his long coat and took out his sharpening stone. The harpoon blades weren't that blunt, so there was no point unscrewing them to give them a proper going over. Peck ran the back of his hand along one razor edge until it bit in and there was a brief spurt of blood. Hardly need sharpening at all.

Come . . .

Tay was still lying on her couch when Keech walked in and stood before her. He glanced at one of the chairs opposite her but did not sit until she waved him to it with an irritated gesture.

'They're self-cleaning,' she said.

Keech blinked as his irrigator worked on his eye. It had been his experience that often people did not like a walking corpse sitting on their furniture.

'Information,' she said. 'I only trade in information.' She closed her eyes.

'I don't know what I can give you,' said Keech.

'You know why I know your name,' she muttered. 'Give

me something unrecorded. Give me something about the eight that I don't know.'

Keech was silent for a long while. Eventually he said, 'Aphed Rimsc killed me and threw my body into the Klader sewers. It took a week for them to find me, and six months of court actions after that before they acted on my will and handed me over to the Cult. Do you want to hear about that?'

'Thoroughly documented. You'd signed up as a member of the Cult of Anubis Arisen some years before. Limitations of mortality, I suspect. There was a legal suit brought to try and prevent your reification, but the Cult backed you all the way. I also know that same suit was brought by Rimsc himself,' said Tay. She had less of a blue tinge to her skin now.

Keech went on, 'Rimsc died when the seal on his spacesuit failed outside the Klader space habitat. His body wasn't reclaimed because the resulting blowout flung him towards Klader. He burnt up in atmosphere before anyone could get to him.' Tay opened her eyes and waited. Keech continued, 'What is not known is why his suit seals failed. They failed because they were eaten away from the inside, just as he was eaten away inside the same spacesuit. Somebody put a pressure-activated vessel of diatomic acid in his oxygen supply. When his oxygen got below a certain level, the vessel opened and flooded his suit with acid vapour. It must have been a very unpleasant death, especially for a Hooper.'

Tay sat up. 'There were rumours about it, but nothing was confirmed. You'd been reified by then hadn't you?' she said.

'Four days,' said Keech.

Tay smiled. 'What do you want to know then?' she asked.

Keech moved over to one of the armchairs and sat. He steepled his bony fingers before his face and regarded Tay with his single blue eye, as his irrigator sprayed, moistening the eye. His face was immobile.

'I know about Rimsc, Corbel Frane, the Talsca twins, Gosk Balem, and David Grenant. I don't know what happened to Rebecca Frisk or to Hoop himself. For two hundred years I've been chasing rumours and myths. When they don't come to nothing, they lead back here. Tell me what *you* know.'

Tay looked up to the ceiling. 'House computer, make a copy of the Rebecca Frisk file to crystal.'

The computer on the desk beeped and a small crystal popped up out of the touch-console. Keech glanced across the room at it. His face twitched and his eye irrigator began working double time.

'You know it was her and Hoop who started out together. From what I've been able to put together they started as art thieves on Earth. From such little acorns . . . ' explained Tay.

Keech continued to stare at the crystal. 'Tell me about it,' he said.

Tay said, 'Frisk walked into the ECS building in Geneva on Earth and told them who she was. When this was confirmed she requested a mind wipe, which she was duly given. After that they gave her a basic overlay personality and she was sent back here. The Friends of Cojan snatched her halfway and fed her into a zinc smelter.'

Keech sat back. 'The Friends are still about? They helped me trace Rimsc.'

'No, they are not still about. This was three hundred years ago. ECS kept a lid on it, but I'm surprised you didn't know about it. You were an ECS monitor before you were killed. Surely you had contacts?'

'I never bothered much about her. She was the least of them. What about Hoop?'

'No . . . Now I want something more from you. Tell me about Corbel Frane.'

'I found him on Viridian, in a castle he had occupied for five hundred years,' said Keech. 'He was a living legend there, and it was difficult for me to get to him. The first time I managed to get through his defences I cut him in half with an industrial shear. His staff sewed him back together again and he was walking within one solstan year. I didn't make the same mistake again. I used Junger mercenaries to assault his castle and when he escaped, I pursued him to the summit of mount Ember. Even an old Hooper cannot survive immersion in magma.'

Tay nodded. 'I like that,' she said. 'You realize I'm recording this meeting.'

'I didn't think otherwise.'

'It doesn't bother you?'

'There is no statute of limitations on the things they did, and I am still officially an Earth Central Security monitor. They were all under sentence of death, whether physical or mental. Now, what do you know about Hoop?'

Tay abruptly stood and went to the wall cabinet. She removed another bottle of the substance she had drunk earlier. This time she filled a glass before returning to the sofa with it.

'Holodrama and VR has them as lovable rogues and dashing pirates. Time will do that to even the most heinous of villains,' said Tay as she collected her thoughts.

'You're telling me this? Hoop and his crew were murderers and thieves. They used this world as their base and the immortality the virus here conferred on them, enabled them to terrorize this whole sector for two centuries. They stole and they killed, and they sold humans to the Prador cored,' said Keech. His words were flat, without inflexion.

Tay looked at him carefully. 'You were on the mission that came here at the end of the war, weren't you?' she asked.

'I was. And the things we witnessed here have made me what I am. I will not rest until they are *all* dead. I will not stop.'

'So there's only Hoop for you to get. What happens when you do get him—when you've killed him?'

Keech looked down at the lozenge of metal on its chain around his neck. 'Option one is that I die completely,' he said. 'I am exploring other options.'

'That is a changer nanofactory?' said Tay, pointing at the lozenge.

'It is. Tell me more about Hoop.'

'The mission you were on drove Hoop and his crew from here and scattered them. With their wealth and the experience of a couple of centuries of life, they established themselves in niches across this sector. The Talsca twins and David Grenant were hunted down and killed by The Friends of Cojan. It's believed they were lowered feet-first into boil-

ing water.' Tay stopped talking when she saw Keech nodding.

'I can confirm part of that,' Keech said. 'I knew Francis
Cojan quite well. He kept a holocording of the event that he
showed me. But I only saw the Talsca twins on that recording. It took them a long time to die and they died hard.'

'I see . . . Gosk Balem returned here and died in the sea.
Hoopers who were the direct descendants of slaves The
Eight kept here, or were original slaves themselves, threw
him into a leech swarm in Nort sea. That one is well docu-
mented. Frane and Rimsc were the ones you tracked down.
Frisk and Hoop fled from the sector and lived on a world in
Prador space for fifty years. That comes from Frisk. She
left him there and just went and handed herself over to
ECS. Attack of conscience? There seems no other explana-
tion.'

'And Hoop? What about Hoop?'

Tay looked at him very directly.

'Hoop is here,' she said.

Keech said nothing. He moved not at all.

Tay went on, 'A hundred and sixty-three years ago a craft
was detected by the Warden. It went into orbit and attempted
a sea landing. It was a very old craft. Unfortunately the
Segre atolls got in its way and it crashed. The wreckage was
found to be that of the Prador landing craft Hoop favoured—
the craft he called *Bucephalus*. There was blood in the craft
and it was Hoop's. There was no trace of Hoop himself.'

'It is not certain that he is still here then,' said Keech.

'It is. No spacecraft have come to Spatterjay since. The
only way out is through the runcible gate on Coram, and the
Warden monitors that. Humans might forget criminal activity. AIs forget nothing.'

'He could be dead, then?'

'He might have been injured enough to bleed, which *is*
unusual for an old Hooper, but he *is* the oldest Hooper in existence, perhaps a thousand years. What do you think?'

'Rumours?'

'I've heard a few. Some have it that he is operating as a
ship captain. Others have it that he went native and became

something . . . horrible. Have you heard the legend of the Skinner?'

Keech gave a slow nod, remembering the thing in Tay's museum.

'The Skinner is a creature that lives on an island and traps any ship Hoopers who land. It seems the one goal in life of this creature is to strip Hoopers of their skins and leave them to suffer in agony for months. The story goes that a lone Captain and an off-worlder went to the island and beheaded the creature, and that this Captain is now said to carry the living head of the Skinner in a box on board his ship. This way the Skinner can never pull itself back together sufficiently to cause the pain it once did. Its living body alone would just be that of an animal. This all happened at the Segre Islands, which have for some time been known as The Skinner's Islands.'

'And this creature, this Skinner, is supposed to be Hoop?'

'Supposedly. Your best course of action now would be to speak to some of the Old Captains. Tell them who you really are. They'll respect that.'

'Would a Captain Ron be one of the ones I should talk to?'

'Oh yes, definitely.'

'And a Captain Ambel?'

'Yes, he and Captian Ron are two of the oldest.'

'Original slaves?'

'So it's rumoured.'

'Why aren't there more of them?'

'Many left Spatterjay. It's an interesting world but it has its limitations for people entering in the latter half of a thousand years of life. Many stayed and died. This world is dangerous even for Hoopers. Many more killed themselves. There's a poison here manufactured from the digestive tract of some of the larger leeches. It neutralizes the virus, and acts on the Hooper body much like that favourite of yours: diatomic acid. A Hooper taking this stuff will come apart in a matter of minutes—spectacularly.'

Keech stood and gazed towards the door. Then he stared at the data crystal Tay had made him.

'If you'll permit me,' he said, 'I'd like to run some searches through your databanks.'

Tay smiled almost hungrily and gestured to her console. 'Stay as long as you like. I'm sure there is much more detail you can fill me in on.'

Keech watched her for a moment, then moved over to the console and sat down. He pressed the data crystal back into place then viewed what it contained on the screen.

Tay stood and walked up to stand behind him. 'Now,' she said, 'describe to me exactly how it was when Aphed Rimsc killed you.'

The woman gazed out across the salt flats to where a plume of dust cut across a range of yellow sandstone buttes. Soon this plume opened into a line, abruptly terminating as the approaching transport turned to head in. Like most Prador methods of transportation, this vehicle, when revealed, bore a close resemblance to the passenger or passengers it carried. It was a ridged teardrop like a spidercrab's carapace, with antennae and sensor arrays mounted to the fore and grab claws folded up as ribs underneath. Beyond this, though, the similarities ended. The transport was bright red and had weapons turrets bulging from the sides. The pictographs of the Prador language adorned every surface, and this vehicle could really move. Behind it the clouds of salt crystals rolled on and settled, and as the vehicle came past the demesne, a double sonic crash shook the crystal windows before the following cloud obscured the view.

The woman turned from the window and for a moment inspected one of her collection of paintings. This particular canvas depicted a similar scene to the one she had just witnessed, and it had been painted by the previous resident of this house, being, as far as she knew, nearly a century and a half old. Next to this was a painting of a man and woman standing on a monolithic rock and staring out to sea, while things that might have been seagulls circled above them. She frowned at this picture before moving to the bar, pouring herself a drink, and then heading out on to the balcony. Here she watched the transport slow and turn. The taste of salt in the air was sharp on her tongue and she sipped her cool-ice to wash it away. Between two security posts the shimmer-shield flickered and went out, and the vehicle coasted in over the blue grass lawns and ornamental ponds. With the rumbling and decreasing whine of thruster motors, it settled by the ramp provided for Prador visitors. The woman went back inside to her comunit to see if there had been any communications yet.

'Councillor Ebulan requesting audience,' said the voice.

The woman looked at the face of the human blank on the screen and recognized it as one she had herself provided. She couldn't remember the female's name, but then what did it matter what name you gave a human shell? To the Prador, a blank like this would just have the title 'Speaker', as so many did.

'I'm always glad to see the councillor,' she said. It would have been impolitic to refuse to receive him. Even with all her wealth, she was still regarded as a second-class citizen of the Prador Third Kingdom. She finished her drink and went into her bedroom. There she discarded her robe and moved to stand before the wall mirror. Still good, after all this time. She had made the right choice with this body. The subject had been a beautiful woman with just the right combination of athleticism and femininity. Before coring, she had apparently been the daughter of an ECS monitor known to that damned Keech. A surprising discovery had been her virginity. The woman smiled at the memory and went to her wardrobe to select appropriate garb.

Three blanks walked up the ramp before the councillor drifted out. Ebulan was an old Prador and all his atrophied legs were gone. He was simply a carapace shaped like a flattened pear with a scalloped rim. Antennae clustered round his fore, and an arc of blood-red spider eyes arrayed the turret front of what might be called his head. Shell-welded to his underside were the four polished cylinders of his AG units. Underneath the slow grind of his mouthparts had been welded the hexagonal control boxes. The woman counted fifteen of them, which meant he controlled fifteen human blanks. In Prador terms this was a sign of prestige: Ebulan was wealthy enough to own fifteen cored humans and had the mental strength to run them all, through their thrall units, simultaneously.

The central blank of the three—the speaker the woman had seen, now clearly identified by pictographs tattooed on her body—stepped ahead of the other two. The woman noted the armour on the other two, and the heavy hand weapons they carried. It wasn't hard to work out what they were for. Prador adults were meticulous about their personal safety. Prador adolescents, who were slaves to their parents' pheromones, and human blanks, had mostly fought the war.

'Greetings,' said Speaker.

'And to you, Ebulan. It's been a long time,' said the woman.

'What is time?' Ebulan asked through the mindless speaker.

The woman smiled and fingered the human-skin jacket she wore.

'Obviously I am honoured by this visit, but I am also curious,' she said.

'A social visit,' said Ebulan, 'and a small return of favours.'

'Then please, enter.'

The woman turned and led the way up the ramp. The three blanks followed her. Then came Ebulan, and after him came three adolescent Prador. Two of these were a twentieth of Ebulan's size and each walked on six long legs. Folded underneath each of them were four arms ending in their hugely complex manipulatory hands, and in front of them were their heavy crab claws. These sexless creatures were loyal to their masters only while they remained sexless. Most Prador now used humans rather than their own kin, who were unpredictable and could not be as loyal as something mindless and under direct control. All high-level Prador like Ebulan had guards of some kind, since Prador politics was never less than lethal. All of the cored humans here, but for the speaker, were heavily armed. The third Prador adolescent was much larger than the others, and his coloration was deep purple and yellow. The woman realized that this one was not much longer for adolescence but unlikely to attain adulthood. No doubt he was soon due to have his legs stripped and his shell broken, which was the destiny of most of his kind.

Settled in the room of her demesne especially reserved for Prador visitors, the woman and Ebulan exchanged pleasantries for as long as it took Ebulan to have his blanks check out the whole area and position themselves. Once he was satisfied a rival had not predicted the visit, and no traps were laid, Ebulan settled down on his AG units.

'Something has occurred,' said Ebulan through the speaker.

'Please tell me,' said the woman.

'The reification has returned, at last, to Spatterjay.'

The woman sat very still as a thousand memories shrieked for attention. She felt a brief nausea as her central core went into nerve conflict with the body she had stolen.

'Does this not interest you, Rebecca?' asked the councillor.

Rebecca Frisk turned and gazed out of the crystal windows towards the salt flats. Keech—always damned Keech. Even after sending her own body, fitted with the brain and spinal column that had been in this current body, to ECS, she could not be safe while he . . . existed.

'He's still alive,' she stated.

'I wonder who you mean,' said Ebulan.

Frisk glared at him. 'I mean Keech.'

'Problematical,' said Ebulan. He shifted on his AG units as if uncomfortable.

Frisk ignored that and stared out of the window again. 'Eight contracts and a hundred subcontracts from them, and every one a failure. Two of them were taken up by Batian stone killers. That bastard almost found out about me when he smeared them,' she said. She turned to Ebulan. 'Does he know about Jay?'

'This I was not able to determine.'

'He will.'

5

Having the ability to taste one part in a million of fresh ichor in the water, also possessing the thickest armour and the most efficacious mouthparts of any of the marine predators there, glisters were rapacious predators and assiduous scavengers. The four—a female and fertilizing males one to three— descended from their slimy home underneath a clump of decaying sargassum, and with tails flicking and flat legs extended as stabilizers, homed in on the delicious taste of dead or dying whelks, and that slightly hormonal hint of turbul in a feeding frenzy—that time in which the big fish became rather careless. The ever-spreading cloud of broken shell, fragments of flesh and essential juices, had lured to its perimeter a shoal of boxies, which fed with frenetic determination and a careful eye on the surrounding depths. As the glisters closed, the boxies fled, but the great crustaceans weren't interested in giving chase to them. Instead, they ground and chattered their mouthparts while contemplating the long meaty bodies of turbul rolling and feeding on whelks—still oblivious to their surroundings. Leeches now were also homing in to latch on to turbul for a moment, then ooze away with a bleeding prize, and even prill were descending from above like flying saucers with particularly vicious landing gear. And the glisters knew they would have to be quick, before their potential banquet became a dispersed cloud of floating canapés.

'Atoll GCV 1232, beginning census scan,' said SM13.
    'You only say that to irritate me,' said Sniper, as they hovered above an atoll like a huge apple core thrust down into the sea.

'The Warden's right, you know,' said the iron seahorse drone. 'You're getting cranky in your old age.'

'And you think counting snails is a worthwhile pastime?'

'No, but it's amazing what interesting items you can find out here and what they'll fetch in the auctions on Coram, and it beats subsumption every time,' replied Thirteen.

'I don't have to be wary of that. I'm a freed drone. I worked off my construction fees and indenture centuries ago. If I want to become part of the Warden, I can. I don't want to, yet.'

'Planting stealth mines on Prador dropbirds was how you paid your way out, as I recollect. You consider that a worthwhile pastime? Some of us are not so inclined to the martial occupation. Perhaps you should try subsumption at least once, it'd straighten out a few of your kinks.'

'I've got kinks?' Sniper paused for a moment. 'What interesting items?'

'Amberclam pearls, fossilized glister shell. I even found a vein of green sapphire once,' replied Thirteen.

'You never told me about this before,' said Sniper.

'Well, after the trouble I got into through snatching thrall units for you, I thought it best to keep quiet for a while.'

After a contemplative silence Sniper said, without heat, 'We gonna count these fucking snails or what?'

The little drone turned towards Sniper with light glinting in its amber eyes, then it turned its nose and tilted it in the direction of one side of the atoll.

'I'll go this way round and you go the other. We'll meet on the other side. This is the last one in sector fifty-two, then we can move on to fifty-three, which should be more interesting. There's molly carp there.'

'Oh joyful day,' said Sniper. 'You know why the Warden wants this census?'

'The way I got it was "A study to assess the long-term impact of runcible heat pollution and on which to base any future plans for environmental restructuring".'

'Make-work,' said Sniper, drifting down to the surface of the sea and lowering his back two legs into the water. The scanning probes in his feet now operating, he slowly began to trawl around the atoll. A subprogram he was running, now counted hammer whelks and catalogued them according to size and species. Sniper then ran one of his military programs to work out the minimum size of charge required to smash certain shells and kill their occupants. He did not test his theories until SM13 was out of sight. The trail of small underwater explosions the war drone left behind him was also undetectable. Five hours later, the two drones met on the other side of the atoll.

'You know, I don't get why you came here to work with the Warden,' said Thirteen, as they cruised on to pastures new.

'Easy enough. I wanted to spend time on a Line world like this: more chance of some sort of action. Nothing's got out of hand in the Polity for a long time now, and things are boringly peaceful. The few Separatist actions are normally flattened by ECS agents before there's any need to deploy war drones.'

Below them the water was the colour of jade, fractured by the occasional white wake from some cruising sea leviathan. The sky was a lighter green shading to blue, and steel-grey clouds held the setting sun as if in a broken pewter vessel. Sniper remembered a day when, above seas very like this, he had been engaged in hunting down two inferior Prador war drones. They had been of old utile design: just flattened spheres of armour wrapped around an AG unit, a mind, and magazines for the antipersonnel guns they had welded underneath. Such was the way of things: when a technology had been taken to its limit of efficiency and utility, you could make it look pretty. This flying brooch next to him was definitely one of the latest examples of that. But those Prador war drones had not reached that point.

Still with a feeling of satisfaction, Sniper remembered catching both Prador drones against the cliff face where they had been hiding. He had spent an hour carefully herding them until he could take them both out with one high-penetration missile. Of course, no one but himself had appreciated the poetry of that moment. The humans and big-fuck AIs running the clean-up operation had posited it as

yet another example of Sniper's flagrant individualism during organized conflict. Sniper had always been the odd one
out—from when his mind had been incepted by a dying AI
warship, up to and including his choice of a body-shape that
scared the shit out of most humans.

'You're ugly inside and out, AI,' said a man who had been
passing information to the Prador, just before Sniper had
snipped his head off.

'Remembering the good old days?' said Thirteen.

'Yeah,' said Sniper, and then began to hum a tune.

'What's that?' asked Thirteen.

' "Ugly Duckling," ' said Sniper then, gesturing ahead
with its heavy claw, continued, 'That one ain't on the map.'

Surrounded by white water was a grey atoll poking out of
the sea like the head of a man tilted to one side.

'Shit,' said Thirteen.

Out of habit, Sniper studied the little drone to try and read
its expression, but obviously to no effect. That use of an ex-
pletive had been very un-submindish, but then SM13 had
not been subsumed by the Warden for quite a while, the last
time being when it had been caught snatching thrall units
from the shore of one of the Segre Islands. Contemplating
this, the war drone followed Thirteen down when it changed
course to sweep in around the atoll.

'Packet-worm coral,' said the little drone. 'Must have
been shoved up in the last year.'

The edifice had the appearance of something on the facia
of a Hindu temple, only subtly distorted until nothing was
recognizably complete, just a wormish depiction of indefin-
able life: limbs and bodies chaotically tangled in organic
stone.

'This mean another census?' asked Sniper.

'It does. We have to count whelks around every above-
surface structure—that's what the Warden said.'

'Great, I really look forward to it.'

'Of course,' said Thirteen, a laser projecting from its neck
ridges to flash a gridded overlay on areas of the atoll, 'this
structure is unstable. You note how top-heavy it is and how
the sea is wearing through that edge lower down?'

'Yeah, I see it,' said Sniper.

'Not long before it collapses back into the sea, really.'

Sniper tilted in midair, smiled, and spat two cylinders from his square mouth. The cylinders slammed downwards drawing black lines through the air, and hit into the sea under the edge of the atoll. Underneath, the sea was lit by two deep red detonations before spuming into the air in a globular cloud. The atoll lurched sideways and with a growing hiss it slid into the waves. Water flooded into the remaining hollow and all around the sea went opaque with disturbed silt.

'Now that is what I call environmental restructuring,' said Thirteen.

'Drone bonding, as I neither live nor breath,' said Sniper, and they flew on.

Erlin leant on the rail shading her eyes against the green sunlight as she studied the distant shapes on the sea. When she heard someone come up behind her, she expected to see Captain Ron—but it was Janer. She checked to see if he was carrying his weapon, since she'd found, over the short period they had been on board, that he tended to forget it. He grinned at her, drew his QC laser from his utility belt, spun it round his forefinger, and then holstered it again. She shook her head and gazed out to sea.

'Here,' he said, 'try this.' He handed her an image-intensifier from the other side of his belt. She studied the device, noting that it had auto-tracking lenses and a magnification setting beyond anything she would be likely to use. She nodded her thanks and brought the device up to her eyes.

The nearest shape on the sea Erlin identified at a glance as a large clump of sargassum—all decaying arm-thick stalks, translucent bladders, and wadded yellow sheets of foliar material. Centring on the next shape out, she targeted it for the intensifier's auto-tracking, and focused on it—the intensifier now automatically correcting for shake. This shape was another clump of sargassum, but moored to it was a ship. After a moment of study, she lowered the intensifier, the chameleon-eye lenses whirring as they tried to keep the distant sargassum centred, and handed it back to Janer. Janer clicked it off and held it in his right hand as he leant his elbows on the rail.

'Any luck?' he asked.

'There's a ship out there, but it's not the *Treader*. It's twomasted and a bit smaller. Perhaps *they'll* know exactly where it is,' she replied, then turned to Captain Ron, who stood up on the forecabin watching them, and pointed out the distant ship. Ron nodded and gave instructions to his helmsman and to the sail. The sail muttered imprecations as it twisted its body on the spars to match the rapid spinning of the helm. It seemed as if there was some kind of ongoing competition between the helmsman and the creature. As the ship quickly heeled over, Janer studied the sail as it performed its duties, the movable spars and mast clonking in their greased sockets. He realized now that there were both fixed and movable spars that the creature utilized, and earlier he had been shown the mechanisms that moved the two other masts: long hardwood chains and hardwood sprockets, cog wheels and shafts running in bronze bearings. When he'd asked the junior greaseboy why their ships didn't have engines, the man had looked at him as if he'd gone quite mad.

'Why *are* they so low-tech here?' he asked Erlin. 'I mean . . . I haven't seen a single aug, wrist comp . . . anything. Everythin made of wood, solid metals, hide and organic fibres. Are they tech breakers, New Luddites, or what?'

Erlin turned and studied the ship as if seeing it for the first time. 'Money,' she explained. 'This is an Out-Polity world so doesn't qualify for any assistance other than free medicare, but that's mostly not needed, and for reasons I don't have to explain to you.'

Janer nodded. He'd not be forgetting that fight between Domby and Forlam for a long time.

Erlin went on, 'There's also very little industry here, because there's so few places to site it and no easily accessible resources, and because of *that* this place is poor. You already know what the exchange rate is with the skind. What we could buy for small change, a Hooper has to work for months to acquire.'

'Yes,' said Janer. 'You said something before about how difficult it is for them to leave this place: they have to work for years to buy passage.'

'And that's the only reason. I don't think the rumours of Polity suppression are true.'

Janer regarded her questioningly.

'It's been said that the Polity is scared of Hoopers,' continued Erlin. 'That ECS prevents technological growth here, and makes it difficult for Hoopers to leave.'

'Plausible though. Keech was saying about how much damage they could do off-planet if they felt so inclined,' said Janer.

'True,' Erlin nodded. 'But an AI like Earth Central wouldn't look upon them as an unhuman threat. It certainly doesn't look at Golem and boosted or augmented humans that way. Its usual recourse is to recruit them.'

'Hooper monitors; what a thought.'

'No doubt an option that's been contemplated. No, the reasons are mainly fiscal, and I'd also say that ECS hasn't tried to change that simply because non-interference is the safest option. Trying to shove a culture up the technological ladder mostly leads to social and environmental catastrophe. That lesson was learnt on Earth centuries ago.'

'So they're in a trap here?' said Janer.

'We might think so, but I don't think they do. When the Polity finally reached here two and a half centuries ago, a ground-base was immediately established, but the Hoopers have been in no hurry to take advantage of the technologies on offer. They're poor, but seem happy enough.'

Janer nodded, reflecting on how that was always the blinkered view of the wealthy. He glanced about at the few crewmembers as they went about their tasks.

'What sort of money do *they* earn?'

Erlin nodded towards Roach. 'Your average senior seaman like Roach there gets about two hundred skind as his share of a three-month trip out, and only then if the trip proves a profitable one. That being said, they can buy the technology.'

'So,' said Janer, calculating, 'something like a wrist comp, something your average autohandler tech could buy for ten New Carth shillings, maybe an hour's wages, would cost a Hooper three months' wages.'

'Not quite, they can get them cheaper here: about a hundred skind,' said Erlin.

'Still a lot of money to them. What about the Captains? What do they earn?'

'Their share is two to three times as much. Though even then they don't seem inclined to spend the money on Polity tech. Ambel could quite easily afford something like that.' Erlin nodded at the QC laser holstered at Janer's belt. 'He doesn't bother though. He sticks with a huge muzzle-loading weapon like a portable cannon. I've never really understood why.'

With the conversation turned to Ambel, Janer contemplatively studied Erlin's profile. 'Why so desperate to find this Ambel?' he asked.

'I'm not desperate. If I don't run into him on this trip I'll head back to the Dome and wait for him to turn up. It's just a decision I've made,' said Erlin tightly.

She glanced at him and he shrugged, bringing the intensifier up to his eyes. Obviously this was a subject Erlin did not want to pursue.

'There's things that look like crabs running about all over that weed,' he said.

'Prill,' she replied. 'If we get attacked by them you'd best get below.'

'Really,' said Janer. Not being reckless was one thing, but he'd be damned if he was going to spend all his time quivering in his cabin. That wasn't life.

Erlin watched him as he rehung the intensifier at his belt, before reaching up to the shaped transparent box on his shoulder. He gave the box a tug and it came free. With care not to rattle about the two hornets inside, he lowered the box to the rail then ran his finger along the side. The box flipped open. Erlin could not help feeling horripilation as the two hornets took off. She watched them fly and hoped they did not try to land on her. She looked at Janer queryingly.

'The mind wants a look around,' he explained.

One hornet shot off over the sea while the other buzzed, around the ship. The crew ignored the insects yet the sail was instantly curious; raising its head from the deck and tracing the progress of the hornet that had remained with the ship.

'Knowing that insects don't live long here I wonder why the mind had you come,' said Erlin.

'Now there's a question,' said Janer.

'One, I take it, that you asked?'

'Oh yes. I ask the mind all sorts of questions, and in return I get all sorts of answers. Not always the answers I'm after, though.'

'Could these hornets be . . . different?' Erlin asked.

Janer was thoughtful for a moment as he gazed in the direction of the hornet that had flown off over the sea.

'They don't live very long as individuals,' he said. 'These two are new ones—replaced before they should have been.' He tilted his head and listened. Erlin did not interrupt the unheard conversation that was obviously taking place. After a moment, he turned to her again.

'Altered,' he said.

Erlin nodded. Hive minds had no compunction about such things. There were stiff penalties for killing hornets, but they did not apply to minds killing their *own* hornets. This would, after all, be like imposing a penalty on a human for killing a few of his own brain cells. She looked at the hornet buzzing round the ship and noted how much attention the sail was still giving it.

'The crew know about hornets, but the sail doesn't,' she said.

'It will learn,' said Janer, uninterested, as he again took his intensifier from his belt and raised it to his eyes.

Later that day the sail did learn, when it snapped at the passing hornet. It howled and rolled itself up to the top of the mast. The crew spent the rest of the day trying to coax it down again.

This time, the humped shape in the water was no drifting mass of sargassum, but a living creature in search of prey. It was ten metres long and, judging by its girth of only a cou-

ple of metres, it had not fed in some time. On its glistening
ribbed back rode prill as hungry as itself. Theirs was a para-
sitic relationship. When the giant leech attached to prey, the
prill swarmed on to it as well to slice off lumps of meat with
their sickle legs. When the leech had fed and was therefore
unlikely to pursue more prey, the prill went in search of another mount. Ambel had his blunderbuss resting on his
shoulder as he gazed out at the creature. The rest of his crew
had armed themselves again.

'Bugger ain't picked us up,' said Peck, and immediately
the leech turned and started heading for the *Treader*.

'I wish you'd keep your bloody mouth shut,' said Boris,
rolling one end of his walrus moustache between forefinger
and thumb, before taking a firmer grip on the helm.

'We may as well take this one,' said Ambel. 'It's not going
to leave us alone.'

His crew-members looked up at him dubiously, then Anne
and Pland crouched to unstrap the five-metre harpoons from
where they were attached below the rail. Peck went over to
the opposite rail where Pland had hung the neatly coiled
ropes, and came back with a couple. He attached one end of
each coil to one of the rings set in the deck. The other ends
of the ropes Pland and Anne shackled to the harpoons. Boris
heeled the *Treader* over and the leech drew closer. The prill
leapt about excitedly on the monstrous creature's back.

'Pland, up here at the helm!' Ambel shouted. Pland
dropped the harpoon he had been weighing and scuttled to
obey. Boris released the helm to him and quickly moved to
the deck cannon. Glancing farther along the deck, Ambel
shouted, 'Gollow, send the young 'uns below. Could get a bit
frantic up here!' He watched as the junior crewman did his
bidding, then frowned as he and Sild returned to the deck.
Their contracts had them down as working twenty years on
the boxy boats and only a few years out on harvester ships
like his own. He considered sending them below as well, then
rejected the idea. They'd learn harsh realities soon enough.

'Keep us just ahead, nice and easy,' Ambel said, hefting
his blunderbuss and sighting it on the back of the leech. The
crash of the 'buss was shockingly loud and it released a

great gout of smoke. Three prill exploded into fragments.
Others fell from the back of the leech then, and swam to
catch up with it.

'Boris!' Ambel bellowed, and the deck cannon bellowed
in reply. More prill flew to pieces and more fell in the sea.
There were, however, still plenty left clinging to the back of
the leech, and it had slowed not at all. Ambel carefully rested
his 'buss against the rail before climbing down to the lower
deck and taking up one of the harpoons. He looked up at
Pland and nodded. Pland steered the ship into the path of the
leech and the sail, at his nod, turned itself out of the wind
and hauled in the reefing cables for the fabric sails. The
Treader slowed. With a couple of thrashes of its long flat tail
the leech was up beside the ship, and there was a grating
engine-sound as it tried to take a lump out of the hull. Ambel
knew that it would rapidly lose interest, and either dive or
swim away. He leant over the side and stabbed half the
length of the five-metre harpoon into its body. Held out his
hand for another, then another. Before any of the prill could
clamber on to the deck, he had put five harpoons into the
leech so it stood no chance of escaping. When it tried to rear
up out of the water, Peck and Ambel drew the harpoon ropes
taut so it could rise no higher than the side of the ship.

After lashing the helm, Pland looked down as one prill
clattered on to the deck. The creature was the size of a dinner
plate and had ten sickle legs sprouting from underneath it.
Eyes like red LEDs zipped around the edge of its carapace as
it crouched for its next leap. Pland snorted, and leapt before it
could. His hobnail boots came down squarely on top of it,
collapsing it underneath him with a liquid crunch. Its spread
legs quivered against the wood as he stepped away knocking
the mess from his soles. The next prill to leap aboard landed
right in front of him. He booted the creature towards Anne,
who shot it once. The hollow-point bullet made just as much
mess as Pland's boots, but by then the sailor did not need his
boots as he had grabbed hold of his hammer and cauldron lid
and could do some real damage. Peck was taking the prill at
the rail with his pump-action shotgun. Ambel just used his
fists and feet, and soon had a morass of prill insides and shat-

tered carapaces all about him. Out of the corner of his eye, he saw Gollow and Sild standing back to back, thwacking at prill with their pangas. They seemed to be doing well enough. The sail had rolled to the top of the mainmast and was keeping a wary eye on proceedings. All the crew made certain no prill made it to the mast, as the sail would flee if the horrible creatures started to climb toward it.

'Ah yer bugger!' was the limit of Pland's exclamation when a prill jammed one of its sickle legs into his thigh. He knocked it down on to the deck and, before it could recover, kicked the creature into the rail where Ambel got it on the rebound and stamped it to slurry—before turning to another balancing on the rail and punching it from the ship. Just then, Boris had managed to reload the deck cannon and fire. The shot fragmented another load of the creatures on the back of the leech.

'Ahah!' Boris yelled and frantically set about ramming another powder charge down the spout, followed by handfuls of stones.

'We're winning, lads!' Ambel yelled as he chased another creature down the deck and jumped on top of it.

'Boris! You bloody idiot!' yelled Pland.

'What!' shouted Ambel, turning from another pool of quivering slurry.

'He got two o'the ropes!' yelled Pland.

Ambel turned toward the rail just as the spout-like head of the leech lifted into sight. This head was just a long tube with a metre-wide mouth at the end. Inside the mouth was a red hell of revolving rings of teeth and reels of chitinous cutting-disks.

'Oh bugger,' said Ambel as the top half of the leech oozed over the rail and went after Anne. Anne leapt back and the leech cornered her against the wall of the forecabin. There was real fear on her face. This was something no Hooper could survive. With her automatic held out in both hands, she emptied the weapon's magazine into the leech's mouth, shell cases clattering to the deck around her feet. Shortly after the empty magazine hit the deck and she was groping at her belt for another one, sure she would have no chance to reload.

'I'm coming!' yelled Ambel. Anne saw him behind the leech with a harpoon in his hands. The weapon came down in an arc behind the creature's head just as it reached for her. The point of the weapon went through. She saw it pass through the grinding mouth, out through the bottom of the head, and punch through the solid deck timbers as she slapped her second magazine into place. The leech heaved against the harpoon and the timbers creaked, but by then Ambel had another harpoon, then another. By the time he was finished, the part of the leech that had oozed over the rail had been stapled to the deck with three harpoons. With shaking hands Anne recocked her weapon and quickly moved away from the cabin wall.

'Thanks,' she said to Ambel.

'Think nothing of it,' the Captain told her.

The last of the prill were those that had been knocked off the back of the leech earlier. Boris sank most of them before they even reached the *Treader* and Peck continued to pick off the rest. Pland went below decks and came back with a knife half a metre long, a bar of the same length with flat pads at each end, some sets of hooks, and crampons. Behind him came the four juniors who had been sent below earlier. They gazed about themselves at the mess on the main deck, at the huge pinioned leech, and nervously fingered their clubs and pangas. Peck, while reloading his shotgun with paper cartridges, glanced at them, then with a shout and a gesture directed their attention to the rail locker containing the mops and brooms.

Pland and Ambel tied the crampons on their feet, and using these and the hooks, climbed down along the slippery body of the leech to where it was widest. In true pirate fashion, Ambel carried the knife clamped between his teeth. When the two of them reached their destination, the rest of the crew moved to the rail to watch. Peck kept his attention on the water around the great body, just in case any prill had been missed.

When Pland was firmly secure with his hooks, Ambel raised the knife and brought it down to drive it deep into the glistening flesh he stood upon. The leech bucked and

writhed, but could not throw him as he held on to the handle
of the knife and steadily pulled it back. In moments he had
opened a gash three metres long, to expose the leech's in-
nards. Pland quickly dropped into the gash and braced it
open with the bar. Ambel passed the knife down to him and
looked up at the spectators.

'Where's the rope then, y'slugs!' he bellowed.

Gollow left his mop against the rail and scurried to get a
coil of rope and hurled one end down to them. The other
end he tied to one of the deck rings. Anne stood over him
as he did this, then, satisfied with his knot tying, returned
her attention to the sea. Pland, meanwhile, was industri-
ously hacking away with his knife. After a little while he
reached up out of the gash and Ambel placed the end of the
rope in his hand. He took this and disappeared for a while
longer.

'Move it, laddy,' said Ambel, just then noticing a glistening hump out at sea, turning and heading in their direction.

'Ready,' said Pland.

Ambel reached down and hauled Pland out by his gore-
soaked jacket. They retrieved their tools and quickly
climbed back on to the ship. Once on deck, Ambel reached
over the side and pulled the harpoons still imbedded in the
body of the leech. The barbs tore out great lumps of flesh,
but it seemed as if Ambel was merely pulling corn stalks. He
then pulled the harpoons from the deck and the leech slid
over the side, all the fight gone out of it.

'Sail!' Ambel yelled.

The sail unfolded and spread its wings, gripped spars and
cables and with much ratchetting and clacking, unreefed the
fabric sails and turned the rig into the wind. The ship slowly
began to move. The rope Gollow had secured grew taut and
the ship shuddered as the leech struggled on the end of it.
Abruptly the rope went slack and they left the maimed leech
behind. The second leech quickly closed in on it, the prill
leaping up and down on its back in anticipation.

'Haul it in,' said Ambel, and the crew got on with what he
could have easily done himself. On the end of the rope was
something bulky, soon revealed, as they hauled it up the side

of the ship, as a greenish fringed organ with the end tied off with the rope, and veins hanging from it like string.

'That's a good un,' said Ambel with a grin, as the leech's bile duct sagged over the rail and flopped on to the deck. Then he looked contemplatively out across the sea. 'No more today. Get the deck cleaned and we'll sort it in the morning.'

The reply to this was a concerted sigh of relief.

The sun had become a green dome nested in turquoise clouds on the horizon and the temperature was dropping very quickly. As he went to his cabin to find his thermal suit, Janer saw that no one else on the ship seemed to notice this cooling. The hornets were torpid in this cold, but the Hive link was alive with speculation and interest. The main part of the Hive, and hence the Hive mind, was many light years away on a planet that remained constantly warm and comfortable for the insects. It was a world the hornets had claimed as their own and given the simple name of Hive. People occasionally made the crack that it would be better referred to as New Israel—while other people often asked them what they were talking about.

'I would say that they were once lovers and that she has come back to renew their relationship. Beyond that I have no idea,' said Janer in reply to the mind's question.

'*But surely this must stem from dissatisfaction?*'

'Yes, of course.'

'*But Erlin has heretofore led a most interesting and satisfying life,*' said the mind.

'How can you know that?'

'*I have studied records of her travels and the places to which she has been, and this place is only one of many. She has been at the forefront of xeno-studies for more than a century and has made many important discoveries.*'

'All you've told me,' said Janer, 'is that she has led an *interesting* life.'

Thankfully the mind remained silent for a while, so he took the opportunity to pull on his thermal suit.

When it spoke again the mind spoke with less certainty. *'Interesting does not equate to satisfaction?'* it asked.

'Perhaps it does to you, but that is not necessarily the case with humans. I think you hit the nail when you said she's been at the forefront for more than a century, she's probably bored, looking for something she thought she once had, trying to return to a happier time.'

'I see,' said the mind. *'It is said that the human condition is one of striving. This then is the case. Success does not equate to satisfaction.'*

Janer had gone at this discussion from every angle since he had been indentured to this mind. It knew all his answers, but he had yet to know all its questions. It kept asking them in different ways to try and gain a further nuance of understanding. He noted the change of 'interest' to 'success'.

'Satisfaction, for us, is only a brief thing. The man who acquires wealth does not reach a point where he has enough. Success for us is more like acceleration than speed. Interest cannot be maintained at a constant level.'

Let it wrap its antennae round that one, Janer thought. But the mind was quick with a reply.

'You cannot stop, then?' said the mind.

'No,' said Janer. 'Except to die.' He climbed the ladder back up on to the deck.

On the other ship, lanterns and braziers had been lit and the smell of roasting meats was drifting tantalizingly across the sea to them. As the sun finally drowned behind the horizon, the pale orb of Coram slowly became visible through thin cloud, and everything turned to shades of green and silver blue.

'You ready?' Erlin asked him as he moved to the rail to stand between her and Captain Ron. Janer nodded, and watched Ron as the Captain snorted in the air and licked his lips.

'I smell roasting turbul, boiling hammer whelk and, best of all, I smell barbecued glister. Captain Drum lays on a good spread for his guests.' Ron looked at Janer. 'I'll bet he's got a barrel of seacane rum on board as well.'

Janer grinned at that and ignored the muttering that came over the Hive link.

Roach and two other crewmen lowered a rowing boat to the sea then quickly scrambled down a rope-ladder to get into it. Ron turned to another crewman who had come out on deck.

'Keep an eye on things, Forlam. I don't want us back drunk to a shipload of prill.'

'Aw, Captain,' Forlam protested.

Janer studied him. He appeared perfectly fit and able only days after having half his hand cut off and his intestines pulled out.

'You do it, Forlam,' said Ron. 'I lost money on you this time and I reckon we might have to go after sprine to compensate.'

There was a sudden silence after this comment.

'Is that a good idea?' asked Erlin, eventually.

'Probably not,' said Ron, turning to the rope ladder and clambering down.

'What's sprine?' Janer asked Erlin before she followed Ron down to the boat.

Quickly Erlin said, 'What's most valuable on a planet is what's most rare. Think about Forlam and what happened to him.'

Janer halted where he was for a moment while he put the question to the Hive mind. Hopefully he would get a straight answer from it.

'OK, what's most valuable here,' he whispered.

'I would have thought that obvious,' replied the mind.

'Well it isn't to me. What is it?'

'Death.'

Janer climbed down to the boat, sat down, and gazed over the side at the oil-dark water. Glisters and prill bedamned.

'Death,' he said to Erlin.

Erlin turned and looked at him. She said, 'Sprine is a poison that can kill Hoopers very quickly. As such it is the most valuable substance on the planet to them.'

Janer nodded in agreement. He was old enough to understand the reasoning behind that. What he wondered about was the reluctance of the crew to go in search of it.

'Where does sprine come from?' he asked the mind, for some reason not wanting to ask these questions out loud with Captain Ron sitting so near.

'*It comes from the bile ducts of giant leeches,*' the mind replied.

'Giant? What, like those ones I saw the other day?'

'*Bigger than that. They can grow up to thirty metres long in the sea.*'

Janer gazed at the sea again and shook his head. It occurred to him that in some situations the weapon on his belt would be of no use whatsoever.

The remarkable hostility of the life forms he found, wherever he managed to land his scooter, was at first a source of amazement to Keech, but it was now becoming a source of extreme irritation. It was not that he had any physical need to rest or cook himself something to eat. What he had was a mental need to stop and take stock; to consider his future moves from a still point. It seemed to Keech that there were no still points on Spatterjay.

Then he saw the rock glinting silver in the light of the moon. The edifice of stone looked like a tower block displaced from a city into the sea. It stood a hundred metres above the waves: a monolith of dark stone, flat-topped and sheer-sided. When he checked the map on his screen he saw that the icon representing himself was now almost upon 'The Big Flint'. He turned his scooter towards it and boosted higher into the air. Here, through his aug, he initiated a light-intensifier program—he did have the option of infrared, but there was no need for that in the light of Coram. Around the rock's base, he could see the usual clusters of frog whelks and prill on steep beaches of flaked stone and shell. In the surrounding sea, leeches glistened in weed-choked water. As he drew closer he saw that the stone of this edifice was indeed a deep glossy black, and felt almost appalled at what this must mean: for a piece of flint this size to form out of chalk beds would take an unimaginable period of time. There was nothing like this on Earth.

Through his aug, he spat a very specific question at the local server. 'How much longer than Earth has Spatterjay had life?'

'One point seven billion solstan years—approximate.'

Keech absorbed that as he circled The Big Flint. After two circuits he slowly, observantly, brought his scooter in to land.

Pink shapes were gathered on the flat top of the monolith and a hundred heads on top of long necks turned to watch him as he approached. He hesitated to land in a clear area to one side of this gathering, until he drew closer. He then recognized these creatures as the strange sails the ship Hoopers used. As far as he was aware, these creatures were harmless, so he landed.

A hundred pairs of infernal eyes glinted at him in the darkness but, beyond this observation, the sails showed no immediate reaction to him. He studied them more closely. They were big; their bodies, with spined wings folded around and behind them, stood at well over two metres and probably massed the same as at least three humans, and their ribbed necks and long flat heads stretched another three metres above that. Below their bodies were splayed large six-fingered foot-talons with which they gripped the rock to hold them secured against the wind. Their necks swayed in that wind like stalks of grass, and the heads that topped them were vaguely crocodilian with perhaps just a hint of praying mantis. Keech supposed that these creatures had as much trouble as did he when they landed anywhere lower, hence their occupation of the top of this rock. Also it explained their arrangement with the ship Hoopers. He put them out of his mind and thought about what he must do next.

He must get to talk to one of the old ship captains, and to do that he must either return to the Dome or seek one out here. Obviously these captains were reticent about their dealings with Hoop, or rather the creature he had become, else Tay would have known more, or at least been certain of her facts. He needed a friendly captain, then, and the nearest he had to that was Captain Ron—or perhaps, through Erlin when she found him, Captain Ambel. In his aug, Keech loaded four names into a standard search program and uploaded it to the local server. The immediate response was two unknowns for the Captains, and the two last-known locations of Janer and Erlin. He dumped this information, then reached out to his touch-console and put the satellite comlink online. The connection was suspiciously quick and confirmed for him who was curious about his activities.

'How may I help you, Monitor Keech?' asked the voice of Warden.

Before Keech could reply, a shuffling movement amongst the sails distracted him. All the heads had turned inward to one of their number; one that appeared bigger than the rest. He kept half an eye on them as he replied to the AI.

'I'm trying to get in contact with Erlin Tazer Three Indomial. Who at present is out on one of the Hooper ships?'

'Erlin Tazer Three Indomial does not carry a personal transponder at this time, and has not filed intended destinations with me,' came the reply.

'How about Janer Cord Anders. He is with her at the moment.'

'Janer Cord Anders does not carry a personal transponder either, and likewise has not filed intended destinations with me.'

Keech paused for a moment, realizing, by the characterless tone, that he was not in direct contact with the Warden itself, but that it obviously had one of its subminds monitoring his transmissions. He was not sure if this was any more reassuring.

'Janer Cord Anders is indentured to a Hive mind. Would it be possible to get in contact with him through his Hive link?' he asked.

'Hive links are for privileged use only. I can put you in communication with the Hive concerned, but it is up to that entity how you might proceed from there.'

'Please do so.'

There was a pause and a strange buzzing issued from the comlink. During this pause, Keech observed the bigger sail leave the group and begin to waddle over to him. The observing heads of the others were swaying from it to him like spectators at a tennis match.

'Yes,' said an echoey buzzing voice from the link.

'My name is Keech. I travelled with one Janer Cord Anders for a short time then recently lost contact with him. I'm trying to get in contact with him again. Can you tell me his present location?'

'I could,' said the Hive mind.

Keech hesitated for a moment, trying to work out what to say next. The sail creature was only a few metres away from him. He drew his pulse-gun and rested it in his lap, as he had recently returned the guard spheres to their case for recharging.

'What is his present location?' he asked.

'I want something in return,' said the mind.

'And what would that be?'

'On the next shuttle from Coram a package will be arriving for Janer. I wish you to pick it up. When you have this package, I will give you his location at that time.'

'What is in this package?'

'This is none of your concern.' The buzzing ceased and the link with mind clicked off.

'You're on our rock,' said the sail, now looming over Keech.

Keech just stared up at the creature. He'd heard a little about sails, but not that they were sentient. When he had been here before, there had been no ships and the sails had only ever been distant shapes in the sky. As this sail now glanced back to its fellows, he noticed that it had a silvery aug on the side of its head. He didn't know quite what to make of that.

'You're on our rock,' said the sail again, louder this time.

'I take it you don't want me here,' said Keech.

'That's right,' said the sail, nodding its head.

'Then I'll leave,' said Keech.

'Last human come here I chucked him over the side,' said the sail.

'A bit drastic, don't you think?'

'He thought so,' said the sail. 'Climbed back up and threw a rock at me.'

More evidence of the indestructibility of Hoopers.

'What happened then?' asked Keech.

'Threw him off again and he buggered off,' said the sail, nodding its head. It squatted down with a slight sigh and tilted its head to one side. 'You smell wrong,' it said.

'That's because I'm dead.'

'Dead?' asked the sail, then, 'But dead is . . . dead.'

'I am a reification,' said Keech.

The sail tilted its head and its eyes crossed slightly. 'Oh,' it said, obviously having accessed its aug for information on the subject. A sudden thought occurred to Keech.

'If you don't mind me asking, how old are you?'

'Dunno,' replied the sail.

'Did you know a human called Hoop?'

'Yeah,' said the sail. 'He bounced.'

Keech just stared at it, and seemingly having made its point it rose up again, turned, and waddled away from him. This sail then was at least seven hundred years old and could be ten or a thousand times that. Keech holstered his gun and engaged the scooter's AG. Soon he was back in the air and heading for the Dome.

Captain Drum was another big thickset man like Ron, though he had a full head of hair that he tied into a ponytail. He ebulliently welcomed them on board and told them to tuck into the food provided. Over a large brazier, Janer noted a large lobster-like sea creature strapped to a metal frame. It was moving as they roasted it, and making low gobbling sounds.

'Not like a boxy,' he said to Erlin.

'Some creatures have evolved defences against the leeches. A leech cannot get through a glister's shell. Glisters in fact feed on leeches,' she replied.

'Do they have the virus in them?'

'No, they've evolved in such a way as to exclude it. I think it's connected to the fact that the fibres normally only enter through wounds, and they don't get wounded too often. Their shells are very thick, and anything that's going to break through is going to kill the creature.'

'Why didn't they kill this one before cooking it?' Janer

asked. The sound the glister was making was beginning to make him feel a little ill. He accepted the mug proffered by one of Drum's crewmen and took a gulp. His eyes didn't water this time. He took another gulp.

'Glisters have psycho-active chemicals in their mouths and brainpans. The only way to kill one, other than by roasting, is to smash its skull. Doing so releases these chemicals into its flesh. Hoopers only kill glisters that way when they really want a party,' said Erlin.

'I think I've lost my appetite,' said Janer.

'That's not the worst of it,' said Erlin, pointing.

A cauldron had been set over a wide brazier filled with glowing charcoal. Fishy steam drifted from this receptacle, and peering through that steam were many stalked eyes. Only on seeing those eyes and how they were vibrating did Janer become aware of the hammering sound.

'What . . . ' he began.

'Hammer whelks,' said Erlin. 'Not such good news to any other slow-moving mollusc. They've got a kick that can crack plascrete. It can also snap human bone easily enough, if you're incautious around them. They *have* to use a cast-iron pot to cook them.'

That was it then: the molluscs were trying to batter their way out of the cooking pot—if 'batter' was the best term to use. Janer took another gulp of his rum to quell the sudden queasiness he felt. Erlin moved away with a fixed smile.

'You told me to warn you the next time,' the Hive link reminded him.

'Yeah, but this time I really need it,' he replied.

Walking past carrying a stack of platters, the crewman who had earlier handed him a drink, glanced at him questioningly.

'Eh, what's that?'

'Private conversation,' said Janer, tapping the box on his shoulder.

The man grunted and moved on. Janer brought his attention back to the hammer whelks as the first set of stalked eyes drooped and sank out of sight. The hammering was getting louder now. He turned away, only to see crewmen swinging the glister's frame from its brazier and knocking out the manacle pins. One of the men used a large pair of tongs to haul the creature from the metal and drop it on to the deck. It was Ron who stepped forward with a large mallet and large flat chisel.

'I get first dibs on the tail-meat,' said the big man.

'All yours,' said Drum.

Janer ate some of the white fragrant flesh of the glister after Ron finally broke it open. When a crewman presented him with a plate piled with steaming purplish body of a whelk, he demurred. This fleshy thing had a large pink foot, ending in a lump of bone, and its flaccid eye-stalks hung over the side of the plate. Thereafter, Janer stuck to the cane rum and tried to avoid seeing the Hoopers gobbling down hammer whelks liberally sprinkled with spiced vinegar, and tossing the foot bones over the side. He was thankful when it was all over and time to return to Ron's ship.

'You all right?' Erlin asked.

'Fine,' said Janer, getting unsteadily to his feet.

She and Ron helped him to the rail then down the ladder to the rowing boat. Once he was in the boat he felt queasy again and leant over the edge in readiness to be sick. The lights from the braziers aboard the ship glinted on the oil-dark wavelets. Janer's nausea subsided and he trailed his hand in the cool water. When he went to take his hand out, he found that it seemed to have stuck.

'Janer!' Erlin shouted.

A glistening body half a metre long came up with his hand and he could feel something grinding through his tendons and bones. There was a horrible keening coming from somewhere and hand hurt very badly. Ron had hold of him and suddenly he was in the bottom of the boat, the glistening thing writhing beside him. Ron's boot came down on his wrist and Ron's hands closed like vices on the leech. It came off stripping skin and Janer saw pink flesh and abraded bone before the blood welled up. I should faint now, he thought, but there was no relief until they got back to the ship and Erlin slapped a drug patch on his neck.

'You know what this means?' she asked as he went under.

Janer didn't know what she meant. All he knew was that the pain was going and that he felt kind of funny.

A hornet came to his bedside as he slept and it watched him with its compound eyes.

The ship was dark and it stank, and it was crawling with the teardrop lice that fed on the scraps Prador dropped when feeding. Her own cabin had extra lights, but these only made the lice hide in her bedding and amongst the few belongings she had brought with her, and still there was the smell and the pervading marine dampness. Knowing what to expect, Rebecca had dressed in a full-body environment suit and, on the few occasions that she slept, she slept with her helmet on. Shortly after the launch she had hunted down all the lice she could find and burnt them with a small QC laser, but soon they had returned and she became bored with the chore. Now she was just plain bored. Time to see Ebulan.

The service corridors of the ship were wide enough for second-children and blanks to pass each other—though she noticed some of the blanks had healing wounds on their bodies where Ebulan's children had passed too close and sliced them with the edge of a carapace or some other lethal piece of shell. When she came face to face with Vrell, a first-child and consequently a larger Prador, Frisk ducked into a wall recess while he passed. The adolescent turned slightly towards her as he clattered by, with some chunk of putrefying human meat held in one of his claws. She stepped out behind him and followed, as no doubt the meat was for Ebulan. Only Prador of his age and status got to sample such delicacies, as not many humans were still bred for meat, it now becoming passé. Adolescent Prador ate only the decayed flesh of the giant mudskippers that were farmed along the seashores of their home world.

Soon Vrell came to one of the main corridors which were wide enough to allow Ebulan himself passage. A second-child saw Vrell coming and dodged to the wall, pulling itself down flat so the first-child would have to extend himself to cause any real damage. Vrell clouted the top of its shell in passing but, obviously on an errand for his father, did not linger to pull off a leg or two. It was this society—utterly stratified and utterly devoid of beneficence—that Frisk most admired about the Prador. The slightest sign of weakness was punished in the extreme. No member of the society deserved any more than it could take. And there was no right to life. She felt there was something clean and pure about it, and it was the antithesis of all those things she detested in the Polity.

Vrell drew to a halt at a huge doorway that was a slanted oval in a weed-coated wall. The doors themselves were a form of case-hardened ceramal; unpolished and still retaining its rainbow bloom from the heat treatment. They cracked in an arc off-centre of the oval and slid, turning as they went, into recesses above and below. Beyond was a chamber lit with screens and control panels that in the Prador fashion had something of the appearance of luminous fungi, and perhaps of rock-clinging insects. On a gust of warm air, rolled out the smell of sea-life, decay, and the sickly musk that only issued from adults like Ebulan. Frisk quickly stepped through the doorway after Vrell, and moved to one side, further studying the chamber as she did so.

Ebulan hovered before a collection of screens, on most of which scrolled Prador glyphs and computer code. A couple of screens showed scenes from the Third Kingdom, and were probably U-space transmissions from Ebulan's agents there. The adult turned as Vrell crouched down to one side of him, holding up the piece of meat, which Frisk now identified as a human leg, then slid forwards, only to halt before presenting his mandibles.

'Why are you here?'

The voice came from Frisk's right, where three human blanks were lined up in readiness to do Ebulan's bidding. He had spoken through one of these. It did not matter which one.

'I'm here because I need one of your blanks to assist me,' said Frisk.

Ebulan slid forwards and presented his mandibles to Vrell. The adolescent dropped the meat across them and scuttled back. It was well for adolescents to be cautious: adult Prador were not averse to, in fact very much enjoyed, eating their

own young, as this was the way they thinned-out the weak-
lings. As Ebulan sliced the meat and chewed on it, Frisk
noted a number of screens fading behind him. Was there
something the Prador did not want her to see? She turned her
attention to Vrell as the adolescent backed up to the side of
the chamber, his carapace scraping along the wall.

'One of my blanks?' said the blank to her right.

Frisk returned her attention to Ebulan. Bits of flesh were
dropping to the irregular floor and lice were scuttling in to
gobble them up. There were also lice clinging around his
mouthparts.

'I have my library console and crystals here with me and I
need some help with some cataloguing,' she said.

'Which of these units do you require?' asked the blank.

Frisk studied the four mindless humans and then walked
over to a heavy-set male. She ran her hand down this one's
bare and heavily tattooed chest then into the front of the
elasticated trunks he wore. The blank farther to the right had
no need of trunks like these to prevent certain items flapping
about, having been neutered some time in the past, probably
because he was not good breeding stock. After a moment,
she slid her hand out and nodded in satisfaction.

'This one will do,' she said.

'He is fully functional,' said Ebulan. 'You may take him,
but be sure he is returned to me fully functional.'

'Come with me,' said Frisk to the blank, and headed for
the oval door. The blank followed her, doglike, as she went
through. Ebulan watched her go then turned slightly towards
Vrell and waited. The adolescent shifted nervously, picking
his legs alternately from the floor before finding the nerve to
speak.

'Why does she require a blank for cataloguing?' he asked
in the humming Prador tongue.

'She does not. She is bored and requires a male blank for
the purposes of recreation,' Ebulan replied.

'Sexual recreation?' Vrell asked hesitantly.

'Yes.'

'Why do you allow her such liberties?'

'You would find, Vrell, should you attain adulthood, that

one gains a certain affection for tools one has had for some time. Also, you would understand and sympathize with the needs for . . . recreation.'

'Yes, father,' said Vrell, understanding not at all.

6

At her instruction, the three male glisters dropped away from their mate and skulked around to the other side of the feeding turbul and, once they were in position, she slammed into the turbul shoal to drive it towards them. She need not have bothered—so far gone in gluttony were the turbul that they hardly noticed her. Seeing their mate grabbing at turbul and tearing off heads had the males hurtling into the mêlée as well—snapping also at prill and goring leeches as they came. Soon all four glisters were in amongst it: moving from turbul to turbul with ruthless efficiency. In no way could they eat all they killed, but their instinct was to kill as many as possible before feeding, for there would always be uninvited guests at the table. For their part, the turbul were still too intent on the taste of hammer whelk, not realizing that none remained, not seeing the sudden flurries of claw and snapping mandible, and their headless fellows now drifting by. The glisters themselves would have been fine, had not all this occurred on the edge of an oceanic trench.

Sometimes Sniper wondered if allowing the Warden to subsume him might be the best and most sensible move he could make. Perhaps then he would become as machinelike in his attitude as he was in appearance. Was it right for a drone such as itself—one of the pinnacles of Polity AI technology—to get bored, `grumpy, and sometimes downright ornery? Did SM13 ever feel that way? He flicked a palp eye round to observe the submind, but the flying brooch was as blank and unreadable as ever.

'GCV 1236, for our delectation and richness of experience,' said Thirteen.

Sniper quickly checked all his outputs and found he was emitting a low-grade mumble from one of his memory interfaces. He quickly shut it off as they slowed to hover over an islet in the shape of a horseshoe. This particular landmass was old enough and had room enough to have acquired some vegetation. SM13 turned and focused its topaz eyes on him.

'That's better—not so noisy now,' said the little drone.

'How long have I been doing that?' Sniper asked.

'Ever since you flew out here. You know you could do with either a deep diagnostic or a memory upgrade. You're so backed-up you're spilling over.'

'I like it that way,' said Sniper. 'So, what have we got here?'

'Usual whelk survey, they're the best environmental indicators, then we check out the molly carp here. They sit at the top of the food chain and pick up all the poisons. But first, we pay a little visit to my sea cave.' With that, the little drone dropped out of the sky towards the island. Sniper immediately followed, his interest piqued.

The seahorse drone decelerated over a grove of stunted peartrunks, then eased in through the sparse green-and-blue leaves and knots of black twigs. Sniper followed, pulling leeches off his metal skin with his precision claw and snipping them in half, not because they might do him any damage, but because on some level it irritated him that they confused him with something living. Once through the branches, Thirteen accelerated to an area where a ridge of old packet-worm coral was crumbling to white powder and glittering nacreous flakes. This mass of coral rested on a slab of basalt tilted up out of black dirt. Underneath this slab was a dark elongated hole. Thirteen turned at forty-five degrees to enter this place, its eyes igniting to light up the interior.

Sniper found the hole less than accommodating and had to smash away lumps of coral with his heavy claw before he could follow the little drone through. Once through he too sent beams of light from the projectors on either side of his mouth.

The two drones were now in a narrow cavern. At the back of this, a cube-shaped hollow had been cut into the rock, and in it rested three large hammer-whelk shells. Thirteen moved forward until it was hovering over one of these. Its ribbed tail uncoiled, split at the end, and gripped the rim of the shell.

'I thought you were only intended for observation,' said Sniper.

'I am,' said Thirteen.

'How did you excavate that?' Sniper asked, indicating the cavity with his heavy claw.

'With a boosted geological laser and patience.'

'And what about your tail? Last I recollect, the Warden didn't allow you any manipulation of your environment . . . ever since those thrall units . . . '

Thirteen gave an aerial shrug above the whelk shell.

'If you have the funds, you can buy the alterations. No doubt that is something you've been telling Windcheater for some time,' the little drone replied.

'I have . . . but does the Warden know about your . . . alterations?'

'No,' said Thirteen, 'nor does he know about these.' With that, the submind tipped the whelk shell to reveal that it was full of amberclam pearls. Sniper shifted forward in the confined space and turned a palp eye to each of the shells in turn. The second shell was full of short rods of translucent pink stone Sniper recognized as fossilized glister. The third shell contained lumps of greenish rock. Only a laser chromatographic scan rendered the delightful news that this substance was pure green sapphire.

'Quite a collection,' said the war drone. 'What do you intend to do with it?'

'To buy my laser upgrade I had to stick a pearl to my tail with amberclam glue and transport it over four thousand kilometres. That took me the best part of a solstan year and I lost four pearls in the process. My tail alteration took five years, by the same methods.'

Sniper gave his deadly grin and backed out of the cave. Dropping the whelk shell back into its place, Thirteen followed him out into the emerald day.

'You still have your account at the Norvabank, then?' Sniper asked.

'I do, though there's not much in it right now.'

Thirteen rose up through the trees at high speed, in an explosion of foliage and leaves. Sniper followed, deliberately going through the thickest branch he could see, just for the hell of it, and smashing it to splinters. Once clear of the dingle the two drones flew out over the bay and settled towards its calm waters.

'So what sort of percentages are we talking here?' asked the war drone.

'There's a gem dealer who comes down from Coram to buy stock from various Hoopers. I got his eddress two years ago and have been waiting for the opportunity to get my finds to him. I can't move this amount without risking being caught by the Warden, and if he catches me, it'll be immediate subsumption and I'll lose the lot. You're a free drone. You've a better chance. It's doubtful that it's even illegal for you to trade in natural gems.'

'You didn't answer my question.'

'Twenty per cent net of profit,' said Thirteen.

'Fifty per cent,' said Sniper.

'You're a robber and a thief!'

Sniper grinned his grin again as they skimmed close to the surface. He lowered his back legs in, and set a subprogram to counting the whelks in the area.

'Seems to me you're all out of options,' said Sniper, at last enjoying himself immensely.

'Watch yourself, Sniper!' said Thirteen, turning in midair.

'Are you threatening me?' Sniper asked, turning also. The little drone must have gone mad. Only at the last moment did Sniper realize to what Thirteen had been referring. The creature looked like a monstrous carp swimming with its top half out of the water. Underneath the water, Sniper knew that this molly carp would have three rows of flat tentacles with which it gripped the bottom to drag itself along. The prow of its head now cut quickly and without deviation towards its target.

Sniper loaded a missile.

'No! Protected! The Warden!'

Sniper knocked the missile out of the air with an EM pulse just as it left his mouth then, too late, tried to lift out of the creature's path. He couldn't even use his fusion booster because this too might kill it. The great mouth gaped and slammed shut, and with a satisfied bubbling the molly carp sank.

SM13 flew in a tight ring then settled down so the sensors on its tail were in the water. Immediately the little drone picked up an ultrasound signal issuing from below.

'Bollocks,' Sniper was saying.

The morning shuttle was due in an hour, and Keech sat in the Baitman nursing his fourth mug of sea-cane rum, his hover trunk resting on the floor beside him. The other customers in the bar had avoided him since his arrival four hours earlier— it seemed this place never closed—and the barman watched him warily from behind his chessboard. Keech tasted each mouthful but otherwise the potent liquor had no effect on him. There were Golem androids that could enjoy the option of insobriety. He had no such option while he retained this body. He often considered, as Janer had suggested, mem-plantation in an android chassis, and just as often he rejected the idea. When he had been reified on the home world of the cult of Anubis Arisen, he had more seriously considered the option then. But being a walking corpse did have advantages, especially if there were people you wanted to fear you. He savoured that moment Corbel Frane had seen him: the atavistic terror the old piratical Hooper had felt. That terror had been integral to Keech's success then. Had he just been human or Golem, Frane would not have fled at that critical moment, and would likely have torn Keech apart. As it was, Keech had chased Frane's AGC out over above Mount Ember, then shot it down. Frane's ending had been suitably apocalyptic.

Keech sipped alcohol through his glass straw and thought about Hoop. Even though the two days with Olian Tay had yielded him little more information of value than he had learnt in the first few hours with her, he was still satisfied with the result there. After seven hundred years, an end was

in sight. The villain would be brought to book, and Keech's
self-assumed mission would end. What then? Keech contemplatively studied the lozenge that depended from a chain
round his neck. Whole avenues opened up before him,
which was more than most dead men could say. Almost, almost he smiled, but there was not enough movement left in
his face. Lost in his own thoughts it took him a moment to
realize that an individual who had just entered the Baitman
was peering at him curiously.

The man was short and very stocky, but not in the least bit
flabby. His appearance had much that was human in it, and
much that was boulder. Like most ship Hoopers, he wore
loose canvas trousers and a loose plastilink shirt with a wide
leather belt around it. Tucked in a loop in the belt, like a
weapon ready to be drawn, was a large briar pipe. His face
was wide and friendly and seemed even wider because of
the great bushy sideburns sticking out below the shiny bald
pate of his head. One look at this man, and at the mottled
bluishness of his skin, told Keech that one of the Old Captains now stood before him.

'Do I know you, boy?' the man asked.

Keech felt a hint of amusement at being called boy. It was
of course perfectly reasonable for this man to assume that
anyone but another Old Captain was much younger than
himself.

'You may know me—or know of me. My name is Sable
Keech and I've been dead for seven hundred years.'

As a line, it was certainly an attention grabber. But that
was what he needed to hook the interest of such a man, and
perhaps then be able to extract information. The Captain *was*
hooked. He looked to the barman, pointed at Keech's table,
then he sat down opposite the reif.

'Sprage,' he said, holding out his hand.

Keech watched the hand for a moment, hoping Sprage
would realize what he was doing and quickly retract it.
When the hand remained offered, he tilted his head to one
side and reached out with his own grey claw. Sprage seemed
unconcerned as he grasped and shook it, then released it to

lean back. He unhooked his pipe from his belt and pointed the stem at Keech.

'Funny to see a reif after all this time,' he said.

'When did you last see one?' Keech asked, curious despite his concerns.

'Oh, way back,' said Sprage, taking a pouch out of the top pocket of his shirt and beginning the seemingly intricate process of filling his pipe. 'A programmed one got sent here in search of his killer, before the Polity put a stop to that sort of thing.'

At least five centuries ago, Keech calculated.

Sprage went on, 'But *you're* not programmed like that. You full AI?'

At this point the barman approached the table and placed a bottle and a glass before Sprage.

'Tab it,' said Sprage when the man seemed inclined to linger.

'Partial,' said Keech, after the barman had moved away.

Sprage now had his pipe filled and he inserted the stem in his mouth. The antique lighter he produced took at least five tries to get going. 'Bloody thing—nothing lasts nowadays,' he muttered, then gazing at Keech through a cloud of tobacco smoke, 'What you doing here, then?'

'Looking for a killer—though not mine,' Keech replied.

'Anyone I might know?'

'Almost certainly. I'm looking for Jay Hoop, perhaps more commonly known round here now as the Skinner. I've been looking for him for a very long time. Any ideas?'

Sprage appeared decidedly discomfited by the question. He puffed hard on his pipe, setting up a glow in it that reflected out of his eyes. Keech wondered what caused such an effect, for normal human eyes were not so reflective.

'Got to be dead, ain't he,' said Sprage.

'From what I can ascertain, killing him has not been an easy option, and has been something people have been reluctant to complete. You wouldn't happen to have something relevant in a box on your ship, would you?' said Keech.

'Not on . . . ' Sprage broke into a fit of coughing. 'Er, not sure I'm with you there,' he finished, when he could. Keech thought that someone of this age ought to be better practised at subterfuge. Sprage poured himself a glass of sea-cane rum and sipped at it to still his ticklish throat.

'Do you know who I am?' Keech asked.

'Seem to recollect a name like that,' said the Captain. He bore a puzzled expression for a moment, then that swiftly cleared. He stared at Keech with widening eyes.

'You . . . ' was all Keech heard of what the Captain said next.

OUTSIDE PARAM FUNCTION: BALM PUMP 30% LOAD INCREASE.

The warning message fed in from his aug through his visual cortex and glowed across his left visual field; also, the vision in his right eye went blurry and sounds abruptly became distant and fuzzy. Everything external suddenly became of secondary importance. He ran an immediate diagnostic from his aug and got conflicting reports from the probes sunk in his preserved flesh. Something was wrong, seriously wrong. Vaguely he heard Sprage saying something with vehemence, and then saw him stand and leave.

Keech ignored this: if now he went into true death, none of it mattered.

OUTSIDE PARAM FUNCTION: BALM PUMP 38% LOAD INCREASE.

Keech reached over and flipped up the lid on his trunk. He removed the cleansing unit and, ignoring the curious stares of the Hoopers in the bar, he opened his overall and quickly plugged himself in. Black balm flooded the extractor tube, and it was some minutes before sapphire balm returned up the other tube.

DROP PUMP PRESSURE 20%, he instructed. Immediately another warning message came up.

OUTSIDE PARAM FUNCTION: EXTREMITY PROBE B23 NIL BALM.

Keech glanced at the cleanser and saw the row of hieroglyphs as a blurred red line. The cleanser was obviously struggling to do its job.

EXTREMITY PROBE B23: STRUCTURAL ANOMALY.

What the hell?

EXTREMITY PROBE B23: STRUCTURAL BREAKDOWN.

This was it; there had always been the chance that his body would start to break down; that the preservatives would cease to be as effective as they had been in the beginning. He had never expected it to happen so fast though. He looked at the lights on the cleanser and saw there was no sign of green.

The next message displayed by his aug was one he had only seen twice before, and then only shortly after he had been reified.

INVASIVE ORGANIZM DETECTED.

IDENTIFY, he told the aug.

A sub-program immediately connected his aug to the local server and a search engine was loaded with genetic code segments. The answer came back very quickly, and flashed up in his visual cortex.

SPATTERJAY VIRAL FORM AI.

The leech that had fallen on him outside Tay's damned museum—that was it, then. The Spatterjay virus was inside him and it was doing untold damage as it tried to assimilate a dead man. He looked at the cleansing unit and saw that there were now two green lights lit up. If he could breathe, he would have breathed a sigh of relief, for now the unit was handling it. He sat back as his vision started to clear and saw that everyone in the bar was staring at him. The barman appeared particularly annoyed, as he walked over to his table.

'I don't know what you said to him, but I've never seen him get that uptight,' he accused.

It took a moment for Keech to realize the man was talking about Sprage. After a long clicking gulp he managed to get out a reply. 'I just told him who I . . . was,' he said.

'I don't care who y'are. The Captains run it here, so I'd prefer it if y'left.' The barman glanced at the cleanser. 'And I want you to leave *now*.' A couple of Hoopers had stood and were walking up behind the barman. Keech knew he had no chance in such a situation. He stood, picked up the cleanser and, holding it close to his chest, walked unsteadily from the Baitman. His trunk closed its own lid and followed faithfully behind.

Outside the Hooper bar the street seemed more crowded than when he had entered and Keech noticed a lot of Polity citizens were wandering about. A catadapt passed close by him and, with a loud sniff, gave him a look of disgust before moving on. Exerting greater control over his joint motors he walked stiffly towards an aircab he saw parked at the end of the street. Another red light had gone out on the cleanser by the time he had reached it. The Hooper inside nodded his head in recognition. He was the one who had ferried them out from the shuttle port.

'Can't take y'mate. Waiting for a fare,' he said.

'I'll give you ten shillings to take me very slowly to the shuttle port,' said Keech.

'Well, why didn't y'say? Get in!'

Keech nodded to his trunk. 'If you could deal with that.'

The Hooper quickly got out of his cab and, using the toggle control on the trunk soon had it in the boot. It gave Keech some satisfaction to see the same catadapt running towards the cab as it lifted and turned towards the shuttle port.

INSIDE PARAM FUNCTION: EXTREMITY PROBE B23 NOMINAL.

Only two lights now remained red on the cleanser.

'How slowly y'want me to go?' asked the Hooper.

'Give me twenty minutes. That should do it,' Keech replied.

OUTSIDE PARAM FUNCTION: BALM PUMP AT 80%

He'd forgotten about that.

INCREASE PUMP PRESSURE TO NORMAL.

Another light changed on the cleanser, but the last red one seemed determined to hold on. The twenty minutes he had asked for were needed in full: the Hooper had done at least five wide circuits of the shuttle port before the light finally changed to green.

SYSTEM NOMINAL — DIAGNOSTIC ANALYSIS?

Keech considered that, but there seemed no point.

NO ANALYSIS.

He detached the pipes from their sockets and fed them back into the cleanser. The lights clicked off shortly after, as he resealed his overall.

'You can land now,' he told the Hooper.

As the man nodded and brought the aircab down to one of the many jetties, Keech closed one grey hand around his lozenge pendant. What he had done was a temporary measure at best. Soon he would have to make a decision he had been putting off for close on a hundred years. Three options remained to him: he could lose what remained of his organic brain—and body—and become fully AI; he could die; or he could take one course open to him that still seemed incredible even after decades of contemplating it.

Keech paid the delighted Hooper and watched the aircab lift and accelerate away in the direction of the Hooper town, no doubt to try and pick up the stranded catadapt. He walked to the edge of the shuttle-pad structure and gazed down the long slope of sea wall at the spindly autoguns as they patrolled above the water line. He observed a mollusc, with a nacreous blue spiral shell, heave itself from the water and begin sliding up the wall. An autogun was poised over it before it got a metre from the water, and flickering red light between gun and mollusc was quickly identifiable as lines of laser light amid the smoke jetting from the many holes punched through the creature's shell.

INFORM: BALM PUMP LOAD BELOW 20%, he instructed.

OUTSIDE PARAM FUNCTION: BALM PUMP 8% LOAD INCREASE.

INFORM: BALM PUMP LOAD ABOVE 20% ONLY.

The message faded and was replaced by a waiting light flickering off to one side.

INFORM: ALL EXTREMITY PROBES OUTSIDE NOMINAL.

The list that appeared had to scroll from the bottom of the visual field in his left eye. It began at B1 and just kept going.

CANCEL, he instructed.

Then he queried the server as to the location of the nearest pharmacy. In his visual field there now appeared a map giving both his present position and the location of a pharmacy only a few hundred metres from where he stood. He looked round and identified a squat building raised above the edge of an empty landing pad. Through its long chainglass windows he saw endless displays of goods, and considered how, on any world he visited, no opportunity for commerce was missed. With his trunk dogging his footsteps he headed over to the metal steps leading up to the building. Here he tapped the 'stay' and 'security' button on his trunk and it dropped hard against the plascrete, with the locks clicking home in its lid. At the head of the steps, sliding glass doors admitted him to a small automart in which aisles of goods tempted the eye. Walking to the first aisle he was immediately joined by an automated trolley. At the back of this trolley was a screen and touch-console. On the console, he punched in the words 'Intertox Inhibitors'.

After a moment, the trolley buzzed and clicked, and immediately led him off to one side. Soon he was standing before shelves racked with a vast display of containers ranging from cards of microcapsules to five-litre bottles and cans. The display glittered with brand names and designs, like a wall of jewels. He walked along this display until he came to a range of cylinders similar to the one that slotted into his cleansing unit. He dropped a couple of these into the trolley and immediately the price came up on the screen. At the exit to the mart, he dropped a couple of transparent octagonal shillings into the trolley's collection tray, before taking up his goods and leaving. Descending the steps he, as was his habit, wondered how such a system dealt with theft. No doubt this mart had an AI keeping a few hundred little eyes on that situation. He had probably been identified the moment he walked through the door. This thought was immediately confirmed for him.

'Message for Sable Keech,' came a voice through the audio input from his aug.

'Go ahead,' he said.

'It has been reported that you purchased Intertox Virex 24. You are advised that all Intertox drugs have a seven-minute active life in reification balms.'

'I am aware of that.'

'Thank you for your attention,' said the voice, and the audio shut off.

Staring out over the sea, with the two containers clutched against his chest, Keech thought it so nice to know someone

cared. What bitterness there was in the thought was muted—
hardly alive.

The morning breeze had died to a flat calm, and the sun had
become almost distinct in the verdigris sky. With nothing
now to do, the sail—bored with hanging on the spars—had
folded its wings and was now perched on a spar munching
on a rhinoworm steak. Crew were either off-shift and sleeping, or catching up on jobs that had been left unattended
while the ship was moving. Anne had a party busy below
decks, checking the caulking and all else that might affect
the integrity of the hull. It was a make-work task as the
tough yanwood did not rot and was infrequently damaged.
Boris was greasing the steering cables, and taking his time
about it, while Pland was supervising a couple of juniors as
they scrubbed stains out of the deck—it was obviously an
authority he relished, having been the one holding the brush
only a few journeys back. Peck cleaned his shotgun with fas-
tidious attention: it had lasted him well this weapon, over a
hundred years, though of course, with all the parts he had replaced, it was no longer actually the same shotgun. He deliberately didn't get involved in anything too laborious, as
he knew what his next job would be.

'Peck, over here,' ordered Ambel.

Peck looked up. It was always himself the Captain called
to help with this stage of the operation—Peck really wished
he would choose someone else. He handed his gun and
cleaning kit to Gollow, who was scrubbing the rails, before
heading over to join the Captain.

'All right, Peck, let's do it,' said Ambel, giving Peck a slap
on the shoulder before reaching down to get a hold of their
second bile duct where it had rested against the wall of the
forecabin overnight. He dragged it across the deck to the
rear winch, eliciting muttered complaints from Pland's
deck-scrubbing crew, then he and Peck heaved the object
into a cargo net and hoisted it from the deck. There it hung
with its tied-off neck pointing down, as Ambel pulled across
the large green-glass carboy he had brought up earlier, and
dropped a big funnel in its mouth. The rest of the crew

stopped what they were doing and moved in to watch as Ambel eased the tie open and thick green bile flooded into the funnel, then into the carboy. The flow of it slowed when the carboy was three-quarters full.

'Water,' demanded Ambel, pulling his sheath knife and driving it into the top of the duct. Pland passed a bucket of fresh water to Peck, as Ambel once again tied off the duct, then transferred the funnel to the slit he had made. Peck handed him the bucket and he poured its contents inside the duct, thereafter moving the funnel back to the carboy and carefully squeezing and kneading the duct to get the rest of the bile into solution. The bucket of water passing through the duct filled the carboy to its brim. Ambel then corked it, sealed the cork itself with wrack resin, and pressed his captain's seal into the resin.

''Bout ten grams o' sprine out of that, I reckon,' said Peck. 'How much does it fetch now?'

'Eighty-two shillin's a gram,' said Boris.

'What's that in real money?' asked Peck, swinging the winch arm out over the sea and releasing the tie on the cargo net. The duct splashed into the waves, but because of what it was there was no concerted rush of creatures to feed on it. Everybody laughed at Peck's little joke, then fell into respectful silence as Ambel picked up the loaded carboy and carried it carefully to the rear deck hatch. Now Peck swung over the winch arm and wound the net down beside the hatch.

Ambel placed the carboy inside the net and secured it before opening the hatch and climbing down into the rear hold. Peck wound the net up off the deck then swung the winch arm across over the hatch and with a clacking of bone ratchets, lowered its precious load into the hold. It was Ambel's job to secure the carboy in its padded frame—indeed, his responsibility. For this was a serious moment. Every Hooper knew the story of the baitman who had dropped a carboy of leech bile. He had been thrown off the back of the ship with a rope round his ankle, and towed through leech-infested waters for a day before the rest of the crew forgave him. Or rather, this was the story senior crewmen told the juniors.

Eventually Ambel came back out on deck, rubbing his hands together. He looked around at his crew and grinned.

'Bugger,' said Peck.

Boris stared at him, then at Ambel. 'Another one?' he asked disbelievingly.

Ambel nodded, still grinning happily. Unfortunately the sail had got the gist of this brief exchange. The steak it was chewing landed on the deck with a sodden thump, and there was a boom of wings opening above them as it chose that moment to launch itself from the mast. It was smart enough to get away before anyone could try talking it out of fleeing.

'Island north five k!' it shouted as it went. Fortunately, sails normally had the decency to tell a crew where the nearest landfall was before they went. It was only polite. Ambel's grin became slightly strained.

'Rowing boat?' Peck suggested helpfully.

Boris, Pland and Anne wore smirks and, noticing these, Ambel turned to give his ship a long slow inspection.

'Yes, the rowing boat,' he agreed. 'And while I'm about that, someone can reef those.' He pointed to the fabric sails, which were hanging slack from their spars. 'I should think that the mast chain and cogs need greasing by now, too. Also the harpoons could do with another sharpen, and this deck needs a *proper* clean.' When he paused, there was a concert of 'ayes' as the crew scattered to their tasks before he thought of any more chores for them. Ambel grinned to himself, then went off to find the reinforced oars.

The great wing of the shuttle slewed in the sky above the landing pads, as Keech yet again unplugged his cleansing unit and packed it away in his trunk. A quick query through his aug confirmed the information that this was the shuttle he was waiting for. He secured the trunk down by the sea wall—its AG set in reverse so it would take a forklift to pick it up—and headed on over to the arriving shuttle. Fenced walkways between landing pads brought him eventually to the one where the shuttle had descended. He avoided the passenger embarkation point, and moved round to where autoloaders were shifting the fresh cargo out into a warehouse. A Golem android—which by his nametag was called Paul A2-18—was standing watching the cargo being shifted.

'Can I help you?' said Paul A2-18, as Keech approached.

This Golem was obviously an old one, constructed before Cybercorp discovered that physical perfection made people nervous. Paul was Apollo descended to Earth and clad in blue overalls.

'I'm Keech. I've come to pick up a package.'

'Ah,' the Golem paused as he, no doubt, sent a query and received instructions. 'Please come this way.'

Paul led Keech to the side of the bay and pointed to a container resting on the platen before a scanner. The container itself was hexagonal in section, and had a single carry handle. The only visible way of opening it was by the coded touch-plate mounted upon it—a device no doubt keyed to Janer's DNA.

'What's inside?' Keech asked.

'I am afraid I am unable to provide that information,' said Paul A2-18. 'The box is scan-proof.'

Keech thought about that. If it had come through the runcible, then there should be no problem with it in legal terms. Why then had this android tried to scan it at all? He was about to ask when he noted that Paul appeared slightly uncomfortable. Though what Keech was seeing was only emulation, and probably conscious emulation at that, he understood what the Golem was telling him and he kept his mouth shut—it was good to know that such Apollonian perfection had its faults. He picked up the container and turned to go, stumbled, and had to support himself against the platen for a moment.

'Are you all right?' asked the android.

'I'm fine,' said Keech, grimacing as he cancelled the warning messages flashing up in his visual field. The Intertox, which had brought the activity of many of his probes back to nominal, but no better, was now breaking down in his balm. He had expected this to happen, but not with such sudden ill effect. Walking back around the shuttle it was with his vision tunnelling that he saw the five very familiar people disembarking.

Batians: for a very long time members of this mercenary race had been trying to finish a job started seven hundred years ago. All of The Eight had employed Batians at one time or another, and Keech had been forced to kill more of them than he liked to think about. Upon recognizing them, he ducked his head and speeded his pace. Unfortunately, it is difficult to disguise the fact that you are a walking corpse. He glimpsed the five of them talking together, then turning as one to gaze in his direction. He could see that they were hesitating, as this particular area would be constantly and closely watched by one of the Warden's subminds.

At that point, he removed his remote control from the pocket of his overalls and pointed it towards his trunk. Instantly the trunk began its miraculous transformation. He reached it in time to pick up his scattered belongings and load them in the luggage compartment, and was in the process of fitting the hover scooter's thrusters when he saw that the five were running towards him. Mounting the scooter he registered them reaching the wall walkway just ten metres or so away from him. He saw how all five had their hands poised over concealed pockets—and were staring at him with ill-contained hatred.

'Another . . . time,' he managed on a clicking gulp, then saluted to them and launched his scooter into the sky.

'Sable Keech, you have broken the law,' came the voice of the Warden from the com in the scooter's console.

'I am aware of the flying regulations around shuttle ports,' he replied.

'I should hope so. You are, after all, a monitor. You realize you have been automatically fined?'

'Yes, I realize, but if I had stayed in the area the five Batians there might have been tempted to try and kill me despite your watching SM—then you'd have had a more serious crime to contend with, one way or another.'

'I see . . . I did note the arrival of those five you mention,' said the Warden.

'But did not see fit to warn me, even though you must have known I was here and must have known my record with them.'

'Even though armed, they were doing nothing illegal.'

'Yes,' said Keech, 'but weren't you hoping they would.'

There came no further comment from the AI, as Keech turned his scooter and headed for the beach from which he had first departed. He set the scooter to land on automatic, as what depth perception he did have—aug assisted—was fading from his eye. With a deal of unsteadiness he dismounted, tucked the cleansing unit under his arm, then staggered across a bank of glossy pebbles, and collapsed on his knees in the green sand beyond.

OUTSIDE PARAM FUNCTION: BALM PUMP 28% LOAD INCREASE.

It was playing out again, only this time the problem was caused by the drug he had used to try and solve the previous problem.

INVASIVE ORGANIZM SCAN, he instructed, and received an immediate reply.

PRESENT.

He was fast running out of options. With hands that seemed flaccid, he opened his overalls and connected the cleansing unit again. The balm coming out of him was muddy brown this time, and it took a long time for the liquid sapphire to return. The blurred line of red lights held his attention, while he thought about what he must do. The option of dispensing with this reified body and going full AI would require his return to the Dome then to the moon Coram, where the only suitable facilities were available. Full death, he decided, was not an option. The remaining option resided in the lozenge depending from his neck chain. What had the Lifecoven woman who had sold it to him said?

'It reads the blueprint and then it sends off its little builders.'

But even that would require his return to very high-tech medical facilities.

'Yes, you need to be in a tank for it to work correctly,' said the woman.

Keech nodded to her, and she stepped back into the dingle at the head of the beach. And he could not quite grasp why this bothered him so, but he was then quickly distracted.

'Why should *you* have any more life,' said a voice beside him.

He glanced across at Corbel Frane.

'Who are you to ask that question?' he replied.

Frane smoothed his moustache. 'In a fair and equitable world we can all ask questions,' he said.

'You can't, because I killed you ages ago.'

Frane seemed affronted as he drifted from hallucination to memory.

OUTSIDE PARAM FUNCTION: CEREBRAL PROBE ERROR.

Cradling the cleanser against his belly, Keech heaved himself to his feet. 'I've got to get help,' he said.

'Not one of your favourite pastimes,' said Francis Cojan, standing at his side.

Keech glanced at the man and saw that he was young, athletic, and smiling, not at all like the last time he had seen him.

'You need friends to help you. Keech doesn't believe in friends.'

Keech turned to see Alphed Rimsc on his other side. It was only his voice that Keech recognized, the man's face having been mostly eaten away by the diatomic acid Keech had put in his suit's oxygen supply.

'This is not real, you're all dead.'

'Really, where you should be,' said Corbel Frane, waving a finger at him. 'I mean, how long has this been going on— seven centuries? Are you mad? How many lives has your vendetta cost?'

Keech gestured at him with a grey claw. 'That's not something *you* would think! That's me!'

He was about to shout out again when he suddenly realized he was utterly alone on the beach.

'Shit,' he said, and gazed down at the two green lights on the cleanser.

REPEAT ERROR MESSAGE, he instructed.

OUTSIDE PARAM FUNCTION: CEREBRAL PROBE ERROR.

In his organic brain—cross-referenced to AI emotional

emulation—he got in the nearest he could get to a cold sweat.
DETAIL.
The reply did nothing to ease that feeling.
Capillary blockage to organic cerebrum/Agglutinate balm/AI viral fibre/Ox-3 starvation.
PRESENT DETAIL.
NOMINAL.
That made him feel no better. Cradling the cleansing unit while it continued labouring to clear his fouled balm, he returned to his scooter and slumped down with his back against it. He'd just come as close as it was possible, for a walking corpse, to having a stroke.

Underneath accreted layers of time, perversion, and monstrous deed after monstrous deed, there lay an earlier self that Frisk knew would be horrified at what she had since become. She even found a certain perverse pleasure in that fact—more pleasure than she was extracting in *this* present pursuit.

The ancient Prador to whom Ebulan himself had been first-child during the Prador/Human war, had maintained that human flesh gained added piquancy from extended suffering. So it was that humans force-grown for meat began to be slaughtered by slow and excruciating factory processes. When they had fled to the Prador Third Kingdom, she and Jay had found satisfaction of their perverse instincts in the holding pens and slaughterhouses there, but only some. For force-grown humans did not have time to acquire the life experience to truly appreciate the horror of their situation.

In later years, after Jay had departed, Frisk had continued to find satisfaction there, but it had decreased as eating human meat had become less fashionable amongst Prador kind. With fewer and fewer force-grown humans available, sometimes years might pass between each sado-sexual release for her. She had tried human blanks before, but always been frustrated.

And thus it was now. The blank, of course, remained utterly indifferent to the things she was doing to him. She realized this was a pointless exercise, but could not restrain herself from carrying it through to the end. Under instruction from his thrall unit, he grew an erection and pumped away at her while she cut and burned him. But because he was also ancient Hooper, the burns quickly scabbed and slewed away, and his skin closed back over the wounds she made like a layer of oil over water, his expression changing not one whit as she inflicted this abuse on him. In the end she grew bored and frustrated at his passivity, and pushed him away. How she wished things were still as they had once been.

'Move back to the door,' she instructed.

The blank pushed himself off her and stepped back as instructed. Lying back, she remembered the games she and Jay had once played: the screams of both agony and ecstasy ringing through the pens, the quintessential pleasure of watching some favourite plaything coming to realize that he or she was no longer favoured, and faced only a future of agony and death, then consumption by the Prador. She remembered how, with the correct drugs and techniques, they could extend such an individual's life for days—even after removing their entire skin. Heady days, now gone for ever.

'Leave me,' she instructed the blank, and turned over on to her stomach as the door closed behind him.

Of course, now she was coming back into human-habited space, there would be a surplus of material for her delectation. Most of them would be Hoopers, true, but they would be Hoopers with minds, and even though durable, they could still be made to suffer—it was all a matter of technique. She understood herself well enough to know that her imminent return to the scene of her most ghastly crimes was not really about Jay or Keech—it was about boredom and *need*.

Feeling movement on her leg Frisk rolled over and batted away one of the many lice that occupied the ship. As she donned her environment suit, she tried to imagine a future where she could continue to let loose the full extent of her malice and have it *responded* to. She tried to relish the prospect, but imagination had become dull, and interest lacking. In this she found another source of anger.

Standing up, she said, 'I will just have to work at it.' But the words seemed to be sucked away by the coldness of the ship surrounding her.

'I *will* work at it,' she said, and smashed her foot down on the louse, crunching it into the floor.

7

The cloud of disturbed silt, broken shell, gobbets of flesh and yellowish chyme now covered five square kilometres of seabed, and when one edge reached the oceanic trench it waterfalled into the cerulean depths. On a good day for glisters, this waterfall would have descended upon certain entities down there and elicited only the waving of siphons like hollowed trees, the contemplative thump of a fleshy foot capable of tipping boulders to see what might be for lunch underneath, and the blink of a slot-pupilled eye the size of a dinner plate. Today was a bad day, however. The monstrous whelk— which had as its minuscule kin both the hammer and frog varieties, for it was into his kind that they tranformed upon surviving long enough to finally become sexually active—had not had a particularly good day himself, nor week either. For longer than had seemed fair, a deepwater flesh-eating heirodont had hunted him through the boulderfields that were his natural home below and, of necessity, he had escaped into the deep crevices found higher up the face of this underwater cliff. Below, encountering such tastes in the water would merely have whet his appetite for one of the huge filter-worms that lived underneath the boulders. Those worms were now far out of reach, and the source of this taste was very close. Rolling out masses of tentacles, with skin so thick and fibrous even leeches could not penetrate, he hauled himself up the face of the cliff and went to dine.

He was on the deck and prill were coming over the rail. There was no one else on board but something shadowy and insectile steered the ship down an avenue made in the sea by the reared trumpet mouths of giant leeches. He backed away from the prill but his fear was more of the leeches and the way their mouths were watching him. Too late he realized he had backed up against the mast and his fear twisted its knife in his gut. He looked up and the sail shrugged at the inevitability of it all before it dropped on him. He tried to run but just could not move fast enough. Sheets of pink-veined skin enfolded him and dragged him down. Only then did it occur to him how ridiculous this whole situation was and that he was dreaming. He woke with the twisting fear in his gut, turning to a gnawing hunger.

Janer opened his eyes and immediately sat upright. He looked at his bandaged hand and flexed it. It was stiff and slightly sore, but not half so painful as he expected.

'How long?' he asked.

'You've missed a day and we are now halfway through a second,' the mind replied.

'I've got the virus in me.'

'Five per cent of visitors here end up infected. The ones uninfected are those who take precautions. You took none, though you were advised at the runcible terminal and took the information pack on offer. Did you scan it?'

'No,' said Janer.

'You *wanted to end up infected,'* the mind stated.

'Perhaps. Not consciously anyway. Fait accompli now. What are the disadvantages?'

'There are few. If you spend sufficient time away from reinfection during your first century, the virus will die in your body, and as it breaks down, will cause most of your major organs to fail. Your sensitivity to pain will be greatly reduced, though some might not consider that a disadvantage. You'll be more susceptible to certain fungal infections. There are three known diseases that would kill you in a protracted and painful way, whereas before you would have survived them . . . There is a long list and it is in the information pack you took.'

'Advantages?'

Extreme resistance to injury. Gradual increase in physical strength. Higher resistance to other viruses—some of which would kill you, had you not had this virus. And, of course, reduced sensitivity to pain—if you consider that an advantage.'

Janer looked at the hornet squatting on the table by his bunk. Minds did not feel pain. How could something scattered between thousands of nests feel pain? How could a mind that once thought at the slow speed of pheromonal transfer understand physical injury?

'Would you consider pain an advantage?'

'I consider anything that increases my sensitivity to the world around me to be an advantage. The unit that is with you now died some time in the night, and all I experienced was the loss of sensory input from that world.'

Janer more closely inspected the hornet. He hadn't realized. He prodded it with his finger and it went over on to its back with legs in the air like a pincushion.

'What killed it?' he asked.

'The same thing you have been infected with,' said the mind.

'I thought you said these hornets had been altered.'

'Two different alterations, one of which I predicted to have a low chance of success.'

'I don't get it,' said Janer. 'How was it infected? It couldn't have been bitten.'

'Insects, unlike humans, cannot avoid infection here. The viral spores which only take hold inside a human after a massive infusion—like through a leech bite—can enter insects through their breathing spiracles,' was the mind's sarcastic response.

'I thought the virus didn't survive for long outside of a body.'

'It doesn't. The spores can enter when the insect feeds on something infected. They can even enter when it lands on something infected, or even flies past it. In the case of insects it only takes a few viable spores for the virus to be established.'

'Why? Why so different from humans?'

'Obviously we are the more primitive life form,' said the mind.

'Oh, you poor thing, you,' said Janer.

'Of course,' said the mind. 'I meant physically, not intellectually.'

'Yes, of course,' said Janer. He slid his feet from under the cover and sat on the side of the bunk. He removed the dressing from his hand and looked at the ugly wound in which it seemed a blue ring had been tattooed. He was a Hooper now. He had the mark.

'What do you want to do with . . . this lost sensory input?' he asked, pressing the dressing back into place.

'Return it,' said the mind. *'There is still much to learn about this virus and its effect on hymenoptera physiology.'*

Janer reached under his bunk and pulled out his backpack. From this he removed a two-pack of brushed aluminium cylinders. Each cylinder was ten centimetres long and three in diameter. One end was rounded and the other end was a spike. He took one cylinder out of the plastic wrapping, pressed his fingernail into an indentation, and a small door flipped open. He used the plastic wrapping to pick up the dead hornet and drop it inside the cylinder. His years of being indentured, and the two decades thereafter, had enabled him to tolerate the presence of these insects but had not relieved him of his fear of actually touching them. He closed the lid and stood. Then he went out on to the deck.

The signal bell from the scooter comunit was chiming, but Keech ignored it as he waited for the last lights to change to green on the cleanser. Shortly after the chiming ceased, he got a message through the audio input from his aug.

'Message for Sable Keech,' it said.

'What now?' he asked.

'Link requested from Hive transponder.'

Keech glanced back at the hexagonal box in the scooter's luggage compartment. He'd almost forgotten about that.

'Permission for link granted,' he said.

First came the buzzing, and then the Hive mind came online.

'Do you have the package?'

Keech replied, 'I have the package, but I won't be taking it to Janer just yet.'

The buzzing took on an angry tone. 'We had an agreement,' said the Hive mind.

Keech watched the last red light change to green, then detached the cleanser and carefully pushed the tubes back into place.

'We had an agreement,' the Hive mind repeated.

'The agreement is off. I need to return to Coram and make use of the medical facilities there.'

'You have a problem?' the mind asked, injecting ersatz concern into its voice.

'I have a problem,' Keech said.

'What kind of problem?' asked the mind.

'At a stretch, you could call it a medical one,' replied Keech.

'Erlin Tazer Three Indomial is with Janer. Perhaps she could help you. I believe she travels nowhere without an extensive collection of medical and pathological research equipment.'

'So nice of you to be thinking of me,' said Keech, bracing his hand against the scooter and standing up.

'Was that sarcasm or irony?' asked the mind.

'Probably both,' said Keech, dropping the cleanser into the back of the scooter.

'I'm never sure which is which,' said the mind.

Keech stared at the scooter, trying to decide if he should risk flying to the Dome. His vision was still tunnelling and there were odd squares flicking up in the visual field fed from his aug. A hissing crack interrupted his decision-making process. Automatically he ducked down, only to stoop into a cloud of smoke that had gouted from his own kneecap.

'You're not going anywhere, reif!' someone shouted.

For one long horrible moment Keech could not decide if this was reality or not. The two Batians who came striding out of the dingle at the head of the beach were like so many others he had seen and killed over the years. Then, to his horror he realized he had forgotten seeing these people earlier at the shuttle port. He tried to dispel anxieties about what this failing memory could mean, as he had more exigent concerns: two Batians here—with, no doubt, the other three not far behind.

'You know, you've made our job so very easy,' spat the man of this pair.

Keech said nothing. He gazed at the woman as she kept her laser carbine centred on him. The man holstered his weapon with a kind of casual contempt. It was the mistake they had always made. They were so very confident in their ability to kill. Weren't they such good shots? But then it was like fire and ash: fire will not burn something that has already been burned.

'Who sent you?' Keech asked, as he had asked many times before.

The man smiled nastily and gave no answer—as before. Keech nodded and drew his pulse-gun from his belt holster.

'Drop it!' shouted the woman with the carbine.

Keech raised his weapon and carefully aimed it. Laser shots punched smoking holes through his chest and through his stomach, but did not spoil his aim. He fired once: a black hole appeared in the woman's forehead, and the back of her skull turned into a blooming cloud behind her. As she staggered back and went over, Keech turned and mounted his scooter. The man just watched this in stunned horror, before thinking to reach again for his own weapon.

'You forget, I'm already dead,' said Keech, before slamming his scooter up into the sky.

A wind was blasting the ship along at a good rate of knots, and spray was coming up over the bow. Erlin watched Janer come up on to the deck and gaze about in surprise.

'Got his sea legs, then,' said Captain Ron.

Erlin turned and searched for a trace of irony in Ron's expression, and found none. She returned her attention to Janer as he walked to the rail and tossed something silvery over the side. The silvery object fell in an arc but, before it hit the waves, it corrected and shot off under its own power. Captain

Ron grunted in surprise and, when Erlin turned to him, he seemed embarrassed.

'Message carrier,' he said, nodding toward the receding object. 'Used to send 'em in the war.'

'What war?' Erlin asked.

'Prador,' explained Ron tersely

'Oh.'

Erlin looked away from him as she absorbed that. Ron was nearly as old as Ambel, and it was well to be reminded of this fact. It became too easy to view the likes of Ron and Ambel as relatively normal. Their apparent simplicity was deceptive, as the Old Captains had centuries of experience, and probably had forgotten more than she had learnt in her mere span of two hundred and forty years. She had actually forgotten that most Old Captains fell into an age range in the upper half of a thousand years. Senior seamen came in at the lower half. Herself? . . . she qualified as a senior, but only that. How easy it was to forget the way things were here. Those of the crew classified as juniors, and whom the likes of Ambel referred to as 'lads', were often over a century old. She wondered then how Ambel viewed her. Was she a child to him? Had the anger she had felt at his seeming complacency been seen by him as a childish fit of pique? What—when she found him—would be his reaction to her? *Stupid child*, she told herself as she watched Janer approach.

'What message?' asked Ron.

'No message,' said Janer as he climbed up on to the cabin-deck. 'Just a dead hornet going home.'

'Told you the fibres clog 'em,' said Ron.

'Apparently so,' admitted Janer. 'Where are we going?'

Erlin replied, 'Captain Drum sighted the *Treader* heading out for the feeding grounds. We're going after it.'

'What feeds there?'

'Leeches—big ones.'

Janer nodded his acknowledgement and grimaced at the scar on his hand.

Erlin turned to Ron again. 'Ambel said he came here after the war. In all the time I was with him I never questioned that, but I do now wonder if he was telling the truth.'

'Couldn't say,' he said. 'I came here a century after it was all over, and didn't meet him until a century after that.'

'You came here a century after the war?' Janer interjected.

Ron glanced at him. 'I was getting old and the geriatric treatments in the Polity weren't so good then. Seemed like a good idea at the time.'

Janer glanced at Erlin to see how she was responding to this—she with her opinion of people searching for 'miracles'. Her expression gave nothing away so he returned his attention to Ron.

'What did you *do* in the war?' Janer asked, parodying himself at the gaucheness of the question, and then wishing he'd kept his mouth shut once he saw Ron's expression.

'I was in a unit fighting out of the Cheyne outer systems. War drones and cyber-boosted troopers. We ran sabotage missions into their shipyards and the barracks where they kept their human-blank troopers. It was all a long time ago.'

Janer was fascinated, but he could see that, as far as Ron was concerned, it was not long enough ago. He glanced at Erlin, hoping that she might have something to ask, but Erlin was gazing out to sea with a slightly lost expression on her face.

'Do you mind saying anything more about it?' Janer eventually asked.

'I do mind,' said Ron, ending the conversation.

Shib stared down at Nolan, and then abruptly holstered his gun. Why hadn't he reacted faster? And why hadn't Nolan's shots brought that bastard down? Just then, Svan, Tors, and Dime came crashing out of the dingle, searching for someone to shoot.

'You missed him,' Svan stated.

Shib glared at her and gestured to Nolan.

'She hit him four times. He simply shot her through the head and climbed on his scooter. He just wouldn't go down,' he said.

Svan stared at Tors. He shrugged—and, in reply to that, she shook her head slowly, then walked over to the prostrate Nolan. She stooped and picked up the laser carbine. After inspecting it for a moment, she threw it to Shib, who caught it with a snap of his hand. Svan then gazed around at all of them.

'I would have thought,' she said slowly, 'that the repetition of events over the last seven centuries would have been enough to inform you about Sable Keech. Well, apparently not.' She studied each of them. 'Do you know how many Batians have died trying to complete the contract on him? No? Neither do I, but I do know that the total is more than fifty—and very probably for much the same reasons.' She pointed at the carbine Shib held. 'That was set on the basic kill level. Keech is a heavy-world reification. He may appear fragile, but you have to remember he has heavy-world bones internally strengthened to take cybermotors.' She walked over to Shib and pulled a small black box from his belt and held it up.

As if she was lecturing idiots, Svan went on, 'That's how we followed him and that is precisely why he's so dangerous. He was a man once, but that's something he hasn't been for a very long time. He's biomech, he doesn't feel pain, and you need nothing less than an explosive shell or full-power laser hit to take him down. Now do I have to engrave these facts on your foreheads?'

The reply was silence. Shib felt especially shamed, as the whole tirade had essentially been directed at him and Nolan. He gazed down at the corpse of the woman he had known only for a couple of days. It was the way of things.

'Now,' said Svan to Dime, 'you and Tors inflate the dinghy, and you,' she stabbed a finger at Shib, 'bury Nolan where she is. I want nothing lying about for the Warden to pick up on.'

Shib gazed again at the corpse. It was not the Batian custom to bury the dead: when you were dead, that was it, and there was no point in giving respect to a lump of meat. However, in this case, he could see the point. Spatterjay was not a full Polity world, but it was on the edge of the Polity, and as such would be very closely watched by its Warden. There would be SMs out there somewhere, and they could be any shape at all. One of them could even be watching them now. He glanced at Svan as she went back to the edge of the dingle, to where she had dropped her pack. He watched her remove black crabskin armour and begin to don it, and then he went in search of something with which to dig a hole.

He had a real bad feeling about all this.

On the map on the screen, it was called 'The Little Flint' and, as is the way with such things, it was precisely as described when Keech was hoping for understatement. There were no sails on this sloping black surface poised less than a metre above the sea, which was fortunate, for had even one been there, he would have been unable to land the scooter. Keech brought the vehicle down with a crash and dismounted even as it slid and caught against a chalky rim of rock. He staggered, fell on his face, and after pulling himself up on to his knees left a wet smear of balm and other less salubrious substances on the glossy stone.

All out of options, and time to pay the ferryman.

Keech surveyed his little island of black stone and thought that there shouldn't be room here for Frane, Rimsc, and the rest. He ignored their acid observations, got himself back on his feet and staggered to the back of his scooter. Once away from it again, now with the cleanser clutched to him like a valued child, he went down on his knees again, on the stone. If what he did next finished him here, then it seemed a dramatic enough place for him to exit. He pulled open his burned and soaking overalls to expose the four supposedly killing holes through his body. There was also a deep burn across the metal shell on his side, but luckily the two cleansing sockets were undamaged. He plugged the unit in and was totally unsurprised at the row of red lights that greeted him. Of course, now, they were irrelevant. He offered a half-hearted prayer to Anubis Arisen and pulled the lozenge of metal from the chain around his neck. After detaching the chain from the end of the lozenge, he stared for a long moment at this lump of golden metal.

'Do I believe in miracles?' he asked the watching crowd, his mind straying back to Erlin's derisory comments on such things.

The replies were as varied as he could imagine, and he

knew they would only be that—what *he* could imagine—as
he still had enough faculties to distinguish hallucination
from reality. Now he had to act quickly before he lost the
ability to make that distinction. Now he had to act before he
lost what remained of his organic brain. He reached down
and affixed the lozenge into the recess made for it in the top
of the unit. The lozenge clamped down, then immediately
grew thin metal tubes from all round its rim, and these tubes
mated with tiny sockets in the cleanser.

INITIATE CHANGER NANOFACTORY UNIT, he sent
through his aug, then swayed back and watched the tubes.
Black balm flooded out of him, and what came back was completely clear. It would not be empty though, definitely not that.
He closed his eye, and waited. He could feel nothing as the
cleanser pumped millions of microscopic factories around
with the embalming fluid in his vascular system. Inside him
he imagined them attaching themselves to the walls of his
veins like little volcanoes, little volcanoes that in moments
would each be spewing out millions of nano-machines, machines that might eventually enable him to live again.

The warning messages were coming up constantly, until
he instructed his aug to turn them off. The system that had
been monitoring his body was a system for monitoring the
stasis of a dead thing. But now the changer factory program
was taking over.

The factories were anchoring themselves and doing their
work. The Spatterjay virus was in there doing its work as
well. He should be in a tank at this moment, being watched
over by one of the more sophisticated autodocs—not sitting
here on a rock being watched by people he had killed long in
the past. He opened his eye and saw that the hieroglyph lights
on the cleanser were all flickering from amber to red and to
blue. He'd never seen them blue before, and he made a croak-
ing sound that might have been laughter. When he then surveyed his surroundings to see what his audience's response
might be to that, he saw that he was once again alone. He now
croaked at the silence, then abruptly turned his head and
stared down at his burnt knee. There was a sensation there.
No, not possible—not yet. It had to be some sort of ghosting

coming across from his organic brain to his aug. The stab of agony that came next, though, was undeniable. He tilted his head back and relished the pain. He knew there would be more of the same as the nano-machines repaired his decayed nervous system. But Keech also knew that, if he survived, he would *remember* this moment; this pain had been the first thing he had really felt in seven centuries.

The molly carp did three circuits of the bay at high speed, and then squatted in a deep trench where the bay opened to the sea. SM13 put this down to an intestinal complaint, and Sniper suggested that the little drone might like to act as a molly carp suppository. SM13 had then suggested it should go off to finish the whelk census and survey of the carp population. Sniper suggested the carp population might be better reduced by at least one.

'You can't do that,' said Thirteen. 'You'll be guilty of killing class-three intelligence and I'll be culpable.'

Sniper did an ultrasound scan of the inside of the carp, found the creature's peanut-sized brain, and wondered just who had made that classification. Also, scanning the other contents of the stomach he rested in, he found the carp had already been guilty of the crime he wanted to commit.

'This one's been eating the others here,' he informed Thirteen.

'That's the natural order of things. We aren't allowed to intervene.'

'Yeah, but how's the Warden going to know this one hasn't been eaten?' Sniper asked.

'If you probe to the back of its skull you'll see why.'

Sniper did this and eventually found a micro transponder direct-linked into one of the carp's main nerve ganglia. He swore yet again, then withdrew his scan to run a diagnostic on himself. Unbelievably, he found that the carp had managed to put dents in his armour. He restrained the urge to put a missile into the carp's peanut, and wondered if by moving about he could make the creature sick.

'Sniper . . . Sniper . . . '

'Yes, I hear you.'

'I'll have to contact the Warden. He'll have to know about this.'

'Don't be silly.'

'I have to. This carp has a transmitter because it's a prime and part of one of the Warden's studies. If I don't tell him, he might get suspicious later on. We don't want that.'

'Oh all right, creep, tell him.'

'There's no need to be like that. Is our deal still on?'

Sniper contemplated that and looked for an angle. 'We didn't actually sort out those percentages. Fifty-fifty, wasn't it?' When there was no reply the war drone was about to continue when he felt his antennae twitching and the invasive presence of the Warden at the periphery of his mind so he clammed up. For a moment the presence was blurred, low signal strength, then the Warden flicked to underspace transmission and included Thirteen in a trifold link.

'So, you cannot even count whelks without getting into trouble,' said the Warden.

'Yeah, that's right,' said Sniper.

'You, Thirteen, neglected to warn Sniper of how partial molly carp are to large crustaceans. That was remiss of you.'

'Sorry,' said Thirteen.

'Very well. You, submind, will now move on to the next sector to continue your survey. You can get going right now.'

Sniper felt the link with Thirteen break. The little drone shot away to the east, and in seconds was beyond the range of Sniper's ultrasound scanning.

'You, however,' said the Warden, 'will stay where you are until nature has taken its course. If this carp is in any way damaged by your incompetence I will get to know about it.'

'I hear and obey,' said Sniper.

Finally, almost reluctantly, the Warden's presence withdrew.

'And molly carp might fly,' the war drone muttered.

The molly carp, its body making swimming motions and its tentacles groping for a bottom that was fast receding, rose to the surface of the sea. It then rose from that surface, and with nose tilted down, accelerated to the east faster than any of its kind had ever travelled before. Perhaps knowing how little control it had over its situation, it closed its eyes and curled its tentacles into knots. Sniper regretted that he could not use his fusion boosters too, but AG planing would have to do for now. After a hundred kilometres, he dunked the carp in the sea again and scanned its body while its skin re-hydrated. The creature's peristaltic heart arteries were fine and the micro transponder had emitted no signal. Other than this, it only seemed a little dazed. For the next jaunt Sniper took it two hundred kilometres—and substantially faster. Again, the carp seemed fine. When Sniper finally started to reach the limit of the creature's endurance he was moving it very fast, and was impressed. These carp were tough. Sniper reckoned on them taking a solstan day or so to reach what was laughingly called civilization on Spatterjay.

Another evening was drawing in and Janer wondered at the steady roll and tranquillity of this ocean life. He'd said something along those lines to Roach earlier on, and the ragged little man had stared at him as if he was a lunatic. After an uncomfortable silence Roach had finally said, 'One the Cap'n always comes out with: "It's like war—long periods of boredom broken by moments of sheer terror." So I don't think tranquil's quite the word.' And at that, Roach had gone off to trull for more boxies. Now leaning on the rail, Janer glanced to one side as Erlin came to stand with him. Unlike him, she did not wear a thermal suit. He wondered if he would be dispensing with his too when the virus took a firmer hold in his system. He studied her profile for a long moment and felt something like yearning under his breast-bone. This woman was so *interesting* and, perhaps because of that, very attractive to him.

'Was this how it was before?' he asked.

She glanced at him before returning her attention to the sea. 'Most of the time,' she replied.

Janer looked thoughtful. 'You know, from what you've said and from what I've learnt from some of the crew, things haven't changed much here in a long time.' He nodded towards Ron. 'Makes you wonder if *they* might be the reason for it.'

'What do you mean?' Erlin asked.

'Well, they're the rulers here in all but name, so perhaps they just don't want things to change. The intention might not even be conscious.'

'You could be right,' Erlin conceded.

'I think I am,' said Janer. The two of them now fell into a comfortable silence. Janer felt calm and relaxed. He hardly noticed the ratchettings and clonks of the ship's mechanisms.

'You were here for quite a while, weren't you?' he asked after a while.

'Eighty years, give or take. I hardly remember a lot of those years. I guess you don't when there's not a lot happening.'

'What about when you first came here and discovered the virus . . . the weird set-up here?' he asked.

Erlin's expression became troubled and she shot him an assessing look.

'Some strange things happened then, but it's been so long that I sometimes wonder if my memory played tricks on me.' She shuddered as if the cold was now getting through to her.

'Well, don't just leave it there. Now you have to tell me,' said Janer.

She stared at him with her expression suddenly hard. 'Why *should* I tell you?'

Janer met her look. 'Because we're the same. We're both coming to that time in our lives when we wonder why we should carry on. You *should* tell me because you may gain some insight, and because you lose nothing by telling me, but you do gain time.'

Erlin's hard expression was broken by a smile. 'You have an unbreakable arrogance, Janer Cord Anders,' she said.

'Yes, which is why I'll live. Now tell me.'

Erlin's expression became troubled again as she turned to lean on the rail, staring out to sea.

'I was young when I came here—young, enthusiastic, curious, and sure I was going to do great things with my life.'

'And you did,' said Janer.

'Debatable,' said Erlin, then after a moment continued, 'You know how seeing that fight between Domby and Forlam brought home to you what this world is really like?'

'Yes.'

'Well, my moment of revelation was somewhat more . . . horrifying than that. I'd been on board the *Treader* only a few days. I'd been ferried out to it by AGC from the Dome—that was when the runcible was planet-based. At that point I hadn't even seen one of the sails, as there wasn't one aboard when I arrived. Anyway, Ambel Peck and Anne went ashore on a little island to get some fresh meat to attract in another sail. While there, Peck got attacked by a leech and, of course, I was fascinated to discover that Ambel had hammered the leech on the ground until it released the plug of flesh it had taken, and that Peck just screwed the piece of flesh back into place.'

'That was it?' Janer asked.

Erlin glanced at him. 'That just piqued my curiosity, and that's when I really started to investigate. I took urine samples, recorded statements, and slowly began to piece together what the ecology of this place is all about: the leeches. I tried to take samples from Ambel . . . but I've told you about that.'

'No blood in him,' said Janer, 'just fibres.'

'Yes, I couldn't even get a sample by opening his arm with a scalpel. Anyway, on we travelled with a sail hanging on the mast and frog whelks leaping on board, trying to take a chunk out of me, and even though I was truly beginning to understand it all, I didn't realize what extremes it could all go to.' She looked at Janer again. 'Have you heard of the Skinner?'

'Skinner's Islands is what I heard. I assumed it was the name of whoever discovered them,' he said.

'No. It's the name of the occupant and his occupation.'

Janer waited for her to continue, and after a long pause she did.

'We lost the sail again because the stored meat had worms in it. Even they were extreme, and I had to hide in my cabin until they were all removed from the ship. Ambel towed the *Treader* to a nearby island and he, Peck and Anne went ashore again after meat—rhinoworms mostly live in coastal shallows. Anne and Ambel came back to the ship without Peck, and started to collect harpoons and other weapons . . . You know, even then most of the crew had a much bluer coloration because they hadn't eaten Earth food for a while. I should have taken that as a clue.'

'Keeps the virus in abeyance,' said Janer.

'Oh yes,' said Erlin. 'But what happens to a human who doesn't get to eat Earth food at all? You know, ever since ECS drove Hoop and his crew away, there has always been Earth food available here. Hoopers could only grow a few adapted varieties that Hoop himself established here, but they were still enough. If such food had not been available there would have been no humans here when the Polity returned.'

'They die without it?' Janer asked.

Erlin gave a humourless laugh and gazed out to where the sun was sinking into a mantel of grey clouds which almost had the appearance of floating mud flats.

'It would be better if they did. They do not: they just cease to be human—we know this because Hoopers have been stranded and unable to obtain Dome-grown food . . . Peck, it seems, had been taken by one of these creatures that had once been human—a creature they called the Skinner, because of its unpleasant habits. I, of course, wanted to see it for myself, and demanded that I go ashore with them in their attempt to rescue Peck. I think what finally persuaded them was the surgical laser I carried. I'd managed to remove its safety limiters and then had an effective weapon.'

'So . . . you went ashore.'

'Yes, we went ashore and we saw this Skinner.' Erlin stared down at the water and proceeded to give a clinical description of the beast. Janer might not have believed her, had he not seen some strange and frightening things in his time. When she had finished her description she paused for a while before going on with, 'When it came at us it was waving something in its right hand. Ambel put a hole in it with his blunderbuss and Anne and Pland got it with harpoons. When I saw what the creature was holding I joined in the fight. I cut it with my laser, and I tell you that was no easy task—then I crawled away to spew up my guts. The other three used my laser to finish the job on the thing.'

'What did it have in its hand?' Janer asked, getting right to the point, even though he thought he might already know the answer.

'It was Peck's entire skin.'

'Jesu! The poor bastard.'

Erlin gazed at him now with a slightly crazy look in her eyes. 'Yes, he was. When you meet him you'll have to ask him all about it,' she said.

'What,' said Janer, 'he survived?'

'Oh yes. Ambel picked up his skin and we went to find him. When we found him, skinless, writhing in a bowl-shaped rock, I tried to put him out of his misery. Ambel knocked the laser out of my hand, then he, Anne, and Pland proceeded to dress Peck again in his own skin.'

'You're kidding.'

'Am I? You know what sticks in my mind the most?'

'What?'

'How they punched holes through his skin to let the air bubbles escape . . . so they could squeeze the air out through the punctures. They carried him back to the boat and out to the ship, but he managed to climb on board himself. There, you see, the raw extremes . . . those are what I saw.'

Janer watched her as she stared into the descending night. Perhaps she was a bit deranged. He did not want to openly call her a liar.

8

The turbul were all either dead or fled, and now the glisters fed with alacrity. As, one after another, they gobbled down turbul bodies, their own bodies expanded hugely to accommodate their gorging but, unlike the frog whelk which had caused all this furore, they had sub-shells which slid into place to protect newly exposed flesh swelling between original segments of shell. It was a rather hasty and frenetic banquet, for a glister feeding on one end of a turbul's body was hard-pressed to eat half of it before coming nose to nose with the uninvited diners. On each occasion this happened the glister might snatch a between-meals snack of prill or leech before moving on to the next turbul—the fish's flesh being so much sweeter and more tender, and definitely to be preferred.

Keech shook with fever. His nerves were regenerating very quickly and when he could stand the pain no longer, he shut down some of the connections to—and in—his organic brain. He did want life, but he wanted sanity too. Even so, with connections closed off, he felt like a diseased wreck. His entire body was delivering to him the message that he was full of infection and decay, and that he was falling apart. The physical evidence of this was how he had swollen, and the plasma leaking from his skin and a creamy fluid oozing from his nose. The cleansing unit was humming now as it worked hard following the nanofactory programme. A pool of volatile balm had puddled on the rock around his knees, having leaked from the holes lasered in his torso. These holes were now filled with nubs of veined, purplish flesh, and a messages light was clamouring for his attention. He decided to view the said messages and turned the system back on.

N-FACT MESSAGE: BALM DRAINED. WATER REQUIRED— 8 LITRES.

The nano-changer program was fully online. Keech got unsteadily to his feet, picked up the cleansing unit and walked down to the edge of the rock. He stared out across the slow dark roil of the sea and thought for a moment that something further was wrong with his vision, until he realized that night was descending. He looked down and saw below the water's surface, whelks of one kind or another, clinging to the stone, their shells seemingly formed of coiled gold and veined jade. He drew his pulse-gun before kneeling and dropping the unit in the water. No reaction from the whelks. Perhaps they became somnolent in darkness—or perhaps they did not consider him edible.

Immediately the unit began taking in water. He could feel it suffusing his flesh and cooling him. Was his bone marrow producing red blood cells now? What would happen first? In seeming answer, his arms began to itch intolerably. As he scratched at them, grey skin began to slew away. His hope of seeing pink skin underneath was dashed when flesh as white as fish meat was revealed. He stopped scratching and inspected his fingernails. Two of them were bent right back. He shook his hand and they fell out, pus now leaking from the ends of his fingers.

N-FACT MESSAGE: DANGER—TANK AMNIOT UNSUIT-
ABLE. ELECTROLYTIC REQUIREMENTS . . .

Keech turned the message off. He wasn't in a tank. The nearest electrolyte he could immerse himself in was this sea, and that seemed a suicidal idea. He'd just have to pray that Erlin could help him. When his irrigator automatically moistened his already wet living eye, he reached up and unplugged it. Some things seemed to be working, anyway. Once the unit stopped drawing in water, he stood, picked it up, and headed unsteadily for his scooter. The nanites could still work on his body while he was in the air, so there was no point in waiting here any longer. He mounted his scooter and dropped the unit between his thighs. From the comlink came that familiar strange buzzing the instant he turned it on.

'Yes?' said the Hive mind.

'I have your package, and I will deliver it,' said Keech, the liquid in his mouth and throat distorting his synthesized voice. A set of slowly changing coordinates flicked up on the screen map, and Keech lifted his scooter from the stone. Once in the air, he keyed the autopilot and sat back. He didn't want to fly manually while he was dripping on the controls.

Through thousands of eyes the Warden observed the people in the base on Coram and on the planet below. When a situation hinted at ramifications that might impinge on its remit, the AI observed it with greater attention, or assigned a sub-

mind to watch it develop. When an SM could not be spared
from its particular vehicle: be that an iron seahorse, floating
cockleshell, or some other more esoteric sea-shape, the Warden loaded a copy or created one for that specific purpose.
Sometimes it allowed these new minds to continue. At other
times it resubsumed them. After all, they were only a pattern
of information—as was all life.

At present, through one of its eyes, the AI was observing
with interest the arrival of an amphidapt from the runcible in
the core ocean of Europa, in the Sol system. The attachment
that came with this woman had her noted down as a separatist terrorist who might be attempting to smuggle leeches
to the strange dark sea that was her home. After only moments of observation, the Warden lost interest and assigned
SM24 to observe instead, as it did not understand how she
believed she might bypass the bio-filters of the runcible. Not
a molecule got through that the Warden was not prepared to
allow through. Now it let its attention wander to a fight occurring just beyond the Dome gate. Just for the hell of it, it
placed a bet for an E with the submind in charge of Dome
security, and got odds that made it wonder if it was time to
subsume said mind—for it obviously knew something the
Warden did not. Shortly after that, the AI received a signal
from a direction whence nothing had come in decades—in
fact from one of its deep-space eyes. It gave the new matter
almost a quarter of its attention.

The ship emerged out of underspace, leaving a coruscating
trail as antimatter particles struck the disperse local hydrogen.
Two of the Warden's deep-space eyes flared out in an EM
shockwave, so of necessity it had to observe from a distance.
Around the ship the stars distorted, as if seen through a lens,
as it fell into the system seemingly out of control. Braking on
ram scoop motors, it threw out a torus of radiation as it
dumped velocity and came down to half the speed of light.

'Please identify yourself,' sent the Warden, as it noted the
pilot was experiencing difficulties. A jumbled theta-block of
pictographic computer language then overloaded all the
Warden's receivers for two microseconds. It took the AI another three seconds to discover that there was little informa-

tion of value in this communication, other than its form. By now the vessel had the Warden's full attention.

'Prador ship. Please identify yourself.'

The ship was tumbling, using ram scoop and ion drive intermittently, as it tried to slow. Leaving a long trail of fire behind it, it arced around the sun. Another block of information overloaded the Warden's receivers. Four seconds later the AI got the gist.

'Nature of U-space generator fault?'

The garbled reply lasted for a couple of seconds, then cut off as the ship went into U-space.

The people in the Coram complex were baffled at the sight of all the exterior windows immediately becoming shrouded in something like an undulating wall of sun-glinting water as shimmer shields slammed into place across them. Internal doors closed—just slowly enough for people to get out of the way. Deep inside the moon, energy buffers went online to take any surge from the arm-thick superconducting cables linked to every essential system in the complex. Through the shimmer shields, ugly weapons turrets could be seen rising out of sulphur and ice.

'Attempting to land,' was the gist of the next transmission.

The Warden immediately direct-linked to the runcible it controlled, ready to transmit itself away should that action be necessary. It knew that if this was an attack, it would itself be the main target. A few seconds later the ship resurfaced in an explosion of antimatter half a million kilometres from Spatterjay, and on the opposite side of the planet from the moon.

Through its satellite eyes the Warden watched as the craft managed to get down to a speed of ten thousand kilometres per second. It skipped atmosphere then tried some sort of aero braking. There was a momentary U-space signature, then a flat antimatter explosion in the stratosphere. After the initial flash and detector overload, the Warden detected a scattering of debris blown into orbit around the planet. It picked up a brief whistling-bubbling sound on com which it tentatively identified from its library as the sound of a Prador getting fried by a high-intensity microwave burst. It

considered the event for a whole six seconds before contact-
ing one of its subminds.

'SM Twelve, you saw?'

'I saw it. I didn't know any visitors were scheduled.'

'They weren't. It was some sort of Prador vessel, but I
couldn't get close enough to identify it. Check that orbital
debris and report back.'

'OK, boss,' said SM12.

From one of its satellite eyes the Warden observed a meagre dot accelerate away from the planet at hypersonic speed,
before flicking its attention elsewhere.

'SM13, I want you moving into your last sector immediately. You are now on full crisis alert.'

With a degree of peevishness the Warden then opened up
its next communication channel.

'Sniper, I do know that a molly carp is not capable of travelling at seven hundred kilometres per hour. If it dies, you
understand you'll be charged with killing a grade-three intelligence?'

'I understand. The carp's fine. What's happening up there?'

The Warden transmitted a condensed information package to the war drone. Sniper might be a pain sometimes, but
did have his uses, especially in any situation that might involve explosions and sudden death. The Warden then flicked
away from the drone to another focus of attention. Now link-
ing through the local server, it accessed a very particular aug
on the planet below. The actions it was pursuing were initiated from a program within itself which it labelled
'nasty/suspicious'. The blueprint for that program had, in
fact, initially come from Sniper.

Sniper scanned around inside the molly carp for breakages.
Dropping it five metres into the sea the moment the Warden
had contacted him had not been a clever idea. Surprisingly
the carp was undamaged, just a bit twitchy. He relinquished
all control of it as he scanned the information package.

Prador . . .

Some very old and unused programs initiated in Sniper,
and as a result he came as close to excitement as it was pos-

sible for him to get. He immediately began running systems
diagnostics and checking his inventory: 121 smart missiles
with coiled planar loads, an assortment of mines, plenty of
carbide fingers for his rail gun, and of course his APW. He
was well armed, but his big problem was his power supply.
Hauling a molly carp all that distance on AG had depleted
his batteries, so his allotropic uranium generator was struggling to bring them up to charge, and his microtok was
struggling to keep the generator running. In drone parlance,
he was knackered. He decided the best thing for him to do
now was sit tight until everything was up to charge.

He did a quick ultrasound scan beyond the fleshy vessel
he was in and saw that a sailing ship had just come into
range. No matter to him unless they decided to hunt down
this carp and cut it open, so he settled down to wait. He was
now in what he supposed might be called the carp's small intestine, and had quite a way to go to reach the final exit.

Using two ceramal-composite oars with blades as wide as a
man, Ambel towed the *Treader* with a rowing boat. Each
time he dipped those oars in and heaved, the hawser connecting the boat to the ship creaked and stretched, and the
ship slowly slid on through the water. The boat itself was
heavily reinforced, especially about the rowlocks. The first
time Ambel had used these oars in an unreinforced boat, his
exertions had torn the sides out of it, and the crew had to
quickly haul him back before the leeches got him. Just in
case of that eventuality, Pland and Anne kept an eye on their
Captain while they supervised work on the deck, and Peck
was in the nest keeping an eye elsewhere.

'What's he doing?' asked Pland.

Ambel had shipped his oars and was staring off to one side.
Both Pland and Anne followed the direction of Ambel's gaze,
towards the horizon. A spreading disk of red fire grew behind
cloud like a skin cancer. It broke and dispersed as they
watched, but it took a long time for the colour to leave the sky.

'What's that?' Pland asked.

'Big meteor?' Anne suggested doubtfully.

They both stared contemplatively at the coloration in the

sky and only returned their attention to Ambel as he started
rowing again.

'Molly carp to starboard!' yelled Peck from the nest.

'Where the hell did that come from?' said Pland.

He and Anne both stared at the creature as it rose out of
the water and came down with a huge splash, seemingly trying to bite the waves. After pausing for a moment it swam
round in a couple of tight circles, then rocked backwards,
apparently examining the boat, before setting off at a frantic
pace to do one circuit of the ship. Those who had been
scrubbing the deck stopped to watch the show, glad of an in-
terruption to their tedium. Once back where it had begun
from, it settled down now to blow bubbles and make strange
grunting sounds.

'That's one confused beasty,' said Anne.

'Bit of a mad moment, maybe? We all get those,' said
Pland.

Anne snorted and gave him a look.

'They used to follow the boxy boats . . . never cause no
harm,' said Sild, leaning on his mop.

Immediately on his words, the carp reared up and suddenly sped towards Ambel's reinforced rowing boat.

'Now that's normally what Peck does,' said Anne.

Gollow and Sild eyed each other in confusion, turned to
watch as she and Pland sped away along the deck, then
abruptly dropped their cleaning utensils and followed.

They all ran around the forecabin to the foredeck and began
winding in the cable that joined ship to rowing boat. Boris
joined them, from the helm, but even with his help, they knew
they would not be quick enough. Ambel shipped his oars and,
holding one like a club, he stood and waited for the carp. The
carp reached the rowing boat when the boat was only four metres from the ship. The creature hesitated in its approach, then,
as if coming to a decision, it lunged. Ambel chopped down on
its head with all the force he could muster. There came a
sound as of a sledgehammer hitting a block of wood. The carp
itself immediately stopped, but its bow wave continued on to
hit the boat, almost tipping it over. Ambel kept his feet and
used all his weight to bring the boat back on an even keel.

When the carp nosed in again, hesitantly, as if not sure what had happened to it, he hit it again, this time high on the hump of flesh located behind its head. Again that solid, bang. Ambel inspected the bend in his oar, then swivelled it in readiness for another blow, perhaps hoping to batter it straight again. The carp shook itself once, then lifted its head out of the water and turned an accusing eye on Ambel.

'That's it! You show the bastard!' yelled Peck from his perch. Anne, Pland, and Boris stared up at him, trying to decide which of the two contestants Peck was addressing.

Ambel rested the butt of his oar in the bottom of the boat as he stared eye to eye with the creature. After a moment, the carp opened its mouth and issued a deep whooshing hoot, then it turned and moved slowly away.

'Captain got its attention, then,' said Boris.

'I thought it was going to try for him,' said Anne.

'Nah,' said Boris, eyeing the junior crew gathered round. 'It knew it couldn't get the Captain down in one gulp, and what'd happen to it if it tried. Molly carp are smart. Remember Captain Gurt's carp? He fed it on leeches, and trained it to catch even bigger leeches for him.'

'He made a lot of skind,' agreed Pland.

'Then there was Alber's carp—used it to tow his ship around,' Boris went on.

Anne said, 'Could be it just didn't want to eat the Captain. That was only a lick on its head it got, no more than an itch.'

'Remember what happened to Captain Gurt?'

'Oh, yeah, they only found his leg, didn't they?' said Anne, then, 'Why they called molly carp? I've always wondered.'

Boris appeared thoughtful for a moment. 'They look a bit like a fish from Earth called a carp. Then there was this Hooper who had a wife called Molly who kept on carping at him.' Boris ignored Anne's wince at this and soldiered on. 'He went out one day and saw this big fat carp and thought it looked like his wife. And that's how they got their name.'

The junior crewmen attended Boris's explanation with dubious expressions, before being shepherded back to their tasks by Pland, now the excitement was over. Anne leaned close to Boris and muttered, 'You don't really know, do you?'

Boris scratched at his moustache. 'Nah, haven't a clue.'

Peck chose that moment for another yell. 'That's it, y'bugger!'

He was waving his fist, but it was still unclear at whom or what he was gesturing.

'Never been the same since,' said Boris, shaking his head.

'Oh, he only goes a bit funny *sometimes*,' said Anne. She pointed at the island to which Ambel was again towing them. 'It's islands—they remind him of the Skinner's Island. He never feels safe near them.'

'He knows he can't be got again,' said Boris, looking meaningfully towards the Captain's cabin.

'Not the point. It ain't logical, but he's convinced it's going to happen again.'

'Well it can't,' said Boris, looking towards Ambel as the Captain continued to tow the ship on in.

In Ambel's cabin the Skinner's head lay still in its box; still and silent, and attentive.

The remaining hornet had been gone for two days now, and the mind had not spoken to him much since his voicing of his concerns about Erlin. Quite dryly, it had asked him just what he found so unbelievable about her story and, when he had tried, it had pointed out all the clues that pointed to the 'extremity' Erlin had described. Since then Janer had been contemplative and had nothing to ask it. Since then the mind had very little to say to him either. It was almost as if an embarrassed silence had fallen between them. When it was broken, Janer jerked as if he had been slapped.

'Now, there's an interesting sight,' said the mind.

'Mind, where are your eyes now?' Janer asked, confused as to why he should have been surprised at the voice. After a pause came a flat reply, without the usual complementary buzzing. He realized this was the reason he had jumped: the buzzing had always served to forewarn of a communication.

'I'm on a rock in the sea. Sails live on it,' the mind said.

'Why are you there?'

There was no reply for a long time and, standing at the rail, Janer started to fidget uncomfortably. He glanced up at Ron, who had a telescope to his eye, then at Erlin, whom the sail had lifted to the nest. Other members of the crew were slowly moving about their business on the deck: Roach, Forlam, a thickset blonde called Goss, who kept giving him the eye, and others he had no name for. Janer studied Goss speculatively. This journey was starting to get a little boring. Perhaps it was time to spice things up a little. Just then, the Hive mind came back to him, but this time the buzzing had returned.

'*Look to the north,*' it said.

Janer did so, and observed a red glow sheeting up behind cloud, wavering like an aurora.

'What is it?'

'*An antimatter explosion. The Warden is most reticent about its source,*' said the mind.

'Antimatter?'

The mind was silent for a while before continuing.

'*I will be with you soon. Keech is coming. Tell Erlin to prepare her equipment.*'

'What do you mean, Keech?' Janer looked in confusion from the light in the sky back to the activity on the deck.

Others were gazing out at the redness and talking to each other in muted tones. But already the light was beginning to disperse, to fade. The buzzing that had accompanied the mind's message faded also, and it gave no reply. Janer looked at Goss again, then he looked up at Erlin. He called to her.

'What did it mean "Keech is coming"?' Erlin asked him, once Janer had related the mind's message.

'I can only think he's in trouble, if it means you'll need your medical equipment,' said Janer.

'What the hell am I supposed to be able to do for him?'

'He is a little past your services, I have to admit.' Janer shrugged and grinned at her. 'Perhaps we should prepare anyhow. The mind doesn't normally get things wrong.'

'OK. I suppose you're right.'

Erlin headed for the deck hatch and Janer watched her for a moment.

'Let me help you. I'm a bit of a spare wheel here anyhow.'

Erlin gestured for him to follow.

Once below decks, Erlin pulled one of her cases from a

storage locker, then put it on the floor and opened it. Janer looked at the mass of gleaming apparatus neatly packed inside. He recognized a nanoscope, portable autodoc, and one or two other items.

Erlin pointed at the autodoc. 'You know how to assemble that?' she asked.

Janer pulled the doc out of the case and proceeded to clip together the hooded cowling and the insectile surgical arms. Erlin allowed a little surprise to enter her expression, nodded an acknowledgement to him, then turned to something else. She then took out a flat box with a gun-shaped object fixed in its upper surface. Janer immediately identified the 'gun' as a hand-diagnosticer, and the box it was plugged into as a portable drug-manufactory.

'Oh hell,' said Erlin. 'I haven't got a clue.'

'Let's just be as ready as we can,' said Janer.

They got ready.

Windcheater flew in a world constructed of information. Eyes crossed and toes clenched he gazed with wonder on a virtual galaxy dwarfing the incontestably vast Human Polity. There was so much to know, so much to see—great minds moved past the sail like sun-bright leviathans, and the financial systems of worlds were complex hives he could lose himself in for centuries. It was wonderful: there was so much to do, *so much to have*. But Windcheater, with a self-discipline and intelligence beyond that of his brothers and sisters, gradually shut all that out and concentrated on the specific. He curled his lip and growled when he located the minuscule antiquities site based on Coram and surveyed the price list. Perhaps Sniper believed the sail would be too dazzled to pick up on things like that.

'Windcheater.'

The voice came from close by and Windcheater uncrossed his eyes and looked around. His fellow sails were all gathered at the other side of The Flint, watching him warily. It had not been one of those that had spoken.

'Sail, I'm speaking to you through your aug. Do you understand me?' asked the voice.

'I hear you,' said the sail. 'But I don't know who you are.'

'Of course . . . you've never heard my voice. I am the Warden.'

'Ah,' Windcheater managed. He noticed then that his fellows were edging even further away from him and were observing him all the more warily. There was nothing he could do about that just now.

'Well, what do you think of the human virtual world?' the Warden resumed.

'It is . . . useful,' replied the sail. 'What do you want?' it then asked, thinking it might be less disconcerting for his fellows if he quickly terminated this conversation. He did not want them thinking him any crazier than they did already.

'Like yourself I want *many* things—and like yourself I understand that there is little to be had without paying a price,' said the Warden.

Windcheater showed his teeth and waited. The Warden continued.

'I see that your business arrangements with Sniper have provided you with some income. I see no reason to prevent that arrangement continuing. It could easily be argued that any artefacts accessible to you are legitimately the property of your people . . . '

'Our property?' Windcheater asked.

'You are, after all, the autochthons of this world,' the Warden observed.

'Does that mean we *own* it?' the sail asked, a couple of strange ideas occurring to him all at once.

'That is something we can discuss at a later time,' said the Warden. 'For now I just want to know if you would like to augment that minor income.'

Windcheater considered the offer for all of a couple of seconds, quickly forgetting his concerns about how his fellow sails might view him. That 'minor income' was the only income he had, and there was so much to *have*.

'Tell me about it,' the sail said.

'I need a pair of eyes, but a pair of eyes in a natural form of this world. Not so much undetectable as unnoticed.'

'What for?'

'You saw the light in the sky to the north?'

Windcheater nodded, then realizing the Warden would have no way of seeing this, replied in the affirmative.

The Warden continued, 'I want you to go and take a look in that area and report to me anything unusual.'

'Like what?'

'Just anything unusual.'

Windcheater considered again: Why not? He could do with the extra credit.

'How much?' the sail asked.

'One thousand shillings for each day.'

By the time the Warden had reached the word 'day', Windcheater was already airborne. His fellows, after watching him depart, turned to each other in great puzzlement and there was much confused shrugging.

As Ambel rested, the *Treader* drifted up behind and nudged the back of the rowing boat. As it did this, he dipped the oars and rowed again for a few minutes. Slowly the ship drifted into a sheltered cove whose visible bottom was smeared with leeches and pinioned by the stalks of sea-cane, which at the surface opened into tangles of reddish tendrils that were kept afloat by chequered gourd-like fruits. An islet, no bigger than the ship itself, slid past to the right of them, and from this the stalked eyes of frog whelks tracked their progress, their grey and yellow shells clattering together in their agitation. Boris turned the helm so that the ship drifted away from these, and Ambel allowed the rowing boat to come back against the side of the ship.

'All right, Pland!' he shouted.

At the bows, Pland, Sild and Gollow heaved the anchor over the side and dropped it into the shallows, where it thumped down, still visible, raising a cloud of black silt. Taking the usual precautions for mooring in island waters, Pland had greased the anchor chain some hours before. The grease wouldn't stop prill as they—should they have the inclination—could scale the wooden sides of the ship using the tips of their sharp legs like pitons, but it would deter frog and hammer whelks, and other of the more common annoyances. Anne lowered a ladder to Ambel while he hitched the boat to the side of the ship and secured his oars inside. As he climbed back aboard, Peck looked down at him disconsolately from the nest.

'Still time to get a worm or two to tempt a sail. Fresh meat's always best,' said Ambel, nodding towards stony beaches and the island with its narrow crown of blue-green dingle.

'I ain't goin',' said Peck.

'You stay and trull for boxies, Peck,' Ambel replied cheerfully.

'I don't wanna stay,' said Peck.

'You could hook us some sea-cane and a few gourds as well. We've a barrel or two to spare, and some bags of dried salt-yeast,' said Ambel, ignoring this.

Peck snorted and returned his gaze to the island. After a moment, he turned away, stepped out of the nest and scrambled down the mast to the deck, from where he again returned his attention to the island. Ambel watched him for a moment, then shrugged and walked over to the wall of the forecabin, from where he unhooked his blunderbuss. He also shouldered a case containing powder and shot. He turned to Anne and Boris, who had just come down from the cabin-deck.

'You two fetch your stuff and get down to the boat,' he said—then, turning to Sild and Gollow, 'You two as well.' To Pland he said, 'Keep an eye on things here,' flicking his eyes in the direction of Peck. Pland nodded, and Ambel ducked into his cabin. Once inside, he closed the door and laid his blunderbuss and bag on the table. After a pause, he went over to his sea-chest and took out the Skinner's box. He opened it and looked at the head inside. Insane black eyes glared back at him from the grotesque object. Ears that looked like spined fins wiggled. There seemed a lot more of them than there had been before. Ambel looked closer and noted lumps growing down the side of the long-snouted end of the thing. They were similar in shape to the lumps from which its tusks sprouted. Ambel stared at it some more, then abruptly came to a decision.

'It's sprine for you,' he said to the head.

The head rose up on its bottom jaw and tried to shake it-self free of the box. Ambel slammed shut the lid and locked it. The head was still banging about inside its box as he closed it in his seachest. He took up his 'buss and his bag and quickly left his cabin.

With a fear gnawing his gut, Peck watched them rowing ashore. Horrible things happened to you if you went ashore. Memory was a feeling. He could feel a long bony finger un-der his skin, working round between dermis and muscle, tugging and ripping. *Why can't a Hooper faint?* he won-dered. Why did the pain have to last for so long? Somewhere deep inside himself Peck knew he was being foolish. The Skinner was finished. Ambel kept the head in a box and the Skinner could no longer do what it had been named for.

The boat grounded on the beach of the cove and the five of them hopped out, secured it, then made their way into the dingle. Rhinoworms would be in the deeper water surround-ing the island elsewhere, so they would have to make their way round there, and out of the shallow cove. Peck looked at Pland, who was standing at the bows with two juniors. The three of them had dropped lines over the side and were trulling for boxies. *Nothing to worry about. Everything was fine.* But then the whispering started again: a kind of hungry pleading.

'Wants some buggering sea-cane does he?' Peck said loudly.

Pland glanced at him. 'Get it from the stern. I don't want you stirring it too much here.'

Peck nodded, then moved to one of the rail lockers, where he pulled out a coil of rope and a grappling hook. He walked then to one side of the stern end of the ship, hurled the grap-pling hook out, and began hauling away. Soon the hook snagged one of the sea-cane plants, and he pulled carefully until it slid up to lodge in the tangle at the plant's head, then he increased the pressure. With a puff of black silt the plant came up out of the sea bottom. He drew it in to the edge of the ship then hauled it up hand-over-hand as far as the rail. With it draped half over the rail, he grasped the stalk, which was as thick as a man's leg, pulled out his panga, and with one blow cut off the hand-like root and anchor stone to which it was clinging. Root and stone splashed back into the sea, while the rest of the plant flopped on to the deck, its gourds thudding down like severed heads, scattering small leeches, trumpet shells, and coin-sized prill across the planks. Peck then spent a happy five minutes stamping on the prill and leeches, and dropping trumpet shells into a cast-iron bait box. During that time he forgot the whispering, but when he had finished it returned stronger than ever.

Come . . .

With a sweat breaking out, Peck clung to the rail—then he swore and headed for the rear hold. Down below decks, he muttered to himself and crashed barrels about with more vigour than was entirely necessary. Two barrels he hoisted out on to the deck before climbing out of the hold and rolling them over towards the sea-cane. After opening the barrels, he stamped on the few leeches he had missed, then began plucking gourds and tossing them into the first barrel.

Need . . .

'Shaddup! Buggering shaddup!'

The stalk of the sea-cane Peck sliced up with single panga blows so each fragrant section fell into the second barrel. The ribbed red-and-green skin of the cane stalk was only a thin sheath covering a gooey yellow honeycomb that smelt strongly of aniseed. Peck scooped up the tangled top and tossed it back over the side, before quickly snatching up the grappling hook and casting it out into the water again. *It's a coward*, he thought, as he yanked in another cane. *It's only this loud when the Captain ain't aboard.* But today the whispering was particularly strong. He'd never known it as persistent as this before. But this time he would resist. It was only when he had dealt with the second sea-cane, which had nicely filled both barrels, that he remembered that Ambel kept the salt-yeast in his cabin. Then the whisper became even more intense, even more *eager*. With elaborate care, Peck returned the rope and grappling hook to the locker before clinging tight to the rail again. He clung there for as long as he could, but a horrible fascination eventually turned him round to stare towards the Captain's cabin. After a moment he walked to the door and—out of Pland's view—he ducked inside.

The pain. The pain had been transcendent. It had taken Peck somewhere he had never before been. There had been a terrible understanding in it, too. It had been given to him so he might understand, yet he had failed. Peck stood over the sea-chest with his sweat dripping on to the ornately carved wood. Here, concealed in this box, was something that all Hoopers—with their ambivalent relationship with pain— could not but fear and worship at the same time.

I mustn't . . .

It was so *hungry*, and if he fed it, the whispering would stop. Peck abruptly turned from the cabin and ran out on to the deck. For a moment he stood there gasping, hoping it would just cease. That subtle voice suggested untold pleasure and pain so intermingled they were indistinguishable. He had to silence it, so if food would do the trick, then food it must be. He reached into the barrel where they kept the sail's feed and pulled out the last, rather putrid rhinoworm steak. He headed back into the Captain's cabin and opened the chest.

It was there in the box; moving about in the box. Peck studied the secured lock and felt a strange relief.

I tried . . .

Then the lock clicked.

Oh bugger.

Gliding on thermals rising from banks of sun-heated coral, Windcheater observed the motorized dinghy as it hurtled for the shore, the wake of a chasing rhinoworm close behind it. Steam and explosions of water blew from around that wake as the figure crouched in the back of the dinghy tried to hit the pursuing worm with a high-intensity laser. Windcheater recognized this because only recently he had been scanning, with wonder and no little dismay, a weapon-dealer's site.

'They're bounty hunters. Batian killers. I already know about them,' said the Warden, as the sail tried to describe what he was seeing—he hadn't yet quite mastered transfer-ring images across from his visual cortex.

Windcheater banked, riding out of the thermal and away

from the island. Hadn't there been something about Batians on that weapons site? The sail resisted the impulse to go back to the place as he had more than enough to chew on concerning humankind. As he flew on, he auged through to any easily accessible information about his own kind, and was surprised to find how much and how little was known.

Polity experts knew that sails fed from the surface of the sea, taking rhinoworms, glisters, prill from the back of leeches—and sometimes leeches themselves. The speculation that they took to the ships for an easier food supply and a less hazardous existence was, of course, entirely wrong. Strange how the humans tried to classify the behaviour of any other species as relating only to 'animal' traits. Windcheater was completely certain that he and his kin had taken to the ships out of curiosity. It was much more difficult working as a ship sail for just a few steaks than snatching a whole worm from the sea and devouring it on the wing. Silly, arrogant humans.

The information section concerning sail mating was of huge interest to Windcheater. He had known for a long time that humans were divided into two sexes, and how all *that* operated—he had often been aboard a ship during one of the frequent Hooper meets, though why it was necessary to consume prodigious quantities of sea-cane rum and boiled hammer whelks before the sexual act, he had never been able to fathom. What he had not been aware of was that his own kind had *four* sexes. Anyway, during the mating season, he had never really had much chance to think about the mechanisms that drove him to such exhausting madness. Three males required to fertilize one female egg, and that egg then encysted and stuck, in its cocoon, on the side of The Big Flint. Hence, what a human far in the past had described as 'that rocktop orgy'.

Windcheater flew on, heading for the horizon of Spatterjay, and all the new horizons he was now discovering. He was but a speck by the time the Batians beached their dinghy in a spray of sand and opened fire en masse on the rhinoworm that reared out of the sea behind them.

* * *

The worm dropped, flaming, back into the sea, writhed there for a moment as if still intent on coming on to the beach after them, and then grew still. Shib let out a shuddering breath, then quickly wiped at the sweat that was stinging his eyes.

'Great idea using an inflatable dinghy to get out here. Real classic, that one,' he snarled.

'Shut up, Shib,' said Svan, as she watched the leeches surfacing to take apart the laser-cooked rhinoworm. 'You know what would happen if we used AG here. The Warden would be up our asses with a thermite grenade about two seconds later.'

'Yeah, but—'

Svan made a chopping motion with her hand. 'Enough. You either handle it or you don't.'

Shib shut up. He knew Svan wasn't suggesting he could pay back the deposit and go home. Employment contracts with first-rankers like her either ended with a large payout or in a rather terminal manner. He nodded when she gestured towards the boat, then slung his carbine from his shoulder and headed over to the vessel. Upon reaching it, he immediately clicked on the little rotary pump. Joining him, Dime hauled out their packs and tossed them on to the pebbled beach. Shib detached and collapsed the telescopic outboard, and then he and Dime stood back as the dinghy quickly collapsed and shrivelled. The rolled-up dinghy was no wider than a man's wrist, and with its motor locked beside it, formed a pack that could be tucked under an arm. Dime carried this to the head of the beach and slid it under a spread of sheetlike leaves growing there. Soon all four of them had loaded up their packs and were heading along the beach.

'Why here?' Tors asked after a moment.

'A location easy to find—and our client has business here,' Svan replied.

Half listening to the conversation, Shib kept his eyes on the dingle. A hideous bird-thing observed him from the branches of a tree with a hugely globular trunk. He had thought the creature dead and decaying until it had moved to follow their progress with its glistening eye-pits. He sup-

pressed his immediate inclination to burn it from its branch.
No doubt Svan would take that as one push too many.

'Do you have any further information on this client?' Tors
asked.

'Same one as has had the bounty up on Sable Keech for
the last three centuries. No way of tracing the transaction
without collecting, and no one has managed that yet.'

'I don't get how he's lasted so long,' said Dime, with an
apologetic glance to Shib.

'Organization, speed, luck and, thus far, seven centuries
of experience. Anyway, Keech doesn't often put himself in a
position where he can be hit. Normally he operates on Polity
worlds well within AI surveillance, and spends most of his
time searching through Polity databases. Not easy to get him
there. When he does come somewhere like this, he's normally well covered. It's surprising that he's here alone like
this. Maybe he's getting careless,' said Svan.

'Or maybe he's just had enough,' said Tors.

Svan shrugged and gestured to a path cutting into the dingle opposite a jetty. 'This looks like it,' she said.

As they turned into the path, Shib could feel the hairs
prickling on the back of his neck. He had been in some hostile places before, some where he'd had to go suited and armoured, and some where nothing less than a fully motorized
exoskeleton would do, but here he felt things were wrong
right from the start. This was a casually brutal place. In the
Hooper town, he'd caught the tail-end of some sort of fight,
and even he had been surprised at how easily Hoopers bore
hideous injury. Then there had been the rush to head for
where Keech had headed, then of course Nolan . . . He
peered round at the surrounding dingle and gripped his carbine tighter. From the dingle floor, spined frog-things regarded him with glinting blue eyes, and the foliage above
bore oozing fruit of a long and slimy variety. Was there *anywhere* here where you could let your guard down?

'This is the place. We secure it and wait for her here,'
Svan said.

'Her?' asked Shib, flicking his gaze forward. Ahead of

them a tower sprouted from the ground, and around it the
churned earth was clear of vegetation, as if the tower itself
had sucked all goodness from it. Shib wondered where the
resident ogre was.

Svan did not elaborate. Instead she turned to them.

'Dime, take out the autogun, and any dishes on the roof.
Tors, I want you to blow the door. You cover him, Shib, and
hit any autos around the door.'

'How many people here?' Shib asked.

'Just one old woman. We're to hold her and wait. Our
client should be along soon. Right, we go *now*.'

Dime dropped a targeting visor down over his eyes, raised
his carbine, and fired four short pulses in rapid succession. As
he fired, Shib and Tors ran for the door. On the roof of Olian
Tay's residence, the satellite dishes on the pylon flared and
sagged. The autogun, which had swung their way at the last
moment, disappeared with a flat crack and flare, out of which
black fragments dropped to the denuded ground. Tors hit the
door and slapped a small disk against the locking mechanism,
while Shib covered him. They both swung themselves either
side of the entrance as the small mine blew and sent the buckled door crashing inside the building. Then they were in.

Svan walked across the clearing, carefully scanning her
surroundings. She watched as Dime ran around behind the
structure, and she listened as sharp cracking sounds and low
detonations issued from inside. The only noise she sensed
came from Shib and Tors. This place was deserted. Either
Olian Tay had struck lucky, or someone had warned her. As
Svan entered the building, Dime moved in behind her. Tors
stood in the central living room, doors broken open all
around, while Shib was coming down a spiral staircase to one
side. She glanced at them and they both shook their heads.

Svan peered up at the ceiling. 'House computer, where is
Olian Tay?'

'Olian Tay, Olian Tay, is over the hills and far away!' The
voice was that of a woman, and Svan had no doubt to whom
it belonged. She made a sharp hand signal to Dime, who
quickly pulled an instrument from his belt and held it up.

'Where are you?' she asked.

'Oh, I see,' said Tay. 'You want me to tell you that just so's you can deliver the flowers my lover has sent.'

'You could say that, but don't you really want to know why we are here?'

'That's the way, keep me talking so's your friend can trace a signal. Not too bright that, considering you destroyed the radio dish.'

'You're somewhere close, then,' said Svan, making another sharp gesture. Shib and Tors made to duck out of the room and search, but Tay's next reply stopped them in their tracks.

'Wrong, this signal is coming through a landline to a pylon on the east of the island. Right now I'm sitting in the Mackay lounge on Coram. Oh, by the way, there's enough explosives underneath my house to launch you four out this way as well, so I suggest you listen very carefully to me.'

'I'm listening,' said Svan.

'Now, I know that somehow you've traced our mutual friend, Monitor Keech. He is not here anymore. The last I heard he was heading off to find some Old Captain to chat to. What I am most interested in is how you managed to trace him *here*.'

Svan gave the other three a warning look. 'If I tell you that you'll let us walk out of here?'

'I will allow that,' said Tay. 'Now perhaps you can explain yourself?'

Leaning her elbows on the rim of the granite outcrop, Tay stared down at her tower. She then studied the screen of her transponder and smiled at the way the mercenaries were frantically gesturing to each other.

Their leader spoke up then. 'We followed Keech with a purpose built tracer that picks up on emissions from certain old designs of cybermotors,' the Batian woman said, holding up some sort of device she had pulled from her belt. Tay peered at her screen. The explanation seemed plausible but she didn't believe it for a moment.

'I don't believe that for a moment,' she said, enjoying herself immensely. Only a small seed of doubt marred her enjoyment: if they hadn't traced Keech by the method they claimed, how had they traced him? As she turned from the granite, with the transponder held up before her face, it occurred to her that maybe they were not here searching for Keech at all. No matter. She walked over to her AGC and climbed into it. When these mercenaries finally went away, as their kind always did, she would return to her home. She dumped the transponder on the seat beside her and reached for the control column.

'Why, Olian,' said the woman who climbed into the AGC beside her, 'you've got it all wrong. They came here to meet me, and I came here to meet you.'

Tay did not recognize the face that smiled at her, but the gas-system pulse-gun pointed at her face had her fullest attention.

'Who the hell are you?' she asked.

'Can't you guess?' the woman asked and, so saying, picked up Tay's transponder and spoke into it.

'Svan, this is your client here. I have Olian Tay and will be with you shortly. I must congratulate you on performing precisely as I expected.'

She clicked the transponder off, tossed it out of the AGC, and then looked at Tay expectantly. Before reaching out to take hold of the column Tay wiped sweat from under her chin and swallowed dryly. Batian mercenaries . . . now there were many people prepared to hire these mercenaries, hence the entire culture of one continent, on an Out-Polity planet, revolving around that frowned-upon profession, but factor in the recent presence of Sable Keech here on Spatterjay, and Tay's own interests . . . Tay did not like where her thoughts were leading her. There had always been something odd about one particular story concerning the demise of one of The Eight.

'What do you want?' she asked.

The woman gave a deprecatory smile and waved the gun at her. Tay could not keep her eyes off the wide silvered snout of the weapon. She knew that, even at its lowest setting, it could probably take her face off.

'Oh, Olian, we can chat about all this back in your wonderful tower. Then you can show me your wonderful museum. I've read quite a bit about it, and have always wanted to see it.'

Tay engaged the old grav motor and lifted the AGC into the air. She considered making a grab for the stranger's gun, as up here might be her only chance. Perhaps this woman did not realize how long Tay had been a Hooper, and just how strong she was.

'You know, Olian, you wouldn't know how old this body is, just by looking at it, and how long it has been Hooper,' said the woman.

Tay said nothing for a moment. *This body*. Not *my* body, not *me*. That one phrase was all the confirmation Tay needed. She felt suddenly very small and vulnerable, even though her captor seemed smaller and more fragile than she. She knew now who this person was, and that there wouldn't be a lot she could do if she did get hold of the weapon. The woman sitting next to her could break her like a ship Captain could.

'You're Rebecca Frisk,' she said.

'Of course I am,' said the woman.

As she brought the AGC in to land on the roof of her tower, Tay became absolutely certain that she would die if she was not very careful. And even then . . .

'Out,' said Frisk, once the grav motor wound down.

Tay climbed out of the AGC, calculating all the way how she might survive this. That Frisk had come to see her out of curiosity, she had no doubt; that she left death and destruction behind her wherever she went was a matter of historical fact.

'What do you want here?' she asked, as Frisk followed her to the stairwell.

'I want to see your museum,' said Frisk.

9

Prill and leeches had gathered in huge numbers, snapping up stray pieces of flesh while adding to the chaos by attacking each other—or the glisters, even though that gained them nought—and tearing the fragments into smaller fragments as they squabbled over them. Visibility in the water was now atrocious, what with all that activity disturbing the seabed and all the spurting spillage from tender organs. This detritus of broken bodies and stirred-up silt was also so thick in the water that little else could be tasted. And, what with the rattling and clattering of prill and the bubbling and hissing sussuration of leeches obliterating most other sounds, what happened next was predictably unfortunate.

'Something coming,' said Ron, his eye to his telescope.

Janer looked out over the sea but for a moment could see nothing. He then discerned a distant dot coming towards them and growing larger. He unhooked his intensifier and quickly focused on the object.

'I'll be damned,' he said.

'What?' asked Erlin.

'He's got an AG scooter,' Janer replied. 'Must have been all those investments he made before he shuffled off. Compound interest.'

Erlin laughed, and Janer chalked up a mental point as he hooked the intensifier back on his belt. It was good to know that he could touch her in some way.

The scooter came to a halt above the ship, and hovered there for a long while. Before anyone could wonder if it was just going to stay up there, it descended and came in to land on the clearest part of the deck.

Janer gagged when he drew close to it. The crusted stinking thing sitting on the saddle was Keech all right, but a Keech somewhat changed since the last time Janer had seen him.

'Too late, I think,' he said.

Erlin approached the reif with her diagnosticer. She pressed it against his arm and the thick scab there cracked and oozed red plasma. She stared at the reading on the diagnosticer, then abruptly took a step back. Keech's head turned towards her, shell-like crust breaking away from his neck to reveal wet and bloody muscle underneath.

'You're alive,' was all Erlin could manage.

Keech just looked at her with his single, weeping blue eye.

With the rest of the crew, Janer just stared. It was Ron who suddenly moved into action. 'All right lads, get him below. Gently, mind,' he said.

'I ain't touching *that*,' said Goss.

Ron looked at her and raised an eyebrow—and Goss was the first one to reach for the reif. As they lifted Keech off his scooter, stinking crusts fell away from him to expose flayed muscle. Something bulked in the front of his overall, and Janer had a horrible feeling that organs were floating about free in there. He was so involved with what was happening that he didn't notice the hornet had returned to his shoulder until Keech was taken below decks.

'He brought a package for us,' said the mind. *'It is in the luggage compartment of the scooter. Get it now.'*

'You don't order me any more,' said Janer out loud, and Ron glanced round at him. Janer pointed at the hornet and Ron nodded, before following the others below decks.

'Please,' said the mind.

'OK.'

Janer went over to the scooter and looked in the back. He instantly knew which package it was. He lifted it out and inspected it.

'Put it somewhere safe . . . please.'

Janer headed for the hatch to his cabin. 'What is it?' he asked.

'Do you need to ask that?'

'No, I guess not,' said Janer, since he had received deliveries like this before.

He took the package below, walking past the crammed cabin, where Keech was stretched out on a table. Reaching his own cabin, he was about to place the box under his bunk when the mind stopped him.

'*Wait one moment,*' it said, as if something had only just occurred to it. In Janer's experience things never 'only just occurred' to a Hive mind. He waited anyway.

The hornet launched itself from his shoulder and landed on the box. It crawled round to the middle plane of its hexagonal front. Immediately a hexagonal hole opened and the hornet crawled inside.

'*You may put it somewhere safe now,*' said the mind. Janer crammed the box under his bunk, and went to see what was happening with Keech. As he arrived, Erlin was clearing the cabin.

'Everyone out. Out, *now*,' she said.

The disgruntled crew shuffled away. The medical technology of off-worlders always intrigued Hoopers simply because of its utter irrelevance to them. Their attitude was something like the attitude of a hospital consultant to the trappings of shamanism. This was yet another strange Hooper reversal.

'*You* can stay,' said Erlin, and it took Janer a moment to realize that she meant him. He walked into the cabin, past Ron as the Captain went out. He stared down at the thing that was Keech.

'What can I do?' he asked.

Erlin pointed at the autodoc. 'That's an idiot savant quite capable of dealing with injuries to a normal human. Right now Keech is making the transition from corpse to living man with the aid of a nano-changer. He's also infected with the Spatterjay virus, which is digesting dead tissue, just as it does in a living creature. The problem is that it started on Keech when he was *all* dead tissue. We've also got a few hundred cybernetic devices to deal with.'

Keech made a clicking gurgling sound.

'He keeps trying to speak,' said Erlin. She seemed at a loss.

Janer did not know what to say. If *she* could not handle this, then there was no way he could. He looked at Keech and felt pity. The only option, it seemed to him, would be to load him back on his scooter and head full-tilt for the Dome. He'd probably be dead by then, but even so . . . Janer focused his attention on Keech's aug. There was an interface plug on it.

'Back in a moment,' said Janer, and ran from the cabin. In the crew cabin he searched his backpack until he had hold of what he wanted, and rushed back. He brandished the small screen and optic cable, then walked over to Keech.

'This should work,' he said. 'It has a voice synthesizer.'

'It *does* work,' said Keech, the instant Janer plugged him into the personal computer. 'Erlin, do not concern yourself with the cybernetics. I will take them offline the moment they interfere with physical function.'

Erlin came up and stood by Janer. She seemed calmer now, and the look she gave Janer made something flip over in his stomach.

'Right,' she said, 'we've got a lot of work to do. We need to rig up some kind of tank. The nanites cannot function outside of a liquid medium, and that's why they're failing to build his outer tissues. The virus needs to be inhibited by Intertox. Keech, I take it you're blocking the pain?'

'I am.'

'Right, we need to make a tank.'

Erlin looked at her box of tricks for a moment, then looked at Janer.

Janer said, 'There's a monofilament mainsail stored in the rear hold. Goss told me it was a gift from some out-worlder who wanted to establish a business here by displacing the living sails. Ron didn't have the heart to warn the man that such replacement sail would require extra rigging as well as extra crewmen. They now apparently only use it to stretch around the hull after an attack by borers. I don't know what borers are, but I can imagine the effect. I should be able to rig something in about an hour.'

'Do it then,' said Erlin.

Janer turned to go, running through his mind the stored materials he had seen for the repair of any damage to the ship. He needed to construct a frame strong enough to support the weight of a few hundred litres of water. Perhaps some sort of hammock arrangement? He did not need to worry about the strength of the monofilament fabric. He'd yet to see it ripped, and knew that little short of a hit from a pulse-gun could puncture it.

'Janer,' said Erlin.

Janer turned at the door.

'I don't know how to say this . . . ' she began.

'Then don't,' said Janer, and went on his way.

The four mercenaries were definitely unhappy. It had soon become evident that Frisk had been watching for some time before their arrival, and had allowed them to act as a crude decoy.

'The warning message—was that you?' Tay asked

Frisk continued to study the looming sculpture of the Skinner and replied contemplatively. 'Oh no, that *was* the Warden. We monitored the signal and made sure there were no subminds in the area. Now, tell me, how did you ascertain the details for this?'

Tay stared at the sculpture and wondered just who Frisk was referring to when she had said 'We'. She also frantically tried to think of some story to turn to her advantage— something to eke out the possibility of escape from this impossible situation. Then she remembered one aspect of the history of Frisk and Hoop: they had once been art thieves and both had an interest in paintings.

'A crewman going off-planet presented me with his collection of paintings. I never believed they were accurate until I went out to the Skinner's Island and saw the reality.'

'Ah, you saw . . . the Skinner, in the flesh?' said Frisk.

Tay looked at her.

'Yes, I saw what Jay Hoop had become,' she said.

Frisk smiled humourlessly and moved on into the museum.

At each exhibit she stopped and stared for an uncomfortably long time. Occasionally she laughed, and occasionally she shook her head in annoyance. All of this performance was precisely that: a performance.

'It is an impressive collection,' she said finally, coming to stand before the model of herself as she had once been. 'You've got *so much* of it right, but there are a few inaccuracies.'

'Such as?' Tay asked.

Frisk made an airy gesture with her hand. 'Eon Talsca was the one who always carried an old projectile weapon. Duon used a fast-feed minigun or one of those bulky old pulse-guns. They often argued over the effectiveness of the weapons they used. I remember them having a competition to see who performed best with their particular choice of weapon. Duon won, of course. He killed fifteen of the twenty ECS monitors we let run loose—though they disputed after about the *artistry* of their weapons' play. Eon brought down his five monitors with clean head shots.'

Tay reached down to her belt for the device clipped there. A hand closed on her wrist and she found herself staring at the flat snout of a small stun gun, belonging to the Batian she now knew to be called Svan. She knew this choice of weapon was meant for her, if she ran. Obviously Frisk wanted her alive—for a while.

'It's only a recorder. I was making sure it was running,' Tay said.

Svan looked askance at Frisk.

Frisk nodded. 'Let her record. She's an historian to the end.'

It was then that Tay knew for sure that she wasn't going to survive this unless she was sharp. Obviously Keech's presence had brought Frisk to Spatterjay and curiosity had brought her to this particular location. Self-preservation, though, would not allow Frisk to leave behind any witnesses to the fact that she was still alive. As Tay watched Svan step back and lower the weapon, she wondered if these mercenaries realized that.

'Well, he did get Jay right, but then I suppose his memories of the Skinner's isle were more recent than those of the Talsca twins,' she said.

Frisk stared at her with the confidence of someone utterly in control of a situation, waiting for her to explain. Tay was aware that the old pirate was expecting some sort of survival ploy. Instead Tay pretended ignorance, or indifference, as she made a circling motion with her hand to encompass all the exhibits.

'The artist,' she duly explained. 'Every exhibit here is based on the sketches and paintings he made. Of course it could be my error giving Duon the projectile gun—the twins are very easy to confuse.'

'Who is this artist?' Frisk asked.

'Name of Sprage, one of the Old Captains,' Tay replied.

Frisk was thoughtful for a moment. 'The name escapes me,' she said, 'though I would perhaps recognize the face.'

'Not that memorable,' said Tay. 'His self-portrait won't win any prizes.'

Frisk glanced around the museum. 'Where are they?' she asked.

'What?' asked Tay, her attention deliberately directed towards the mercenaries, as if searching for a way past them. If Frisk clicked to her ploy, that was it—all over.

'Where *are* these paintings?'

Tay glanced at her as if surprised at her interest, then quickly cleared her face of expression. 'I don't have them. Sprage has them still,' she said quickly.

Frisk smiled at such transparency, and Tay dared to hope.

'Where do you keep them?' Frisk then asked. 'Don't lie to me. You know your life might depend on it.'

Tay hesitated before saying, 'I keep them in a vacuum safe. They were done on kelp paper, and some of them are very old. I didn't want to risk putting them on display in here.'

'You could have vacuum-sealed them in here,' said Frisk.

'Yes, but they're also susceptible to light damage,' said Tay—then, quickly changing the subject, 'What . . . what else have I got wrong in here?'

Frisk was not to be distracted. 'I want to see these paintings. Show them to me.'

Hooked, thought Tay, though she was uncomfortable with just how easy it had been. None of The Eight had been quite this stupid, and these Batian mercenaries certainly weren't. Perhaps they were all simply confident that any ploy she tried would be ineffectual in the face of their combined abilities. Tay scanned about herself as if seeking, yet again, for some way out. Finally she stared directly at Frisk.

'I'll let you have them if you let me live,' she said.

'What makes you think I want to kill you?' Frisk asked.

'I know your history, remember?'

Frisk affected an expression of boredom.

'Take me to these paintings *now* or I will have Svan here cut your fingers off one at a time until you do,' she said.

Tay stared at the Batian who was tapping a small curved knife strapped to her side. Giving a sharp nod, the historian moved to the door. Two of the other Batians closed in on either side of her as she stepped out into emerald sunlight. Perhaps they thought she might try to run now. She did not, and instead stumbled on the bare soil, obviously demonstrating how fear was making her weak, then walked as slowly as she could—delaying the inevitable. The mercenary Svan shoved her in the back, and she stumbled again. As she righted herself and continued, she felt the skin on her back crawl. This was her only chance, and it had to be done just right. Soon they reached the ruined front door of her residence, and Frisk went in ahead, with one of the mercenaries following behind her. Svan shoved again, and Tay followed them. Soon they were all gathered in the main living room.

Frisk turned and regarded Tay. 'Well?' she said, utterly in control of the situation.

'I need to address the house computer,' said Tay in a hollow voice.

Frisk nodded to Svan, who stepped up beside Tay and pressed the snout of her stun gun against the back of the historian's head.

Tay swallowed dryly before speaking. 'House computer, open false wall.'

Immediately a wall that seemingly held two windows, began to slide sideways. The windows blinked out, at the last re-

vealing themselves as screens. Behind was revealed an oval
door completely free of any apparent locking mechanisms.

'House computer,' Tay began again, pausing when the
stun gun was pressed harder against the back of her head.

Frisk nodded for her to continue.

'House computer, cancel lock-down and open atmosphere
safe,' Tay finished.

There came a deep clonk, then, with a low clicking and a
hiss, the oval door swung aside. As it opened it was revealed
to be almost like a barrel bung, such was its thickness. Inside
lay a polished spherical chamber. At the centre of this chamber rested two long coffin-like cases.

Tay very carefully gestured towards one of them. 'There
they are. We can take a look if you wish,' she said.

Frisk was immediately suspicious. 'You—Shib, isn't it?
Go in there and bring that case out,' she said, pointing.

With his laser carbine held one-handed, its butt propped
against his hip, Shib cautiously stepped inside the chamber.
He squatted and pulled at a handle fixed to one end of the
case, then glanced back questioningly.

'It's palm-locked to the floor,' explained Tay.

To Svan, Frisk said, 'Take her in there to unlock it, and
then bring it out.'

Svan pressed the gun again into the back of Tay's head and
the historian advanced while Shib stepped out of the safe and
moved to one side. Tay ducked slightly as she stepped over
the safe's threshold—then drove her elbow back as hard as
she possibly could. The Batian woman grunted and stepped
back a pace. Tay kicked out, catching Svan hard in the groin,
and then turned and slammed her hand against the touch control beside the door. The door began to swing closed, but not
fast enough. There was a flash and searing pain in her thigh—
one of them had hit her with a laser. She staggered against
the case and glanced back in time to see Svan raise her stun
gun. Only half the blast hit her as the door relentlessly drew
closed. As something like a hammer of light flung her to the
back of the safe, Tay could hear Frisk screaming imprecations. The sound of the door locking down told her she knew
she might live, then she lost consciousness.

* * *

Ambel boarded first, and leant over the side to catch the rope cast up to him. Hand over hand, he hauled up a huge cluster of hide sacks sodden with fresh purple blood. As these squelched on the deck, Anne followed him up. Pland looked askance at the bloody slashes in her clothing.

'Fucking prill,' she muttered.

The others soon following her had similar slashes on their clothing. Gollow and Sild wore the same somewhat bewildered expressions at they disappeared below to tend their wounds. Boris remained on deck, pressing his hand to a deep, seeping wound across his stomach. He was chewing one end of his moustache; a sure sign of irritation. Ambel, Pland now realized, had slashes in his clothing too. There was no blood of course, since Ambel healed too quickly to bleed. Erlin, that Earther woman Ambel had taken a shine to some years back, had even wondered if he contained any blood at all. Pland chuckled at the thought and went over to help them lower some of the bags of meat below decks, and then to fill the sail's food barrel from the remainder. He glanced around for Peck, then spotted him at the stern rail, stooping over another barrel to empty a sack of salt-yeast into it, and yelled to him. Peck tied off the yeast sack, dropped it to the deck and wandered across. He began to silently assist Pland and the others, while Ambel single-handedly hauled the heavy rowing boat up the side of the ship and tied it in position.

'Leave a few lumps out on deck, lads. We might get us a sail tonight, then we can go after that other big'un,' said Ambel.

There were groans from all of the crew—except for Peck, who was strangely silent.

'You all right there, Peck?' asked Ambel.

'Buggered well shoulda gone with you,' grumbled Peck.

'Next time,' said Ambel, giving the crewman an estimating look. 'How'd you manage with the sea-cane?'

'Barrel of cane and one of gourds,' said Peck grudgingly.

'Good,' said Ambel, reaching out to give him a slap on the shoulder. 'We'll have some mash to sell at the Baitman when we get back, and later I'll have you boil us up a batch of resin. Now get 'em sealed and down below.'

'He been all right?' Ambel asked Pland, as Peck went to do as bid.

'Bit noisy,' replied Pland. 'Shouting and muttering—but that's nothing new.'

'Mmm,' Ambel nodded.

In the night, the boom of wings woke Boris from the light snooze he was enjoying while on watch. He observed the long neck and crocodilian head of a sail questing about below the mast, gobbling up the rhinoworm steaks deposited there. He then observed the curious sight of the sail dropping a half-chewed steak and staring intently out to the sea.

'Who's that?' growled the sail.

Following its gaze, Boris saw that the molly carp had surfaced a short distance away and was now returning the sail's stare. The sail clamped its mouth shut with a snap, and remained utterly motionless. It was almost as if the two creatures were engaged in a staring competition. Boris shook his head, dismissing the scene, and rested his head back against the rail. On the following morning, spread across the spars with meat digesting in its transparent gut, the sail—one of the largest Boris had ever seen—was ready for work.

It watched with interest as one by one the crew roused and came out on to the deck.

Peck came first up from the crew quarters, to empty a bucket of slops over the side, watch the commotion this caused in the sea below, and then urinate after it.

'Mornin', Peck,' said Boris.

Peck merely grunted at him before heading to the water barrel for a drink, then moving on to his tasks about the deck. By the time Anne, Pland and some of the juniors came out, Peck had a brazier set up and was blowing on the charcoal in it. Every so often, he would stop to cough, or wipe at his watery eyes and mumble imprecations. Anne stood staring at him for a moment, arms akimbo and with obvious annoyance in her expression. When he finally noticed her she glared, took up the slop bucket he had left on the deck, and retreated below.

'What?' Peck asked Pland.

'If you don't know by now, you never will,' said the crew-man, coming over with a small jug and a hide bag. Peck shrugged and continued at his blowing while Pland poured oil into a pan and set it on the brazier. When Peck was satisfied with the glowing charcoal, and rocking back on his heels, Pland dropped square slices of boxy meat into the pan. The sudden sizzling and waft of savoury smoke across the deck was Ambel's signal to come out of his cabin.

'Ah, boxy,' he said, then with a glance at Pland, 'We got any of that Dome bacon left?'

Pland nodded and wandered off to investigate. Ambel watched him go, reflecting how it was strange that the stuff was still called 'bacon', it never having been within a light-year of a pig, or any other animal for that matter. He turned his attention now to the sail, who was audibly sniffing at the smoke from the pan and looking dubious.

'How are you called?' Ambel asked it, as was proper courtesy.

The sail turned its head towards him, and Ambel took an involuntary step backwards when he realized just how big the creature was. It exposed its teeth in what might have been a grin.

'Windcheater,' it replied, and all the crew on deck stood still with their mouths open. They'd never before encountered a sail without the name 'Windcatcher'. True, they'd heard rumour of a sail that had actually grasped how a name could be an individual thing, but like so many other Hoopers, had dismissed the rumour as nonsense.

'Only kidding,' said the sail. 'It's Windcatcher really.'

They closed their mouths and got on with their work, quickly trying to forget this upset to the natural order of things.

'Pleased to make your acquaintance, sail,' said Ambel, giving the creature a look. He had already noticed the bean-shaped device attached to the side of its head, and he knew precisely what it was.

The sail snickered and shook its wings.

Windcheater surveyed the ship with intense interest and re-called when, long ago, he had been here last. The Earther human woman had been aboard then, and he remembered how he had tried to bite her when she sneaked up on him to remove a sample of his skin. Memory of that brought back to him the memory of what had happened afterwards. The Captain, with some crew and the woman, had gone ashore, and after traumatic events he had only learnt about later, returned aboard carrying a certain box that was still here now.

Windcheater could even hear the whispering. The man he once threw from the top of The Big Flint was here now . . . in part.

The sail tested the movement of the spars and found that they were well greased in their sockets, and that there was little scope for slack movement between the three masts. Pulling on the reefing cables, he released the fore and aft sails and checked the movement there. Again, everything seemed fine. He lowered his head so as to inform the Captain, then abruptly pulled away from the smell of charring meat. He had never quite understood this human preference for incinerating perfectly good fresh meat prior to consuming it. It was like so many other things the humans did that he could not quite get a handle on. As he watched them eating their food, he thought back again to a time long ago.

Windcatcher had been the cleverest of all the sails and the most curious about these strange creatures that had descended from the sky, but the autoguns and intruder defences they had installed around the island they occupied had been enough to deter the most inquisitive, and thus the situation had remained for a very long time. Then had come internal strife, after the arrival of more of the same creatures, and the defences were gone and these creatures, these humans, came out into the world. Windcatcher's curiousity became almost a painful thing when these humans built movable shells out of peartrunk and yanwood timber in which to float about on the seas.

At first he had flown at a safe distance, but sometimes close—especially in the night—and listened to the sounds they made to each other. He'd realized from the start that these sounds were a language much like that of the sails, and had quickly memorized it all. Learning what the words actually meant had taken somewhat longer, nearly one human century, and even then it had been difficult to grasp that they only had so few words to describe the wind. And as for names . . .

When Windcatcher had seen a ship drifting in the sea, without its sail of normal fabric, he had quickly grasped the opportunity this presented. Settling on the spars of the ship, he had gazed down upon the bemused crew and told them, 'I am wind catcher.' And so it had all begun. The other sails had soon joined him in this diversion—it was substantially more interesting than sitting on a rock discussing the weather. They, like the then original Windcatcher, had not grasped the concept that individuals could possess individual names and by the time they did, the tradition of them being called 'Windcatcher' had been established. The first sail to break with this tradition had been the original Windcatcher himself, when he had changed his name to 'Windcheater'. But then he had always been one to break new ground.

After reminiscing, he accessed, through his aug, a communication channel that had been opened in the night. The first communication then being, 'You still into dodgy artefacts, sail?'

'Are you still there?' he asked over the ether, still finding it difficult to talk without actually opening his mouth.

'I ain't going nowhere until this fucking fish has a bowel movement,' replied Sniper's irritated voice.

'Aren't you controlling that crazy carp, then?'

'Nah, I'm recharging in readiness for that bowel movement. Molly here's just got a bit confused, and seems to want to hang around the ship. Understandable, as it's a long way from home. Tell me, how much you say the Warden's paying you for this?'

'A thousand a day.'

'Yeah, thought so. But what the hell is there to see on that ship?'

'Nothing much. I was hungry and needed a rest so I thought I'd stop by. The way I see it, the longer I'm out here, the more money I'll get. If the Warden tells me to move on,

then I will. Don't see the point in putting in too much effort,'
said Windcheater.

'You like the idea of wages, don't you?' said Sniper. 'It
ever occur to you that a few steaks is pretty cheap payment
for the work you do as a sail? Without you, they'd need a
fabric mainsail, extra rigging and extra crew.'

Windcheater blinked and surveyed the *Treader*. Boris was
at the helm, steering the ship, but the others were scattered
about the deck at minor tasks. That had not really occurred to
him. Yes, over the ages he had seen the design of the Hoopers' ships changing and, until this moment, had only viewed
those changes as ones intended to more easily accommodate
his kind. It seemed almost a reversal now to realize that the
benefits were really a bit one-sided. Through his aug, he accessed a text on Hooper ships and sailing practices.

'The crew-members all take a percentage of the ship's
profits,' he said.

'A sail could demand that, too' said Sniper. 'But, he'd probably have to agree to stay with the ship for the entire duration
of the voyage.' Sniper then transmitted the address of a particular site, and Windcheater studied with interest the sample
work contracts there displayed. He decided then that, when
the Warden was done with him, things were going to change.

The wound on her hip was now hurting less than the after-
effects of the stun blast. Parting the burnt fabric of her
trousers she saw that already the hole had filled with pink
scar tissue, which was slowly welling to the surface of the
wound. The Batians and Frisk, in their overconfidence in
their abilities, had forgotten that she too was a Hooper with
quite a few years behind her. Had she been a normal human,
her surprise blows would have had no effect on the one called
Svan—Batians were tough. Anyway, she had survived. The
distant sound of a couple of explosions had long since faded,
as had the wail of her house computer when it was blown. No
doubt they had tried to either cut or blast their way through
this door, but once it had closed she knew she was safe. The
amount of energy required to penetrate a metre of what had
so far only ever been described simply as 'Prador armour'—

the superconductive and highly impact-resistant exotic metal that had been one of the reasons that ancient war had dragged on for so long—would have been sure to draw the attention of the Warden, and Tay was certain Frisk was not prepared to risk that. She wondered just what Frisk had thought about her having such an incredibly impervious safe installed here, but then Frisk did not know how valuable was the item Tay kept here. The historian grasped the edge of one of the coffin-cases to haul herself to her feet, then pressed her palm to the lock in the case's surface.

'Open viewing panel,' she instructed.

In the surface of the case a rectangular section faded from shiny chrome to transparency, revealing that the case indeed served a purpose similar to a coffin. There had been no paintings here.

'Well, I did get all of your features right,' said Tay, gazing down at David Grenant. She then, with a stab of her fingers, initiated a touch-console beside the window and began studying the readouts. The feeding system was still being utilized and Intertox levels were being maintained—like this he could last almost indefinitely. She touched in a sequence she had not used in a little while, then waited. After a minute, Grenant's face twitched—then, he opened his eyes. For a second he appeared utterly confused, then he started to jerk and shake and whip his head from side to side. She'd previously noticed how it always took him a little while to remember precisely what his fate *was*. Now she stared at him calmly as his silent screams frosted the underside of the viewing window. Grenant's entombment had been one of the more imaginatively horrifying of Francis Cojan's punishments, and Tay saw no reason to change that: it was history after all. She then reversed the touch sequence and he slowed to immobility and finally closed his eyes.

Glancing across at the other, empty, coffin-case, she contemplated the fortuitous workings of fate. When, if her plan evolved over many years came to fruition and she got to open her museum on Earth, this one exhibit would be the making of her fortune. Perhaps an additional exhibit would ensure this success. She smiled to herself, then sniffed at the air. First she had to get out of here, before the air—no longer renewed by the house computer—turned bad.

Tay pushed herself upright and limped over to the control panel she had used to close the door. There she paused. She had no way of knowing what might lie on the other side of the door. Frisk could be waiting for her, even though a few hours had already passed. Tay hesitated, and in that moment the opening light on the panel flickered, and she listened to the clicking as the lock mechanism disengaged. No, surely she hadn't touched it. Frisk! Tay turned and stared in horror at the door, as it swung open. She would not now be able to close it again until it had reached its fully open position.

Grenant! She limped over to his coffin-case and slapped her hand down on the palm lock.

'Open!'

Black lines quartered the lid of the coffin-case and those quarters began slowly to spin aside. Inside the case, Grenant was fully dressed, his fingers clawed above his chest, where he had been scraping at the lid. At his hip was an empty holster. Damn! She'd forgotten that she'd previously moved his weapon to the model she had constructed of him in the museum, mainly to prevent him trying to draw it and use it on himself here—the little projectile weapon would not have been sufficient to drill a hole in his coffin. She hardly dared look up now as the door clunked into its fully open position.

'I thought you were advised to get away from here,' spoke an irritated voice.

Tay stared out into the ruin Frisk and her Batians had made of her home, then focused on the object visible in the doorway. Here hovered an iron-coloured cockle, half a metre across.

It opened its bivalve shells to expose glimmers of greenish light as it spoke again. 'You're lucky to be alive,' it said. Then, 'Who's your friend?'

'Who are *you*?' Tay asked, slapping her hand on the coffin's locking mechanism.

'I'm SM Twelve, the one they usually send to clear up other people's messes,' it informed her. 'Now, I can see there's quite a mess here. Perhaps, through me, you'd like to tell the Warden all about it?'

'Close,' Tay instructed the coffin-case, then watched it do so before moving away. As she walked to the door of the safe, the drone retreated into the room beyond and hovered in midair. With a touch, Tay had the safe door closing behind her, and then she stood surveying the wreckage. It was vandalism, plain and simple, like someone had gone berserk with a gas-system pulse-gun. The furniture was burnt, even the floor, ceiling and walls were distinctively scored, cabinets smashed. Books, some burnt and some still burning, were strewn all about, and the computer console was a hollowed-by-fire ruin.

'It seems they had some sort of grudge against you.'

The voice that now issued from the mollusc drone was no longer its own, Tay realized instantly, but that is what it wanted her to know. Picking her way through the debris, she moved to the entrance hall—the drone trailing along behind her.

'A grudge?' she asked.

'The Batian mercenaries that came here—presumably in search of Sable Keech,' replied the Warden.

'Oh, I don't think they had a grudge,' Tay replied, stepping out into soft green light.

'There does seem an excessive amount of damage here.'

'Not done by them, I should think. It's not part of their remit. That lot,' Tay gestured over her shoulder with her thumb, 'was probably done by their employer, once she realized she couldn't get at me. She has a long history of throwing spectacular tantrums. And now, of course, she's quite mad.'

There was a long silence from the drone as Tay headed for her museum. Shortly before she reached the structure, the drone hummed ahead of her and zipped inside. Following it in she was pleasantly surprised to see no damage here at all. The drone was now hovering above the head of the Skinner, and together they presented a sinister apparition.

Tay stared up at it. 'No explosives? No booby-traps?' she asked.

'None,' now replied the voice of SM12 again.

'I thought not. Her arrogance and self-regard would not allow her to destroy this, though her love of inflicting pain and terror would have let her destroy me—though she would have labelled it an act of self-preservation.'

'Who is this employer you refer to?' asked the voice of the Warden, quickly returning.

'You haven't worked that out?'

'I have some idea, but I would like to hear the answer from you.'

'Rebecca Frisk,' said Tay, swinging her gaze down to the model of that very person. 'She must have cored herself and swapped into another human body. It must have taken some deep re-programming to have whoever she put into her own previous body play the part of Frisk herself, but then she would have had access to Prador thrall technology, and without any compunction or moral restraint. She would have dearly relished breaking another's mind and turning it to her own ends.'

'The woman we thought was Frisk, and who was mind-wiped on Earth, was innocent, then' said the Warden.

Tay wondered if the Warden was deliberately appearing to be slow for her benefit. Perhaps AIs sometimes found it difficult to assess the intelligence of the human minds they were addressing.

'Well, now you've stated the obvious, what are you going to do about it?'

'Nothing at present. I have no real jurisdiction here.'

Tay grimaced and turned to glare up at the drone. 'Do me a favour. Your average Polity citizen might believe that crap, but I do not.' The iron cockle tilted itself towards her and its shell opened slightly wider. It was an action that could only be interpreted as a grin. As it closed again the Warden's voice became significantly abrupt.

'SM Twelve,' demanded the Warden, 'analysis.'

Tay could only assume that the AI *wanted* her to hear this conversation. There was no other reason for it to remain audible, since Warden and drone could communicate many thousands of times faster than human speech—or even become one entity.

'The debris I analysed was that of a post-armistice Prador in-system cargo hauler. She probably used a small tactical to blow it, then under cover of the explosion jettisoned herself in an escape pod,' explained the SM.

'Olian Tay, why do you think she is here?' the Warden asked.

Tay took a moment to catch up. Perhaps she *was* a bit slow.

'To get to Keech, is my first thought,' she said. 'Then, again, she might be here to find her husband, or simply on a whim. Someone like her is not easily predictable. Why do *you* think she's here?'

'I cannot really say. It is difficult to assess such an ancient personality. But I do know that someone wanted it to be known she is here. Before confirmation of her presence by you, I have observed agents of untraceable employ disseminating rumours and stories of her arrival here. Curious, don't you think?'

'Must be some enemy of hers, then,' said Tay.

'Maybe.'

'What else? You know what the reaction here will be?'

'Oh, I know, and I observe it now,' said the Warden. 'Already the Old Captains have called a Convocation—no doubt to make arrangements to hunt her down and throw her to a leech swarm.'

Tay turned and walked out of her museum, and then stood glaring up at her tower.

'I suppose the bitch destroyed my AGC,' she said.

'Do not despair, Olian Tay. Sprage is coming here for you even now, knowing you would not want to miss out on this.'

'You told him,' said Tay. 'How did *you* know about this . . . to come here, I mean?'

'Your house computer called me just before it died. It also gave me the locking code to your safe. Be well, Olian Tay.'

Tay glanced round at the drone as it came level with her shoulder. 'Wait, you didn't say why you thought Frisk might be here,' she said quickly.

Just then the SM jerked, shaking itself like a wet dog. 'Well, there he was, gone,' said SM12.

'Did he answer my last question?' Tay asked.

'The boss don't know why she's here, but says it could be any of three clear reasons or combinations of them: to kill Keech, to find her husband, or to die here. He says the last is a certainty—through her choice or otherwise.' And with that, the drone gave her its green-light grin again and shot up into the air.

10

The first male glister noted a vibration and a shifting of currents but recognized these as being no threat to itself. It continued to tear and feed, comforted by the knowledge that there were few creatures in the sea that could penetrate its adamantine shell. The presence of a large boulder to one side of it—revealed as one of these shifting currents dispersed the organic cloud for a moment—was something it puzzled over for only a moment before getting its nose down to its meal again. Its puzzlement increased when it soon noted how this boulder seemed to have got much closer. When the boulder suddenly heaved up and huge eyes observed it through the murk, the glister had time only for a few seconds of confusion, before it too became a crunchy mouthful.

Keech was a blurred shape behind silver monofilament. He had coiled himself into a foetal position, and the autodoc clung to his side like a chromed crab. Umbilici and cables snaked from the surrounding fluid to Erlin's drug manufactory, Keech's cleansing unit, Janer's computer, and other jury-rigged hardware.

'That's the best we can do for him,' said Erlin.

Janer noted that her hands were shaking. He himself had slept for a couple of hours, but she hadn't stopped working all night. She slumped into a chair and sat staring at the floor. Janer walked over to her and took hold of her upper arm. She stood without him having to say anything, turned and rested her head against his shoulder.

'Best you get to your bunk,' he urged.

She nodded her head, still resting against him, and allowed him to lead her to the cabin she shared with Goss and seat her on the bed. She showed no inclination to do anything more.

'You'll keep an eye on the read-outs?' she said.

'I will.'

'You're a good man.'

'Debatable.'

He reached down to her and tried to turn her over so she could lie down. Her arms came up round his neck and, before he knew what was happening, she was kissing him. After a time, they parted.

'Is this a good idea?' he asked.

She unzipped the front of her coverall and gazed up at him.

'It's what I want,' she said. 'What about you?'

He looked at the light blue circles visible on her dark skin. There were only a few of them. He put his hand on her neck and ran it down to cover one small breast. Her nipple was hard against his palm, as she lay back.

'Help me off with this stuff. I'm too knackered to do it myself.'

Janer pulled her coverall down from her shoulders, and over her hips when she raised them. He tugged off her shoes then slid the overalls off completely. She now lay naked, staring up at him, stroking a hand over her belly.

'Stress always makes me horny,' she confessed.

'Me too,' said Janer, nearly breaking his neck in his hurry to get undressed. The fit of giggles that followed unmanned him for a while. But Erlin was warm and, although with the body of an eighteen-year-old, brought to their love-making the experience of over two centuries. This experience for Janer, himself only just into his second century, was enlightening. He soon discovered that there was nothing Erlin did not know about the human body, and how best to use it.

Alternately rubbing his eyes and his belly, Captain Drum left his cabin. He felt he'd maybe overdone it on the hammer whelks and sea-cane rum—just a tad, but not enough to cause any real damage. What had finished him off had been those glister brains on toast. The ensuing hallucinations had been of the flying kind and had continued throughout the night. He felt sluggish and slightly ill, as if the virus inside him was punishing him for his excesses. It was a moment, therefore, before he realized that what he was now seeing— mostly submerged next to the island of sargassum—was no Spatterjay leviathan he recognized.

'Orlis, get that anchor up, nice and easy, lad.'

Drum moved to the rail to get a closer look at the initially unfamiliar shape. His vision was still a bit blurry, and some part of himself was trying to deny what he was seeing. Finally, he could deny no longer that he was observing Prador pictographs impressed in golden metal armour.

Jack, the first mate, walked up and stood beside him. 'What's up, Cap'n? . . . Oh!'

'That,' said Drum, 'is a Prador light destroyer, armoured with that damned exotic metal that always made 'em so hard to blow.' He looked round to check that Orlis had the anchor in, then hurried to take the helm. 'Wake up, Windcatcher!' he shouted, and tried to turn the wheel. When it did not move, he pushed harder, then felt wood beginning to break in his hands, so he eased off.

'Boarders!' Jack yelled, suddenly.

Before Drum could react, a shape in black crabskin armour was on deck, levelling some kind of weapon. There was a flash and a thud and, trailing smoke, Jack went flying over the opposite rail. Before he hit the water, he blew apart and Drum saw one of his legs go cartwheeling across the surface of the sea. Another black-clad killer came over the rail—then another.

'Get 'em, lads!'

Orlis threw the anchor at the last one to come on deck.

With a sickening crunch, the anchor folded that one, and he just lay down to die. With a roar, Orlis charged the next one, but something suddenly lifted him from his feet and flung him four metres back. He lay on the deck staring at the smoking wound in his stomach.

'Hey! It's only—'

A flat detonation curtailed his observation, and spread bits of him all over ship.

Drum picked up a harpoon head that Banner had been working on, up on the cabin-deck, and moved to join the fray.

'One step further and you're dead.'

Drum stopped exactly where he was, and looked around. The woman standing there held a heavy pulse-gun trained on him, and he knew she wasn't kidding—it might take her two or three shots, but he'd certainly go down. Whoever these people were, they had come prepared for the durability of Hoopers.

The woman seemed surprised for a moment. 'You . . . ' she said, then, 'I suppose you don't recognize me, Little Skin.'

Drum had not been called that in more years than he cared to remember. And even then there had only been a certain group of people who ever used the nickname. A sick feeling grew in his stomach as he guessed who this woman must be. Immediately he put her appearance down to cosmetic surgery, but quickly realized that had to be wrong. Whoever had given herself up to ECS needed to have the right genetic code for ECS to be fooled. That meant the woman before him had either cloned herself, or actually sent her own body. Drum *knew* which she had done, and why she looked so different now.

'The sail, secure the sail!' the woman yelled as she moved up behind him.

Three loud thumps followed, and he glanced down to see one of the armoured figures beside the mast, with some sort of bolt gun. The sail screeched and struggled in the spars— ratchets and chains clanking below and the foremast slamming back and forth. Another detonation followed and Banner's head went bouncing along the deck.

Drum swore and threw the harpoon head at the woman. The gun stuttered in her double-handed grip, and Drum staggered under the impact of ionized gas pulses hitting his torso. It hurt like hell and there was a smell of burning flesh in his nostrils. She fired again and it felt to Drum like he'd been hit in the chest with a shovel. Losing his balance fell back towards the ladder, where a third hit sent him over towards the deck. His head struck the hard timbers and the world went dark—so thankfully he did not see the rest of his crew being slaughtered.

Rebecca Frisk gazed down at the three Batians as they removed their breather helmets and went to check on their comrade. Svan, Tors and Shib were all heavy-worlders, and all quite capable of tearing an Earth-normal human to pieces. Dime also, and the anchor thrown at him had nearly cut him in half. Svan, the woman whom Frisk had initially hired, soon saw that there was nothing to be done for her comrade, and turned to climb the ladder on to the deck which formed the roof of the forecabin.

'They are dangerous and strong. It's a shame we weren't sufficiently acquainted with that fact before meeting Olian Tay,' said Svan, once she was face to face with Frisk.

'You *were* warned this time,' said Frisk, a glassy smile on her face. 'You have now also been provided with weapons suitable to the task, rather than those silly carbines you had before.' She pointed to where Dime lay. 'It seems that even such a warning and such weapons are not enough.'

Svan turned from her and stared out over the sea to where the Prador ship was surfacing, its chameleon skin of exotic armour now taking on the colour and texture of the nearby island of sargassum, so that it now appeared to be an extension of that island.

'We will be more careful in future.'

Frisk congratulated herself on choosing these stone killers. Ebulan had offered her some of his human blanks, but she doubted he could control them as well as these Batians controlled themselves. Very fast reactions were needed to deal with Hoopers. She glanced at her hand and noted it

was shaking. She put it on the rail to still it, and ignored the closing slit in her cheek where the harpoon had just missed slicing her head in half.

'As for when you take the Captain aboard,' said Frisk, nodding to a small wedge-shaped transport that was on its way over from the Prador ship, 'full-restraint harness. Remember: a Hooper his age is about twice as strong as you are, and a lot more durable. Be prepared to hit him with a level-six stun if he so much as quivers.'

Svan went down to the lower deck and supervised the fixing of the ceramal restraint harness on Drum. With a feeling of melancholy, Frisk watched the proceedings. How ironic that so long ago she had saved this same man from coring in order to make him her personal body slave—and now to do this? She stared for a moment then took a cloth from her pocket to wipe away the small spill of blood on her cheek. As the cloth touched blood, she convulsed violently, dropping her pulse-gun on to the deck. Svan glanced up at her, but Frisk stepped quickly out of sight, pulled an injector from her belt and pressed it to her neck. The shaking stopped shortly after, but the feeling of dislocation, of not quite knowing whom she was or *why* she was, persisted. Bad nerve conflict. Partially under control, Frisk moved back to the rail.

Speaker and two guard blanks came aboard to collect Drum.

'We have experienced previous difficulties with the coring of long-term Hooper humans,' said Speaker, staring up at her.

'You just need to be as quick as you can, and not worry about extraneous damage,' Frisk informed the Prador in its ship. 'Don't bother removing the cerebrum either, just cut in and use a spider thrall unit.'

'Yes,' said Speaker.

They never nod or use any hand gestures, Frisk observed for perhaps the thousandth time.

'Oh, and don't worry about his injuries. Hoopers heal very quickly,' she added as they hauled the Captain over the side. Then she pressed a hand against her mouth to suppress a giggle.

* * *

A wind from the east began blowing with greater and greater intensity, rolling the cloud into grey threads across the sky's jade face. With the occasional imprecation and much skill, Windcheater and Boris tacked the *Treader* out of the cove, then rounded the island and ran before what seemed the start of a squall. The morning was gone before the island was out of sight, and a persistent drizzle sheened Windcheater and soaked the crew. Boris stood at the helm in a long waxed-cotton coat and sou'wester, and grumbled when the rest of the crew went below for shelter. Windcheater held his head up and was enjoying the moisture and cold.

Ambel came and stood beside Boris for a little while before turning to him. 'I'll take over in a couple of hours, but I'll send Peck up with some rum tea before then,' he said.

'Aye, Captain,' said Boris, quite used to long lonely watches at the helm.

Ambel stood there uncomfortably for another moment, then asked, 'You got any sprine, Boris?'

Boris gave him an odd look before replying. 'Don't carry it, Captain. Anything happens where I might need it, and I'd likely get no chance to use it,' he said.

Ambel nodded, moving to the ladder.

'Try Peck,' Boris advised. 'He'd be the one.'

Ambel nodded again, climbed down, and swung at the bottom to drop himself before the door of his cabin. Once inside he immediately opened his sea-chest. He didn't attempt to open the box containing the Skinner's head—just stared at it for a while before closing the chest and leaving his cabin. Clumping across the deck, he opened the hatch leading down into the crew quarters, and went through. As he descended, he could smell rum tea being made.

'You got any sprine, Peck?' he asked.

Peck looked up from the little stove, shook his head, and returned his attention to the kettle. Ambel reckoned he was lying. Any Hooper who had been through the kind of experience Peck had endured would carry sprine just in case such a situation should recur.

Ambel didn't push it. 'Any of you others got some?' he asked generally.

'Got any what?' asked Pland, who lay on his bunk with a book propped on his knees.

'Sprine, you idiot,' Anne replied, from the bunk above him.

'I ain't that rich,' complained Pland.

Ambel looked next at Anne and she shook her head. He leaned back and glanced over to the junior's quarters, then decided not to bother. No chance young 'uns like that had any sprine. You didn't really get to think much about dying until you were reaching the end of your second century.

'We'll have to refine some then,' he said.

Nobody asked what for. They all knew what Ambel kept in his cabin.

'We'd need a steady mooring for that,' observed Pland.

Ambel said, 'We'll cross Deep-sea, pick up one or two more on the way across, then moor at the west atolls. We can do it there.' He gave them an estimating look. 'Take an hour or so off, then I'll want you up on deck and ready.' And, with that, he climbed back above.

An hour later, he was up on the cabin-deck, scanning the sea with his ancient set of binoculars, when a humped shape slid into view.

'We got one!' Ambel yelled. 'Hard to port!'

Boris drained the last of his rum tea, and hung his tin cup on his belt, before steering the ship towards the distant shape.

Windcatcher adjusted himself accordingly. The rest of the crew clambered up on deck, but as the *Treader* drew closer to the shape, they all realized something was wrong. There were no prill visible there, and the hump was too steep, too immobile.

'Yer molly carp again,' said Peck.

They were silent for a while as they watched the great fish parallelling their course, then, because they were now on deck anyway, they slowly began to set about their normal duties. Anne sharpened harpoons and knives. Peck had a

couple of juniors helping him repair ropes, and making new
ones from a bag of fibre beaten from sargassum stalks.
Pland worked in the hold, salting rhinoworm steak, and
Boris had the helm, of course. Other crew continued with
that constant round of tasks which kept their ship seawor-
thy: the constant repairs to the superstructure; the greasing
of chains and sprockets; the tightening of chains, cables,
and bearing shells, besides the endless scrubbing and pol-
ishing.

As they worked, the crew-members considered what they
already knew. They had all heard stories about molly carp—
about their tenacity and the odd things they did. They were
aware that to have one hanging around while they were hunting giant leeches could be dangerous. Through his ancient
binoculars Ambel watched the molly carp for a while longer,
then turned his attention elsewhere. The drizzle had ceased
and the sun was burning the sky a lighter green, when he was
able to yell out another warning. A group of three leeches
had come into sight and they immediately headed for the
Treader.

'Twenty degrees to starboard!' Ambel yelled. 'Hold it
there.'

As the ship hove over, Pland came up on to the cabin-deck
and quickly went to replace Boris at the helm. Boris meanwhile went to load the deck cannon with its powder charge
and stones. The others brought out their own weapons and
readied them. Ambel slid down the ladder, dived into his
cabin, and came out with his blunderbuss tucked under one
arm.

He looked around. 'All juniors below!' he yelled, eyeing
Gollow and Sild. The two men looked set to argue with him,
before nodding acquiescence. It was fair enough: none of the
juniors was as strong as any senior, or anywhere near as
strong as Ambel, so they could easily get killed during a
leech hunt. Gollow and Sild, who had done well enough during a previous hunt, were still suffering from the injuries
they had received when going ashore with Ambel after the
last rhinoworm—for juniors also did not heal as quickly as
older crew.

Once they were gone, Ambel scanned those who remained. 'We'll take the last one, lads.' He glanced up at Boris. 'You hear that?'

'I ain't deaf, Captain.'

Boris sighted down the deck cannon at the last of the three shapes rapidly approaching. Ambel watched them for a moment, then turned his gaze to the right. Further out in the sea, the molly carp held station and watched.

The incursion of prill from the first leech to arrive was short-lived and quickly repelled. The leech itself, after grinding at the wooden hull for a moment, lost interest and swam away with most of its prill remaining on its back. The same happened with the second leech, but the third one arrived only moments after the second had turned away from the ship, so the attack of prill from both was unrelenting. Boris managed to fire three times on the back of the final leech. Ambel managed to get off two shots before taking up the first of the harpoons and planting it in the huge creature. He continued methodically planting four harpoons deep into its body, hauling tight the ropes to each, and bringing the leech hard against the side of the ship.

Prill were mashed and smashed and blown apart. Bits of prill still managed to crawl to the scuppers and drop through into the sea, but what remained on board no longer had any mobility. Anne and Peck washed this mess out through the scuppers after the rest, where no doubt some of the larger pieces would grow into more prill again.

'This is a good one, lads,' said Ambel, rubbing his hands together.

He scrambled down the rope with his crampons fixed to his feet and hooks hanging from his belt. Pland followed with the knife and bar and they were soon out standing on the slippery mound of the leech and making the first incision. At one point the leech convulsed momentarily, and Pland fell and began to slide down its side, before Ambel caught hold of his collar and hauled him back up. Soon they had the incision braced open and Pland was inside groping about in the bloody morass of its intestines. The leech con-

vulsed once again, sinking down at its tail end. Ambel
looked back and saw a large swirling in the water there. The
humped crown of the molly carp suddenly surfaced. The
creature regarded Ambel for a moment, then it sank out of
sight again.

'Crafty bastard,' he muttered.

Meanwhile, the juniors, hearing that the shooting had
ceased, came back out on to the deck to help in any way they
could. But really, at this stage there was little they could do.
They would just get in the way, so they stayed back and
watched.

Peck next threw out the rope and Ambel caught it and
lowered the end of it to Pland. When the leech shook again,
Pland let go a stream of curses. He was on his way out of the
incision when the molly carp got a firmer hold on the leech's
tail and gave a hard tug. As the bracing bar slipped, the incision closed on Pland like a wet mouth. Ambel slipped and
fell and caught himself only a metre from the sea's surface
by driving one of his hooks into the side of the leech. One
harpoon came free with a sucking crackle, and the leech now
had enough of its mouth end free to investigate the damage
being done to it. Luckily, that end oozed back past the creature's main body, in the sea underneath Ambel, to where the
molly carp was attacking it.

'Pull on it! Pull on it!' yelled Peck.

He and Anne took up the slack in the rope Pland had tied
to the severed bile duct inside the beast. The tension on the
rope reopened the incision enough for Pland to get one leg
out, but suddenly the leech rolled, snapping the remaining
harpoons that secured it, and both Pland and Ambel went
underwater. Boris grabbed hold of the rope as well, and the
three crewmen pulled with all their might. Sild and Gollow
joined in as they heaved. The rope went slack for a moment,
but they were soon hauling in their gruesome catch. The bile
duct was a large one, and clinging to its outer surface was
Pland, with a carpet of small leeches clinging to him. They
hauled him quickly up on deck.

'Get 'em off! Get 'em off!' yelled Pland.

The crew gathered round him and wrenched the leeches

off, one after another. The larger ones they beat on the deck until they released the plugs of flesh they had taken. Pland began screwing these pieces back into place, swearing angrily all the while.

Peck meanwhile leant over the rail with a rope in one hand, to which he had hastily tied a grapple. As he searched for his Captain, he muttered under his breath. The leech drew away from the ship; its back end a ragged mess now where the molly carp still tore at it. Searching elsewhere, Peck turned his attention to the ship's wake, where pieces of prill floated and writhed. Abruptly he cast the grapple there, hauled it quickly in, cast again. On his fourth cast, he hooked something large.

'Give us a hand, yer buggers!' he yelled.

Anne and Boris were quickly at his side, hauling on the rope as well, while Pland leant back against the cabin wall, whimpering as the remaining leeches were removed from him. In a pool of sticky blood round his feet, lay more plugs of flesh, and kneeling in that blood Sild collected them and passed them up to Gollow, who screwed them carefully back into place—Pland himself no longer having the strength to do it.

Hauling on the rope, the three seniors saw an indefinite shape reach the surface, and pulled it in.

'It's the Captain,' croaked Peck.

They hauled it towards the side of the ship. Abruptly there was a swirl in the water behind the shape, and it was rapidly shoved right up next to the hull. The crew quickly pulled in the remaining slack and, as they did so, they saw the swirl circle back round towards the leech.

Anne glanced questioningly at Boris.

'Molly carp,' he said, and shrugged.

It was indeed Ambel under a thick layer of writhing leeches. Once he was on the deck, the crew proceeded to do the same for him as they had done for Pland, except for screwing back plugs of flesh. Ambel's wounds closed too quickly for that, and there was no blood loss. When they had finished, Ambel lay still on the deck. The grapple was still hooked through his thigh, and it took two of them pulling

hard on it to get it out. His clothing was in tatters, there were
new scars layered across the many he already possessed, and
with the recent loss of flesh, he looked smaller.

'Captain?' said Peck, tentatively.

No reaction for a moment, then Ambel abruptly opened
his eyes and sat bolt upright.

'You all right, Captain?' asked Boris.

Ambel stood up and started for the rail. Peck tackled him
before he could get there, and brought him down.

'Bloody Hoop! Bloody Hoop!' Ambel yelled, hammering
Peck with his fists.

The others heard bones break in Peck's body, and they
quickly leapt on Ambel to hold him down—but to no avail.
He threw them off as easily as bed covers, and was at the rail
in a moment. There he stopped, gasping heavily, his hands
gripping and crushing the wood. As the others watched and
waited, Pland came away from the cabin wall where he left a
smear of blood, and stood with them.

Ambel turned from the rail and stared at them. Then he
walked straight past them and went into his cabin. He locked
the door behind him.

'That could have gone better,' said Windcheater, as he turned
himself into the wind and observed the crewman called
Pland being helped below.

'Well, it was your idea to move this damn molly up behind
the leech,' replied Sniper.

'You wanted a bowel movement? You'll soon get a bowel
movement,' said Windcheater, remembering the last time he
had himself eaten a load of leech meat, and the unfortunate
effect of that meal. He also remembered the unfortunate
consequences for the crew of the ship he was over-flying
shortly after.

'I think you're right. There's about a tonne of chewed-up
leech sitting in this molly's stomach, and some very strange
sounds coming from there. Surprising it attacked. Surely it
knows the effect?'

'Molly carp will attack anything that's moving right in

front of them, but they prefer glisters and prill,' said Windcheater.

'I'm aware of their love of crustaceans,' growled Sniper.

'Why the hurry to get out anyway? The Warden'll only
have you counting whelks again.'

There was a long pause before Sniper replied. 'Something
going down,' said the war drone. 'We just had a Prador ship
blow in orbit. That's probably why the Warden sent you out
here for a look. He's always too cautious—should have this
area covered by a network of war drones by now.'

'Ah,' said Windcheater, turning his attention back to the
deck of the *Treader*. Peck and Anne were now draining the
latest bile duct. The Captain was still in his cabin, and it
seemed unlikely he would be coming out for a while. The
sail wondered if he had made the right choice in coming to
join this ship.

'What do you think's happening?' he asked.

'Dunno, but sure as fuck that explosion was no accident.'

Windcheater thought about it. Maybe there might be an
angle here. Maybe there would be some chance to add to his
Norverbank account. He'd have to keep an eye on the situation.

Keech floated in a warm comfortable place, and considered
what he must do next. In the morning he'd go and check that
lead in Klader. He was sure he was close to Rimsc now. The
old pirate had been clever in leaving a number of false leads,
but Keech felt he was getting to the end of them now, after
using the new search program Francis Cojan had sent him.
As he contemplated what he would do to Rimsc when he
found him, a coldly analytical part of himself was saying
that Rimsc was dead, that he, Monitor Keech, was dead.
There was also the feeling that a long time had elapsed. His
thoughts, such as they were, seemed to have been broken in
two; as if separated over that time.

N-FACT MESSAGE: EPIDERMAL GROWTH 65% COM-
PLETE.

What was that? It seemed to come from that cold part of

himself. He tried to move and encountered resistance. His body moved, but it was not moving how he wanted it to move. What this all meant was too painful to contemplate, so he concentrated on the task in hand.

The man in Klader claimed he had seen Rimsc and knew where he now was. The man's information would cost, but that did not matter to Keech: he would have readily paid for it himself if he had not had ECS funding. Rimsc had to die for the things he had done—just as *all* of them had to die.

N-FACT MESSAGE: HEART RESTART.

A sudden thumping drowned out all coherent thought. It was his heart, of course, yet something was telling him that he hadn't heard it in a long while. He felt sick now, and there was a huge pressure growing in his head. A sudden swirling all about him made him aware that he was submerged in some kind of fluid. *I'm in a tank, I'm injured*, he told himself. But surely that was wrong? He was dead. He knew he was dead.

Suddenly the fluid was draining away from all around him. As it went, he found himself lying at the bottom of a slimy hollow in a tangle of tubes. He stared up at the two faces hovering above him and he could feel the machinery attached to his body. This wasn't right. Who were these people?

ERROR MESSAGE: PHYSICAL RESISTANCE TO CYB-PLANT.

DISCONNECT.

Keech tried to ask them who they were, and what was going on. A colder part of himself already knew, and it tried to tell him as fluid jetted from his lungs and from his mouth. He felt he was drowning, and started to struggle

You are the reification Sable Keech. You have been dead for seven hundred years.

Keech gave a liquid gasp, and the sound he next made was more of a croak than a scream. The cold part of himself acknowledged that there was only one thing to do.

MEMPLANT MESSAGE: FULL DOWNLOAD TO ORGANIC BRAIN.

The memories began to return. As they returned, Keech could no longer fight: he was paralysed. A door opened before him and he walked into the apartment, drawing his EC-issue thin-gun. The stink he recognized from Spatterjay: the almost savoury smell of charred flesh. He only recognized his contact because the man was still wearing the bright green shirt he was wearing when he'd left the com message. The face itself wasn't recognizable, as there was no face. Whoever had done this had obviously taken pleasure in it: they'd tied the man to the chair and done it slowly. This much was evident by the way the man had torn off his own nails by clawing at the chair arms.

Keech moved on into the room, then checked all the doors leading off from it. Nothing he could do here now; he'd come back with the forensic team and go through this room at microscopic level. But he didn't need the evidence they'd find to know who had been here earlier. He stepped out of the apartment and closed the door behind him, as well as he could, the lock being broken. Holstering his thin-gun he moved to the elevator, stepped inside, and descended the twenty floors to street level. Outside the building, one of those heavy rains that seemed to fall only in Klader was shining the hydrocar streets and running streams past the pavements. Keech folded up his collar and headed for his battered police hydrocar. Would this be another dead end, in more ways than one?

His answer stepped out of the alley next to his car.

'Sable Keech,' the man sneered.

He was short, thin-faced, and bald-headed, the heavy coat he wore not concealing the fact that he possessed a physique that appeared boosted. But it wasn't boosted, not in the usual sense. Keech didn't bother to respond with words. He pulled his gun and fired, and Alphed Rimsc went over backwards, with a smoking hole through his middle. Keech walked over, his thin-gun down at his side. Just like that: got him.

Rimsc sat up and smiled, and casually lifted the gun he had been holding all the time. There was a flash, but Keech heard no sound. Something smashed into his side and spun him around. Next thing he knew, he was sitting on the pavement in the rain, broken, and unable to move his hand to retrieve his gun that had fallen next to him. The virus: the damned virus. Keech managed to find the strength to tilt his head and glare upwards at Rimsc. The man was still smiling as he narrowed the aperture on his heavy pulse-gun. Last thing: the snout of the weapon cold against Keech's head, a blow, blackness. That was all for a while.

Out of blackness, Keech woke to the grey. He was not alive and he knew precisely what had happened. He had prepared for this: he was now a reif. *I am dead.* The years of searching came back to him: the killings and the questionings, the terrible purpose that was empty of feeling. He had hunted down Hoop's crew with the tenacity of a mining machine digging into a cliff. Rimsc first—it had been a simple thing to rig his suit once he had located him. There had been no restraining morality then as Keech had not considered himself a monitor any more. Killing Corbel Frane had been a high point. In between there had been lesser kills; many of those who had worked for The Eight, and those sent by Frane and perhaps by Hoop himself. So many of them, and so many years. Keech wanted to cry and felt the circuit that activated his eye irrigator becoming live, then going off again. The years of it all continued to download into his newly repaired and activated brain.

In the darkness, Windcheater observed Ambel unsteadily leaving his cabin. All but the helmsman, Boris, were back below decks. When Ambel walked over to Windcheater's food barrel and methodically pulled out steak after steak and munched them down, the sail considered, then rejected, the idea of complaining. He just watched as Boris spotted the Captain then, with a lantern hung from his belt, climbed down from the forecabin and walked across.

'You better now, Captain?' Boris asked.

Ambel wiped purple blood from round his mouth before replying. 'Bad memories,' he said.

'Happens like that sometimes. Got shot with a vis gun 'bout twenty years back. The wound healed in a day but I was real nasty for months after.'

Ambel just looked at him and waited for him to continue— as he did.

'It was on account of me first wife shooting me with one, ye see.'

Ambel nodded. 'You remember it all?' he asked.

'Mostly,' said Boris.

'I don't. I've got a piece missing as long as you're old, and I don't want it back. I know what it is, but I don't *want* it.' Ambel looked very closely at Boris. 'There's bits, though. Bits keep coming back.'

'How'd you lose it?' Boris asked.

'Lost it in the sea, Boris. In the sea.'

Windcheater blinked and remained utterly still. Unlike most human conversations, this one he did not understand at all. He recognized the expression of disbelieving horror on the helmsman's face, and understood that the man had not shuddered because of being cold. But beyond that . . .

After a long silence Ambel said, 'In the morning we'll be at the atolls, and there we'll refine us some sprine. With that, I'll free meself of one of those bits. Time the Skinner went to his locker for good.' He took another steak out of the barrel and began eating it.

'You shoulda done that long ago. Don't know why you didn't. You know it whispers in the night?' said Boris.

'I know. Does it to Peck, mainly. Makes him all skittery.'

'That don't take much.'

'Yeah.'

They both eyed each other knowingly, then Boris nodded and turned to walk away, swinging his lantern in the night. Its light glinted on the open eyes of Windcheater as the sail watched Ambel move to the rail.

'What was that all about?' the sail queried through his aug.

'Memory loss through intense pain,' replied the Warden.

'Oh, so glad I asked,' said Windcheater.

'It's interesting that you chose *this* ship,' the Warden told the sail. 'Why *did* you choose this ship?'

'It happened to be in the area,' said Windcheater. 'And you wanted me to look out for anything unusual in this area.'

'And what have you found?' the Warden asked.

Windcheater, with his long understanding of human language, was not immune to sarcasm. 'Well, I've found the ship with Jay Hoop on board, and I've found a molly carp with a big lump of scrap metal inside.'

'I heard that!' interjected Sniper.

'Yes, I know you're here,' said the Warden. 'Is that molly carp well?'

'Think it might have a bit of a stomach upset. Reckon it ate something that disagreed with it, and I don't mean me,' replied the war drone.

The Warden was silent for a moment, then, 'You, Sniper, will stay with this ship and keep watch. When you're free, I may have further instructions for you. You, Windcheater, will leave this ship in the morning and fly to Olian Tay's island. By then Captain Sprage's ship will have arrived. You'll join it and keep watch. I'll want constant reports.'

'What's happening?' asked Sniper, unable to keep the frustration out of his communication.

'The exploding Prador vessel was a cover for the arrival of Rebecca Frisk. Where she is now I have only a rough idea. The Old Captains, who are aware of her presence, are gathering for a Convocation.'

Sniper hissed excitedly, 'Frisk here?'

'Yes, she is here.'

'She won't be alone,' said the war drone.

'She is not,' said the Warden, and withdrew contact.

'Come on, you damned haddock! I want out of here!'

Windcheater turned his attention to where Captain Ambel had focused his. There was a disturbance in the sea, and white water glinting in the dark, as the molly carp swirled and rolled and thrashed its tail against the waves.

11

The second male glister flicked clumps of hairlike organs on its head, registering the tail-end of a low-pitched squeal in what served it as ears, but so stupefied was it by its current pleasure in gustation that it could not identify the sound. Perhaps this was understandable, since it had never heard a brother's death-squeal before. Waving its antennae, it detected only an overwhelming taste of whelk, but that was perfectly understandable—so many of them having recently been torn apart in the vicinity. It gave a lobsterish shrug, and went to take another bite of the wonderful bounty of flesh strewn before it. The wall of flesh that rolled over it and its meal, as well as uninvited leeches and prill, was as yielding as old oak—the great mouth behind just hoovered them all up.

The pinioned sail kept mouthing obscenities, until Shib cut its tongue out. That made it thrash about so much that he had to put a couple of more staples through its neck and into the mast to keep it secured. He was the right one to do it: he had been very vocal in his dislike of this place and its fauna. Without ceremony, the three Batians then dropped the body of their deceased comrade over the side. Dead, he was as much rubbish as the rest of the human debris scattered over the deck. Frisk watched the corpse dragged down as countless leeches attached themselves to it—and then she went to see how Svan was getting on.

'How much longer!' she shouted down into the aft hatch. There was no reply so she climbed down to have a look. Svan was crouching in the rear of the ship, over the open casing of the motor she had just bolted to the keel. There were twists of wood shavings all over the floor where she had bored the bolt holes, together with those holes required for the intake pipe and outlet jets. Two pipes went straight through a bulkhead to the bow of the ship; Frisk assumed they were for braking.

'Fucking Prador diagnostics,' Svan snarled.

'What is it?' Frisk asked.

'This whole motor is just a pain,' Svan said.

'Will that be a problem?'

Svan closed the casing and locked it into place. 'Shouldn't be unless it goes wrong. But I don't see why it has to be so complicated. This ship isn't exactly high-tech.'

Frisk stepped out of Svan's way as she began to unreel a length of optic cable from the motor. She followed the Batian as she climbed the ladder on to the deck, across this, then up the next ladder to the cabin-deck. Here, Svan plugged the cable into a throttle-lever attached to the helm.

'Is all this really necessary?' Svan asked.

'Not completely,' Frisk replied. 'It's just the way I want to do things.' She took a device from her belt and peered at its small screen. She nodded at the coordinates displayed there, then quickly put the device back on her belt when her hand began to shake. She forced a grin.

'Why not just take your Prador's ship straight there and blow them out of the water?' Shib asked Frisk, coming up on to the deck. She stared at him and her grin collapsed. Was he really that stupid?

'Because if the Warden detects a Prador war-craft moving about down here, we just might never be able to get away,' she said. 'So, Ebulan will have taken his ship down deep and out of sight.'

Svan glared at Shib, then turned back to Frisk. 'I see your point there,' said the mercenary, 'but why not use one of the little transports?' Frisk appeared confused for a moment. Svan went on, 'Why all this?' she asked, gesturing at the helm.

Frisk glanced down to where the transport bumped against the side of the ship.

'It was Ebulan's idea . . . to get us close to Keech. He'll be naturally suspicious of strangers. All the Old Captains are familiar figures to each other. This way we'll be able to get close without rousing too much suspicion.'

This reasoning sounded specious even to herself. Frisk had indeed considered using one of the transports—until she had been dissuaded—but now, now she liked things this way. She glanced over as Speaker came aboard leading Captain Drum. It gave Frisk a buzz of pleasure to see the Captain, standing here on his own ship, reduced to a human blank: his spinal column disconnected and his body run by a spider thrall. This was *power*. This was everything Jay Hoop had taught her. Her grin came back: a rictus that stretched her split cheek. She didn't mind the pain; it told her she was real.

He felt *everything*. The breeze against his skin almost hurt, and each step he took on the wooden boards of the deck sent a jolt through his entire body. His breathing sounded like waves hissing on a shingle beach. The air tasted of metal and vinegar and carried a thousand scents, some putrid, some sweet. The thumping of his heart was controlled thunder in his breast, and the images coming in through his eye seemed to imprint themselves on the back of his skull.

Keech stopped where he was, and thought for a moment. One eye. He reached up and pressed his fingers into the cartouche on his aug unit. With a sucking click it came away and rested warm and heavy in his hand. Doubled images slowly pulled together as his new eye focused. Erlin had repositioned the connections while he had been in the tank—as it seemed the nanites had been intent on growing him another eye, whether there were connections into what remained of his optic nerve or not. Vision was now painful. Taste, sound, the texture of the rail on his hands: it was a beautiful pain called life. And now he had it, Keech wanted to keep it.

'How are you . . . feeling?'

Keech glanced round at Janer, who was standing just behind him.

'Alive,' said Keech.

'A novel experience,' said Janer.

Keech turned to Erlin as she came up on to the deck. 'Thank you,' he said.

Erlin smiled, glanced at Janer, and abruptly appeared uncomfortable. She turned back to Keech. 'Thank *you*,' she said. 'This is the most involved I've been in anything for decades. I . . . ' she paused, and again glanced at Janer, 'I enjoyed it.'

Keech nodded and gazed down at the sea. These two were like teenagers who had discovered sex for the first time—or was that just his perspective? Was this how the Old Captains felt? Did most people seem naive and silly to them? He studied his pink hands, then his body with the monofilament overall clinging to it. He felt a vague twinge of embarrassment when thoughts of sex and the feel of the material against his skin conspired to give him an erection. He stayed where he was by the rail.

'What's that?' he asked after a moment, and pointed to a humped shape in the sea.

Erlin stepped up beside him and peered at where he was pointing. 'It's either a transitional leech that tried to take a large prill, or Hoopers have been hunting here,' she said.

Keech waited for an explanation.

To try and cover her earlier embarrassment, Erlin took on a didactic tone. 'Small leeches feed by taking a plug of flesh from their prey, and whatever fluids they can suck out.'

Keech noted Janer rubbing the distinctive scar on his hand.

'As a leech gets bigger it takes to the sea after bigger prey, also because the water there can support its larger body. In time, it begins to outgrow its prey, so it makes the transition from plug feeder to a feeder upon whole animals. The problem with eating animals whole here is that they tend not to die very quickly, so can cause a great deal of damage to a predator's insides. Therefore big leeches produce a poison in their bile which can kill virus and prey at once.'

Before Erlin could continue, Keech said, 'And a transitional leech is one that isn't yet producing the poison, but still needs to feed on whole prey.' He nodded at the leech floating past. 'Hence, that could be one that has fed on something that tore its way out of it again.'

'Exactly,' said Erlin, studying him carefully.

'Why *do* Hoopers hunt leeches?' he asked.

'Sprine,' said Janer.

'That's the poison,' said Erlin. She said no more, and gestured Janer to silence when he seemed about to explain.

'Difficult to obtain, also rare, and it kills Hoopers,' said Keech. He turned away. 'No wonder they hunt these leeches. They'd probably do much more just to get hold of it.'

'Why are you here, Keech?' Erlin asked, suddenly.

Keech considered lying to her for only a moment. 'I'm here to find and kill Jay Hoop,' he said.

'Why?'

'Because he is a criminal. Because I must. Because it was . . . *is* my job.'

Erlin stared at the back of his head. She thought about where they were going, then about Ambel and about what he kept in his cabin. She'd hated that low morbid whispering. It was part of what had driven her away.

'In a day or so we may well reach the ship that has . . . Hoop aboard,' she said.

Suddenly Keech was facing her again, one hand gripping her collar, his other hand rigid for a killing strike. He had moved fast, faster than she could move. Alive, Keech must have been a very dangerous man. And now . . . he was alive again.

'Explain,' he said.

'What *remains* of Hoop is kept on that ship,' said Erlin.

Keech released her and suddenly stepped back. He seemed confused, and his hands were shaking. Spittle ran from the corner of his mouth.

'No . . . I don't believe that. I don't believe that story.' He shook his head once, shook it again. Abruptly his body began to spasm, and he fell over on the deck like a falling door. His aug unit bounced on the deck beside him, and a green light on its surface turned red as the reattachment delay finally ran out and it began to power down.

'Quickly! Get him below!' Erlin yelled.

'What is it?' Janer asked as he helped her carry the spas-ming man below.

'His organic brain's taken over control of his cyber im-plants and now his muscles are fighting them. We'll have to restrain him till he gets control.'

'What about his aug?' Janer asked.

Erlin shook her head. 'Wouldn't work. He'd end up fight-ing it like he is his implants.'

Janer gazed down at the convulsing face. But for the metal interfaces inset in Keech's cheekbone and above his eye, he looked utterly human and vulnerable. Janer wanted him to live, not to suffer—found that he cared for the man.

'Well that's a first,' said his Hive link.

When Janer angrily questioned it, it retreated to its distant buzzing, and he wondered just *how* much it was picking up from him through their link.

Darkness and pain, and the smell of the sea and of things de-caying. He fought the harness and, though stronger than most men, he was weakened by his wounds and could only flex ceramal that in other circumstances he could have bro-ken like chalk. The blanks dragging him back were as iron as he had been, and his struggles were all but ignored. He was just a difficult parcel that they dragged to the table and threw down upon it. Then began the bubbling speech of the Prador and, in flickering nightmarish luminescence, a huge first-child entered and poised itself over him, its mandibles flicking as if it might like to *taste* this particular morsel. A claw closed on the harness, gouging into his back as it lifted and suspended him.

'Why? Why did you kill my crew?' Drum asked.

The Prador's translator box groaned and crackled as it replied. 'Kill your crew . . . I did not kill your crew,' it stated.

'Why—?' he began, but before he could question further it threw him face-down, looming over him. Something clicked and detached from the harness, and now he was able to move his head. He turned his head to see the underside of the creature's body: the ridged carapace and swiftly moving manipulatory arms. In one of those hands he saw something like a grey metal spider, wriggling its legs as the first-child brought it down behind Drum. He started to bellow as small legs like pitons burrowed into the back of his neck. Then his whole body went entirely slack, but not, unfortunately, without feeling. The cutting sensation continued, and the pain rolled out in waves which soon grew dull and distant. Blackness welled up inside him and took him away: stood him aside from the world.

Then, in time, he came back.

Drum would have normally looked around, but no longer had that choice. He continued to steer his ship and check the compass, but these actions were not at his own instigation. Hunger and thirst were constant, but he could do nothing to slake them. He could feel the horrible ache of healing injuries, and he could see, and he could taste the salt in the air, but beyond sensing the world around him he could not influence it. Straining to look round where he was not directed to look availed him nothing more than a little hope: for there was still *something* physical to strain against—and something at the back of his neck repositioned itself each time he tried.

Frisk screamed and flung the biomech detector to the deck. Before anyone could think of trying to stop her, she stamped on it until it broke. As she stepped back, its power pack discharged into the planking, and set the pitch caulking on fire.

She stood there with her hands shaking. 'How did he fucking know! How did he know!'

Svan and Tors stood back, kept their faces without expression. When Frisk pulled her pulse-gun, Tors slipped a hand down to his own weapon—before Svan gave him a cautioning look. He didn't take his hand away from it though.

Frisk crashed out of the cabin, swearing repeatedly. She glared up to where Drum stood impassively at the helm, and fired off three shots at him. The first shot seared the side of his face. The second punched a smoking hole through his chest, and the third shot set the helm burning. He showed no reaction but just continued to steer, his hands sizzling where they touched the burning wood. Frisk screamed with rage and went storming down the deck. She burnt holes through the planking as well as the rail. Eventually she came to the mast and glared down at the head of the sail. It tried to move out of the way as she directed her weapon at it, but with three staples through its neck it could not move far. Frisk altered the setting on her weapon and let off a volley of shots into its face. It made a gargling hissing sound as it struggled, and its wings boomed against the spars. It grew still, eventually.

'You waste useful tools.'

Frisk turned and rammed the barrel of the gun up under Speaker's chin.

'This is not your tool to waste,' said Speaker.

Frisk pulled her arm down in a jerky motion, holstered the weapon, pulled her injector from her belt and placed it against her own neck. Her right leg was quivering and her cheek had started to ache again. These nerve conflicts were becoming more and more frequent. Was it being here? The stress? The excitement? The priozine soon flooded her system and stilled the rebellion of this body she had stolen.

'Stupid,' she said to herself, then glared down along the deck to Shib.

'Get that thing secured,' she ordered him, with a nod at the sail's body hanging in folds where it had released its holds during its convulsions. Shib looked with distaste at the sail, then went to obey. From where they stood, outside the cabin, Svan and Tors gave each other a look.

Once Frisk was out of hearing, Tors said, 'If the detector is not picking up Keech's aug that means it's off, and he's probably dead. Doesn't she realize that?'

'Maybe . . . whatever. She pays the money and we do what she says. Mad as a pan-fried AI she may be, but she's got the shillings,' replied Svan, and went off to assist Shib. Tors stared up at the Hooper Captain, and after a moment fetched a bucket of seawater to throw over the smouldering helm.

Drum continued, mindlessly, to steer his ship.

Using the deck winch, Ambel brought the first carboy up from the hold. Using muscle and great care, he detached the

cargo net it was contained in and took it over to below the
forecabin ladder. After attaching a rope, he climbed up on to
the cabin, then hauled the carboy up there, where he tied it to
the rail before breaking the seal and extracting the bung with
a large corkscrew. Anne and Pland grimly watched the proceedings, while Boris finished setting up the spinner and lu-
bricating the cogwheels with turbul grease.

Peck came up on deck with a coil of tube looped over his
shoulder. He threw one end up to Ambel, who caught it and
inserted it in the carboy. On the lower deck, below the rail,
the three armour-glass vessels Ambel had purchased at great
cost twenty years before stood wedged in a rack. Peck
sucked on the tube and watched carefully as the green bile
came up out of the carboy and started to descend towards
him, then quickly took the tube out of his mouth and put his
finger over the end. Leech bile in the mouth wouldn't kill a
Hooper, but it would make him sick for months. Actually
swallowing the mouthful would kill, though. Taking his finger off the end, he inserted the tube into one of the vessels.
The bile flowed on down and it began to fill. Peck took this
opportunity to put on his gloves. Once one vessel was full,
he pinched the tube and transferred it to the next, careful not
to get any of the bile on himself. The contents of the carboy
filled all three.

'You ready there, Boris?' Ambel asked.

'I am, Captain,' said Boris, pulling on his own gloves and
going over to help Peck transfer the vessels to the horizontal
wheel of the spinner, and clamp them in place.

'Let's get winding, lads,' continued Ambel.

Gollow and three of the other juniors were the first to
come to the double winding handles, as Ambel came down
from the forecabin. They put their weight against the handles and heaved. Greased cogs began to turn and the chain
leading in underneath the spinner began to move. Slowly at
first, the wheel began to turn. Peck and Boris removed their
gloves and waited their turn at the handles, as did Anne and
Pland. Ambel waited as well. He always went last, and he
turned the handles by himself. It was an adequate demonstration of the difference in strength between juniors, se-

niors, and the Old Captain. They had a long day ahead of
them.

Morning dragged into afternoon, and it was the next turn
for Pland and Boris at the handles. The wheel was whirring
around nicely, and the bile was just beginning to separate in
the vessels. In the bottom half of each it lay thick and green,
with a layer of cloudy fluid above it. When it came to Ambel's
turn, there was a thin layer of clear fluid at the surface. As he
worked the handles some of the crew fished for boxies, and
others went below to rest their aching limbs.

By mid-afternoon a centimetre of clear fluid rested at the
top of each vessel. At this point Ambel released the handles
and let the spinner wind to a stop. He called Peck over and
together they siphoned this clear fluid into a smaller, open-
topped vessel. This container they took into Ambel's cabin
to place in a secure framework he had earlier clamped to his
desk. It wouldn't do to lose all that work to the first squall
that came along. The stuff remaining in the larger vessels,
they tipped over the side.

'Should be ready by tomorrow morning,' Ambel stated.

'Aye, the bugger,' said Peck in the same grim tone that all
of them had taken on this day. It was a serious business plan-
ning to kill something a thousand years old, no matter how
evil it might be.

SM12 scanned the three ships and found nothing to make it
suspicious. It recognized the crews of each vessel, having
come across them many times before in its travels. Com-
pleting its circuit of Tay's island, it experienced dronish
frustration. Where was she? The Batian's deflated dinghy
still lay under the sheet-leaves where they had beached and
there had been no signs of any other landings on the other
beaches. Nothing in the air either, so that left one choice.
The iron cockle dropped out of the sky with the aerodynam-
ics of a brick, entered the sea with a huge splash, and
switched on its sonar. Immediately it picked up signs of
movement all around it, but nothing with a metallic signature. It accelerated, kicking up a cloud of silt behind, and

ran electrostatic scans for as far as it could. It really needed some help. Taking an instant decision, it shot out of the water and broadcast.

'Where's SM Thirteen?' it asked.

'SM Thirteen is hypersonic and will be with you directly,' said the Warden. 'You are having trouble locating Rebecca Frisk?'

'Has to have gone into the sea. She's not on the island,' Twelve replied. It then dropped, and started scanning once again. It was soon tracing something it thought might be promising when there was a splash above it, and soon an iron seahorse was cruising along beside it.

'Want a hand?' asked Thirteen.

'Yes, I'm on to something now,' said Twelve.

'You realize that hammer-whelk shells have a slight piezoelectric property?' said Thirteen.

In chagrin Twelve said, 'Well, aren't you the whelk expert. Take the north side. If she's using an escape pod as a submersible, there should be ionic traces. She's probably heading away fast. We need to get on to this.'

SM13 tilted and shot for the surface. Shortly after it was gone, SM12's underspace transceiver opened.

'Anything?' asked the Warden.

'Nothing yet, but I'm sure we'll find her,' replied Twelve.

'I'm glad you're so confident,' said the Warden. 'I have to wonder if there's not something we're missing. No matter— she will never leave.'

'They've gone to the atolls,' said Captain Ron, thumping a finger down on the chart.

'How can you be sure?' asked Erlin.

Janer stood back and didn't question. His concerns were all with Keech, strapped in his bunk below, fighting to regain control of his body. His convulsions had not let up for twenty hours and it seemed his return to life might only be temporary.

'Ambel's got his own refining gear. If he's having a good hunt this early, he'll want to refine what he's got, then see if

he can get some more before the season ends. For refining he
needs a stable mooring. Anyway, we'd have found him by
now if'n he'd been here.'

Erlin shrugged. 'I bow to your superior knowledge,' she
said.

'And so you ought,' said Ron, tipping Janer a wink.

As they left the cabin, Janer asked, 'What now, when you
find your sea captain?'

'I don't know,' said Erlin. She looked Janer up and down.
'It could be nothing has changed, and it could be everything
has. I won't know till I find him.'

Janer nodded. He wasn't about to argue with her. So
they'd had sex a few times: it had been fun, but nothing to
get all emotional about. He liked Erlin and he found sex with
her intensely stimulating, but there would be other Erlins
and there would be other sex. Just a little more thought along
those lines, and he felt sure he would convince himself.

Janer followed Erlin below decks, to the cabin where
Keech lay strapped to his bunk. The monitor's convulsions
were less severe now. But perhaps he just didn't have the energy to fight any more. Erlin stood over him and started to
lift one of his eyelids. Both Keech's eyes abruptly flicked
open and he looked from one to the other of them.

'Getting it,' he managed, before the next convulsion hit.

Erlin checked the reading on her diagnosticer then
plugged it into her drug manufactory. In a couple of seconds
it provided her with a drug patch, which she slapped on
Keech's chest. He relaxed; his arched back settling to the
bunk and his jaw unclenching.

'How's he doing?' Janer asked.

'Getting it, as he said. He seems to have control of his
limbs now. I should think in another ten hours or so he'll be
able to get up and move about. If he lives that long,' she
replied.

'Why the doubt?'

'He took a hell of a risk using that nano-changer. They
shouldn't be used without AI supervision with full and constant scan. All it would take is one rogue factory in his bloodstream, and he could end up with nanites floating about doing

untold damage. That could happen at any time in the next week or so, until the changer programme has run its course.'

'He's been dead before,' Janer observed.

Erlin went on without acknowledging his comment, 'The nanites could do *anything*. Rogue bone-repair nanites could ossify his entire body. Nanites building blood cells could turn him into a pool on the floor.'

'You don't have much confidence in them, I take it.'

'I do not. The more miraculous a technology is, the more prone it is to catastrophic breakdown.'

Janer studied her very carefully. Sinking back into her didacticism, she had abruptly become distant from him. He considered taking her in his arms there and then, and rejected the idea. He didn't really need the complications. Without a word, he left her alone to tend to Keech, and returned to his bunk in the crew quarters.

Once there, Janer pulled the box that Keech had delivered earlier from under his bunk. He studied it for a while, then pressed his fingertips against the touch-plate on its side. When nothing happened, he lay back on his bunk, holding the box up before his face.

'Why here?' he said.

There was no reply.

'I could easily take this box and throw it over the side of this ship. I wouldn't be killing anything, as no doubt the contents are in stasis. In fact, I think I'll do that now,' he said, and began to sit up.

'Why not here?' the mind asked him.

'I can think of a number of reasons. This is a primitive world. Hornets have to be adapted to survive here . . . The main reason, of course, is that it's not a Polity world and that you'd piss off an awful lot of people,' said Janer.

'Not half so many as on a Polity world,' the mind replied.

'OK, let me reiterate: why anywhere?'

'Humans establish their colonies where they will. Why should I not?'

'No answer to that, but it's not often you establish a nest without a reason, beyond that of colonization. . . . Tell me, the remaining hornet was successful here, wasn't it?'

'*It was.*'

'So you had it transfer its genetic imprint to our friend here in this box.'

'*I did.*'

'How long will this queen live?'

'*As long as any other. The adaptation completely prevents any invasion by the fibres. For that I took a snip from a glister—a creature that also exists here without the viral fibres in its body.*'

'So what's the point?' Janer asked, weighing the box in his hands.

The mind warned, '*If you throw the box over the side I'll have another brought in by another agent.*'

'You're not going to tell me,' said Janer.

'*Not yet.*'

'Now, why do I get the distinct feeling that you're up to something you shouldn't be up to?'

The mind did not reply, and Janer snorted, then reached over and placed the box on the floor beside his bed—before closing his eyes and settling down, intending to sleep. Before sleep could claim him though, he opened his eyes again.

'The hornet with me possessed the pattern for survival here. OK, it's imprinting the queen—but that's not enough, is it? You have some other edge?' he said.

'*You will be told eventually,*' said the mind.

For a while, Janer stared at the bunk above him. It occurred to him that he might live to regret not throwing the box over the side, then reporting things to the Warden. It also occurred to him that the AI probably knew a lot more about what was going on here than he did. Soon, he slept.

From the promontory, Olian Tay watched the three ships slide over the horizon and come in to moorage beyond the reefs. She continued to watch for a while, expecting that once a rowing boat put out from one of them she would have plenty of time to wander down to meet it. That Sprage had come here for her was unsurprising to her, as they had been friends for many years and he was one of the few Captains ever to visit her and acquaint her with the doings of the rest of the Old Captains. That those same Captains had done nothing in which she felt interested for many years had never really interfered with their relationship. Now, of course, the Captains were involved in something *very* interesting. To capture coming events, Tay had all her portable recording equipment with her, hooked on her belt.

Still no rowing boats left the ships, and Tay was getting fidgety when she observed the sail circling above her. Soon it came lower and, with a booming of wings and a stirring of dust clouds, it landed further along the promontory. She knew that sails had landed here in the past. This fact was evinced by the scattering of broken glister shells, and the black spinal columns and articulated skulls of rhinoworms. She had only ever seen them from a distance, though, and they had always departed immediately at her approach.

This sail did no such thing. After folding its wings, it waddled over to her and gazed down upon her with its demonic eyes.

'Sail, you have an augmentation,' Tay said, trying not to sound as nervous as she felt.

'The name's Windcheater,' said the sail, and Tay immediately clicked a switch on her belt. From the top of a flat rectangular box attached there, a device the shape and size of a candy bar launched into the air and began slowly to circle the two of them. The sail tracked the course of this device for a moment.

'Remote holocorder,' he declared. 'X-ten-fifty, full spectrum plus anosmic, with a transmission range of five hundred kilometres. Why you want to record me?'

'Because you're a legend, and obviously part of the whole story,' Tay replied.

Windcheater shook his head. 'If you like,' he said. 'Right, you ready?'

'What?'

The sail made a low growling sound, then abruptly launched itself. Tay yelled in shock and closed her eyes against the dust. The next thing she knew, long bony claws had closed around her waist and her feet had left the ground.

'What the hell do you think you're doing?'

Windcheater gave no reply.

'Put me down, dammit!'

Windcheater snickered. 'You sure about that?' he asked.

Tay looked over her shoulder and down, to see her island rapidly receding.

'OK, don't put me down,' she said. Even though angry and not a little frightened, she felt some satisfaction in seeing her holocorder speeding along beside them, recording every moment.

Sprage drew deep on his pipe and chuffed out a cloud of smoke that drifted down the length of the *Vengeance* like a confused djinn. He rocked back in his chair, clumped his boots up on the rail of the foredeck, and gazed across the white water marking the reefs around Olian Tay's island. Though now certain that Rebecca Frisk was back on Spatterjay, he was in no screaming hurry to find her. A brief conversation with the Warden had confirmed that she would never be leaving the planet. He and the rest of the Captains could take their time, in deciding how to deal with her—not that there would be a lot of debate on that, as she would most certainly end up in a fire—then slowly and inexorably they would hunt her down. Sprage gave a grim smile at this thought.

'That sail's got something,' said Lember from the cabin-deck.

Sprage glanced at the creature winging out from the island. It had probably caught a rhinoworm, though why it was heading out from a landward direction he couldn't say, unless it had flown with its prey from the sea on the other side of the island. Watching its continued approach as he pondered what must happen in the coming days. The *Jester* and the *Orlando* were moored up, and by now, through the slow message-carrying of the sails and, in some cases, through Polity-issued radios, nearly all the Old Captains should know—barring those still out in Deep-sea. Soon the rest of them would be arriving, and it would be time for the Convocation. Before then, Sprage would send for Olian Tay, as she would be a pain for years if he let her miss this. Then would come a slow but sure search, island by island, atoll by atoll.

Sprage felt sure it would be the Warden who would detect Frisk first, but that would not stop the Captains from searching, even though the Warden had assured him that they could have her eventually. All of those who had once been slaves of Hoop carried just too much emotional baggage to keep out of it all.

'Hey, it's carrying someone!' shouted Lember, now gazing through Sprage's tripod-mounted binoculars. Sprage dropped his feet from the rail, stood, and walked to the front ladder of the forecabin, puffing on his pipe. Soon he was up standing beside Lember.

'Spot who it is?' he asked.

Lember jumped back from the binoculars, and glared at his Captain. Sprage might be ancient, but he certainly moved soft.

'Can't really see,' said the crewman.

Sprage gently pushed past him and, moving his pipe so it jutted sideways from his mouth, he put his eyes to his binoculars.

'Olian Tay,' he said, and stepped back to watch the sail come in to land.

This sail was a big one, and the boom of its wings had its smaller kin on the spars flinching back. It deposited Olian on the main deck then, hovering above her, it stretched out its neck towards the other sail.

'Bugger off,' it said succinctly.

The smaller sail hurriedly released its grip on the spars, furled its wings, hauled itself higher up the mast and launched away from Windcheater. The bigger sail now descended and quickly settled himself into position.

'Interesting,' said Sprage.

Lember watched as Olian climbed to her feet then came stomping towards the forecabin.

'Yeah,' he agreed. 'You don't often see them doing that.'

Sprage faced him, pointed a finger to one side of his own neck, then pointed down at the sail's head.

'Ah,' said Lember, squinting at the aug Windcheater had acquired.

Sprage moved away to the ladder and climbed down to the

main deck. As Tay approached him, her face was flushed and there was a touch of exhilaration in her expression.

'I was just about to send for you,' he said. 'Interesting times.' He turned to regard the new sail, that had swung its head round the mast to watch the two of them.

'They are that,' agreed Tay.

Just then, Sprage spotted the holocorder sliding around them in a wide arc.

'I would guess *you* know about Frisk?' he said with a raised eyebrow.

'I know about her—and I want to be in at the kill.'

'Like you were with Grenant?' Sprage asked, fixing his attention back on the sail.

'If possible,' said Tay, trying to keep an impassive face.

Sprage nodded as he once again puffed at his pipe. After a moment he said, 'Welcome aboard, sail, how are you called?'

'The name's Windcheater,' said the sail. 'And I'll want paying for this.'

The sun edged over the horizon, and turned umber clouds to turquoise silk. About their business over the sea, three sails glided across the face of this orb as its light revealed a ship far out on the water, and decked it blue with gleams of emerald. Ambel stared at the vessel for some time, then turned to Peck, crouching by the rail and staring down into the water. Peck looked distinctly unwell in this morning light. The scars on his face were livid and his eyes were dark with blood.

'What is it, Peck,' Ambel asked him at last.

'Bugger,' muttered Peck.

Ambel waited for him to continue. It took him a while.

'It *calls* me, Captain,' Peck said.

'It calls to us all. It'll call to any who listen.'

'It called and I went,' Peck confessed.

'What have you done, Peck?' Ambel asked calmly.

Peck rested his forehead against the rail. 'Wouldn't stop. It had its hunger. I fed it to shut it up,' he said.

Ambel glanced back at his cabin and considered, having

spent the night in there, how the head had been strangely silent.

'Did you release it?' Ambel asked.

'No, Captain.'

'What did you give it, then?'

'Remains of the baiting steak.'

Ambel was about to make a reply to that when Boris yelled down from the nest, 'It's the *Ahab*!'

Ambel shaded his eyes to gaze out at the distant ship.

'Now what's Ron doing out here? Last I heard he was off after a load of turbul,' he observed.

'Maybe it calls him, too,' said Peck.

Ambel stared down at his crewman and wondered if that might be true—for the Skinner called in different ways. Perhaps Ron was coming to deliver some long-avoided Convocation decision on the matter. But he would soon know, as the *Ahab* was heading straight towards them. Ambel walked back to the door of his cabin and locked it. The next time he went in there, he would take with him a harpoon wet with sprine. He didn't like to think about what might be going on inside his sea-chest.

'Get a cask up, lads,' he yelled generally. 'You know how thirsty Ron can be.'

And general laughter greeted this comment, though it was subdued.

The rowing boat approaching from the *Ahab* had six people in it. Ambel immediately discerned the large, bald-headed shape of Captain Ron at the tiller, and he guessed the two at the oars to be Forlam and Goss. The other three were dressed like off-worlders, and for a moment he didn't recognize any of them.

So he felt a momentary flush of pique when Boris recognized her first.

'It's Erlin!' the crewman yelled from the nest.

Ambel squinted his eyes at the Earther woman. The last time he had seen her, she'd told him he was dead inside, and she seriously doubted if he was human any more. He won-

dered what she wanted of him now. Was she starting to comprehend things beyond her own small compass? Was time
now doing to her what it had done to him so long ago? Ambel doubted it. He shook his head and concentrated his attention on the other two off-worlders. The blond-haired man
wore the utile clothing of a seasoned traveller, and he wore it
with the casual air of one who had not just donned it. That
one might be an interesting person to meet. The other man
looked ill—or as if recovering from a long illness. He was
bald and scrawny, though his bone structure was that of a
heavy-worlder. He was wearing monofilament overalls—
utile garb again, but the kind worn by Golem androids and
the like: individuals that did not worry too much about either
the temperature or their appearance. Was there something
familiar about this man? Ambel felt the nag of memory and
a surge of both apprehension and excitement. Perhaps he
was from *before*? No, unlikely: there were few off-worlders
of that age. Ambel tried to dismiss these thoughts, but he
still felt a nagging doubt.

The boat clunked against the side of the ship and greetings were shouted back and forth as a rope was thrown up
for them to secure it, then a ladder lowered. Ron was first
over the rail and Boris thrust a jug into his hand. Ron
downed it in one and handed it back for a refill.

'How are y', Peck m'boy!' he bellowed at Peck, after he
had bellowed greetings at each other member of Ambel's
crew.

Peck just stared at him, and Ron turned to Ambel.

'Still a bit . . . y'know?' he asked, making a wiggling motion with his hand.

Ambel nodded.

Erlin was next over the rail and, while each member of the
crew greeted her, she kept her eyes fixed on Ambel. When he
winked at her, a slow smile spread across her face. Goss immediately started to come on to Boris, and Boris suggested
showing her around the ship. Anne stared speculatively at
Forlam, then filled a jug and took it over to him.

Ambel watched the blond man as he came over the rail as-
sisting the bald one up behind him. The look blondy gave

Erlin told Ambel all he wanted to know. He allowed himself a little smile, as it wasn't important. He stepped forward to greet the two new off-worlders.

'Welcome to the *Treader*,' he said.

With deep blue eyes the bald man stared at Ambel, and an immediate shock of recognition ran between them.

'This is Janer Cord Anders and this is Sable Keech,' said Erlin, still smiling.

Ambel had only time to raise one hand before the first energy pulse slammed into his stomach. The next burnt a hole in his chest and the next blew away part of his shoulder. Collapsing, he turned and ducked to protect his head. Another pulse hit him in the back and he lost it for a moment. As he came to, he groaned and rolled over, agony blurring his vision and sapping his strength.

He looked up to see Keech glaring at him with flat hatred, while he tried to bring his weapon to bear again. Ron, Forlam, and Boris were all three having trouble restraining him, which was very surprising. His struggles against them lasted only so long as it took Ron to get a hand free to slap him on the side of the head. As Keech went down, Ambel tried to rise, but that was not a good idea. He felt the blood draining from his face and just had time to see Erlin crouching over him, peeling open a drug patch, before he lost consciousness for the second time.

Keech regained consciousness to find himself roped in a chair, with his head throbbing and an ache in his torso that evidenced the fact that someone had put the boot in as he went down. He sat for a moment with his teeth firmly clenched against the vomit that threatened to rise into his mouth. As the nausea slowly started to recede, he tested the rope and found it strong enough to restrain his human muscles. Next, he found that direct brain-to-cybermotor link that had nearly killed him, and tried again. This time the ropes stretched and the chair creaked. But still he did not have the strength, augmented or otherwise, to free himself, so he scanned the cabin for some other means of escape.

No knife was lying handy on the desk and there were no

useful sharp edges anywhere else, as was to be expected in a ship's cabin. There were cupboards that might contain something he could use, but what chance did he have, without being heard, of manoeuvring his chair to one of them and opening it? So he waited and, as he waited, he became aware of a sound . . . or something like a sound. The sea-chest by the wall drew his attention. Before he could wonder what it was about this chest that increasingly riveted his attention, the door slammed open and Ron stomped in.

'Give me a reason why I shouldn't let the boys chuck you to the leeches,' growled the Captain.

Keech tested his bonds again then let out a sigh. 'My name is Sable Keech,' he said.

'I know that, but it don't sound like reason enough for me.'

The Captain was angry, and Keech knew what damage an angry Hooper of his age could do. He suspected that if he didn't explain himself soon, he wouldn't even reach the sea in one piece.

'I first came here seven hundred years ago, with the ECS mission that released Hoop's slaves. I was part of the attack force that raided Hoop's stronghold—and I was the one who subverted the program running the slave collars Hoop was using.'

In shock, Ron stared at Keech, then stepped back and sat down on the sea-chest. He shook his head, appearing confused for a moment, then realized where he was sitting and abruptly stood again.

'Keech?' he said. 'I came here after the war, but I know about you.'

'I'm the same Keech who killed Frane and Rimsc, and I can recognize one of The Eight no matter how scarred and changed they may be. Ambel—a ridiculous anagram. So *you* don't recognize him, even though you were present when the ex-slaves threw him into the leech swarm,' said Keech. He spoke with the calm of utter certainty.

'Gosk Balem,' whispered Ron.

Keech awaited some explosive reaction, but there came none. Ron looked thoughtful for a moment, then he shud-

dered. He rubbed a hand down across his bare chest, where
the leech scars were thickest.

'Are you going to release me now and let me finish what I
started?' asked Keech.

After a moment Ron said, 'No.'

Keech felt a momentary sick anger. Had he misjudged?
Could it be that Ambel was not the one he thought him to
be? Or was Ron not who he thought either? So many memories crowding in his mind—so many to sort, to know.

'Why not?'

'Because he's not Gosk Balem,' said Ron.

'What makes you so sure of that?' Keech sneered.

Ron advanced to stand over him, placed his hands on the
arms of the chair.

'It's the sea, Sable Keech. It takes.'

With that, he turned from Keech and left the cabin. Keech
stared at the door for a moment then slowly began to work
his arms and legs against the rope. Motor and muscle. He
broke skin and ignored the pain. The chair began to creak.
From the sea-chest there came sounds of movement—and
that other sound, that whispering.

Keech worked harder at loosening his bonds, a sudden lu-
dicrous idea occurring to him as to what was inside that
chest.

12

*The third male glister—the last one of this particular family
had he but known it—was feeding with the female upon a turbul the size of a rowing boat. It sensed that something was
very wrong, just before a hawser of a tentacle wormed into
view, coiled and crushed the female, then snatched her backwards, squealing, through the murk. This last remaining male
fled as fast as his flat tail and paddle legs could propel him.*

Another tentacle whipped out and slapped his side, cracking his armour, but driving him beyond the predator's reach. The monstrous whelk was unconcerned about this escape, as it crunched down the female glister, then turned its attention to the plenitude of turbul corpses and their concomitant crop of leeches and prill. Perhaps it should have been more concerned about the heirodont, irate at having been deprived of the giant whelk it had been pursuing, and now ascending through the waterfall of organic detritus in the hope that its source might quell the grumbling of its gargantuan stomach.

With so many eyes keeping watch for it in so many places, the Warden did not feel any guilt in allowing its attention to stray beyond Spatterjay to observe such momentous events. In this particular observation it was not possible to easily maintain a direct link, so it created a submind ghost of itself that it sent hopping for lightyears: from runcible to runcible and onwards to AI ships and ship's drones, until it reached its destination. Here, as just one of many thousands cramming together to view one scene, it watched through the eyes of a Golem—linked by virtual fingernails—while the essence of the ghost ran itself in the huge processing spaces of the thinly disguised AI battleships poised above the Prador world. It recorded the momentous events, the AI reactions and net-space discussions, and relayed them back to itself every few seconds—a veritable age in AI terms.

A hundred Prador transports were parked along the edge of the flat, and salt dust glittered in the eddies of air disturbed by the cooling of their engine cowlings. Grand Prador adults, with their retinues, were gathered in protective groups on the cracked and pinkish hardpan: trusting each other less then they trusted the ECS monitors and the sector AI which, in the form of this Golem, had come to negotiate and hopefully agree terms.

'There can be no meaningful dialogue between us while this continues,' said the sector AI. 'Would you ever consider trade with us if it was our habit to use Prador carapaces as receptacles in which to take our ablutions?'

The concerted reply from the gathered Prador was both amused and angry. The Warden noted an open message sent by one of its fellow AIs to its homeworld, informing certain high-ranking humans to 'lose the decorative bathroom suites', and the brief discussion that followed would perhaps have shocked some humans who considered AIs to be without humour.

They settled down, though, when the speaker standing out in front of the Prador addressed the sector AI. 'Would you deprive us of our hands?' asked the male human blank on their behalf.

'You had hands before you encountered humankind,' replied the Golem, 'and your own cyber technologies could provide you with hands more efficient than those of human blanks. In truth it has become only a matter of status amongst you.'

After a long pause came the concerted reply through their speaker. 'We must discuss this.'

Humans, Golem and AIs together watched while Prador shifted about like huge draughts on some unseen board. A couple of shimmering fields flickered into existence and there came the stuttering crackle of a single railgun. One Prador, surrounded by its children, and attended by more blanks than most of its contemporaries, hissed out a bubbling scream and crashed to the hardpan as its AG cut out. Control units on its outer carapace detonated, and that carapace deformed and cracked, flinging fine sprays of dark fluid across the salt.

Railguns now opened up again, and blanks and second-children exploded into a mess of shell, flesh and numerous legs. By now the humans where hazed behind projected fields, and autoguns were spidering out of the heavy-lifter and up its sides to get an open field of fire on the assembled Prador. A single first-child ran gibbering towards these screens, until a missile hit it from behind and the explosion separated upper carapace from lower. Its lower half ran on for a little while longer, perhaps not yet realizing it was dead, then it keeled over like an unbalanced pedestal table. Before the human side could feel sufficiently threatened by this violence, the speaker blank held up a hand and spoke, his voice amplified all around.

'The discussion is ended. We now feel we can negotiate,' he said.

Erlin kept Ambel unconscious while she worked on his wounds. She didn't need to work to save his life, only to prevent the formation of ugly scar tissue, and to do this she had to cut again and again in a race with the rapid healing of his fibre-filled body. Had Keech managed a headshot, the Ambel she knew would have been dead and what remained of him would not have been human. Sprine would have then been administered, and the corpse buried at sea with all due ceremony. As it was, the Captain was bound to recover. Even with these wounds, Erlin reckoned on the healing process normally taking about a day and a night. But Ambel had obviously suffered other injuries recently, as his body weight was down and there was an excessive blue tinge to his skin. She allowed him to wake just after she finished repositioning the flesh of his shoulder and as the wound there closed like a startled mollusc.

'Erlin . . . who is he?' he asked.

'Goes by the name of Sable Keech. He claims to be an ECS monitor over seven hundred years old. He was a reification until only a few days ago, so that might be true. The bastard. I saved his life and he goes and does this. His brain must still be rotten—probably thought you were Hoop or something.' As she spoke, Erlin searched Ambel's expression with a kind of desperation.

'He isn't Hoop,' said Captain Ron behind her.

Erlin turned to see the Captain and Forlam entering the room. Forlam held a length of black cord she recognized as something used in ship wedding ceremonies and divorces. Ron nodded and Forlam stepped up beside her. He reached down and tied one end of the cord around Ambel's wrist.

'What the hell!' Erlin yelled.

She moved to stop him tying the cord, but Ron caught hold of her shoulders and gently pulled her away. Ambel watched impassively as Forlam bound his wrists together.

Erlin tried to understand what was going on. Surely they knew that nothing less than a steel hawser would hold Ambel. Forlam stepped back after he had tied the final knot.

'By my right as member and captain,' said Ron formally, 'I call you before Convocation, Captain Ambel. I want your parole until the time of the Convocation. Do you give it?'

'I do,' said Ambel.

Ron made a cutting motion with the edge of his hand. Ambel snapped the cords binding him. Ron turned back to the door, with Forlam following him.

'Do you *know*, then, Ron?' Ambel asked.

'I know,' said Ron, without turning.

'I'm not *him* any more. It was five years, Ron.'

Captain Ron turned and stared at him. Erlin thought she had never witnessed such an expression of horror on an Old Captain's face. She thought there was little in the world that could produce such an effect on such a man.

'You'll tell it, then,' said Ron.

'Now?'

'No, the monitor must hear it as well. He's owed that.'

Ron went on his way. Erlin noted that Forlam appeared as confused as she herself felt.

The rope stretched just enough for Keech to slide his hand free, but it only slid because he had lubricated it with his blood. As he held it up before his face to inspect the damage he had done to himself, the sounds from the sea-chest became more audible. Keech then worked on the knots tying his other wrist to the chair. His lack of fingernails made the task a lot more difficult than it should have been. Small nubs of nails were already growing from the quick of his fingers, but they were of no use as yet. He also found that his skin was too soft. It was like a baby's skin and—yet to thicken and acquire the calluses of age—it was easy to tear. He swore quietly as he persevered.

Keech had almost worked his left hand free when he noticed how the noises from the sea-chest had ceased. With his skin crawling, he slowly looked up and peered across the room. The lid of the chest was partly raised, and two evil black eyes were watching him. As the lid rose higher, Keech tried not to believe what he was seeing. His chest felt constricted and painful and that tightness was only relieved by a hiccuping hysterical giggle.

. The thing crawled out of the chest and landed with a heavy thump on the floor. It made a snorting sound, then rolled over on to the six spatulate limbs it had grown. Keech felt the urge to giggle again, but the giggle dried up in his throat when the thing rolled its lips back from jagged blades of teeth that it licked with an obscene black tongue.

Then it hissed, and Keech started yelling.

Frisk occupied her time by luring leeches to the side of the ship with lumps of the sail's feed, then hitting them with her pulse-gun. When she eventually got bored with this game, she dropped a weighted line overboard and, after a number of tries in which she caught only boxies, she managed to hook a frog whelk from the seabottom. This she pulled up and swung on to the lower deck, to see how her pet mercenaries would react to it.

Tors saw it first and laughed at it, as it tracked him with its stalked eyes. He pointed it out to Shib who laughed too, until it jumped the entire length of the deck to land next to him, then leapt again to take off a couple of his fingers. Shib yelled, swung his weapon to bear one-handed, and blew the whelk to pieces just as it jumped again. Later, as Shib stomped about the deck with a dressing on his hand, Frisk wondered how, some time soon, she might lure in a prill or two. That would make things more interesting.

'We have something,' said Svan, coming up the ladder.

Frisk turned from the rail with her gun still in her hand. Tors had been giving her some funny looks lately, and she didn't like it when people came up behind her so quietly. For a moment, she aimed the weapon at Svan's chest, then she gave a flat smile and holstered it.

'What do you mean, you "have something"?'

'All the equipment we brought along, we also brought a spare for,' said Svan, keeping her expression blank. 'So we brought a spare biomech detector—to replace the one you trashed.'

Frisk considered killing her right then, but decided that would be wasteful. Anyway, she could later do the job at her leisure, when Svan was no longer of any use to her. Perhaps just an injury for now . . . ? Then she comprehended what Svan was telling her.

'What have you detected?' she asked.

'Somebody is using cyber-joint motors about two hundred kilometres north-west of here. We had an intermittent signal for some time, but we couldn't pin it down. It has since become constant.'

'Show me,' said Frisk, tempted to berate Svan for not informing her earlier.

Svan pulled from her pocket the twin of the detector Frisk had smashed and flipped out its screen. She turned it round to show to Frisk. On the screen was a definite trace, with slowly drifting coordinates. Their source was not a ship under sail then, and if they were quick, they could reach it today. Frisk swivelled to face Drum's back.

'Turn the ship to the north-east and increase speed,' she ordered.

Drum swung the helm and pushed forward the throttle lever. The ship began to drone as the newly installed motor opened up. It left a foaming wake behind it and the wind pushed the sail back against the spars, belling rearwards.

'Is this as fast as it can go?' Frisk demanded. When Svan did not answer right away, Frisk turned to glare at her.

Quickly Svan said, 'This is about half speed, but go any faster and the ship might break up. It's not made for this kind of treatment.'

'Might?' asked Frisk.

'There's no way to—'

'Full speed ahead!' Frisk yelled.

There was no action from Drum, so she pulled her pulse-gun and put a shot in his back. He lurched forwards then straightened back up into position.

'I said "Full speed",' Frisk hissed viciously.

Svan stepped up beside Drum and pushed the lever all the way forward. She cast Drum a speculative look before leaving the cabin-deck and going to find something to occupy herself with, preferably something well away from Frisk. Drum continued staring ahead, seemingly unaware of the recent damage done to him. Frisk walked round to look him in the face.

'I *know* it hurts,' she said with relish. She nodded towards the mercenaries below. '*They* think it was a full coring, but you and I know better, don't we? How is it, I wonder, to be utterly under the control of that nasty little spider thrall, yet able to see, hear, and feel *everything*? How much does *that* hurt?'

She stared at him for a long moment as she tried to discern a reaction in his expression. But nothing—just like the blank on Ebulan's ship. Pressing her gun against his side, she fired off another pulse. Drum whoomphed, moved sideways, but just straightened up yet again. Something that time? No, still nothing. Frisk shook her head, suddenly bored with this game, and strode to the ladder. Behind her, Drum's eyes tracked her progress for a second, before flicking back to the fore as she turned to climb down. His wounds wept for a while, before slowly closing.

Janer stopped by the hatch to help Erlin out. She gave him an annoyed glance, before the two of them rushed to the fore-cabin, trailing behind Forlam and Ron.

'I thought you had the key,' said Ron.

Forlam searched his pockets, then gave Ron an apologetic look. Inside the cabin, they could hear Keech yelling, and then there was a crash. Ron swore as he straight-armed the door. This was the first chance Janer had to observe how strong the Old Captain really was, for Ron's hand went straight through the door, rather than bursting it open—as had been his intention. He swore again, and reached inside to tear the door off its hinges, then stood for a moment with the door hanging from his arm before shaking it to the deck.

Forlam ducked into the cabin ahead of him, but quickly backed out again. Janer stepped up behind Ron and peered around him.

'What the fuck is that?' he asked, turning to Erlin. She was backing away, shaking her head—her eyes fixed on the thing on the cabin floor.

In his struggles Keech had tipped his chair over. The Skinner creature turned like a bull terrier from savaging his arm and hissed at the spectators. Ron tore a length of wood from the doorjamb on his way in, swinging at the creature and striking it hard. The monstrosity slammed back against the cabin wall, then dropped to the floor while Ron discarded his now shattered club. But the creature merely rolled back on to its feet, shook itself, spat out a couple of teeth, then shot between Ron's legs and out of the door. Janer aimed a kick at it, but it darted out of his way before pausing to snarl at him.

'Skinner's out!' Forlam yelled.

Crewmen converged from every part of the ship. Goss threw a harpoon head that opened a wound on the Skinner before it ran again. Janer was only thankful it did run.

'Skinner?' he queried, but everyone was too busy to reply.

Next the Skinner aimed itself at Peck who yelled and threw a bait box at it. The lid flew off the box, and the bait leapt out and scuttled away in every direction to make its escape. One of the trumpet creatures came at Janer who, remembering Erlin's warning, stamped on it before it sought refuge in his trouser leg. It let out a pitiful squeaking as he ground it into the deck.

'Get the bugger!' Peck shrieked.

A gun went off with a staccato cracking. Janer glanced round to see Anne opening up on the Skinner with an ancient automatic pistol. Her first shot knocked it over. The next two shots splintered the deck—as it got upright again and scuttled towards the mast. A junior swiped at it with a panga but missed, then it stumbled over backwards, reared up and hissed at him. Someone else threw a club and knocked it tumbling. The Skinner again landed on its feet and glared from side to side as the whole crew closed in. Abruptly it turned and leapt for the mast, where it started scrabbling its way up. A knife thudded into the woodwork below it and it accelerated. The crew dispersed to lockers and cabins in search of further weapons, as the evil creature climbed outwards along one of the spars. The spar it chose was a movable one, and turned when it was halfway out so the Skinner ended hanging upside-down like a dislodged caterpillar, its spatulate legs detatching, one after another, from the wood. The crew closed in below, eager to take it apart once it hit the deck.

Just then the Skinner lost its grip and plummeted. There was a sudden soggy snapping sound as it opened out ears grown into stunted wings. It glided out over the sea, jerking each time Anne managed to hit it with her automatic. When Boris opened up with the deck cannon, bits of the Skinner fell away, and the thing dropped ten metres before correcting. But it glided on, in a steadily descending course, and penetrated the surface of the sea a hundred metres from the ship. The crew silently watched the place where it had gone under.

It did not resurface.

Janer no longer knew how he felt about Keech, now he had seen him try to kill someone. It gave one a very different perspective when you saw someone behave like that. You realized how, on an emotional level, they amounted to more than the sum of what you had previously seen, that they had connections and commitments to a life of their own in which you played just a bit part. As for the monitor, Erlin was tending to him: sealing up his arm with a portable cell-welder, closing a wound that reached right down to the bone.

'Janer, my boy.' Ron came up to stand at the rail beside him.

Janer eyed him, this jolly hey-ho bit seeming a bit contrived. 'Not the happy ending we were aiming for,' he commented.

'No,' said Ron, 'we've just discovered some endings long overdue.'

Janer studied him more closely. 'You mean Ambel?'

Ron shook his head. 'I don't mean endings in the terminal sense—at least not for him, but for the Skinner, yes.' He paused, studying Janer's puzzled expression, then continued, 'It's not dead, you know, and we know where it'll go.'

Janer pursed his lips to keep his immediate retort reined in. He'd just seen a disembodied head sprout wings and fly right into the sea, so he wasn't going to argue about its likelihood of being alive.

Ambel had now come out on deck and was looking about himself with a guarded expression. Janer noted that some of the crew were deliberately facing away from the Old Captain, and the cold way that Keech was staring at the man.

'So what now?' Janer asked, as Ambel approached them.

'We go to the Skinner's Island,' said Ambel.

'And there we hold Convocation too,' Ron said.

Ambel nodded slowly. 'I'll be wanting to sail there as a captain, not as a prisoner. Might be the last journey I make.'

Ron nodded. 'I'll leave any who don't want to come with us on the *Ahab*, and I'll send the sail across here.'

'Thank you,' said Ambel, then, 'How you going to call it . . . the Convocation?'

Ron turned to Janer. 'Your link? Through it you can communicate with the Warden?'

'You getting this?' Janer asked the Hive mind.

After a brief buzz the mind replied, 'All of it—and very interesting it is.'

'Will you contact the Warden?'

'I can, but nothing is for free,' said the mind, which puzzled Janer until it went on.

'OK, I'll consider it,' he said, once the mind had finished. He turned to Ron and Ambel. 'What do you want of the Warden?'

'The Warden can call the Convocation for us,' said Ron. 'Some of the Captains possess transceivers, so word can be spread quickly enough.'

Janer nodded, and again listened to the dull flat buzzing, which went on for a little while before being interrupted by another voice. 'A Convocation has already been called on another matter,' said the Warden. 'It is little enough trouble to have them relocate it. I will inform Sprage immediately. The Captains should be with you at the Skinner's Island within days.'

Janer informed the two Old Captains of this latest news,

then watched them exchange a look before turning back to him.

'Why was this *first* one called?' asked Ron.

Janer waited for an explanation, but all he got from his link was the flat buzzing. He shrugged. 'Didn't say.'

Ron sighed. 'Best we get things moving.'

There were ten ships now moored beyond the reefs, with two more coming over the horizon, and yet another sweeping round from the other side of the island. Tay climbed aboard, then turned her attention to the creaking winch being used to haul up her precious cargo. That Sprage had even agreed to let her bring aboard this empty coffin-case was indicative of the fact that he had been one of Hoop's original captives. For all such men agreed that no punishment was excessive when it concerned The Eight. Sprage moved to her side as the case swung over and was lowered. It was too big to drop through into the hold, so some crewmen worked to secure it to the main deck with straps and rope.

'Old Cojan was an imaginative fella,' observed Sprage.

'He was that, and I think it was imagination that finished him in the end. He could never forget, and that's why he committed suicide,' said Tay.

'He didn't kill himself,' argued Sprage.

'No, he did not. He *did* suicide though, by allowing himself to be killed. It's the same way a lot of people in the Polity go. When they're very old they look for more and more danger, thinking this is intended to relieve them of boredom, when in truth it is to relieve them of life.'

Sprage only grunted noncommittally. Tay noticed the Old Captain was peering beyond her towards the forecabin. Turning her attention in that direction, she saw Lember carrying the Captain's rocker down to the main deck. The crewman positioned the chair by the mast, directly facing Windcheater's crocodilian head.

'I take it you've yet to cut a deal with the sail?' she asked.

'Thought I'd wait for you,' said Sprage. 'It's history.'

As Tay stared at Windcheater, she wondered if having to hold its head in that position—its neck curving back on itself—was a physical strain for the sail. She grimaced at the thought of its discomfort. Sprage's crew were now gathering round the mast. These Hoopers wore bemused expressions, but there was almost a party air about the gathering. This was something *different*; few of them had ever before encountered a sail like this.

Tay pulled out her holocorder unit, tapped instructions into it, then detached the holocorder itself and tossed it into the air. It stabilized immediately, then panned around, before Tay had it focusing in on the mast area as Sprage moved to his rocker and sat down.

'So,' said the Captain, taking out his pipe and starting to fill it. 'You told me that you do the work of five crewmen and a fabric mainsail, so should earn an equivalent percentage of the ship's profits.'

'Yes,' agreed Windcheater.

'Let me see then . . . Most captains, being the owners, take the first twenty per cent, and the rest is equally divided—in the case of this ship, amongst ten crew. So you consider yourself worth five of my crew. By my calculation that's the remaining eighty per cent divided into fifteen, of which you take five shares, one-third. Am I right?'

'Yes, I get *five* shares,' said Windcheater, but the sail now sounded a little less sure of itself.

'So you are telling me you deserve twenty-six and two-thirds per cent, which is even more than a captain's percentage? I don't think so. The sail you scared off earlier was quite prepared to work just for the meat we provided. Why should we deal with you?'

'Because you have to—just as *all* captains will have to deal with other sails in the future.'

'Ah, so you speak for all sails now?' said Sprage. He put his pipe in his mouth, flicked at his lighter for a while, then swore quietly and gave up. Taking his pipe from his mouth he studied Windcheater.

The sail went slightly cross-eyed for a moment. 'Yes . . . I will be speaking for all sails,' he explained.

Sprage frowned and shot a look at some of his crewmen.

'In that case,' he said, 'it'd be best we get the bargain

struck now, though it'll have to be ratified at this coming
Convocation. But I'm prepared to offer any sail the same
amount as is given to crew. Eight per cent of the journey's
net take, and the same contractual obligations apply.'

'What obligations?' asked Windcheater.

'Well, I think the one that mostly applies here is that if
you go AWOL you forfeit your percentage. Too often we've
been left without a sail, because the one we had got bored
and flew off.'

'Twenty-five per cent, and I want to see the contract.'

Sprage turned to Lember. 'In my desk—you'll find a
sheaf of them,' he said.

A dark-skinned and lanky individual clad in canvas
trousers and a sleeveless leather shirt, Lember shook his
head in amazement and moved off.

'I guess I could go as high as twelve per cent,' continued
Sprage.

'You're a robber and a thief!' said Windcheater, and this
statement seemed to dispel some of the crew's bemusement,
as they now felt back on familiar ground. 'I'll not go below
twenty, and you know you're getting a good deal.'

'Twenty—are you mad?' Sprage asked. He flicked hard at
his lighter, but still had no luck. Tay took pity on him and
reached into her belt pouch, removed a burnished metal
cylinder and passed it to him. He took the object, studied it
for a moment, then held it over the bowl of his pipe. When he
pressed the button on one end, red light flickered and his tobacco was soon glowing. He puffed out a cloud of smoke and
grinned with delight, and then, holding up the cylinder, he
looked questioningly at Tay. She waved for him to keep it.

With satisfaction, he dropped the laser igniter into his top
pocket and returned his attention to the sail. 'Perhaps I can
go as high as fifteen per cent,' he suggested.

'How would all your ships fare if not a single sail came in
to land on them?' asked Windcheater.

Sprage eyed him, but since getting his pipe lit, seemed
less inclined to argue.

'All right, seventeen per cent.'

'Eighteen and we have a deal,' said Windcheater.

Sprage was silent for a moment. Then he nodded.

Just then, Lember returned with a printed contract and a pen. He held these out midway between Sprage and the sail, then seemed at a loss as to what to do next. Sprage grabbed both pen and contract and scribbled in his signature and the percentage.

'You have an aug, so I presume you can read. But can you write, sail?' said the Captain.

In reply, Windcheater reared up in the spars and turned himself so that his foot claws came down to rest on one of them. He then stooped down, extending one long wing, and wriggling the two spider claws at its last joint.

Sprage handed the contract and the pen to Lember, who then handed these two items up to Windcheater. The sail raised the contract up to his demonic eyes and squinted at it.

Tay almost burst out laughing when it held the cap of the pen in its mouth and chewed on it gently. Sprage turned to regard her. 'History in the making,' he said.

'It is that,' she replied distractedly—another two ships had appeared on the horizon. Returning her attention to the sail, she watched it signing the contract. Once that was done, the sail put contract and pen in its mouth, then up-ended itself on the mast, spread huge its wings, and reassumed its normal working position before depositing pen and contract in Sprage's lap. The sail had signed its name in block capitals so neat they were almost indistinguishable from the print of the contract.

'But of course,' said Sprage, 'that percentage is of the trip you happen to have signed on for.'

'Yes,' said Windcheater. 'And I do realize *this* trip is without profit. I am just establishing a precedent.'

Sprage folded the contract and dropped it into his top pocket. He nodded slowly. 'You're a wise sail.'

Windcheater tilted his head for a moment and his eyes crossed. When they uncrossed, he said, 'The Warden tells me that this trip is not yet over.'

Sprage paused in his rising from his chair and stared at the sail questioningly.

The sail went on, 'Captain Ron has called the Convocation to the Skinner's Island. The Skinner is out and it has been revealed that Captain Ambel is in fact Gosk Balem.'

There came exclamations of surprise from the crew—but Tay was curious to note how Sprage displayed no surprise at all.

'That old chestnut,' he muttered.

Disdaining assistance, Keech clambered aboard the *Ahab* and moved quickly to his hover scooter. One-armed, he began to loosen the ties holding it to the deck. His other arm, though cell-welded and now without gashes, was still bruised and painful. Ron, as soon as he was aboard, walked up to the sail. Behind him, Boris, Goss—and other crew who had not wanted to be part of the coming quest—climbed aboard.

'There's fresh meat over there on the *Treader*. Will you go over there for us?'

'Might,' said the sail.

'How can I persuade you?' asked Ron.

'Boxy meat. I *like* boxy meat,' said the sail.

'Well, we can always get that,' said Ron.

The Captain had heard of the sail called Windcheater, but not how he behaved. Had he heard, he would have been unsurprised, Windcheater was unique, but not that unique. Ron turned from the sail as it furled itself and climbed to the top of the mast, and faced Roach, who had snuck up beside him.

'What's happenin', Cap'n,' said the little man.

Ron gazed down at him, then at the juniors who gathered beyond him.

'Ambel *is* Gosk Balem, and the Skinner's out, and we're going to the Skinner's Island to kill it—and also have a Convocation to decide whether or not we throw Ambel into a fire.'

Roach squinted at him. 'No, but really, what's happenin'?'

Ron gestured to Goss and Boris. 'They'll tell you all you need to know. Now, can I trust you, Roach?'

'Of course,' said Roach, sticking his chest out.

Ron eyed the little man dubiously before going on. 'OK, I want you to stay here. As soon as another sail comes along, I want you to follow on as fast as you can. No stopping for meets, and no going after turbul. This is important,' he emphasized.

'Aye, Captain,' said Roach trying, but not managing, to not look sneaky.

Ron then turned to Boris. The crewman was sombre, and Goss, who walked at his side, looked annoyed.

'You might think different when you hear what he's got to say.'

'No,' said Boris. 'Gosk Balem ran the furnace. My dad went to the furnace.'

Ron nodded then stood, staring pensively out to sea, with his thumbs in his belt, as if unsure of what to say next. After a moment, he freed one thumb and pointed.

'That,' he said, 'is one very persistent molly carp.'

They all gazed out at the humped shape in the sea—between themselves and the nearest atoll.

'It crossed with us earlier. Had a go at a leech we got. Helped us get the Captain back in when he fell in the sea,' said Boris. 'Probably head back to its island in the night—unless there's good hunting here.'

'Helped Ambel in?' asked Ron.

'Well, we think so,' said Boris.

Ron turned to Roach. 'Keep an eye on it. You never know what one of them might do. I'll be off.' He turned and walked over to Keech.

'Ready?' he asked.

Keech nodded and climbed on to his scooter, Ron climbing on behind him. Keech lifted the scooter from the deck and, one-handed, guided it out over the sea to the *Treader*, which was already turning into the wind.

'You'll hold to your promise?' Ron asked as Keech slowed the scooter over Ambel's ship.

'I'll not kill him yet,' said Keech.

'You *may* change your mind when you hear what he has to say,' said Ron.

'I doubt it,' said Keech.

With the wind blowing through her hair, Rebecca Frisk stared out over the waves, and smiled happily. Come the morning, she would have the pleasure of slowly cutting Sable Keech into pieces and feeding those pieces to the frog whelks. This pleasure would be somewhat marred by the fact that Keech had long been beyond pain—but there would always be others on hand to satisfy that need. She hoped Keech had a partner to whom he had some meaningful attachment. If not, then the crew of his ship would have to do. She smiled again as she contemplated what she might do. The disadvantage in torturing a Hooper was their high resistance to pain: it took huge injury to cause sufficient pain to elicit a scream or two from them, but the advantage was that Hoopers could survive huge injury. Burning was the best method of torture. Over a slow fire, a Hooper could last for days.

Frisk started to mentally recount the many slow fires she and Jay had lit, but her pleasurable contemplation was interrupted.

'All stop! All stop!' Svan yelled from the front rail. 'Hard to port!' She shot past Frisk to Drum, whose hand was on the control lever, and tried to pull that lever over. With interest, Frisk studied Drum, as Svan tugged at the Captain's hand. There was a sudden rending crash and the ship shuddered to a halt. Tors yelled as he flew over the front rail. Frisk and Svan fell and slid across the deck to the side as the ship tilted.

Something huge thrashed in the sea in front of the ship. The vessel slewed sideways, and Frisk heard the sound of many hard, scuttling feet. Tors began to scream.

'Too fucking fast!' Svan yelled, then looked up as a number of hard disk-shaped creatures leapt up on to the rail, red dots of eyes skating round their rims.

'Prill!' Frisk shouted from where she lay. Then laughed, drew her pulse-gun, and began shooting down at them. Svan rose to a crouch and drew her own weapon. After their volley of fire cleared the rail, she leapt to the edge of the cabin's desk and looked down to one side. Below her, oozing past the side of the ship, a great glistening body heaved, and over its surface swarmed eager prill. On that slick surface, a vaguely human shape thrashed and screamed as the prill tore it apart. One creature made a run that uncoiled intestine. Another three were fighting over an arm that swiftly detached.

'Tors,' Svan whispered, then began firing again, but within a moment she did not know where to aim as Tors came apart and the prill fed on pieces of him all over the back of the giant leech. The ship lurched again as the leech itself began ponderously to pull away.

'We're flooding!' Shib yelled up from the lower deck.

Svan, hearing the panic in his voice, knew he was losing control since that damned whelk creature had taken his fingers off. She went over to Frisk and dragged the woman to her feet. 'We have to use the AG,' she said.

Frisk laughed in her face, and Svan slapped her. Abruptly Frisk became sober. She backhanded Svan across the chest so Svan crashed through the back rail to the lower deck. There she lay stunned. *Augmentation?* She wondered, as Shib got to her side and helped her sit up. She leant against him and struggled for breath.

'We're sinking,' said Shib, sweating. He had his handgun drawn.

'Get to the motor. Turn on the AG. We've no choice now,' Svan gasped.

Shib nodded and ran for the hatch.

Svan tried to stand, but for a moment could not manage. Beside her hand, the deck suddenly burst into flaming splinters. She looked up at Frisk, standing in the gap of the broken rail and waited for the killing shot. It didn't come. More prill swarmed up on to the deck and instead Frisk started shooting at them.

'Fucking lunatic,' muttered Svan, and dragged herself towards the hatch. Once she reached it, she fell through, catching a rung with her hand so she turned and came down on her feet on the tilted floor below.

Shib was waiting for her. 'Tors,' he said.

'Dead,' she replied.

He nodded and looked up towards where they could hear Frisk still blasting away at prill.

'She'll have to pay,' he said. He held up his hand with its missing fingers. 'And for this too.'

'Later,' said Svan. 'Four thousand grams of Prador diamond-slate, remember? We complete the contract, collect our payment, then we burn her.'

Shib nodded, but his attention was wandering.

Svan peered down towards the bows of the ship, where water gushed in and timbers were groaning.

'Let's get that AG going,' she said, and the two of them headed up the sloping deck to the motor. Once they reached it, Shib popped the casing, and Svan flipped down a control panel underneath. She hesitated over the controls.

'There's no other way,' urged Shib.

'Might bring the Warden down on us, and we don't need that,' replied Svan.

'Better that than swimming in this sea,' said Shib.

Svan nodded and punched a control. The ship juddered, and spillover from the field made her face tingle. The motor now produced an AC hum and the creaking and groaning of the ship increased. Svan watched the fixings bolted into the keel of the ship. If those tore free, the motor would smash through the deck above, before it righted itself. But they wouldn't tear free: she had done them herself. When the ship heaved again, she regained her balance before making further adjustments to the motor controls. The field tilted, and now the ship was coming level, pivoting at the point of those fixings, which loaded them even more. The gushing of water into the bows ceased for a moment, and then went into reverse. Svan made a final adjustment to the control panel, then closed the cowling over the motor. She stood up as the flooring finally levelled out.

'I've set it to lift us clear by about a metre,' she said. 'Let's go and look at the damage.'

She pulled her weapon and walked to the bows, Shib following a pace behind her, and it irritated her that his breathing sounded heavy with fear. He'd never seemed xenophobic before. Yes, it paid to be cautious around the lethal fauna of this planet, yet the creatures here were nothing compared to an armed human—and he had dealt with plenty of *them*.

Frisk reluctantly holstered her weapon when it seemed she had disposed of the last of the prill. The ship was level now and the water quite a way below the rail. She stared at it for a long while before she realized what had happened. She thought about why it had happened—thought about some of her decisions over the last few days. She cringed inwardly and pressed a hand to her throat.

'What's happening to me, Jay?' she asked.

But Jay wasn't there to answer her, nor to back her up, and sometimes she just did not understand why this was so. They had been happy on that Prador world hadn't they? Why had he felt it necessary to leave, in the end? Why had he been so angry with her? Yes, sometimes she had behaved a bit irrationally, and of course that was to be expected: you couldn't live together for as long as they had without sometimes encountering something like that. It had been her idea that maybe their crimes could be forgiven and that they could return to Earth which had thrown him into his rage. In retrospect she realized that had been a silly idea, but his reaction had been excessive.

She remembered him sneering at her. *'Another excellent idea from your superior mind, dear. I would put that on a par with your one about opening a gallery on Circe. Do you think for one second that ECS has stopped searching for us? Do you think for one second we can breeze easily through the Polity avoiding both capture and getting mind-wiped?'*

'But Jay, darling—'

'I used to enjoy your little whims and sudden enthusiasms. I think I ceased to enjoy them the moment you ceased to be you. Why did you do it? Why the hell did you do it?'

'Jay darling.'

'Don't touch me. You disgust me.'

There was a taste like iron in her mouth that she tried fruitlessly to spit away. That she had no longer possessed the body he loved, she understood. But, in the end, it had been because she no longer had the same mind. She gave a dry laugh and squeezed tears from her eyes, but, deep inside she knew she was going insane. Because she'd lived too long in a body not her own, she'd seen and caused too much horror, she'd lived too long amongst aliens, and because—in the end—she'd lived too long.

* * *

Janer stepped over the wreckage of the door and into the
cabin. He reached down and righted the chair to which they
had tied Keech, then carried it to the desk positioned below
the brass-rimmed portal. He sat down and studied the two
sealed flasks contained in a rack clamped to the edge of the
desk. Each flask contained a number of red rhomboidal
crystals resting under a clear fluid. He removed a bung from
one of these and sniffed at the pungency released. It reminded him somewhat of old coffee, perhaps with a background of something putrefying.

'Just *one* crystal?' he said.

'*Yes,*' said the mind, and Janer wondered if he was imagining a touch of avidity in its voice.

'I suppose that if I don't get it for you, you'll get hold of it
some other way.'

'*Yes,*' said the mind.

'I'm not going to do this,' said Janer, reinserting the bung
and tapping it home with his forefinger.

'*Why not?*'

'Because I've worked out what you're up to. "Get me a
sample of that unusual substance in Ambel's cabin." Do you
think I'm entirely stupid?'

'*I do not.*'

Janer sat back in his chair. 'Why do you want to go this
route?' he asked.

'*Power,*' explained the mind. '*It was tried before using cu-
rare. That failed, and the hornets in question were wiped out.
The mind concerned still hasn't regained its consciousness.
But it is the way.*'

'The same could happen again,' said Janer.

'*Not here,*' said the mind. '*This is a primitive society. It
will work.*'

'Well, not with my help,' said Janer. He stood, pulled the
small jewelled Hive link from his ear, and dropped it in his
pocket. He gazed at the two flasks of fluid out of which pure
sprine was crystallizing, shook his head, then left the cabin.
Once outside, he climbed up to the cabin-deck—to go and
listen to a story.

* * *

'Captain Sprage,' said Ambel looking round at Ron. Ron nodded from where he leant against the rail. Ambel turned to face the sea again. Gathered behind him, on the main deck, were Keech and Erlin, Forlam, Pland, Peck and Anne, and behind them, the rest of the crew. Even the sail had extended its neck so it could turn an ear to what Ambel said.

'It was him named me Ambel, and I've always thought he knew.'

'We should ask him.'

'Yes, we should—now. I've always been afraid to before.'

'Is there a point to this?' asked Keech flatly. He hadn't taken his eyes off Ambel since mounting the cabin-deck. His right hand rested on the butt of his pulse-gun. In his left hand he held three steel spheres.

Ambel stared at him. 'Gosk Balem was a slave, then he was slave master. He became like Hoop and his crew because that was the only way to survive here then. Slaves were regularly cored, and had their cored brains and spinal columns thrown into a furnace. It was just like Hoop to put Balem in charge of that furnace,' he said.

'You should know,' said Keech, bitterly.

'But I don't,' said Ambel.

'Explain,' said Keech.

'You came here with the ECS force that freed those slaves that hadn't already been cored. But you weren't as prepared as you ought to have been, and Hoop and all his crew escaped. So Hoop, Frisk, Rimsc, the Talsca twins and Grenant escaped off-world. They left Gosk Balem behind to face the consequences of his actions. The surviving slaves hunted him for a hundred years, and he was finally caught out here, by Sprage and Francis Cojan, who later went on to form The Friends of Cojan, whom you yourself knew.'

'I knew Cojan himself,' said Keech. 'He got hold of the Talsca twins and boiled them alive.'

'I heard that,' said Ron. 'What happened to him, then?'

Keech turned and stared at Ron.

'Batian mercenaries got him with a thermite bomb,' he said. But only because he allowed it. He was tired of the run-

ning and tired of the killing. He told me this only days before his death, when he transferred all his funds to one of my
accounts.'

Ambel nodded then continued. 'When Gosk Balem was
caught, he first Convocation was called. All the slaves were
by then captains of their own ships, and the population here
was swelled by their children, and by off-worlders coming
through the gate. The Convocation decided unanimously to
carry out the ECS sentence of death on Balem. They didn't
have sprine then, and at Cojan's instigation they decided
against burning. They decided instead to throw him to the
leeches that were swarming at the time. On the dawn of the
following day, they took him to the rail of Sprage's ship and
threw him into the sea. He screamed for four hours before he
went under. The Convocation was broken and the Captains
went their separate ways, assuming Balem was dead.'

'Evidently he wasn't,' said Erlin. Janer studied her, wondering what she *now* thought of her Captain.

Without turning round Ambel said, 'No, Erlin, he wasn't.
The durability of the older Hoopers was something not fully
understood then. The leeches fed on Balem's skin and outer
flesh, whittling him down until he was a stripped fish. He was
just like a turbul or a boxy—only a turbul or a boxy that can
experience pain. Pain of that intensity drove him insane. I
have no doubt he wanted to die, yet having the fibres in him,
his body could not die. He fed, on boxies, turbul, whatever. He
regrew flesh, nerves, skin—regrew them, and had them eaten
off him again and again. This went on for five years. In that
time he died in the only way he could die. His mind died.'

Ambel gazed around at them with a haunted expression.
'My first memory is of Captain Sprage standing over me and
asking, "Jesus, is he alive?" I'd been harpooned and hauled
out of the sea. I was almost skinless and had very little muscle. In places I was right down to the bone. I was told later
that I then had a leech mouth rather than a tongue, and that I
took a chunk out of Sprage's forearm. They tied me to the
mast and fed me mashed Rhinoworm steaks and Dome-
grown corn. The leech mouth slowly turned back into a
tongue. It took only ten minutes or so before my lungs

readapted to taking oxygen out of the air rather than out of the sea, but it was a couple of days before I was able to scream again. I screamed for a while, but even that uses too much energy, and apparently I stopped after an hour or so. It was two weeks before I'd regrown all my skin and muscle. Sprage then asked who I was and I had no reply for him. I didn't even have language—I had nothing. I was an infant who had to be taught not to shit on the deck. Sprage taught me how to speak, taught me how to read, how to learn. I was on his ship for twenty years before I got some intimation of who I might once have been.'

The only sound now was that of the waves slopping against the side of the ship. Peck, Anne and Pland could not look at their Captain; Forlam's expression displayed a strange avidity; Ron was without expression.

Keech turned to Erlin, who was looking slightly sick. 'Is this possible?' he asked.

Erlin nodded.

'A Hooper of Ambel's age can't die unless most of his major organs are destroyed simultaneously. The leech mouth was the result of lack of Earth food. It's due to the Spatterjay virus. Not only does it infest the body, but also it reprograms the DNA of that body for optimum survival—and keeps on reprogramming. Adrift in the sea, with his muscles eaten away, he needed *some* way of feeding. The virus grew him a leech mouth so he could attach to other animals that got close to him.' Erlin shook her head and stared down at the deck.

'What about his mind?' asked Keech.

Erlin said, 'His nerves would have been regrowing all the time. He would have been suffering varying degrees of agony all the time that was happening to him. It would work in much the same way as the overload employed in a mind-wipe, though that's done by shooting a full sensory overload down every nerve channel, and takes only about ten seconds.'

Keech studied Ambel. 'Then you're like the Talsca twins and Rimsc,' he said, and pocketed the three spheres he had been holding.

Ambel returned his stare and waited.

Keech said, 'The sentence pronounced upon you has been executed.'

'Does this mean you won't try to kill me?' Ambel asked.

Keech stared at him expressionlessly. 'Probably not.' He turned and left the cabin-deck.

One after another, the blanks were now walking away from the gathered Prador towards the heavy-lifter. One of the Warden's fellow AIs was ruminating over the huge possibilities now, perhaps, opening for such corporations as Cybercorp, and wondering if this had been the sector AI's purpose in coming to the Prador home world in the form of a Golem—Cybercorp could certainly provide the Prador with more efficient hands than those of the human blanks, and perhaps commence trade in Golem and robot technologies. Another AI was observing that trade in such technologies would give AI a foothold in the Prador Third Kingdom, so that it would not be long until it was absorbed into the Polity. The Warden of Spatterjay acknowledged all this and shifted its attention away from the sector AI Golem and to the interior of the heavy-lifter.

The blanks' control codes were being switched over to the control of subminds that had been briefly initiated by the sector AI, then dowloaded into the blanks' thrall units, and these minds were moving them into cold-storage lockers on the lifter. As each one went into storage, sampling drones the size of flies took snips from their skin, which were instantly taken for analysis.

Joseph Best, ECS monitor, lost in action . . . Erickson Sewel, medical orderly on the obliterated Hounger Station, lost in action . . . Seben Daes, housewife, disappeared . . . and so the list scrolled on and on, as DNA was matched to ancient records and those records then completed and closed down.

The Warden now pulled further back, to get an overview of yet more heavy-lifters landing and taking off on other Prador worlds, as the thousands of essentially dead were taken away for respectful disposal: a transmigration of the undead—a ghoulish chapter that should have closed the Prador war, though that war had ended long ago, but did not.

The final closing words, the Warden knew, would be written on Spatterjay. And so it continued to watch and send information packages back there—to itself.

13

The surviving male glister, having come within a whisker of falling prey to one of the deep-sea denizens, instinctively headed for the shallows where such creatures never came, and where it might digest in peace the hundredweight of turbul flesh now cramming its gut. It was this last huge meal, putting excess pressure on the network of blood-vessels lacing the creature's body, which forced one such vein up against a sharp fragment of its own damaged shell. This circumstance would not have proved so unfortunate had the creature stayed in the depths; but the drop in external pressure, as the glister rose to the surface, caused the vein to expand, sawing against the shell as it swam. The vein burst just as the creature reached the surface near a small isolated atoll. The injury, in itself, was a minor problem for the glister and would have healed in a few days, had not the leakage of blood left a trail for the molly carp resident close by. Feeling a surge in the water behind it, and tasting molly carp—a taste that elicited only terror in it—the glister accelerated away from the shallows towards open sea, though it was sluggish after its gorging. Swimming over a declivity into deeper water, the glister experienced something like relief, assuming that the carp pursuing it from the shallows would be unlikely to pursue it any further. But when it flipped its tail to dive, the tail remained rigid and its body moved up and down instead. Sculling in panic with its flat legs it found itself rising inexorably out of the sea. As the carp somersaulted it into the air, its last view in this world was of a large mouth gaping where it would rather have seen ocean.

The adolescent Vrell mistook the grinding of Ebulan's mandibles as an indication of hunger, and nearly lost a leg trying to feed the councillor a nicely decayed hock of human meat. Sliding on his AG, Ebulan slammed Vrell up against the weed-pocked stone-effect wall.

'An adult Prador initiates and manipulates. But what does an adult Prador *not* do?' Ebulan asked.

'An adult Prador does not physically intervene, Father,' Vrell signed.

Ebulan again slammed the child against the wall, putting a crack in Vrell's carapace as a reminder, then backed off to let the child escape. As the adolescent scuttled away, Ebulan accessed Speaker's thrall unit and looked through the blank human's eyes. Prill everywhere, water rushing in through a hole in the hull, screams and shots; chaos. Stupid human.

It had all been so simple: send Frisk off in pursuit of Keech, let it be known there that she was on-planet and, using adulterated eonides, destabilize her nerve linkages with her host body so that she operated below efficiency. He had predicted how she would quickly be captured and a Convocation called. In such circumstances all the Old Captains on-planet, as well as Keech and Frisk, would be assembled in one place. And in that same place, he would have a Prador multipurpose motor with totally improbable antimatter power supply—and that with a little tab of planar explosive stuck to the side. Ebulan ground his mandibles again and quickly sent four of his more heavily armed blanks hurrying off to his shuttle.

Then he summoned Vrell again. The adolescent edged his way into the chamber and waited, shivering, for instructions.

'Things have not entirely gone against us. We have enjoyed some of what the humans call "luck". A Convocation has been called, so we must be sure that the motor gets to its location.'

'What about Frisk . . . Father?' asked Vrell.

'The motor is of main importance. Frisk we must retain in case this Convocation is broken off and we need some method to set up another.'

'I understand, Father.'

'You will go along with the four blanks to assure the fruition of my plan.'

Vrell suddenly stopped twitching and went very still.

Ebulan went on, 'Take the ship to that Convocation. Go along with Frisk's plans unless they begin to interfere with this purpose. As it is primary. I do not expect you to return.'

'I understand, Father.'

The chamber was a thirty-metre sphere of mirrored glass, with a floor of black glass. The runcible itself stood at the centre of this, mounted on a stepped pedestal. Its apparent similarity to some kind of altar had long been the subject of holodrama and VR: gleaming ten-metre-long incurving bull's horns jutted up from the pedestal, and between them shimmered the cusp of a Skaidon warp: an interface with the supernal. When asked why this was so, most AIs gave equivocal replies. The Warden's reply to this question was uncompromisingly direct. 'What design do you expect, from someone who calls a tachyon "pea-green"?' it always retorted.

Through the cusp now stepped four people. The Warden noted the presence of an ophid-adapted human, two women dressed in the utile garb of seasoned travellers, and a free Golem android. Tourists, doubtless. No ECS monitors as yet, though it expected them at any time. It flashed its attention down to the planet's surface and took in multiple views through its thousands of eyes positioned there, noting nothing more untoward than a fight between a couple of Hoopers, then returned all its attention to the eye mounted on one of its satellites.

The AG reading was coming from a ship, and this was all it could ascertain through the thick cloud layers. It wasn't a registered antigravity device, of this the Warden was certain, and it wasn't one of the many unregistered ones it already knew about. It took the AI less than a second to interpolate the likely source of the device. It opened its 'anomalous' file and inspected more closely what it found there—focusing on the instant before the antimatter explosion. The Prador ship had passed through the cloud layer, and been effectively hidden by the ionized gas it left behind it. It seemed entirely likely that the explosion had been a subterfuge covering more than just the jettisoning of an escape pod. Something more significant than Frisk's arrival here had occurred. As a precaution, the AI sent a coded underspace transmission of activation to a satellite on the other side of Spatterjay.

That satellite, a polished cylinder twenty metres long, jetted out two blades of fusion flame and began to change its orientation. Inside it, systems came alive, and ten matt-black objects began to draw energy. The Warden now turned its attention elsewhere.

SM12 and SM13 exploded from the surface of the sea and shot into the air.

'I don't know who is aboard that sailing ship, but it seems unlikely that whatever is going on down there is unconnected to the arrival of that Prador vessel. You, Thirteen, have chameleon-ware—though I don't remember approving it. I want you to get on board and report everything you see. Twelve, I want you scanning the entire area for anomalous signals—anything,' the Warden ordered.

'It might not be Frisk. If it is her, though, there's no way she could have got that far merely in an escape pod used as a submersible,' said Twelve.

'I am aware of that,' said the Warden. 'If it is her, then it seems likely she has had more assistance than that of a handful of Batians. If it is not her, then you can return to your search for her, or work from that point, should there be a connection. Twelve, I want you to confine your scans to very low power, as I do not want you detected. Thirteen, you will transmit direct to me via underspace. For now we just watch and learn.'

'You got it, boss,' said Twelve as the Warden withdrew.

'Creep,' muttered Thirteen as they sped on through the sky.

Prill had entered through the gaping hole in the ship's bows. Bits of their bodies lay smoking round that hole, though some of them had made it further in before being hit. A legless prill lay on a coiled pile of rope, its red eyes still shooting round and about its carapace. Svan thought how like an adult Prador it seemed, and equally vicious. She looked to where Speaker sat against a bulkhead, a pulsed-energy weapon on her lap and a cord round her right upper arm, above where the limb had been cut away.

'Need any help?' asked Svan, forgetting herself. She glanced at Shib, who was staring at the legless prill with a horrified fascination.

'It is unfortunate that this unit has lost its arm,' said Speaker, and Svan stared back at her, reminded that this Speaker was not actually a human being; she was just a tool of the Prador in its ship; its eyes and ears, and . . . hand. She shook her head in annoyance, then ignored the blank while she inspected the damage to the ship.

'Do we have enough equipment to deal with this?' she asked Shib, gesturing at the breached hull.

'I'll rig a couple of sheets—inside and out—and fill the gap between with crash foam. Shouldn't be a problem,' he said, still staring at the prill.

'There is a more immediate problem,' said Speaker. Both the Batians turned and looked at her as she removed the cord and dropped it, then stood, holstering her weapon. She continued, 'Rebecca Frisk has been going into deep nerve conflict with her body for some days now. She carries the drug to alleviate this problem, but since arriving here has not taken it with any regularity. The nerve conflict is therefore causing in her a psychosis with schizophrenic episodes.'

'Pan-fried AI,' said Shib, turning from the prill. Svan was glad to see that he seemed to have himself under better control now.

'What are we supposed to do?' asked Svan.

'She must start to take the drug regularly. If she does not she could become a further danger to this ship. Also, while she is acting like this, you will find it difficult to effect repairs, and we do not want it running on AG for much longer.'

'You go and tell her to take her damned drug,' said Svan. 'She just took a shot at me out there.'

'It should be possible for you to bring her down with a high-energy stun setting,' said Speaker.

'Right,' said Shib, rolling his eyes.

'I repeat, if you do not do this, she will become a danger to herself as well as to others.'

'Tell me about it,' said Svan, turning back to inspect the hole in the hull.

'Also, if you do not do it,' said Speaker, 'you will have to find some alternative method of transport from this planet.'

The Batians stared at her.

'What's your interest, Prador?' asked Svan. 'Her I can understand. She wants Keech off her back. She wants him dead. What's in it for you?'

'Friendship,' said Speaker.

'Answer the question then I'll do what you ask,' said Svan with contempt.

'You don't believe I do this for friendship's sake?' asked the Prador through its Speaker.

'No, I don't.'

'Very well—politics. Our Kingdom is slowly but certainly developing closer ties with the Polity. As these ties grow, I become ever more of an outcast in my own society because of my connections with the trade in cored humans. I have come here to sever all such connections.'

'But Frisk is one of those connections,' said Svan.

'I do have a certain affection for her,' said Speaker.

'Keech is also one,' said Shib, 'but surely you could have left him to her, to us.'

'There are others too,' said the distant Prador.

'Who?' asked Svan.

'Anyone who was once a slave here when the coring operation was being run. They are still here, many of them. They are people like Drum: the Old Captains.'

'All witnesses,' said Svan, nodding in understanding. Shib eyed her questioningly. She explained, 'It's the nature of Prador politics. Since anything written or recorded can be falsified, only the verbal statements of witnesses are given any credence in law. It basically works out that you can get away with anything so long as you leave no living witnesses to it.'

'In this you are correct,' said Speaker.

'Be difficult tracking them all down,' said Shib.

'For really important events, all the Old Captains come together in Convocation. The presence of Hoop's mistress here would certainly bring about such a Convocation.'

'Then what?' said Shib.

'They are very primitively armed here.'

'Point taken,' said Shib.

Svan pulled her stun gun from her belt and altered the setting. Shib watched her for a moment, then did the same with his own.

'Let's go put our leader to sleepy-byes then,' she said.

Up on deck Frisk was still blasting away at this and that— and giggling at things only she could see.

'I can't even begin to imagine such suffering as he experienced,' said Janer, watching the sun descend into dull sunset.

'None of us can,' replied Erlin. 'It's beyond even *his* understanding—which is why his mind died, why he became Ambel.'

'I'm confused,' said Janer.

'That's not surprising,' said Erlin. 'It's a very long and involved story.'

'No, not about that—just about a couple of other points,' he said.

Erlin watched him and waited.

He continued: 'I know Hoopers have a very high pain threshold, but obviously they *do* suffer pain.' He nodded towards Forlam who stood at the stern, near Keech. 'I saw him get his guts pulled out in a contest, yet that was an arranged bout he got into willingly. Was it just for the money, or what?'

'Some of them do have a strange relationship with pain,' said Erlin. She seemed uncomfortable with the knowledge.

'What kind of relationship?'

'Some of the neural pathways get mixed up. Severe injury can cause it. They get hurt time and time again, then find themselves going on to put themselves in more danger. It's unconscious, mostly, though some of them begin to realize what they want.'

'They *want* pain?'

'It makes them feel alive.'

Janer shook his head and stared down at the sea.

'Maybe that's why they want to keep on pursuing that dreadful thing,' he said.

'Maybe, but it is something that has to be done. It must be killed.'

'Why?' asked Janer, surprised at her vehemence.

'The head will go to where its body is, and its body is on the Skinner's Island. They intend to go there and destroy the Skinner completely.'

'This Skinner is Jay Hoop, then? You know I never believed that story until now.' He paused for a moment. 'And now it's . . . heading for its own body—?' He allowed himself a weak grin at the unintended pun.

'To rejoin it, yes. And that cannot be allowed to happen.'

Janer studied her for a long moment. He felt as if someone must have shoved him into one of the weirder type of VR scenarios. Every time he thought he had a handle on the situation, it just got stranger.

'What about this Convocation?' he asked, trying instead for a discussion of the prosaic.

'The Old Captains will meet and sit in judgement on Ambel. They might decide to throw him back into the sea—or into a fire. But they might decide he's suffered enough.'

Janer studied her again.

'How do you feel about it?'

'I don't know,' said Erlin.

Janer nodded and toyed with the Hive link in his pocket. He did not know how he himself felt either. Ambel he considered a rival for Erlin's affections but, like Ron, with his slow, huge power and calm assurance, the Old Captain was difficult to dislike.

Frisk playfully burnt holes in the deck as Svan dived for cover. The shot Svan returned splayed mini-lightning along a rail but caused no damage. Her second shot hit Drum, and the Captain coughed as if slapped across the chest, but he remained by the helm as steady as a monolith.

'Come out, come out, wherever you are!' shouted Frisk,

and burnt a couple of holes through the captive sail. The sail's wings hung flaccid, but its stapled neck quivered.

'Frisk!'

Frisk turned just in time to see Shib straddling the port rail. The pulse hit her in the chest and knocked her backwards. She tried to raise her weapon, but a second and a third pulse struck her. She staggered away while Shib made an adjustment on his weapon. Then the fourth pulse slammed her back against Drum, and blackness engulfed her.

'Got her,' yelled Shib, and went to stand over the woman. Svan came out of hiding and climbed on to the cabin-deck. She glared down at Frisk.

'What setting?' she asked.

'Six,' Shib replied. 'Hooper.'

'No sign of leech marks on her though,' said Svan, 'but maybe that doesn't mean anything. We'll have to remember that.' They both turned as Speaker made her way precariously up the ladder.

'What now?' Svan asked.

'Repair the damage to this ship. Using AG will bring us unwanted attention. Then we wait for my shuttle,' said Speaker.

'One thing,' said Svan as Speaker turned to go. 'To bring about this Convocation, you spoke of the Captains needing to know that Frisk is here. Our pursuit of Keech brings you no closer to that goal.'

'The Captains do know that she is here, but even that is now unnecessary since a Convocation has been called at our next destination. It would seem Rebecca is not the only remaining member of Hoop's crew here, beside himself. Gosk Balem has been found, alive.'

'Hoop is here as well?' said Shib, but Speaker descended to the lower deck without replying, then quickly returned to the hold.

'I'll watch her,' said Svan, nodding at the prostrate Frisk. 'You go and get on with the repairs.'

Shib glanced down at his mutilated hand. After a moment, he stepped closer to Frisk and trod his heel down hard on her face. He was about to do so again when Svan pulled him back.

'I wouldn't bother,' she said. 'If she's Hooper, she probably won't even notice when she wakes. Now, as I said, the repairs?'

Shib stared at her hard.

'She'll pay,' he snarled.

'Repairs,' Svan repeated, her voice flat.

Shib retained enough survival instinct to recognize her tone, and moved off to do as he was told. With her hand resting on the butt of her pulse-gun, Svan watched him go. Unnoticed by the both of them, a seahorse the colour and texture of the sky, had drifted to the top of the main mast and settled there. It immediately changed appearance to the colour and texture of the mast, providing it with a baroque and somewhat odd adornment. The sail opened one crusted eyelid to expose a dark red pupil, then quickly closed it. Drum's glance flicked impassively to the top of the mast, then down to his hands on the helm. With painful slowness, he lifted one finger from the wood, then returned it. At the back of his neck, a hole had appeared, exposing the dull metal of the spider thrall.

With a fair wind in all her sails, the *Treader* moved out of the atolls and into Deep-sea. The sun set in a silent viridian explosion and thick clouds hauled a deeper darkness up behind the ship. Keech shivered at the rail, testing the fingers of his injured arm.

'Hurt?' asked Forlam with undue interest.

Keech nodded, closing his hand into a fist. He wanted to be fully functional for what was yet to come. He hadn't decided about Ambel yet—but if his eventual decision went against that of this Convocation, he wanted to be ready and able to carry it through.

'The Skinner gives pain,' said Forlam.

'You don't say,' replied Keech.

Forlam went on, 'They say it caught Peck, stripped him completely of his skin and ran around waving it about like a set of overalls. Peck's never been the same since.'

Keech didn't suppose he would be. He also wondered about the reason for Forlam's intense interest.

'Why was it allowed to live for so long? Didn't you all know about it?' he asked.

Behind and to either side of the ship, the sea reflected a yellow glow as Peck and Pland moved about lighting lanterns. Keech glanced around the ship. Anne was standing by the mast, cutting up rhinoworm meat for the sail. Janer and Erlin had gone below, and Keech wondered if they would be sharing a bunk this night. From the cabin-deck could be heard the low murmur of Ambel and Ron in conversation. Ambel was at the helm: his huge bulky shape silhouetted against the sunset. When Ron moved up beside him there was little to distinguish between them.

'Not everyone knew about it. Kept it to 'emselves' said Forlam, as if bemoaning that the location of some treasure had been withheld from him.

'Who did, then?' asked Keech.

'The Old Captains mostly.'

'That still doesn't tell me why it was allowed to live.'

'I guess it don't.'

'Balem knew and he did nothing,' said Keech, testing.

Forlam appeared distracted as he said, 'Its final death— maybe a Convocation decision, not just Captain Ambel's.'

Keech let that ride: there had been no Convocation decision to pursue and kill the Skinner *this time*.

'How many Captains?' he asked.

'Twenty-three at last count,' Forlam quickly replied, lost now in some strange abstraction—his eyes wide on the dark.

'And your Ambel is one of the most respected of them.'

'Yes, he is that.'

Keech nodded and turned to head for his bunk. This man made him feel uncomfortable as there was something definitely not quite right about him—which was an interesting assessment from someone who had only recently been a walking corpse. Also, Keech felt tired and even with all his doubts and wonderings, he was relishing the experience. Even unpleasant sensations were better than having no sensation at all.

'No action,' the Warden decreed.

'But they've put a thrall unit in him,' argued the submind.

'No action.'

'But they're criminals. She's Rebecca Frisk. I *should* do something.'

'No action.'

'But—'

'I can always recall you, and send SM Twelve instead,' suggested the Warden. 'He too has chameleonware—which, incidentally, was approved by me.'

An incoherent mutter came from the drone.

'What was that?'

'Nothing, Warden. I hear and obey.'

The Warden shut down communication and considered its options. It logged the situation with ECS as low priority, and ran a quick summation of the facts that were certain. The spacecraft being blown in orbit had, apparently, been a cover for Rebecca Frisk's arrival on Spatterjay. And she had come shortly after the arrival of Sable Keech. Here she had met her mercenaries, and set out after the monitor. That all seemed quite simple until you started factoring in some other items.

Firstly, agents of unknown employ had been disseminating the information that Rebecca Frisk was on-planet, which information had led to a Convocation being called. Frisk had moved rather quickly to join the sailing ship she was now on, and had installed an AG motor. This was worrying, because the spacecraft that had supposedly been blown was only capable of carrying a certain class of escape pods, which in submersible mode could not move as fast as she had. What was going on?

The Warden decided to widen his logic field. Results: the immediate consequence of Frisk's presence here being known had been the calling of a Convocation of the Old Captains. That made no sense. But perhaps something to do with the Prador? The Warden opened its Hoop files and began to check Prador associations, and to compare them with present events in the Third Kingdom. Ebulan, a human name given to a very old adult Prador, seemed the most prominent name. Slowly, the Warden began to discern a possible scenario emerging.

* * *

SM13 continued its silent vigil. It watched as Shib hung two sheets of plass across the gaping hole in the front of the ship, moulded them to the shape of the hull by means of a small heating unit, then injected crash foam in between both sheets. The foam set instantly, then Shib went to carefully shut off AG. The ship settled back into the sea, and the patch-up held firm. Thirteen momentarily considered introducing a few weaknesses around the repair but found it didn't have the nerve to defy the Warden. It turned its attention elsewhere.

The sail was slowly recovering, though the damage done to it had been severe. Its brain had been partially cooked, but not completely destroyed, and was now regenerating. It could do nothing as yet, by dint of it having had its neck stapled to the mast, but it was working on that: methodically flexing its neck muscles against the strips of metal securing it.

Drum was a much more interesting possibility. Thirteen had noted the Captain's finger movement and, listening in on conversations between Shib and Svan, it surmised that the accident was in some part due to Drum not immediately obeying a verbal instruction from Svan. It also noted the typical Prador metal exposed at the back of Drum's neck, and surmised that a spider thrall had been used on him, but that the Captain had not been *fully* cored. Now, his virus-filled body was attempting to reject the device controlling him— just as the body Frisk had stolen was attempting to reject what remained of her. Such endless possibilities.

At present the sail and Drum were in no immediate danger, however. Yet, if either of them became capable of any more decisive action, they would likely put themselves in mortal danger. Then, the submind decided, it could act, despite the Warden's orders. So it sat up on the mast, with the AI equivalent of smug satisfaction, and awaited events. Then it saw the one-armed woman climb out of the hold and, when it read the Prador glyphs tattooed on her body, it suddenly realized that something very important had been missed.

'Warden! Prador blank!' was the extent of the message it

shrieked, before other events came upon it rather abruptly. A
flash of intense light haloed the ship, and a thunderclap
shook it. Thirteen had just detected something metallic in
the sea—before its senses whited out and a power surge
fused its AG.

'Damn,' it managed, before tumbling from the masthead
and axing down into the deck timbers.

Shib drew a bead on the baroque metal drone. The seahorse
wobbled in the splintered planking and little gusts of smoke
puffed from a couple of its small vents.

'Drone shell—probably loaded with one of the Warden's
subminds.' said Svan. 'That was an EM burst hit it. So it
won't be getting up again.'

'What do I do with it?' Shib asked.

'Throw it over the side.'

Shib lowered his weapon and moved towards the drone.
He tried to pick it up with his injured hand, and then had to
holster his weapon and use both hands to tug the device from
the deck timbers. When he finally lifted it, he found it as
heavy as a cannon ball. It was hot as well, continuing to puff
smoke and make small buzzing sounds. He tossed it over the
side, watched it rapidly sink—and then turned quickly,
drawing his weapon at the splashing sound behind him. He
lowered his weapon on identifying the wedge-shaped Prador
transport rising out of the sea on the other side of the ship.

The transport drew level with the rail, and opened like a
clam. Out of it, in full war harness, sprang the large adolescent Prador he had earlier seen inside the destroyer. The
creature rocked the whole ship as it hit the deck, the armoured spikes of its feet driving like daggers into the planking. Throwing up splinters, it turned—and demolished a
section of rail with a sweep of its claw. Quickly following
the creature through this gap came four heavily laden human
blanks, just as fearsomely armed.

'Get us back on course—now,' rasped the Prador's translation box.

'And if we don't?' said Shib.

He did not even have time to duck. An armoured claw,

reeking of the sea, closed round his neck and lifted him from the deck.

'All are dispensable,' Vrell rasped. 'All.'

As Vrell lowered him back to the deck, Shib glared at the Prador with hate and disgust. When finally it released its hold, he glanced up to the cabin-deck where Svan stood at Drum's shoulder issuing instructions. The motor churned the sea behind the ship, and Drum swung the helm over, turning the vessel away from where it had been drifting, the transport attached limpet-like at its side.

Moving away from Drum, Svan watched cautiously as one of the blanks came up the ladder. The blank looked straight into the polished barrel of Svan's weapon, then went and crouched down by Frisk. The blank pulled the injector from Frisk's belt and quickly hurled it over the side. Using a new injector, the blank gave the woman a dose, before substituting the injector in her belt with the new one. As Svan watched this she realized immediately that she had been lied to—then she climbed down to the lower deck and moved up beside Shib. They watched silently as blanks started bolting armament and defences to the deck. Their transport, now empty, sank back into the sea.

'Getting a little complicated,' observed Shib, staring at the Prador, with beads of sweat on his forehead.

'Next chance we get, we're out of here,' murmured Svan.

'Nice to get a chance,' said Shib, still rubbing at his throat.

The Warden registered the message, and the EM blast, and then all its speculations and calculations slammed together in a logical whole. There was a Prador *adult* somewhere on the planet below. There had to be one, to run a human blank. Now, all of a sudden, Rebecca Frisk and the events on Drum's *Cohorn* were only important in how they pertained to the presence of that Prador.

'SM Twelve, keep away from that ship. I won't tell you again,' warned the Warden when it detected the little drone moving in close again.

'Sorry, boss.'

The Warden went on, 'Did it occur to you that the debris

you scanned earlier might have been planted in orbit, that in fact no ship was destroyed in the atmosphere?'

'No, boss.'

The Warden scanned back over its visual files, only confirming that—of course—none of its eyes had been close enough for it to identify what kind of vessel had approached Spatterjay.

'Obviously didn't occur to you either,' interjected another voice.

'Sniper, this is a private channel,' said the Warden.

'Yeah, and your security sucks. Come on, when are you gonna get with some direct action?'

If the Warden could have smiled, it would have done so then. It had only taken the smallest chink in its armour for the war drone to break through, and then from under the sea, in the belly of a molly carp: proof that even after all this time Sniper had still not lost his edge.

'Our priority is to trace the Prador vessel. SM Thirteen was knocked down by an EM burst shell, the kind of weaponry often found on their war craft. That, combined with the tricky manoeuvring it executed on the way in puts it at nothing less than an attack ship.'

'Yeah, so whadda you doing about it?' demanded Sniper.

'SMs numbers one to ten, activate and upload to drone shells in defence satellite Alpha, and run diagnostics,' said the Warden.

'Now that's more like it, but is it enough? That lot are only police-action spec. You want soldiers not enforcers,' said Sniper. 'Why don't I come and play, too?'

'You will remain exactly where you are unless the situation becomes critical—though there is something else you can do for me.'

'What?' said Sniper grumpily.

'I want an overlay program from you. You know the kind I mean.'

Sniper's reply bounced through subspace: a tight package of viral information. The Warden studied its format and its pasted-on title, then beamed it directly to the cylindrical satellite that was now moving into position. One of its long ports opened and ten black coffin-shapes dropped out of it. Hitting atmosphere they started glowing like hot irons.

'SM Twelve, I want you there in position to shepherd them. They'll be a bit erratic to begin with.'

'Yes, as I can hear,' said SM12.

The Warden listened in to the close chatter between the ten SMs.

'Let's kick arse!' was the gist of their excitement, overlaid on sounds as of mechanical projectile weapons being loaded and primed. With the amused tolerance of a parent, the Warden watched their continued descent to the surface of the planet. Subminds that had previously only been used for ecological, geological and meteorological surveys had changed very little even when they uploaded into the newest enforcer shells. Sniper's overlay program had immediately changed that. But then that program had, after all, been called 'attitude'.

No matter how hard he tried, Ambel could not go back behind the pain. His first screams on the deck of Sprage's ship all those years ago had been his birth screams. *I'm Ambel now, I'm not this monster that fed Hoopers to the furnace— they'll recognize this.* But even as he thought these things, he could not rid himself of the memory of the look of hurt betrayal Boris had given him. Yet there were no lies: *I am not Gosk Balem. I'm not.*

'I'm for bed,' said Ron. 'Wake me in a couple of hours.'

'Use mine,' said Ambel.

'I'll do that,' said Ron. He patted Ambel on the shoulder as he went past him to the ladder. Ambel listened for the sound of a door closing then abruptly remembered that there was no door any more: the Skinner was away and all secrets were out. He glanced back and saw that Sable Keech, too, had finally gone to his bunk. The only ones remaining on deck were a single junior checking the lamps, and Anne and Forlam, who by the attention they were giving each other, would be heading bunkwards soon anyway. An aberrant thought crossed Ambel's mind: Ron could be a problem to him, but a harpoon dipped in sprine would quickly solve that issue. The rest of them he could kill with ease, with the possible exception of Keech. There was no telling what kind of weaponry the Earth monitor carried. Ambel shook his head. Did others ever think such thoughts?

Did he think such thoughts because, underneath all those years of being Ambel, he still really was Gosk Balem? No. He believed others *did* think such things. The test of character was in what you did, not what you thought about doing. He could no more actually murder these people than could a molly carp fly.

'Deep thoughts?'

Ambel glanced sideways at Erlin as she slipped up on to the cabin-deck beside him. He hadn't heard her approach. He looked down at her bare feet, then to the thin slip she wore, then at her face.

'Boris calls them "long thoughts", because if you think too deep you lose sight of the point. Full of daft comments like that is Boris,' said Ambel.

'He hurt you,' said Erlin.

'It hurt, but I expected nothing else. I'm surprised that Anne and Pland still call me Captain and still act friendly. Either they feel no betrayal or they're just waiting for their chance to shove me over the side.'

'I doubt that. You're not surprised at Peck still calling you Captain?'

'Nothing Peck does surprises me. The Skinner turned his skin inside out and turned his head inside out as well. He stepped off the far side of weird long ago.'

'He'd kill for you.'

Ambel turned his calm gaze upon her for a long moment, then faced forward, nodding slowly. Erlin moved a little closer and rested a hand on his arm.

He said, 'I'd best have a little talk with Peck. Don't want him doing anything drastic.'

'Do you want to know why I came back?' Erlin asked.

Ambel turned to look at her. 'I guessed you'd get round to telling me in your own time,' he said.

Erlin pulled her hand away, annoyance flashing across her face. 'Do you even care?' she asked.

Ambel glanced at her. 'Of course I care. The critical question has to be: do *you*?'

She took a breath and started again. 'Then you *know* why I've come back,' she said.

'Yes,' said Ambel, his hands resting easy on the helm, his face almost tranquil, 'but it's best you tell me all about it.'

Erlin took another slow shuddering breath, but all her rehearsed words dissipated like smoke. 'I came back because it gets so empty out there,' she said. 'Sometimes I can't see the point of going on. Achievement or failure? After a time you don't care about the difference . . . ' Erlin trailed off and stared at Ambel in the hope that he might understand.

Ambel nodded. 'I've felt that too, and I'll feel it again maybe. In the end, you find a calm centre and you just keep on living. You live for friendship and a bright sunrise, for a cool breeze on your face or a peppered worm-steak. You take as much pleasure in the taste of sea-spray as in the discovery of the hyperlight drive or the saving of a human life. Because you can live for ever you take pleasure in the *now*. You don't have to rush about living on account of having only a finite span. That's trite, but true,' he said, his words rolling out as rhythmically as the slow splash of waves against the hull of the ship.

'I hear what you're saying, but I don't feel it,' said Erlin.

Ambel regarded her thoughtfully. 'I can't help that. It comes with the years or it doesn't come at all. There's twenty-three of the Old Captains here, and that don't mean just the ex-slaves of Hoop. The Old Captains are those of us that have managed to "live into the calm" as they say. Some are only five or six centuries old. Including those off-planet, we reckon on there being a hundred or so of us. The rest . . . ' Ambel shrugged.

'It's why I need to be with you.'

Ambel waited.

'I need help. I need a guide. I already know the figures: it's fewer than one in a hundred who "live into the calm". Those same figures apply to people stretching all the way back to Earth.'

'You want to live, then? That's the best point to start from,' said Ambel straight-faced.

'I'm not sure I do,' replied Erlin.

'If you don't, you'll probably regret it later,' said Ambel.

Erlin laughed. Out of the corner of his eye, Ambel noted the abrupt easing of her tension. He continued to steer the ship, content in silence, at his still point.

'Janer . . . ' Erlin began hesitantly.

'I know,' said Ambel. 'Nothing lasts, you know. Even *we* change over the years. There's joy and pleasure in that, if you think about it the right way. Stay with him for a while then come see me. Anything that keeps you interested keeps you alive, and right now you need to accumulate years. In my experience, most suicides occur before the three-century mark. Deaths after that are usually due to accident or someone else's intent. Survive that mark and you'll likely carry on, unless you've got some enemies I don't know about.'

'I don't think so.'

'Good,' he glanced at her. 'In a way this is academic. I myself might not be around in the near future. I might be back in the sea, or in a fire . . . Can we make a pact here and now?'

'What do you want?' Erlin asked apprehensively.

'If the judgement is in my favour, I promise to do everything in my power to help you to live: to bring you to your calm and still point. In return I want a promise from you, should the judgement go against me.'

'Tell me.'

'In my cabin are some crystals of sprine. You must bring me a crystal before they throw me in the sea or roast me. I came here out of a world of pain, and it's not somewhere I wish to return to.'

'I can promise you that.'

'Good, Erlin. Go to your hornet man now.'

Erlin smiled and went off to do as he told her. Ambel watched her go, and smiled as well. The breeze was cool on his face and he could taste the salt of sea-spray on his tongue.

14

Whelks, as they grow in size and calorific requirements, descend deeper and deeper into the ocean, their bodies adapting to the intense pressure there. Its slow ascent, of hiding in crevices and clamping down hard to rock faces whenever the heirodont got near, and a long concealment in that final crevice until the heirodont grew impatient and went away, had enabled this particular whelk to slowly adjust to the decreasing pressure, and not experience the whelkish equivalent of bends. Unfortunately, due to other conditions, such as differing salinity and temperature, and the extreme change of diet, the giant whelk was now beginning to feel rather queasy, and wished it had just returned to the depths in search of filter worms. So thinking, it began to slide towards the edge of the trench. It was a few metres from its goal when the heirodont rose out of the depths before it—even more irritable now that leeches had begun attaching to its body.

Boris tried, without much success, to accept that his life had changed now and that there was really nothing to regret. Because of his tetchiness resulting from his failure to come to terms with it all, Goss had kicked him out of her bunk.

'And don't come back until you've figured out what you really want!' she'd shouted, then turned over with her back towards him.

As he climbed up on to the deck of the *Ahab*, he wondered just what exactly she had meant by that. He greeted Gollow and a couple of Ron's juniors, who were sitting playing cards below a deck lantern, and then went to the port rail to urinate over the side. When he was rebuttoning his trousers, he glanced over at Roach, standing at the helm, and the man gave him a knowing grin.

Boris turned away. Obviously the man had heard Goss shouting at him. He decided then that he would try to patch things up with her, rather than talk to this weasely man. He didn't like Roach. He didn't like this ship—felt uncomfortable aboard it. Did he really like Goss all that much? Most importantly, did he really hate Captain Ambel? Regret was there—there was no escaping it. He stood on the crux of indecision, and while he pondered, he noticed the approach of the other ship.

'Vessel to starboard!' he yelled at Roach, and refocused his attention on the ship. There was something wrong with it, its lights had a much whiter tint than was usual, and they lit a wake that indicated the ship was travelling at a hell of a rate. Yet there was little wind, and from what Boris could see of its sail, it was belling in the wrong direction.

'That's Drum's *Cohorn*!' Roach yelled back at him.

Boris hurried back towards the forecabin. 'What's he doing out here? Last I heard, he'd got a full load of turbul on and was heading back for port,' he said as he approached the ladder.

'Drum's a changeable fella,' commented Roach.

Boris climbed up and joined him on the cabin-deck. 'I don't like this,' he said.

'Sail ain't right . . . Take the helm for me,' said Roach.

Boris did as instructed while Roach went over to Captain Ron's telescope. He swore once, took his eye away, and then put it back.

'I see Drum at the helm, but there's others there that ain't his crew.' Roach turned from the scope and shouted down along the deck. 'Scart! Get everyone up on deck, and get 'em up armed!'

'Aye, Captain!' one of the card players yelled back.

'"Captain"?' said Boris, and Roach gave him a sour look. Boris then nodded towards the deck cannon. 'That loaded?' he asked.

'No,' said Roach.

'Might be needing it,' Boris observed.

'Best you load it, then,' said Roach, squinting at the lower deck to see if his orders were being carried out.

The *Cohorn* rapidly closed in while Boris packed the deck cannon with a paper-wrapped charge, then a bag of stones. He noted, as he worked, that the prow of the approaching ship was white and misshapen; it had many things on its deck that should not have been there. One of those things was moving about, and seemed to have too many legs for comfort.

'Goss! Get yerself on deck! And bring up the guns!' Roach yelled.

'Biggest prill *I* ever saw,' said Boris, taking a box of sulphur matches from his pocket and striking one on the rail.

'That ain't no prill,' said Roach, who was a century older than Boris. 'That's a buggering Prador.'

Boris grimaced as he got the cannon's igniter wick smouldering. It hadn't been necessary for Roach to tell him that. Boris had seen plenty of pictures of the creatures, and heard quite enough stories from drunken Hoopers in the Baitman.

Goss charged up on deck clutching a handful of ironmongery, which she began to distribute. After this, she studied the approaching ship for a moment, then ran for the ladder. Boris leant over and accepted the weapons she handed up: two pump-action shotguns and one pulsed-energy handgun. The handgun had to be Ron's. No one else but an Old Captain could afford such a thing.

'Maybe they don't want trouble?' said Roach with what might have passed for humour.

'In your arse,' said Goss, feeding shells into one of the shotguns.

There was no warning. Something flashed, leaving shadowy afterimages in their eyes. There was a dull crump, the ship lurched, and a spar crashed to the deck. Next, there was a double flash and one rail exploded into splinters. On the other side of the ship the other rail sagged, where it too had been broken, and was now being pulled down by the weight of the ship's rowing boat. Boris pointed the deck cannon, fired, and had the pleasure of seeing two figures keel over on the *Cohorn*.

Goss began firing shells at the approaching ship. But then all of them were rocked back as something crashed below and sea-spray fogged the air. Boris looked over the side at the hole blown in the hull, just above the water line, and the fires burning within.

'We're gonna sink,' he said to Roach.

The little man just appeared angry as he aimed again at the figures visible on the approaching ship. Boris picked up another paper cartridge, then stepped back from the cannon when it suddenly began to smoke.

'Huh?' he said brilliantly, as heat spectra travelled the length of the barrel, and it blued, then began to glow. Abruptly he realized that there was either a laser or some sort of inductance weapon being pointed at it. He ducked at the same time as Goss, and she slid the other shotgun across to him. Roach was now down beside him aiming with the handgun, a dangerously furtive look on his face.

'They're just playing with us,' he said. 'We've had it.' Through the cross rail he shouted down to the main deck, 'Scart! Gollow! Cut the boat free and get the rest of 'em into it!'

'But, sir!'

'Do as you're bloody told! You reckon you can take 'em on with that club?'

Boris looked down to see Roach's orders being obeyed. Two of the juniors were busy at the sagging rail, trying to untie the rowing boat. Something else hit further along the ship and a lantern went down spreading flame across the deck. A third crew-member joined the two at the boat and hacked at the ropes with his panga. That was Gollow, and Boris felt unaccountably proud. The ship's boat crashed into the sea and those on the lower deck quickly began to follow it down. Goss stood upright now, a wild look on her face, as she provided covering fire.

'Goss! Get down!' Boris yelled.

She staggered back then stared at the smoking hole under her breasts.

'Shit,' she said—and was blown in half.

Boris yelled and stood up again, firing at the ship as it

swung alongside, then blasting at the figures that came leaping across. One of them was the bloody great prill!

Something hit him right in the stomach and sent him stag-
gering. He felt it exit through his back and heard it clatter to
the deck. Both he and Roach stared at the small black cylinder, just before it exploded. The blast threw Boris over the
rail, so he found himself hanging off one side of the ship.
Roach, who had been knocked back against the remaining
rail, struggled upright, then reached over to catch Boris by
the scruff of his neck. He was about to start hauling him
back onboard when a huge armoured claw closed on his
arm, and something cold and metallic was pressed against
the back of his skull.

'Shit,' he said—just like Goss had done.

The claw clamped shut, making a sound like a vegetable
knife going through a carrot. Roach yelled as his bones shattered and muscle was crushed. His hand went flaccid, and
Boris yelled out and plummeted into the sea. Then, hand-
things like iron pulled Roach around and hurled him aside.
For a second he thought he too was going to end up in the
sea, but instead he slammed against the main deck, and
bounced. Then someone grabbed him again and flung him
against the mainmast. He slid down it, waiting for that terminal shot. But it never came.

'Oh look,' someone sneered. 'They're escaping.'

Roach turned his head to one side and dimly made out the
silhouette of the ship's boat out on the gleaming sea. The
Prador now loomed over him as it moved forwards and brandished a weapon in one of its main claws. The object was
long and heavy-looking, and was fed by tubes and cables
from a pack strapped underneath the creature's body. There
followed a whooshing roar, and the sea all around the escaping boat turned white. There was no time even for screams,
as the rowing boat and everyone in it disintegrated under
rail-gun fire.

'Bastard,' Roach managed, just before a hand closed in his
hair and slammed his head back against the mast. He
thought how the woman would have been attractive if her
face wasn't so twisted by whatever it was inside her.

'Now, you and I are going to have a little chat,' she told him.

With a feeling of chagrin, Janer watched as Erlin slept in a tangle of sheets, then he rose from the side of the bunk and took up his clothing. As soon as he was dressed, he shoved a hand into his trouser pocket and took out the jewelled Hive link. *Some new species of loneliness,* he wondered, and then fixed the link back into his earlobe. There came a vague clicking as it induced a signal in the receiver imbedded in the bone behind his ear—for the visible ear stud was not the actual link, rather it acted as the on/off button—but he received no communication from the mind. Still none came as he left the cabin, passing Forlam in the gangway, and headed for the ladder. The link only buzzed into life once he was on deck, watching the slow grey roll of the predawn sea.

'*It was foolish of you to cut communication with me. You are now in extreme danger,*' warned the mind. This was not what Janer had expected.

'What do you mean?'

'*There is a ship now coming towards you. Aboard it is one Rebecca Frisk, with two Batian mercenaries, and possibly others. They are coming to kill Sable Keech, and no doubt any others who are with him. They have Prador weaponry.*'

'That's not so good,' said Janer, at a loss for anything else to say.

'*It is not good,*' agreed the mind. '*I would suggest that you tell someone.*'

Janer glanced up at Captain Ron standing at the helm, then around at the morning activity on board. All seemed so slow and tranquil that what the mind had just told him did not gel for a moment.

'*Now would be a good time,*' urged the mind.

'Oh fuckit,' said Janer and trotted down the deck to the fore-cabin. As he mounted the cabin-deck, Ron gave him an amused look that suggested he might want to slow down a bit. Without more ado, Janer told him the mind's wonderful news. Ron's expression lost its humour and he looked over Janer's shoulder as Ambel joined them.

'Seems we got problems,' said Ron.

Ambel gazed enquiringly at the two of them.

'We got Rebecca Frisk and some Batian mercenaries with Prador weapons coming right up our backsides,' said Ron.

Ambel glanced around at the open sea. 'We don't stand a chance out here,' he said.

'The island,' Ron stated.

'Seems the best option,' said Ambel.

'What do you mean?' asked Janer.

'Does your Hive mind know how long we've got before they reach us?' asked Ambel.

The Warden informs me that at present they've stopped to . . . that they have halted their journey. You still have time to reach the island,' said the mind.

'We've time to reach the island,' echoed Janer, wondering exactly what their pursuers had stopped to do.

'Alert the others,' said Ron. 'Tell them to get their gear together. We'll be at the Skinner's Island in about five hours.' He turned to Ambel. 'Might not be time to ferry everyone in.'

'Beach her then,' said Ambel, his hands tightening hard enough on the helm to make the wood groan in protest.

Janer went to do as bid encountering Keech on the main deck and telling him what was happening.

'I thought it a bit improbable that she handed herself over to ECS,' the monitor said.

'How'd she manage it?' Janer asked.

'Not sure, but I'd bet she's now not wearing the face I knew her by.'

Janer brooded on that as he rushed to wake Erlin up and to find Pland. Anne had by now joined Ron and Ambel on the cabin-deck.

For the next hour, there was a continuous flurry of activity as supplies were brought on deck and weapons were taken out of waterproof packaging to be checked over. Keech cut the lines holding his scooter to the deck. From its baggage compartment he took out his attaché case and opened it.

As Janer approached him, Keech tossed him an item from

the case. Janer nearly dropped it, finding it heavier than he'd assumed.

'Never seen one of these in real life,' he muttered.

'Give your handgun to one of the crew. You won't be needing it now. That's a QC laser carbine. Half an hour continuous fire, thousand-metre kill range, and auto-sight.'

Janer handled the weapon as if it had suddenly turned into a snake. 'Bit drastic,' he said.

'You might well need it,' said Keech.

Janer turned to Forlam, who at that moment came up beside him.

'Here,' he said, passing over his handgun. Forlam stared at the weapon for a moment, then suddenly looked pleased and thrust it into his belt. Janer thought it was rather a strange grin the crewman wore.

Forlam pointed at the weapon Keech was quickly assembling from the case. 'What's that?' he asked.

Keech clicked the twin barrels—as of a shotgun—into place, then the folding stock, before opening out the fan of cooling fins from the main body of the weapon. He gave it a slow visual inspection then carefully took up a gigawatt energy canister and screwed it into place underneath.

'This,' he murmured, 'is completely OTT.' With that, he mounted his scooter, pulled the leg straps across his thighs and secured them in place, then slammed his vehicle up into the sky. He gave no one time to ask where he was going. No one needed to ask.

Amazingly, one of the juniors, who had either somehow survived the burst of rail-gun fire or had gone over the side during the attack, now yelled nearby as darkness seeped out of the sky. Before dawn, one of the mercenaries, perhaps out of boredom, finally shot a shell into him. Roach wished they would do the same to him.

Through a haze of pain, he tried to concentrate on what she was saying.

'Now I want to be utterly sure of this. Think about it a little before you reply,' said the woman he now knew was Rebecca Frisk.

He'd thought about it a little when she'd asked him the last time, and the time before—and on every occasion he'd told her the truth. She didn't care about truth, though. She wasn't doing this for truth. She was doing it because she liked to see suffering. Roach bit on his tongue as she played the laser, on wide beam, over his feet and legs. He'd screamed the third time she'd done this, in the hope that would satisfy her. But it hadn't. She'd just go on until there was nothing left of him to scream. It was Frisk's way, just as it was the way of her husband, or what was left of him.

'Think carefully now,' warned Frisk.

She seemed oblivious to everything else—had a crazy look in her eyes and jerky shudders running through her body with metronomic regularity. Roach did pretend to think carefully, while he listened to the low conversation going on behind her.

The mercenary woman was speaking to the Prador. ' . . . time for this?'

'Delay . . . Convocation . . . does not matter.'

'Fucking lunatic.' That last came from the male mercenary. He seemed to find Frisk's pursuits contemptible, but then his kind tortured people only for business, not for recreation.

'Tell me again about Jay,' demanded Frisk.

Roach leapt at the chance. At least while he was speaking, she wasn't burning his legs.

'Ambel . . . y'know, Balem Gosk, kept the head in a box in his cabin. I reckon Peck musta—aaaargh!'

'Oh I know all about that. Tell me something new, something *interesting*.'

'AG vehicle approaching.'

Roach could not identify from where that voice had come. The others were blanks, so perhaps it was their master speaking. He knew that this Prador on board wasn't an adult. It still had all its legs.

'Rebecca Frisk, we must return to our vessel,' grated the translator box of the same Prador.

Roach prayed that this would mean the end.

Frisk stood up and confronted the Prador, angry that her little game had been interrupted.

'I want to take him with me,' she spat.

'We do not have time. To the vessel—now.'

The Prador turned away. The blanks were already leaping from the *Ahab*, ahead of it. Frisk seemed about to rebel. Abruptly she turned, walked up to one of the mercenaries, and snatched his weapon from him and thrust her carbine into his hands instead. This is it, thought Roach. This is when I end up spread all over the deck.

Frisk, though, did not shoot him. She moved to the deck hatch, kicked it open releasing gouts of smoke, and then fired shot after shot below. Roach could feel the ship shuddering. When she was finished, she grinned at him with satisfaction, before following the Prador from the ship. The mercenaries went last, and without looking back.

Roach couldn't believe it: he was going to survive. All he had to do was work on these ropes tying him to the mast . . . It was then that he realized what the smoke meant, and what Frisk had been doing. He saw how smoke was also wisping up through the holes in the deck and could hear the crackle of flames from below. He continued to struggle at his bonds, but the torture had weakened him too much and he only had one arm to work with—his broken arm still being dead meat from the shoulder down. He listened to the sound of the *Co-horn* pulling away, its flaccid sail booming in the wind of its passage, and wondered which would get him first: the fire or the sea.

'You bitch!' he yelled, and heard her laughter growing distant. He sat panting for a while, then had another go at his bonds. Doing so, he heard sounds coming up from beside the ship, and had a horrible vision of prill clambering aboard. He stared over at where the ship's boat had been suspended and saw a rope there jerking. The sound, he began to realize, was a continuous cursing monologue. Shortly after, Boris hauled himself over the rail, the bottom half of his body covered by a writhing mass of leeches. With further cursing and the occasional yelp, Boris began to detach them, one by one. Roach didn't even have the energy left to yell at him to hurry up, even though he could feel the deck getting hot underneath him.

Keech stared down at the wrecked and burning ship, and the two figures remaining on its deck, then he turned his image intensifier to examine the second ship. Over there, a Prador and a number of humans—any of which might be Frisk herself. He set his scooter on hover, took up his weapon, and aimed. Half charge: he'd flame the deck.

Keech pulled back one of the three triggers, and lit the air between himself and the target ship with a line of purple fire. Seawater erupted and flashed into a ball of flame that splashed across an invisible disk.

'Shields,' was all he managed to say before his scooter dropped out of the sky. Letting his APW hang by its strap, he grabbed the controls, and saw the message flashing up on the screen: 'EMERGENCY DIVE: EVASIVE'.

A missile screamed past overhead and made a slow turn beyond him. Keech slammed the control column forward and put all the scooter's power into the dive. Gs threatened to steal his hands from the controls, and tried to drag him from the seat, but his leg straps held him in place. He went into cyber mode as his flesh began to fail, and used his arm motors to pull the scooter out of the dive at the last moment. The missile streaked past two metres below him, entering the sea with a crack. An explosion lit the underside of the waves, with a rapidly spreading disk of light. He was a hundred metres up from the surface when it erupted. No time for self-congratulation, he told himself, as another two missiles sped towards him.

Keech slammed the control column forward again and sped away from the two ships. As he departed, he took two of the guard spheres from his pocket, and held them in his hand. Glancing back he spotted the noses of two missiles like two chrome eyes. The ships themselves were still visible. He went into rapid descent. Only a second or two more and he'd be out of sight. Only a second or two more and the missiles would reach him. He tossed the two spheres up in the air and they shot away behind.

* * *

'Fuck you, monitor!' Frisk yelled, shaking her fist at the double explosion on the horizon. She turned to Vrell, grinning maniacally. After a moment of gazing at a creature with no emotions she could identify, she sobered and turned towards the forecabin.

'Bring us about,' she instructed Drum.

'No,' said the Prador—and the ship did not deviate from its course.

'We have to check,' said Frisk.

'There will be nothing to see,' replied Vrell.

'We have to be sure!' Frisk yelled.

Vrell did not consider this worthy of further reply.

'This is what we're here for, you shell-brained prawn!' Frisk yelled and kicked out at something on the deck. A metal staple went skittering across the timber and the sail cautiously opened one red eye to track its progress. But no one seemed to have noticed.

'Restrain her,' ordered Vrell.

Abruptly several arms closed about both of Frisk's. She whipped her head from side to side at Svan and Shib—who were doing the restraining—and considered freeing herself until Svan shoved a gun up under her chin.

'I've had about enough of you,' said the Batian woman, then looked to Vrell.

'Take her away and confine her in one of the cabins. She may yet serve a purpose.' Vrell turned with a complicated scuttling of legs, and regarded Drum still stationary up at the helm. 'Continue on course, no deviation.'

Drum reached up to scratch at the back of his neck, then nodded and continued with what he had been doing anyway. The Prador noted this unprogrammed action but thought nothing of it. It did not have the experience of humans to know whether such scratching was an autonomous action or not.

'Well, there went the cavalry,' said Boris.

'Yeah,' said Roach, and gritted his teeth while Boris put in another stitch to close the split in Roach's arm. It seemed a somewhat pointless exercise, what with a fire raging below and gouts of steam hissing through the holes in the deck.

'That was Keech,' explained Boris, now applying the needle and thread to some of the more embarrassing rips in his own tattered trousers.

'Yeah,' said Roach and, feeling a vague tingling in his fingers, he tried to flex them. He managed a little movement, but there would be no real strength in either his hand or his arm until flesh and bone began properly to knit. He thought it would be nice if they enjoyed the time to do so.

'Should we try and put it out?' Boris wondered.

'No chance. This ship's bound with sea gourd resin. Once you get that alight, you ain't gonna get it out again,' Roach replied.

'Maybe the ship's boat'll come back,' Boris suggested, while studying Roach's expression.

'The boat ain't coming back,' said Roach.

Boris nodded his head once at this confirmation—he hadn't seen what happened to the juniors in the ship's rowing boat, but he'd a damned good idea.

Abruptly, the deck tilted, and swathes of steam roared out of the open hatch. Boris and Roach peered over the side at the swarm of leeches attracted by the commotion, and by bits of Goss floating in the water. Beyond this writhing mass, the molly carp was cruising.

Boris instantly dropped his needle and thread and scuttled across to pick up the handgun Roach had dropped earlier.

'I'll not have happen to me what happened to my Captain,' Boris swore.

'I ain't neither,' said Roach, thinking what a waste of time it had been to sew up his arm. It had kept the boy occupied anyway. He stared at the water, ignoring the weapon Boris was handling so nervously. He tried not to wince when Boris reached over and pressed the warm snout of it against his head.

'Wait a minute,' he said.

'No point delaying,' said Boris. 'Only makes it harder.'

'I said *wait* a minute,' said Roach, angrily knocking Boris's hand away.

'What for?'

'Look,' said Roach, pointing at the sea.

An iron seahorse had just risen to the surface, the seawater fizzing all about it, and leeches jerking spastically in their hurry to get away. It tilted so as to glare up at them with one topaz eye, the other one burnt black.

'We should attack 'em, splash 'em, kill 'em, hit 'em . . . ' was the essence of the communication between drones one to ten with 'attitude'. All ten of the drones, now they were in atmosphere, had extruded stubby wings to which were attached their weapons pods. In one part of itself, the Warden agreed. Frisk's ship had encountered one other and left it burning. Sable Keech's seven-century search for justice and vengeance had ended in a few brief explosions, and it seemed unlikely there would be any chance at another reification for him. But all these were emotional issues. On a flat calculation of life and death, the sailing ship was unimportant. First, the Warden had to find the Prador spacecraft, for from it could issue destruction perhaps an order of magnitude greater.

'SM Twelve, I want them in pairs, covering the relevant eight sectors—same division as for geostudy. I want all signals reported. Specifically I want thrall-unit carrier waves and command codes. It won't be a direct transmission, as that would be too easy to trace should we get hold of any thrall units at the receiving end. Somewhere down there, the enemy will have secondary and perhaps tertiary emitters.'

'Coded U-space signals are difficult to detect,' observed Twelve.

'*Almost* impossible, would be a more accurate summation. It is not the signal itself you will detect, but overspill from the secondary emitters before the signal starts tunnelling. On detecting this overspill, you will have found an emitter. I want no action taken against emitters located. Just transmit everything you get to me.'

'Yes, Warden,' said Twelve.

The muttering from the other drones, which formed a backdrop to SM12's reply, made the Warden wonder just how good an idea it had been to load Sniper's little program into them. No matter—the AI returned its attention to the information packages coming in through from the submind ghost of itself trawling the loose AI net forming around the Prador worlds. These packages now detailed the rabid progression of events in the Third Kingdom and were fascinating. It seemed that the Prador were almost desperate for closer ties and trade opportunities with the Polity and, as had been demonstrated quite graphically before the sector AI, with such drastic changes in the offing, the old guard there was having trouble hanging on to power. Already some further high figures among them had not done so well. Three had been assassinated by direct methods: in two cases by explosives and in the third case by an injection of a putrefying virus. Two others had been killed by their own blanks after control programs had been subverted. Now *that* was what the Warden had found most interesting.

Ebulan, one of the highest-ranking Prador in the Kingdom, was also of particular interest to the Warden. It was he who once had dealings with Hoop and his merry crew, and who had become rich and consequently powerful on the trade in human blanks. This hideous practice was now becoming frowned on in the Prador Kingdom, because of the change of zeitgeist that had led to this aim for closer ties with the Polity. So Ebulan's power was waning.

Ebulan—that name came up repeatedly. Could it be that agents of his were the ones here on Spatterjay? If so, what was their purpose?

Floating just below the surface of the waves, the turtle-shaped remote probe folded its emitter dish and switched to passive observation. Twenty similar devices scattered across the surface of the sea performed a similar action, only two of them remaining in the relevant areas to maintain the U-space signal relay. They were not AI these machines—the Prador neither liked nor fully understood such technology—but they had proved more than sufficient to their limited task. Now that would have to change, however.

In his ship deep in an oceanic trench Ebulan watched the pictographic information sliding in on one screen then

turned his attention to another screen showing a real-time
image. Foam bubbled from his jaws as he chewed on a lump
of putrid meat, and then spat it out for the delectation of the
lice skittering round the floor.

The Warden had to know that a ship was down here, or it
would not have brought out this kind of firepower, though
the AI obviously did not yet realize just what kind of ship it
was dealing with, else it would be screaming for help right
now. Ebulan disconnected one control box—the human
blank concerned slumping at a scanning console—and
direct-linked into a rear hold. There, through the box, he got
an image of the four heavy-armour drones he carried with
him. Each was a flattened ovoid four metres across, armed
with rail-guns, missile launchers, and screen projectors.
These, again, were not AI: the intelligences inside each of
them derived from the surgically altered and then flash-
frozen brains of four of Ebulan's many children. They were
totally loyal, fixed as they were in a state of constant
adolescence—enslaved by their parents' pheromones.

As Ebulan sent a signal, red lights ignited in recesses in
the drones' exotic metal shells. The hold was flooded with
muddy seawater and rapidly filled up, then a triangular door
opened on to the deep ocean. The four drones motored out
into the murk, the images viewed by their recessed eyes
coming up on the screen before Ebulan.

'Children,' Ebulan said to his four kin. 'You will assume
the roles of remote emitters, once you are in position. If detected you must defend yourselves, then immediately reposi-
tion. I want the signal maintained at all times.'

'Yes, as you will,' they replied as one.

'Skinner's Island,' indicated Captain Ron as, out of misti-
ness across the sea, the purpled mounts of the landmass
came into sight.

The atmosphere on the ship became even more subdued
than it had previously been, and the crew, about their tasks
on the deck, proceeded with the care of people not wanting
to wake someone, or something, from sleep. As they drew
closer, Janer tried to study their destination with a clinical

eye. Was it this place's reputation that made it seem so sinister, or was it just sinister anyway? he wondered. The island appeared little different to the others he had seen: a rocky mass thrust out of the sea, shallows and beaches and then a thick wall of dingle. Janer scanned the expanse of sea between the ship and the island's beaches. Out of the shallows jutted sandbanks on which frog whelks and hammer whelks clustered like herds of sheep, while small molly carp and occasional glisters patrolled the waters around them. And there were leeches of course—always plenty of them. He couldn't nail it down: the same yet not the same. There was something *brooding* about this place. An air of menace emanated from that deep dingle and the rocky outcrops.

Ron steered the ship for a suitable cove and kept right on going.

'Brace yourselves, boys!' he shouted.

The *Treader* slid into the shallows, the sandy bottom speeding underneath liberally poxed with leeches. It passed a mound that seemed entirely composed of frog whelks, and a hundred stalked eyes followed the ship's progress. Janer braced himself for the crash, but none came. First there was a deep vibration, then a grating, then the ship was slowing and he was gradually dragged towards the bows by his momentum. Peck caught hold of his belt and didn't let go until the ship had shuddered to a halt five metres from the shore.

'Let's be doing it then, Captain Ron,' said Ambel.

'Right with you, Captain Ambel,' said Ron, sliding down the forecabin ladder.

Ambel moved to the prow and dropped the anchor over the side, towing its chain—now wiped clean of grease—after it. Janer couldn't see why the chain had been thus cleaned, or why the anchor had been dropped at all, as the ship was unlikely to drift.

'Shoo, bugger off,' Ron told the sail.

The sail snorted in indignation, released all its various holds and, in a folding of spines and sheeted skin, it hauled itself up to the top spar, and from there launched itself into the sky. Janer watched it go, then turned back to observe Ambel—but Ambel had gone.

'Right with you,' said Ron, and leapt off the prow of the ship.

'What the hell?' muttered Janer, moving down the ship to the bow rail. He got there in time to see Ambel wading ashore through the metre-deep water, with Captain Ron following just behind him. The two of them dragged the anchor chain ashore and once there quickly stripped the leeches from each other and stamped the creatures to slurry.

Erlin moved up to stand beside Janer. 'This is what brings it home to you,' she murmured.

The two captains then took up the anchor chain, Ambel in front and Ron behind, pulling on it until it grew taut. Janer doubted he would have been able even to take the curve out of the heavy chain.

The Captains looked at each other. 'On the count,' said Ron. 'One and two and three . . . '

Janer realized his mouth was open, but couldn't think straight enough to close it. With a deep grinding the ship itself began to move. He saw that, with each step the Old Captains took, their feet sank deep into the sand. Two, three metres, the ship moved. Ron and Ambel dropped the length of chain they were holding at the edge of the dingle, then moved back to take up another section of it at the shoreline.

'One and two and three.'

The prow of the ship was heaved up on to the beach, then the two captains dropped the chain. They pulled themselves out of the sand and walked back to the vessel, as casual as if having just completed some very menial task. The rest of the crew had not even bothered to watch, but continued gathering together supplies.

'Collect your stuff,' Erlin advised Janer.

'It is estimated that a Hooper in his third century has the strength of a three-gee heavy-worlder,' the Hive mind observed. *'But no one has measured the physical strength of an Old Captain.'*

'How much does this ship weigh?' Janer whispered to it.

'Its dead weight is considerable,' said the mind, and Janer translated this as meaning it didn't know. It went on with, *'Obviously, being partially supported by the sea, and with it*

being dragged, there are matters of friction and so forth to be factored in.'

'All I asked you was how much the ship weighed,' said Janer.

'Not less than thirty tonnes,' the mind replied, almost grudgingly.

'Oh, is that all,' said Janer. 'There I was thinking it might be a lot.'

It took a quarter of an hour for them to get supplies, weapons and most of the crew on to the beach. It took another ten minutes for Ambel to persuade Peck that it was in his best interests not to stay on board. Janer could not understand why the ship's rowing boat had also been lowered, until they were all gathered on the sand, where Ambel and Ron addressed them.

'Too many of us crashing about inland there'll spook the Skinner, and we'll never catch him,' said Ron. 'So some of you boys'll not be coming.'

Janer glanced around at gathered crew. The strongest reactions came from the juniors, as it was obvious where Ron's speech was leading. Some of these Hoopers wore looks of disappointment; however, most of them looked relieved.

'Thing is,' said Ambel, 'you lads cannot be hanging about here in full sight, what with that lunatic woman coming after us, so me and Ron here think it best you take the ship's boat round to the east of the island'—he gestured in that direction—'and find yourselves a handy cove to moor up in.'

'Now, I know you're all disappointed,' said Ron, 'but that's the way it's got to be. Any questions?'

Some of the crew-members addressed were already heading back towards the ship. A few hung back, Sild amongst them.

'What is it, lad?' Ambel asked the man.

'I'm not a lad. I was a hundred last birthday and I know me own mind,' Sild grumbled.

'And?' Ambel asked.

'I'll go,' said Sild. 'I know we ain't got your muscle, and I don't want meself stripped by no Skinner. . . . but I just want to say that you're my Captain, and you'll always be that.'

Ambel seemed at a loss to find a reply and he stood there dumbly as Sild moved off with the others. After a moment he shrugged, then turned to face Janer and Erlin.

'Best you two go with them,' he said.

'Not one chance in hell,' said Janer, and Erlin just shook her head. Ambel nodded, expecting this response, then, hoisting his blunderbuss up on to one shoulder, turned towards the dingle.

Ron took up a huge machete, advanced on the wall of vegetation, and set to. Ambel followed, and the rest of them, after taking up their packs of supplies, followed after him.

Beyond the first thick layer of dingle, things began to get a little easier, though there were numerous peartrunk trees, with their concomitant crops of leeches, to get past. Janer clutched Keech's carbine to himself and kept a wary eye on the dingle. There were things moving around in the bluery— big, slimy things with buzz-saw mouths.

'Mask,' Erlin warned him at one point and, not having encountered putrephallus weeds before, he was a bit slow to cap the filter mask over his face. He nearly filled it with vomit.

'What's that?' he asked when he had recovered enough to point at the horrible baggy bird-thing clinging to one of the phallic flowers.

'Lung bird,' Erlin told him. 'They're about the only creatures here that other creatures won't eat. They stink worse than their food, and are full of toxins. No one's figured out how they manage to stay alive. But no one's really wanted to get close enough to find out.'

'And those.' Janer pointed again.

'Frogmoles. Don't step on one. They've got barbed spines that'll go through just about anything, and you'd need surgery to have them removed,' said Erlin.

'Charming.'

Beyond the peartrunk trees and stands of putrephallus, yanwood trees reared into the sky. Below them the ground was clear of new growth, though thickly layered with oily oval leaves that smelt of kerosene. With the vegetation now thinning sufficiently for Ron to put away his machete, they picked up their pace and soon came to a place where ahead of them reared something like a grassy slope. What was growing on it—though the same green as ordinary grass—consisted of small translucent spheroids that popped when trod upon and let off a smell like coffee and curry powder combined. They were also slippery underfoot when burst, so climbing the slope became hard going.

At the crest of the slope, bare rock jutted up like bones flayed of flesh. Here they halted, mainly to let Janer rest, him being only a newly made Hooper. Sitting on one of the rocks he gazed down another incline into dingle like a green and blue sea resting between mounds. This landscape beyond stretched on into a haze of distance and was lost. Strange hootings and squeals came up regularly from this tangle of vegetation.

'Bigger island than I thought,' said Janer. 'How'd they expect to find the Skinner here . . . if he is here?'

'He's here,' said Erlin.

Before she could go on, Peck muttered, 'Bugger'll find us, I'll be buggered.'

'That's a comfort,' said Janer, standing up and shrugging his pack into a more comfortable position on his shoulders. Ambel and Ron glanced back at him for a moment, then set off down the slope towards the dingle, Ron already drawing his machete in readiness.

'Another point to note is how easy we'll be to track, if Rebecca Frisk does come here,' said Janer.

'If?' said Erlin.

'Well, Keech might have solved that problem for us.'

'Emphasis on the "might",' muttered Erlin.

They continued on down the slope, after the others.

For most of the afternoon, Ron hacked a trail for them, and Ambel took over thereafter. He did not take over the chore because Ron was tired, but because he was bored with the task and Ambel had got bored with just walking behind him. They slogged on until it was getting too dark to easily dodge the leeches falling from the peartrunk trees. Then Ambel hacked out a clearing in an area with few overhanging branches, and marked its perimeter by jabbing sticks into the ground.

Pland lit a fire of peartrunk wood while Anne prepared rhinoworm steaks to roast over it. They ate in silence as the moon, Coram, rose into the sky like a mouldy pearl, and then laid out their bedding.

'You take first watch, Janer. Don't let any leeches past the perimeter. If anything comes that's too big for you to handle, wake me or Ron,' instructed Ambel.

Janer patrolled the perimeter with his carbine held ready. With this weapon he doubted there would be anything too big for him to handle. The smaller leeches—the ones about the size of his arm—he kicked back into the undergrowth. Frogmoles kept well clear, their eyes glinting from the fire-light out there in the darkness. No one warned him about anything else.

Keech found the best way to keep himself out of the water was to use what power the remaining thruster possessed to drive down towards the sea, then up again and away in one burst. Thereafter he drifted along fairly levelly until the thruster cooled down enough for him to use it again. A problem was the scooter's tendency to try to flip over whenever he applied thrust. Further problems consisted of the failing AG, which was taking him closer and closer to the surface despite his use of the thruster, the fact that the thruster was taking longer and longer to cool down each time he used it, and also that there were some horrible noises and occasional sprays of sparks emerging from under the cowling. His burnt back and mauled arm now seemed of secondary importance. And all these hindrances were of less importance than the fact that he had miscalculated.

Both missiles aimed at him had been of the EM-burst variety. Not only did they have the capability of turning an enemy vehicle into a disperse spray of molten metal, but they released a burst of radiation that scrambled any electronics in the vicinity of the explosion. The thruster had burnt out after taking in a cloud of ionized gas; the EM had not been kind to the AG coils, and com was completely out; the screen had melted and buckled.

Keech had been in worse situations than this—after all, he wasn't dead yet, and he'd been in that one before. So he nursed the scooter along, using manual and jury-rigged controls and a modicum of prayer, wondering if he was imagining seeing eager movement in the sea whenever the scooter dropped lower.

15

The giant whelk's immediate response to the presence of the heirodont, was to spit out the last leech-covered turbul body it was chewing, and attempt to clamp itself down against the bottom. But up here the bottom was comprised of a thick layer of stones and silt and broken shell, so that there was nothing firm to hold on to. With a flick of its tale the heirodont drifted forward, eyeing the desperate creature as it struggled to find purchase, then cruised round it in a slow circle. The whelk turned as it did this, stalked eyes keeping its nemesis in view. The heirodont finally seemed to comprehend its luck, and suddenly drove into the whelk and tipped it over. Flailing its tentacles, the whelk opened huge wounds across the heirodont's head, but to a creature quite used to being fed upon by leeches every day, these were as nothing. With its mandibles the heirodont gripped the rim of the whelk's shell and twisted it over so it was forced upside-down into the treacherous surface it had been unable to grip; driving its snout into hard flesh with teeth admirably suited to the purpose, the heirodont began to chew.

The heavy resinous yanwood of the ship was not buoyant. Like a steel hull holed in the same manner, it started to go

down, water breaking through smashed timbers and gouts of
steam blasting from the deck hatches. Boris emerged from
one of those hatches, hauling up two sprine carboys on a
rope behind him. Once on deck he danced about and swore
as he beat out his smouldering clothing. When the ship suddenly lurched and tilted he grabbed the carboys and slid
them to the edge, pounded the corks to make sure they were
secure, then tossed both containers over the side, down to
where the drone floated below. Lying by the shattered rail, to
which he had crawled, Roach peered down into the water.

'This a good idea?' he queried.

'The only one,' confirmed Boris as he helped him to his
feet.

Roach was about to say something more when the ship
lurched again. Without more ado, they leapt into the sea and
splashed towards the carboys. Near the fizzing seahorse the
water tingled with an electrical charge and was warmer than
expected.

'Aargh, that smarts,' yelped Roach.

Boris just grunted an acknowledgement and stared at all
the creatures swarming beyond an invisible perimeter. He
looked beyond them to where the water swirled occasionally
as a large rhinoworm cruised by, snapping up stray leeches.

'Must tell the Captain he needs floats,' said Roach.

'You'll have to tell him he needs a new ship,' said Boris.
As if to reinforce his words, the ship groaned, slowly tilted
further to one side, and water surged inside it, extinguishing
the last of the fires. Soon its whole deck was awash, and as if
making one last attempt to stay afloat the ship righted itself
as it went down. The two masts slid last into the sea, and the
water was turned into foam all around by escaping air—not
just the activity of leeches and other creatures as they moved
in to investigate. For a little while there were remarkably few
of these in the water immediately surrounding the two men,
but they knew this situation would not continue.

Roach looked alternately thoughtful and sneaky.

'Ain't my fault,' said Roach, both reflection and sneaki-
ness in his tone.

'No, I guess not,' said Boris, peering at the little man in

the halflight and thinking how it didn't really matter any more, as he'd soon be joining Goss and the rest of the crew, chewed up in the stomachs of leeches and prill. He checked again that the laser was still in his belt, though exposure to water might prevent it from working.

As the leeches returned from inspecting the empty ship, their cordon appeared to be narrowing and it seemed to Boris that the fizzing around the seahorse had subsided—either that or the leeches were becoming inured to it and slowly moving in on them.

'Cavalry's back,' said Roach, pointing.

Boris couldn't quite grasp what he meant, until his eyes followed the direction of his companion's finger and, after first discerning the glow from a malfunctioning thruster, he witnessed the erratic approach of the AG scooter. Both men stared at it in dubious silence for a moment before shouting and waving. Soon the machine was close enough for Keech to spot them so he brought it in right over their heads and tried to keep it hovering there.

Boris watched open-mouthed as it slowly sank towards them.

'Jump on as quickly as you can!' Keech yelled. 'We'll only get one chance at this!'

'Great,' said Roach flexing his half-dead arm.

'You go first,' said Boris.

The scooter continued to drop towards them, now tilting in the air so its rear end met the surface of the water first. Roach shoved down on his carboy to lift himself up enough so that he could grab the rim of the luggage compartment with his one operable arm. He was hanging there, unable to pull himself further, until Keech himself reached back with one hand and grabbed him. The scooter sank half a metre into the sea as Roach struggled up on to one of its wings beside Keech.

Boris then snatched at the same area, and began pulling himself on to the other wing. Keech reached back intending to help him, then abruptly turned away to slap some control in the partially dismantled console, as the AG's hum became a vibration. Boris found it easier boarding with two operable arms, and soon the two crewmen were squatting either side of the driver's seat, clinging on to whatever they could. Meanwhile Keech manipulated the controls, but seemingly to no effect.

Abruptly the seahorse leapt out of the water and landed with a thud in the luggage compartment. The scooter now rested deep enough in the water for the occasional wave to splash in after it.

'Here goes,' said Keech, very carefully upping AG. The motor under his seat issued a grating hum, then spat out a couple of black smoke rings. The scooter rose briefly, until its back end was just clear of the water, then slowly began to sink back again. Keech then opened the tap that supplied pure water to the thruster still functioning. It cracked out a brief blue flame that had them drifting across the surface of the sea. Again, he tried AG, but swore when it failed to lift them clear.

'Can't you give us some lift?' he said.

Behind his back Boris and Roach looked askance at each other.

'What can *we* do?' Boris whispered.

'We ain't got no lift,' added Roach.

Keech ignored them and turned to peer down into the luggage compartment.

'Did the EM burst get you as well?'

The seahorse gazed straight back up at him, with its remaining topaz eye flickering. It emitted a stuttering crackle that sounded vaguely apologetic. Keech swore once again, then turned to Boris. 'What about the rest of the crew?' he asked.

'Dead,' said Boris.

'Tell me what happened,' continued the monitor as he nursed the scooter along.

In a flat tone, Boris began to tell the monitor about the Prador, about the human blanks and the weapons they carried. At one point Roach interjected a bitter monologue about Rebecca Frisk, while eying an ominous swirl in the water behind them.

The big leech turned up when even Ron's and Ambel's drain-cleaner snoring had ceased to keep the others awake.

Janer was over on the opposite side of the perimeter when it surged out of the dingle and bore down on those he was guarding. Even so, he hesitated before taking aim. He'd never seen anything quite like this; the huge slimy creature was the size of a hippopotamus and the gaping tube of its leech mouth as wide as a bucket. It didn't move fast, but it moved deceptively. One moment it was oozing over the perimeter at full width. The next moment it drew itself out thin and long, then flowed forwards again—and was poised over the curled-together bodies of Anne and Forlam. Not familiar with the settings on the weapon he held, or even which trigger to pull, Janer aimed it and fired.

The carbine made no noise whatsoever, and there was of course no kick. Drifting smoke from the fire vaguely traced out the pulsing path of a beam of coherent light the width of Janer's wrist. Where it struck the leech, bright flame flashed, and its slimy flesh melted away. The beam cut through the creature like boiling water poured on ice, smoke and steam condensing in a flat cloud in the air immediately above. The leech made no sound other than a hiss that could have emerged from its boiling insides, and it oozed its way out of the clearing just as fast as it had oozed into it. Janer kept firing at the monster until he could no longer see it behind the clouds of smoke and steam.

The frogmoles quietened, and other sounds issuing from things Janer had no name for, ceased as well. He stood gasping with shock, nausea churning his stomach. He realized his back was right up against the perimeter and leapt away from it, turning his weapon on the dingle. No movement. Nothing. After a moment the nausea subsided and he looked around at his companions. Ron and Ambel were still snoring loudly on opposing sides of the clearing. Forlam and Anne had not even stirred, while Erlin was still sound asleep in her padded sleeping bag, and Pland was showing no signs of life either. The only one to move was Peck, and that was just to grunt and turn over. For a moment Janer couldn't believe that not one of them had woken. Then he grinned to himself and stood up straighter. What a rush!

* * *

The molly carp surfaced ten metres behind them, and sculled along like a faithful dog until Boris managed to get his gun out of his belt, but the creature submerged before he could draw a bead on it. A sinuous swirl appeared five metres to one side of it, and the pink snout of a rhinoworm broke the surface.

'We got problems,' muttered Boris, aiming at its snout, but electing not to fire when it also resubmerged.

'How observant of you,' said Keech. He had the side of the AG motor cover hinged open so he could inspect the burnt-out control system. After a moment he pulled an optical IC and plugged in an optic cable from the control column. The motor surged for a moment, lifting them a metre above the waves. A quick burst from the thruster had them skating away, and they were fifty metres from the two escorting creatures before the scooter started to lose height again.

'Fsk pock . . . help?' said SM13 and the three of them turned to stare at it.

'Self-repair?' asked Keech.

'Sprerz-sprock,' said Thirteen, and rose a few centimetres out of the luggage compartment before dropping back.

'It speaks?' said Roach.

'They often do—but usually only to say *"Take that, fucker"*. But then my own experience of SMs has mainly been restricted to those uploaded into war drones. They don't normally employ a wide vocabulary. They don't really need one,' replied Keech.

'Sprzzz carp Sniper.'

'Makes no sense at all,' muttered Boris. 'What's SM stand for anyway?'

'Submind. So the Warden's obviously taking an interest in what's happening down here. We'll probably be seeing a few of this one's brothers and sisters some time soon. Pass it here.'

Boris hefted the probe out of the luggage compartment and handed it carefully to Keech. The monitor grabbed it in one hand and shoved it under his seat, on top of the AG motor, which was now letting out faint wisps of black smoke.

'It might be able to give us some lift in a bit. We're going to need it,' he explained.

'Scugger-fuck,' said the probe. It thumped against the underside of the seat, and the scooter lifted fractionally. Keech gave the thruster a quick burst, and the scooter surged forward just enough to avoid the rhinoworm that had chosen that moment to try for a mouthful of Roach.

'We ain't gonna make it,' whined Roach.

Keech passed him the weapon he'd used against Frisk's ship. 'This still works, but be careful; there's no control system, so it could fire in any mode. Don't use it unless you really have to,' he warned.

Roach held the weapon in one hand and pensively inspected its controls. He peered down the silvered insides of the twin barrels, then quickly pointed them away from himself.

'These are illegal, ain't they?'

'Yes, does that bother you right now?' asked Keech.

Roach aimed the weapon at the two following swirls. 'Not particularly,' he admitted.

When Pland took over the watch he began by joyously zapping even the smallest leeches that entered the clearing, until Janer thought he'd never get to sleep. Sitting up, wrapped in foil-like heat blanket by the fire, he opened his pack in search of a suitable pill. For a moment he eyed the hexagonal package he'd brought along at the mind's insistence, then closed his pack again, as he'd decided against the pill. He didn't want to fall into a heavy sleep, with things like that huge leech out there. He lay down again and stretched himself out on the lumpy ground.

'Anything from the Warden?' he whispered.

'I'm allowed to speak now, am I?' asked the mind.

'I didn't want you distracting me while I was on watch.'

'You did not want me talking about the packet of sprine crystals Captain Ambel has brought along.'

'That too,' said Janer.

'Just one crystal in the front of the box and I will cease to . . . bug you.'

'Very funny.'

'Would independent finance be a suitable motivation?'

'Explain.'

'At present you are effectively in my employ. You travel where I wish you to travel, and you take my eyes with you. Ten million shillings paid into your private account would make you independently wealthy and you could travel wherever you wished. You could go to Aster Colora, as you have always wanted. You could return to Earth any time you wished. There are many things you could do.'

'Ten million just to put one crystal in the front of your little box?'

'Yes,' the mind replied.

'That can only mean your intentions are against Polity law, and I'd probably be charged as an accessory. Accessory to multiple murder would mean being mind-wiped at best.'

'Spatterjay is not within the Polity.'

'It is not in the Polity yet, and are you telling me your hornets will stay here on-planet?'

'No crime has been committed.'

'Yet.'

'You argue that, yet under Polity law any Polity citizen may bear arms.'

'Within limits,' said Janer.

'The only proscribed items are explosives and energy weapons. That proscription is very specific as concerns weapons in the gigawatt range, which, incidentally, is precisely the level of weapon that a representative of Polity law has already been using here.'

'What?'

'The monitor, Sable Keech, was in possession of an antiphoton weapon capable of a gigawatt burst. The penalty for owning such a weapon is moral reconditioning.'

'So that's what it was,' said Janer.

'I would be in possession of no such weapon. What I would possess would merely be for personal defence.'

'I'd like to go to sleep now.'

'You have no way of refuting my arguments. Consider this: you get ten million in your account and my aims are

*achieved now. The alternative is that they are achieved in the
next solstan year and you do not get ten million in your account. You would, in fact, have to seek gainful employ with
someone else.'*

'Threats now.'

'Promises.'

'I just don't think it's a good idea to inflict this planet with
hornets carrying sprine in their stings. Individual hornets are
still just insects and they'll react to defend themselves unless
directly under your control. A lot of people here could die.'

'Ten million shillings.'

'I'll sleep on it,' said Janer guiltily.

The mind made a buzzing, self-satisfied sound.

When Janer woke again, he felt as though he'd only been
asleep for a moment—until he noticed that he could now
distinguish sky from dingle. He looked around to see who
was on watch, and saw Forlam sitting at the perimeter, the
carbine resting across his lap, and his back turned to the dingle. The crewman looked tired and bored—no doubt Pland
had scorched all the leeches in the immediate area earlier in
the night—and much in need of relief.

Janer was about to call out to him, when he realized he
must still be asleep and dreaming. Standing behind Forlam
was a blue man—or rather the body of a man. This figure
stood about four metres tall, and impossibly thin and long-
boned. His hands looked like giant harvestman spiders, his
torso a long arc of ribs, and his arms and legs seemed to possess more joints than they should do. Also, he had no head.
This is what persuaded Janer he must be dreaming—that and
the slow and silent way the blue man moved. Anyway, surely
Forlam would not court disaster by sitting with his back to
the trees, would he? As Janer tried to wake up, tried to call
out, he became aware of Ambel's snores, and connected
them with some kind of reality.

Suddenly he realized this was no dream. Between the blue
man's shoulders sprouted a questing leech's mouth, and
Janer now knew who this man had been.

'Forlam!'

But his cry came too late. One long bony hand reached down and took Forlam up like a doll. Forlam yelled once and the carbine dropped to the ground. Then he saw what had hold of him and suddenly went silent, mesmerized. The man-thing raised him to its horribly eager leech-mouth and that mouth attached to Forlam's torso.

Forlam screamed.

'What the bloody hell!' Ambel sat upright.

Janer leapt across the still-prostrate form of Captain Ron and dived for the carbine. He seized it just as other questions were shouted. Ambel's blunderbuss went off with a huge bang and the sound of its shot striking the man-thing was the slap of a spade on flesh. The blow peeled back skin which immediately rolled back into place. The thing kept grinding at Forlam and Forlam kept on screaming.

'Bugger! . . . Bugger! . . . Bugger!' yelled Peck, pumping his shotgun and blasting away with each repetition of the word. Each hit slewed away fragments of the creature's skin and punched a grey hollow, but each hollow quickly refilled and blue skin slid back into place. There were other shots, Janer did not discern from whom. He aimed at blue gut and fired. The creature's torso smoked and it jerked backwards, skin charred away to expose knotted woody fibre underneath. As Janer fired again, it pulled Forlam away from its mouth and hissed out a cloud of blood. A third shot charred skin from its legs, but seemed to cut no deeper than that. It suddenly dropped Forlam to the ground and took a long stride back into the dingle. It was gone in a moment.

'Oh god, it was *him*.' Erlin shuddered.

'Bugger!' Peck yelled again, and went roaring across the clearing after the man-thing. Ambel caught him by his jacket collar and flipped him on to his back. With a sick expression on her face, Erlin grabbed her medkit and went over to where Forlam lay moaning in the undergrowth. Ron chose that moment to snort awake and sit upright.

'What's going on?' asked the Captain.

Janer stared at him, then cracked up. This was all just too bizarre. He sat on the ground and laughed so hard his stomach hurt—this inappropriate hilarity ending with a fit of coughing. Ron stared at him with a puzzled expression, then transferred his attention to Ambel, calmly reloading his blunderbuss, then to what Erlin was doing. Pland and Anne were holding Forlam down while she worked on him. She had picked up Janer's heat sheet and was cutting it into wide strips. Nothing else was big enough to suffice as a dressing for the hole in the crewman's body.

'Bugger,' said Peck, sitting upright.

Ron stood up and walked over to examine Forlam. There he exchanged a few brief words with Erlin before coming back, obviously irritated, to Janer and the rest.

'Best get packed and moving,' he said.

'Forlam?' asked Janer.

'I'll carry him. We gotta catch that thing afore its head finds it,' explained Ron.

'Catch it?' said Janer, but Ron was no longer listening. He had his attention fixed on Ambel who had pulled on gloves to open a waxed packet secured at his belt. Ambel then took out a single red crystal and crumbled it into the sheath of his knife. He then spat into that sheath and replaced the knife.

'Best be moving,' he growled and stared towards where the Skinner's body had vanished.

The Hive mind chose that opportune moment to address Janer. '*Frisk's ship has moored in the cove,*' it announced.

'Better and better,' Janer spat.

Rebecca Frisk stared at the open door, and the two human blanks waiting there. The leading one, a heavily muscled man with virus-blue skin and a mass of scar tissue down the side of his face, gestured at her with the nerve-inducer he held. She rose and walked forwards, and the two of them parted to allow her past. She considered trying to snatch a holstered weapon, then shelved the idea. These blanks were as old as the Captains and, like all the other bodies she and Jay had supplied to the Prador, had been infected with the Spatterjay virus from the moment of capture. Their bodies would be much stronger than the body she inhabited, since it had been infected for several centuries less than theirs. She might be able to knock the Batians about, but not these two.

Vrell waited for her on the lower deck, turning to watch as she climbed through the hatch. To one side the two mercenaries stood glaring. Frisk immediately noted that they had been disarmed.

'You will go ashore,' said Vrell. He gestured with one of his legs to a ship beached there. 'Ashore are Sable Keech, Gosk Balem and the thing that was once Jay Hoop. It does not concern me what you do there.'

'I'll get Jay,' said Frisk.

'That does not concern me. You will not remain aboard this ship.'

'Why not?'

Vrell turned away from her, and she felt the hard hands of the blanks close on her upper arms. They moved her over to where the two Batians stood.

Vrell continued, 'You no longer serve a purpose. The Convocation has been called and all the Old Captains are coming to attend it. Within days they will all be here, to discuss the fate of Gosk Balem. I must keep this ship here until then. You pose a threat to the completion of my task merely by being on board. You are not under my control—nor are your mercenaries. You will all go ashore.'

'Will you let us have weapons at least?' Frisk asked.

While Vrell considered the matter, it was Speaker who replied.

'She and her mercenaries may indeed take weapons ashore. They will not be able to get back through your defences.'

'Ebulan! What is this? What are you doing? I thought we were friends,' cried Frisk.

'You wax sentimental, human. You have been an inefficient tool I tolerated only because there was no easy replacement for you. You became a living proof of what I achieved during the war with your kind and a demonstration of the source of my power. I brought you here to serve another purpose, even though you had become an embarrassment to me and a danger to my political ambitions. As Vrell has stated: You no longer serve that purpose.'

Rebecca Frisk stared expressionlessly at Speaker, and

then turned to the rope ladder leading down to the ship's boat. One of the blanks filled a rucksack with a selection of weapons and tossed it over to the Batians. Svan picked up the sack with a glare at the heavily armed blanks. With a final look of hatred flung at Vrell, she followed Frisk down the ladder. Shib went after her with a similar expression.

'Isn't it dangerous to let them live?' asked Vrell, as he watched the boat being rowed ashore by the male Batian.

'Not really,' said Speaker. 'And it pleases me for things to end this way.'

'I do not understand, father,' said Vrell.

'I do in fact retain some feeling for Rebecca Frisk and find in myself a reluctance to kill her, as would be logical— here and now. So it pleases me that she is going ashore, since I know that it will please her to hunt these allies of Sable Keech. It also pleases me that humans will be running around killing other humans; that there will be so much irrelevant drama. In the end they will *all* die: the Old Captains, Gosk Balem, Hoop, and our dear Rebecca too.'

'They may try to seize this ship,' warned Vrell.

'The weapons they now have are not sufficient to the task. You are safe where you are, and you are sure to complete your mission successfully. You will be remembered,' said Ebulan.

'Thank you, father,' said Vrell.

'The Convocation—that was the reason, nothing else,' said Svan.

'I don't understand,' said Frisk, eyeing the weapon Svan held trained on her while Shib rowed them ashore.

'Of course you don't. For too long you've thought the world revolved around you. Ebulan has his own agenda, and you've been incidental to it all along. I had that figured as soon as Vrell came on board. Ebulan brought you here because only the presence of someone as notorious as you would be considered important enough to bring all the Old Captains together in Convocation. Coincidentally Gosk Balem was also discovered still to be alive, and a Convocation already called. That probably happened even before

Ebulan's agents finished spreading the news that you were on-planet.'

'Ebulan wouldn't do that,' said Frisk, just for form's sake. She eased herself into an apparently more comfortable position—one that put her hand closer to Svan's weapon. As Svan backed away and slowly shook her head, Frisk showed her teeth in what might have been a grin.

'Ebulan, like all Prador, thinks of humans merely as prosthetic limbs,' added Svan dryly.

'Why does Ebulan want a Convocation?' asked Frisk. 'What can the Old Captains, those old humans, possibly do for him?'

'They can die,' said Svan. 'The Prador is severing all his prior connections with your coring trade in a permanent manner. I find it surprising that he let you live like this, considering that you are one of the strongest connections. Perhaps that Vrell creature will be sent ashore to mop up the last of us, once it's finished wiping out the Convocation fleet, and once we've meanwhile finished killing each other.'

'Great, so where do we go from here, then?' asked Frisk, a sneer in her voice. She shifted closer again, testing Svan's tolerance, pushing it.

Svan leant back and fired. Frisk jerked back as the beam scorched the side of her face, then reached up to probe the burn with her forefinger. Svan watched her, the flat snout of the QC laser directed at her eyes. Frisk glared back, then carefully settled down where she was, and didn't try to get nearer again.

'I'm not sure where we go from here,' said Svan, as if nothing had just happened. 'The Warden knows about all three of us so there's no way for us to get off-planet via the runcible. If we handed you over, however, I imagine the Warden might be inclined to be lenient. The only alternative seems to be to stay here, and I do not like that alternative. The Warden would hunt us down. It'd hunt us for the rest of our lives. It would just put a submind on the task, making it that mind's one purpose of existence. Wardens can be very patient about things like that.'

'There is another way,' said Frisk, 'if you dare to trust me.'

Svan said nothing and waited. Frisk went on.

'Off-planet I have billions of credit units in numerous accounts, all easily accessible. I have agents and whole organizations under my control. All I need do is get to a net access point and send a few coded transmissions. I could have a ship here in a matter of months,' she said.

'Burn her,' said Shib. 'She'll do us at her first opportunity.'

'I'm thinking about it,' said Svan.

Frisk said, 'You both know how lenient the Warden would be. These Polity border AIs don't always stick to the rules. Its "leniency" would probably consist of giving you a choice between slow mind-wipe, the furnace, or being handed over to the Old Captains.'

'Burn her,' Shib repeated as he brought the rowing boat up against the beach.

Svan said nothing while he pulled the oars in, stood and, with the rucksack of weapons slung over his shoulder, hopped over the bow on to the sand. Svan slowly stood and backed away from Frisk. The mercenary felt her way with her feet and did not stumble once. She too stepped out on the sand while Frisk remained seated in the boat. If it came to the worst, Frisk reckoned on diving over the side as her only option.

'Come ashore,' ordered Svan, as if reading her mind.

Frisk hesitated, then quickly followed the mercenaries on to the sand. Svan flicked a glance at the ship beached further down the shore.

'You can't keep me at gunpoint all the time,' said Frisk.

Svan said, 'Ebulan upset your nerve linkages deliberately with the intention of making you behave irrationally. You were set up as a target, like a wounded animal. But it was a miscalculation that jeopardized his primary mission. The drugs you now possess should stabilize you.' Svan could not help resorting to sarcasm: 'Are you stable enough to understand you are unlikely to get away from here on your own?'

'That bastard crab,' said Frisk, glaring back out to the ship they had left before returning her attention to Svan. 'I'm stable enough—stable enough to offer you the same fee for your hire as I did before. Do we have a deal?'

Svan glanced round at Shib, who now held a laser in his hand.

'Give her a weapon,' she said.

Shib reached in the sack and took out one of the short black shell-projectors they'd brought along specifically for Hoopers. He pointed this weapon casually to one side as he tossed Frisk the laser.

'I'm sure you won't be needing much more than that,' he said.

She caught the weapon and held it aimed at the ground for a moment. After that hesitation, she slid it into her belt and glanced towards the beached vessel.

'What now?' asked Svan.

'We get Jay,' said Frisk.

'Is that entirely necessary?' asked Svan.

Frisk turned back to her. 'That's part of the contract. We go after Jay and those hunting him. There's clearly Old Captains in their group who must have pulled this ship ashore. Them we don't kill. We bring them back here to relaunch this ship, then we head back for the Dome.'

Shib looked askance at the ship and snorted.

'You got any better ideas, mercenary?' snapped Frisk.

'We have no better ideas,' admitted Svan. She nodded towards the path cut into the dingle. 'They should be easy enough to track.'

Frisk stared at the two of them for a moment, then abruptly turned and headed for the path, the two mercenaries lagging behind her. Shib attracted Svan's attention, pointed at his weapon, and made a twisting motion with his hand. Svan gave him a smile he did not notice, for by then he was too busy watching the dingle.

Forlam was white and as unmoving as a corpse. He wore the expression of the brain-damaged, and the dressing made from Janer's heat-sheet was stretched tight across the hideous injury under his rib cage. His trousers were stained with blood, and other substances. *What now?* Janer wondered. How does the man live with half his guts missing from his body? While watching Anne and Pland strap the drained crewman to Ron's back, he put this question to Erlin.

'He'll live,' she explained. 'The question is whether or not he'll be human, though. He might become something like . . . something like the Skinner's body—like the Skinner himself.'

'What about nutrients, liquid? . . . How can any body heal with half its internal organs missing?' Janer persisted.

'In Hoopers internal organs can grow and heal much more quickly than damaged or missing limbs. The Spatterjay virus alters DNA to optimize survival. An arm is unnecessary, a digestive system *is* necessary. Think of that monster we just saw. In survival terms the most essential item missing from it wasn't the brain, it was the mouth—so it grew a mouth,' she said.

'Surely a brain is necessary, and what about the senses located in the head—hearing, smell and sight?' said Janer.

'It'll have the same senses of a leech: heat and vibration. As for a brain, it'll have some rudimentary ganglion at the top of its spine. That it was standing upright tells me it has grown an inner ear, and that it could continue to use its limbs tells me that same ganglion may even be as complex as an insect's brain. It's likely that such alterations required less energy than converting a basically human body into the body of a leech.'

'That can happen, then?' Janer asked, ignoring the filthy comment that came over his Hive link at Erlin's reference to 'an insect's brain'.

'Oh yes, the virus optimizes survival, optimizes flesh growth: the leech's harvest. This isn't necessarily what's best for humans, though. Flatworms are better survivors than us humans,' she said.

'Well, that's nice to know,' said Janer, thinking he really didn't *want* to know any more. Erlin continued remorselessly as they followed the others away from the overnight camp.

'The worst thing is when a human mind ends up in the body of a leech. That didn't happen to Ambel, probably because he was fed upon too much to build up the energy to make that change; and when Sprage hauled him up out of the sea, he was fed Dome-grown food to prevent it. When the transformation does start to happen, and can't be prevented, Hoopers feed the victim sprine. For all of them it's their greatest fear: to end up being only able to feel vibration, heat, pain, or hunger.'

'Could there be many of them about?' Janer asked, thinking with horror of the huge leech he'd burned during the night.

'There could,' said Erlin, offering no comfort.

As they stomped on, deeper into the dingle, Janer began to notice pronounced changes in the flora and fauna. The swollen trunks of the peartrunk trees were larger, and they often had large splits running through them, so that they seemed more like barred cages than solid trees. The leeches in their branches were dark red rather than the usual brown of coastal or sea-going leeches, and here the frogmoles were absent. After a time, Ambel no longer needed to use Ron's machete, as the growth of foliage became steadily higher. The large flat leaves that grew at ground level near the coast now sprouted at the top of thorny trunks standing five metres tall. It was dark here and the ground was coated with soggy rolls of leaf and brittle white twigs. Fungi were scattered amidst this like droplets of orange blood. Now the leeches falling from above were not their worst problem; it was the leeches lurking in the fallen foliage that oozed towards one's ankle if standing in one spot for too long.

When Ambel suddenly called a halt, Janer thought this a foolish place to choose, until he realized they were pausing only to allow another denizen of the dingle to pass.

Through the shady trunks came a huffing squeal and something huge moved painfully into view. To Janer it looked like a lizard made in the shape of a buffalo, but with some extreme differences to either creature. It did not have hooves or claws, but huge flat pads; the horns on its head were repeated in rows along its neck, and it had no tail. Janer mistook it as being four-limbed until he spotted the mandible limbs folded under its three-cornered mouth. Its tough hide was heavily pocked and Janer realized that the circular marks he had assumed were scales, were in fact healed leech scars.

The creature lumbered on past, flinging only a glance at them with its single double-pupilled eye. At the shoulder, it stood twice the height of a man and seemed a formidable creature. That it was a vegetarian, was evident when it halted by one of the thorny trunks and ground a lump out of it with its serrated mandibles. The vibration this caused had leeches falling on to it out of the tree. They immediately attached themselves and bored into its back. It grunted on finishing the mouthful it was chewing, then turning its head each way it used its mandibles to pull off any leeches it could reach. It then champed another mouthful—and more leeches fell.

'We'll go round,' said Ambel.

'Is that thing dangerous?' asked Janer, his carbine held in readiness.

'No, but they are,' said Pland, pointing to the leeches wriggling on the ground or oozing back up the tree trunks.

'What is it?' Janer asked Erlin, as they gave the huge creature and the rain of leeches it was causing a wide berth.

'Its name? I think it's called a tree pig or something.'

'Wood pig,' Pland corrected her.

She nodded and went on, 'It's one of the heirodonts. There's thousands of different kinds—some no bigger than a pin head. That's one of the largest types you'll find on land. It's rumoured there are oceanic ones that grow larger, but that's never been proven,' she said.

'Does it have any predators?' asked Janer, wondering about some of the sounds he'd heard in the night.

'There's only two predators here on land: us'—she pointed up into the foliage—'and them.'

'Why only two?'

'The leeches and the virus evolved together. There may have been other land predators at one time, but the leeches left no room for them. I'd guess that the leeches took to the sea only a few million years ago, so that's why you find other predators there. Give this place another couple of million years and there'll be nothing in it but vegetation, herbivores, and leeches.'

'A grim prospect.'

'It's life,' said Erlin simply.

In time, the vegetation began to thin and sprouted closer to ground level again. Janer saw Pland pointing at something, and it took him a moment to distinguish, amid the surrounding trunks, what he was indicating. It was an octagonal metal post, half a metre wide and higher than a man, its surface thick with grey corrosion.

'We're closer than I thought,' said Ron.

Janer glanced at him, then at Forlam who was now showing some interest, and staring at the metal post. 'Perimeter,' the crewman managed to utter.

'What is it?' asked Janer, puzzled.

'Slave post,' said Ambel.

Janer was still none the wiser, but he saw Erlin nodding in understanding. Before he could ask her what Ambel was talking about, the Captain led them out of the dingle, and she had moved back to escort Forlam.

They came out on to the crest of a hill sloping down to a valley. Below them, a river rumbled between red-brown boulders. On the other side of this stood structures built of the same stone: tall many-windowed buildings sprawled like a disjointed medieval fort. Crenellated walls stretched between them and there were signs, under thick vegetation, of what had once been a moat. To one side the ground had been levelled, and the vegetation there was having trouble getting a hold on the glassy surface. A wrecked landing craft of very old design stood decaying on that same surface.

Janer moved up beside Ambel and stared.

'Hoophold,' said the Captain.

'And those posts?' Janer queried, gesturing behind with his thumb.

'The posts broadcast a signal to activate the explosive collars his captives and slaves wore. Here was where he kept them imprisoned, then cored them, and from here he shipped them out to the Prador,' Ambel explained.

'You think that . . . the Skinner has come back here?' Janer said.

'I don't have to think,' said Ambel, and pointed.

Squatting on a merlon of the nearest stretch of wall was something that could have been taken for a gargoyle—until it shifted its position and briefly opened its stubby wings. The head of Spatterjay Hoop was watching them approach.

It all came down to Prador politics, the Warden realized now. It continued observing through the many eyes of the enforcer drones below, and saw the ships of the Convocation fleet moving towards the Skinner's Island, and far ahead of them the ship Frisk had siezed. Of course: Ebulan wanted all living witnesses dead so he could claw back power in the Third Kingdom. One large explosion, when that fleet reached the island, and all the Prador's problems, here at least, would be solved.

'SM Twelve, I want four enforcers to get between the main fleet and that ship. If it shows any sign of moving from its present location I want it destroyed.'

Accessing Windcheater's server took a little while longer, as the sail was deep into studying a political history of Earth and obviously quite fascinated. Though it might cause Windcheater a headache, the Warden broke the sail's connection and linked in.

'Windcheater.'

'Yes, what, wadda y'want?' snapped the disgruntled sail.

'I want you to tell Captain Sprage that he should halt the fleet at least ten kilometres out from the Skinner's Island. I myself will inform those captains who possess radios or augs.'

'And why should I tell him that?' asked the sail, still irritated.

'Because if you do not, that whole fleet—and you yourself—will end up as a crust of ash spreading on the ocean.'

'Why's that?'

'Because I think it highly likely that waiting for that fleet at the Skinner's Island is a CTD. You should have no trouble finding information on such devices through your aug. If you do have trouble, then try "contra-terrene device".'

As the Warden withdrew, Windcheater had no trouble locating an encyclopaedia entry concerning CTDs. After reading it carefully he suddenly felt very vulnerable and very small. Snapping his head up from the deck he tried to locate Sprage. However, the Captain was in his cabin, so the sail shifted his head up behind Olian, who stood at the rail gazing out at the growing number of ships. He nudged her in the back with his snout.

'What is it, Windcheater?' Olian asked him.

'Did you know,' said the sail, 'that a CTD the size of a coffee flask can erase an entire city?'

'That's common knowledge to us, and we've lived with it for centuries now. Did you know that during the Prador war five entire planets were destroyed with them?'

Windcheater went slightly cross-eyed for a moment. 'This fleet must not get closer than ten kilometres to the island, so the Warden warns. He claims there's a CTD waiting for it there. I suppose it will be a relatively small-yield device, but even that's too much. I think that if we continue to move any closer I'll consider my contract void and get straight out of here.'

Olian's face went a little white as what the sail had just told her slowly impacted. She pushed herself back from the rail and hurried to Sprage's cabin.

Windcheater lifted his head higher to scan the many ships now under sail. Eighteen so far. He thought deep and hard about all of the things he had learnt over the last few days. There was the Polity, huge and embracing thousands of worlds; there was the Prador Third Kingdom; and beyond these there was probably an awful lot more. His own kind, he realized, needed to gain some real leverage—in terms of political, economic, and possibly military power. Not so they could become major players in the grand scheme of things, but just to make sure that others would not inadvertently wipe them out.

And, so brooding, Windcheater began to make plans for *his* people and *his* world.

16

The huge whelk shell was now nearly empty of flesh and the heirodont felt sated enough to return to the depths. Soon all the leeches clinging to its surface would be turned to mere threads by increasing pressure and, unable to feed, would detach and rise back to the surface. For the heirodont, leeches represented the bane of its life: never having evolved the nerveless fleshy covering of turbul or boxies, it was put in constant pain by the onslaughts of smaller leeches, and could even be killed by some of the larger ones. This last danger should perhaps have made it more observant of its surroundings but, though intelligent enough to know that this giant whelk had been the same one that had evaded it earlier, it was also stupid enough to concentrate on its meal too closely. It still had its nose deep inside the cavernous shell, tatters of flesh hanging about it like cave moss, when an enormous leech struck it from the side.

SM3 likened its appearance to a Harrier jump-jet, an ancient flying machine it had spotted on an 'historical weapons' site, but SM4 argued, on surveying the same site, that it looked more like a helicopter gunship. At their inception, the two subminds had not possessed sufficient mental differences from each other to have anything to debate, but as the hours rolled on they slowly began to develop individuality.

'Why do you think the boss put that nancy in charge of us?' Three asked its companion as they searched their assigned sector.

'Well,' said Four, who was becoming the more dominant of the two enforcer-drones, 'I reckon it's all down to prior physical experience of this world. We got the programming but we ain't got the experience.'

Flexing its nacelles, Three harrumphed.

'Yeah, Twelve might have done a bit more than us, but it ain't got the firepower.'

Four, who had been playing 'devil's advocate', moved into the defensive. 'It's not all about what you can do, but about what you can understand.' Even as it said this, the drone was not quite sure what it meant.

'Twelve might have more experience of the physical world, but he sure ain't got the watts to handle it. That's what *we're* for,' argued Three.

'Well,' began Four—and then fell silent for a moment. 'Did you get that?'

'Sure did!' said Three excitedly.

The enforcer drones dropped low, and decelerated on ribbed fusion flames. Below them, the sea was kicked up in two tracks of white spray when they turned as one to nose back along the course they had been following. They moved more slowly now and slid apart, their dishes and antennae swivelling as if scenting prey.

'There: underspace signature,' said Four with satisfaction.

The drones turned again and hovered over the seawater like a couple of wasps zeroing in on a fizzy drink. They bobbed in the air as they attempted to read something from the tightly beamed signal—trying to pick something up from it by inductance, without interrupting it.

'We *have* something!' Four bellowed across the ether.

Flashes of quaternary code flashed through from their receivers, as they tried to nail down some sequence of the code.

'Direct transmit all you are receiving,' SM12 instructed them.

'We're getting it!' shouted. Three, as it tried to pull together something coherent to pass on. Then, 'What's that?'

Four did not get a chance to answer its companion, as a black line cut from the surface of the sea directly towards SM3. The drone fragmented round a disk of light, its weapon nacelles cartwheeling across the waves. Four blasted away from the surface, and something detonated below it. Then, to one side, a Prador war drone broke from the surface and headed towards it. Four released two seeker missiles and planed away. One missile exploded way out of range, but the remaining one blew just ten metres from the Prador drone and swallowed it in fire. Four slowed then abruptly accelerated, as the Prador drone came through that flame with only a coating of soot on its armoured skin.

'You cannot survive,' the Prador drone transmitted.

Two missiles came shooting after Four like hunting garfish. The drone blasted higher, only to be slammed sideways as its path intersected that of a stream of rail-gun fire. Pieces fell from Four's body as it tried to swerve out of the way of this hammering fusillade. But the gunfire tracked it, and the drone could do nothing but sling power into its fusion engine. The EM shell extinguished the drone's engine only fractions of a second before the two missiles came up at it from below. Four didn't even see them. It disappeared in a double explosion, nothing of it larger than a fingernail surviving the twin blasts.

The shore was already in sight as the rhinoworm chose its moment to attack. It thumped against the scooter, slewing it sideways, and its beaked mouth clamped over Roach's foot. Roach let out a yell, and promptly dropped Keech's antiphoton weapon into the water. Keech reached over and caught hold of Roach's jacket, while Boris lunged over the driver's seat to link his arms around Roach's chest.

'Shoot the fucking thing!' Keech yelled at Boris.

'I can't! He'll go in!'

Keech swore, and tried reaching for the weapon in Boris's belt.

'I ain't going! I ain't going!' Roach yelled.

'Hang on!' Boris yelled pointlessly.

Keech's arm felt leaden as he tried to move it with its cybermotors, then his face became a mask of pain as something crunched in his wrist. He finally managed to pull the weapon free and aim it at the rhinoworm.

'Damn! I can't pull the trigger! Try to hold him aboard!'

Keech released his hold and swapped the weapon to his
right hand. Boris, still holding on to Roach, was dragged
over the seat when the worm tried to haul his companion
into the sea. Keech's first shot burnt a hole into the worm's
head. It paused in its tugging only to blink at them, then
started pulling again. Keech fired again, then a third time,
opening a smoking crater in the bone between the worm's
eyes. Abruptly the creature released its prey and rose up out
of the water like a cobra about to strike. Keech took aim at
the underside of its head: one shot that blew open something
soft and yellow. The worm went rigid, coughed, then
dropped into the sea like a puppet with its strings cut.

'I told you I weren't going!' Roach shouted at the creature
floating limply beside the scooter.

'Oh shit,' said Boris, staring in another direction.

Keech and Roach turned and gaped at the approaching
mound of molly carp.

'This isn't going to stop it,' said Keech, holding up his
pulse-gun. 'What we need is something like my APW.' He
glared accusingly at Roach, who tried his best not to look
sneaky.

'I can't help it. Me arm ain't working properly,' the crewman protested.

'This is it, then,' muttered Boris.

The molly carp surged up to the scooter, but turned at the
last moment and snapped up the rhinoworm. Because of its
unusual mode of propulsion, it was able to stop dead once it
had hold of its prey. It rested right beside the stationary
scooter watching the occupants with one eye while it noisily
munched on the rhinoworm's head.

'Nice molly,' soothed Roach, while Keech tried to gener-
ate enough AG to lift them clear of the waves that were beginning to swamp his vehicle. The motor merely whined and
grated.

'Sprzzck burnt-out, safe Sniper,' said SM13 from under
the seat.

'Can you give us more lift?' Keech asked it quietly.

The SM thumped against the seat's underside and jerked

the scooter free of the waves. Roach swore as he nearly fell off again, but pulled himself back on while muttering about 'talking lumps of scrap'. Keech eyed the molly carp as he reached for the tap that fed pure water to the one working thruster. He opened the tap and the thruster coughed and began to smoke. As areas of it began to turn red hot, Boris hurriedly shifted his feet off it.

'What about thrust?' Keech whispered.

'No chance,' said SM13.

The thruster coughed again, and spat out something that skated hissing across the surface of the sea before it sank.

'There goes the grid,' said Keech.

The thruster began to belch steam and pure water started to pour out of it. Keech took his hand away from the tap and watched this steady stream.

'Might as well leave that tap on. It'll bring our weight down.' He leaned over and peered under his seat at the SM. 'You're all that's left now. I suggest you try something.'

'It's finished eating,' said Roach.

The three of them glanced over at the molly carp as it sucked in the last bit of the worm's tail. About now, thought Keech, it should belch loudly. The carp did nothing so amusing. Instead it turned towards the scooter, with a movement so abrupt it appeared surprised by it itself, and came shooting at it head on. Before Keech could raise his pulse-gun and fire, the creature struck the scooter and propelled it over the waves. A second time it rammed against the scooter, still driving it before it.

Keech took aim at its eyes, but Roach caught hold of his wrist.

'It's only playin'. Won't do to annoy it,' he warned.

The scooter tilted over as the carp shoved it towards the shore. It was now travelling faster than it had moved for some hours, waves slapping against its underside while the AG motor puffed out smoke and whined alarmingly. The molly carp abruptly stopped propelling it, the scooter continued on, only the occasional wave slowing its progress.

'Beach ahead!' yelled Boris.

The scooter skipped over a mound sticking out of the wa-

ter, smearing frog whelks with its underside. It continued to
skip waves like a skimmed stone and the AG finally started
to give out. The probe said something nonsensical that nevertheless sounded obscene. The scooter ploughed right into
the beach, flinging its three passengers on to the sand.

Keech swore, sat up and spat out a mouthful of sand.
Boris groaned and stayed lying on his back. Roach was the
first to his feet and limped unsteadily to the waterline. The
molly carp rounded the mound they'd just bounced over,
cruising in close to the shore where it drew to an abrupt halt.

'Did it mean to do that?' asked Keech.

'I reckon,' said Boris.

'Like hell,' said Roach.

The carp now started shaking violently, so that the water
foamed all around it. It then tilted back, opened its mouth
wide, and made a loud groaning sound.

'Weird,' said Boris.

Suddenly the beast sank out of sight—but not for long. It
exploded from the water, straight into the air, and seemed to
hover there, hanging nose-down for a moment, before crashing back into the sea.

'I ain't never seen one do that before,' observed Roach.

'Me neither,' said Boris.

Keech stared at the creature in perplexity. The way it had
hung there in the air for a long moment had been . . . well,
very strange. The carp was out of sight again, but left evidence of where it was by the gas and silty detritus bubbling
to the surface. A putrid smell wafted in across the waves.

'I reckon it isn't well,' commented Boris.

Just then, something exploded from the water with a
whoosh and flash of light and shot over to hover above them.

'I see,' said Keech, though he wasn't sure he did.

Sniper settled lower, opened his heavy claw, and dropped
the monitor's antiphoton weapon to the sand. He flexed his
legs and shook himself. Rancid pieces of meat fell from his
scarred armour. Keech felt a stirring of memory: hadn't
there been something like this involved in the clean-up operation here all those centuries ago? This was a war drone of

very old design, he realized, and though ancient and without human expression it certainly managed to appear pissed off.

'You all right?' grated the drone.

Keech was about to give an answer when a movement caught his eye. He glanced down at the seahorse SM, as it made a buzzing sound and flipped itself upright on the sand, balancing on its tail.

'Sprzzt, kill 'em,' the little SM managed.

Sniper turned and faced out to sea, then turned back to them.

'Fucking Prador drones,' he said. 'Let's see how they handle a real war drone.' And with that, Sniper racketed into the sky, opened up his fusion engine and was soon just a dot on the horizon.

'What was that all about?' Keech asked, studying the SM. The effort had obviously been too much for Thirteen, who went over sideways on the sand with a thump.

'Prador drones?' Keech queried the two Hoopers. Boris and Roach appeared just as confused. Keech went over to retrieve his weapon.

'Maybe they're back here. Maybe the war's on again,' said Roach.

Keech shook his head as he moved to the luggage compartment of the grounded scooter. From it he took out the portable medkit Erlin had given him, sat down on the sand, then injected and bandaged his wrist. This was the problem in using cybermotors ungoverned by an aug: they could over-reach the strength of the bones they were attached to. As an afterthought, he looked up at Roach.

'You need this kit?' he asked.

Roach flexed his hand then batted at his legs. Thick scabbing fell away from the burns exposed through his charred trousers, and clean skin was revealed underneath.

'Don't need none of that stuff,' he said.

'I thought not,' said Keech.

When he had finished working on his wrist, Keech stood and turned towards the dingle. The sudden and disconcerting appearance of that war drone he had to dismiss as irrelevant, simply because he had no explanation for it. Now he must concentrate on the matter in hand. It occurred to him that if Frisk thought he was dead, she might leave Spatterjay. Then again, she might also have come here in search of Jay Hoop, and Keech wanted both of them.

'Ambel and the others should be here somewhere, searching for your Skinner,' he said.

'That's so,' said Boris, staring contemplatively at Thirteen.

'How do we find them?' Keech asked.

'They'll have landed on the other side of the island,' said Boris.

'Best we head over there, then.'

He fired his APW into the dingle. There was a blinding purple flash and a thunderclap. Once the debris had settled, Boris and Roach got up from the sand and glared at Keech accusingly. Keech gestured to the avenue he had opened up lined with burning trees. He grinned and went stomping on in there. Roach limped after him and Boris moved to follow, hesitated, then went back to Thirteen. He picked up the SM before hurrying after the other two.

'Sprzzt thanks,' said the submind.

Pieces of bubble metal floating in the sea pinpointed where the two drones had died.

'That Prador drone won't be here,' said Sniper. 'You realize it *was* your secondary emitter and that there'll be more of the bastards?'

'I am aware of that, Sniper,' the Warden replied.

'You also understand that you've got no chance of pinning down that signal until we've thinned a few of them out and whoever's sending it starts getting desperate?'

'I am aware of that also, Sniper.'

'What is it you're after, then?' asked the war drone.

'Enough code to decipher, then I can break into the transmission.'

'To get that's gonna mean a stand-up fight. These bastards ain't gonna hang around while we record their overspill.'

'How fortunate, then,' said the Warden, 'that you are no longer anally retentive, so to speak.'

'Look, we need to work out how to do this,' snapped Sniper.

'What would you suggest?'

'I suggest we find the fuckers and blow them. The more we blow, the less of them can act as secondaries. That way we're sure to get more and more of their code.'

'Well, that sounds like a good plan. How do you suggest we locate them?'

'Sarcasm don't help,' said Sniper. 'I know Prador, and if there's one here, it's in the deepest hole it can find. So what's the deepest hole in Nort Sea?'

There was a long delay before the Warden replied, and its tone had somewhat changed when it did. 'Yes, there *is* one very deep trench down there.'

'And I'd bet that where I am now has a clear and direct line to the bottom of that trench.'

'Why is that relevant?' asked the Warden. 'Underspace transmissions go *under* space. They are not affected by anything less than a planetary gravity well.'

'It's relevant,' Sniper lectured, 'because Prador stole U-space tech from us. They still think like they're using realspace transmitters, and in terms of direct links and control. That's their psychology. Put a mountain in the way of the signal, and a Prador will think it's not quite in control of that signal's recipient. Your secondary emitters will be found in an area above that trench.'

'Very well,' said the Warden. 'SM Twelve, stay with drones Seven to Ten at the ship. The rest of you move into sectors immediately over the Lamant trench. Sniper, you take command there.'

With this communication came a deep-ocean map and Sniper saw immediately where he must go, and that it was not far. Slowly he slid up high above the ocean, with his antennae waving and a dish extruded from his stomach plates. As he travelled, he activated a system that he had not used in centuries, and bled power from his U-charger. Slowly, laminar gigawatt batteries built up to a huge charge inside him. Over the sea, he grinned his antiphoton grin. Soon he would get a chance to show his teeth—but he did not realize how soon.

Radar returned four signals as the enforcer drones the Warden had sent out came into the area.

'Spread out singly and search. Stay up high to give your-selves time to respond to any attack.'

'Sure thing!' the drones responded eagerly.

'If one of them comes at any of you, you don't try to take it alone. You run for me.'

Their response this time was less enthusiastic.

Sniper watched the four signals separate and spread out, and then, from memory storage, he downloaded differing programs into his carousel of smart missiles. He knew that nothing less than a direct hit by one of these on that Prador armour would do the trick, and even then . . . These Prador drones were certainly not the pushover they had been in the old days. Sniper accelerated and was soon at the precise cen-tre of the area to be searched.

'Shit!' shouted SM1.

Sniper received a fragmented picture of explosions, and one fleeting image of a Prador war drone. On radar he saw that SM1 was hammering towards him at Mach II. Close be-hind this SM came another signature that did not show up so clearly on radar. Sniper froze that second signature and stud-ied it.

'Exotic metal . . . right,' he said. Then, 'SM One, go higher, then straight down into the sea once you're a kilome-tre out. I will give you the signal. Don't deviate, you'll have incoming straight over you.'

'Poxingmissileupassgunning!' was the SM's reply.

Sniper opened up his fusion engine and sped towards the drone in trouble. After calculating vectors, he spat out one missile and watched it accelerate away. By the time it reached its intended target, it would be doing over Mach V. Little time to manoeuvre for either target or missile. Next Sniper cruised to the right and opened up with his rail-gun. A swarm of carborundum fingers, needle-pointed and weighted, sped out in front of him. In seconds SM1 came into sight, swiftly pursued by the Prador drone. Sniper watched the missile making small corrections to its course, then sent the signal. SM1 dived, pieces falling away from it as the Prador hit it repeatedly with rail-gun fire. The missile flew over SM1, straight into the Prador's face. It managed to shift aside only slightly before it was struck. Sniper tracked it as it came tumbling out of the explosion, its armour glowing white-hot. It corrected and swerved towards him, only to run straight into the swarm of carborundum fingers. As they struck, it shuddered in midair, jets of metal vapour issuing from its softened armour as the fingers penetrated and smashed its insides. Sniper turned in on it like a raptor as it dived for the sea. He allowed it to get within ten metres of the surface before grinning his grin. Violet fire speared the Prador war drone. It hit the surface and rolled along it like a droplet of water on a hotplate. Then it blew, scattering fragments that bounced and sank in clouds of steam.

'Take that, fucker,' said Sniper, as he jetted above those fragments.

The disembodied head dropped away before Janer could acquire it in the autosight and centre the beam on the thing's perch. Stone flaked and exploded away, as he tried to follow its course. In a moment it lost itself in the vines growing over the ruin. Janer only stopped firing when Ambel placed a hand on the barrel of the carbine.

'The power supply isn't endless, lad,' said the Captain.

Janer lowered the weapon and studied its displays. He swore when he realized there was only a quarter of a charge left.

'We'll go in after him,' said Ron, undoing the straps that held Forlam to his back. 'Erlin, Anne an' Pland can stay here with Forlam.'

Janer surmised that this meant he himself was included in the hunt, so there'd be a use for that quarter-charge yet. He watched as Ambel removed a packet from his belt and handed it to Pland.

'Wet your knife for the body if it turns up,' said the Captain. 'Same for the head.'

Pland nodded and gingerly accepted the packet.

Ambel pointed to the QC laser in his belt. 'That'll burn either of 'em, but it won't kill 'em.' Now he turned his attention to Peck, who stood clutching his shotgun and looking surly. 'You wouldn't stay here if I told you to, would you, Peck?'

'Buggered would I,' said Peck.

Ron laid Forlam on the ground, with his back resting against a rock.

'Feelings bits betterst,' said Forlam.

There seemed something funny about his tongue. Ron studied him dubiously for a long moment, before turning to Erlin.

'He's not well,' said the Captain meaningfully.

'I'll get some more Earth nutrients into him,' she said.

'Let's go then,' said Ron.

The four of them set off down the slope towards the river, and the ruin beyond. Janer walked with his nerves jangling, and his attention flitting to every movement in the undergrowth. Peck proceeded with his shotgun close to his chest, and Ambel plodded stoically along, with his blunderbuss resting on one shoulder and his hand on the hilt of his sheath knife. Captain Ron ran a stone across the edge of his machete as he walked. Once they were halfway down the slope, he pocketed the stone and held out his hand. Ambel passed across one of the small packets of sprine.

In the river, leeches clung to the bottom, looking just like trout swimming against the current. In the deeper water, Janer spotted a creature that had the appearance of an onion with spider legs, and though it showed no inclination to come out of the water after him, he kept a wary eye on it. They crossed by using the boulders as stepping-stones and shortly reached one of the overgrown moats extending below a crenellated wall. Peck stared down into the moat and spat. Janer also gazed into it, and saw only stagnant water filled with a tangle of white branches. He was about to move on after the others when he realized that branches were not what he had just seen. He took another look at them and realized that what he was seeing was a tangle of human bones.

'They shouldn't be there,' he pointed out.

'Hoop's place,' reminded Ambel.

'But that was centuries ago.'

'Human bone don't rot here, not unless it's Hooper bone,' said Ron.

Janer was about to ask why, but realized Erlin was not here to answer him.

'A more suitable monument than that, I guess,' he said, referring to the Hoophold.

'Bugger,' said Peck, with reference to nothing in particular.

They walked on, moving parallel to the moat, until they came to a place in the wall where there had once been a steel door. Some fragments of corroded metal still jutted from the stonework and the earth below was stained red with rust. Here, Ron scrambled down the slope to the edge of the stagnant water. He tucked his machete under one arm, pulled on his gloves and squatted down. He dipped the blade into the water then with great care sprinkled a few sprine crystals on to the wet metal before grinding them all to paste with the stone he had retained. After smearing the paste all along the razor-sharp edge, he tossed the polluted stone away.

'Cross here,' he ordered, holding the machete carefully away from his body as he waded through the stinking water.

Ambel quickly followed, then Peck. Janer halted at the edge, trying to detect movement below the oily surface.

'No leeches there. The bones have poisoned it,' said Ambel.

Janer decided to take him at his word and waded across. He tried to ignore a skull that they had disturbed from the bottom, which was now bobbing about in the silt like a Halloween novelty.

Once they had climbed the other side of the moat, they entered Hoop's demesne through the rusted door. The wall was two metres thick and above their heads were open murder holes the purpose of which, in an era long before this place had been built, would have been to pour molten lead over unwelcome visitors. Janer wondered if Hoop had ever used them for such a purpose. Probably yes, just for the hell of it.

Inside, was an open courtyard, with stairs all around leading up to the top of the walls. Beyond this lay a further confusion of walls and buildings. Ron led the way across the courtyard then halted to point down at the flagstones. No one commented on a long distorted footprint clearly visible in the dust. Hefting his machete, Ron gestured for them to continue. He guided them through a long tunnel into yet another courtyard, then beyond that into an overgrown garden.

Janer stared around him at familiar Earth plants that had managed to survive here, seeding and reseeding themselves down the centuries. Wild rose covered one wall and some sort of orchid sprouted from the black ground below a tilted sundial. The wall bordering the far end of the garden had some kind of vine embedded deeply in its strange decorations. On top of that wall rested the Skinner's head.

Janer raised his carbine just as the head moved, and he realized this was the second time he had been mistaken. The head was actually behind the garden wall, not resting on it. Behind the wall—and reattached to the long body that was now stepping into view.

'Oh bugger,' said Peck, more pertinently this time.

The Skinner was complete again and Janer had never before witnessed such a terrible sight. For here was a real monster: a blue man four metres tall and impossibly thin, hands like spiders, a head combining elements of warthog and baboon with much of a human skull, evil black eyes and ears that *were* bat wings, spatulate legs depending underneath the long jaw like feelers and, when it opened its long mouth, row upon row of jagged black teeth.

'Only just reattached itself,' said Ron calmly. 'Look at its neck.'

Janer gazed at the neck and saw a leech mouth located where an ordinary man would have his Adam's apple. He raised his carbine again, wondering how Ron could sound so analytical.

The Skinner roared, and came charging at them in ridiculous but horrible loping strides. Peck was already blasting away with his shotgun before Janer could fire. Janer's hit burnt skin from the monster's chest and seared one bat-wing ear. Yet the Skinner didn't even slow down, so Janer kept firing—as an arm like softball bats joined by pieces of elastic came sweeping in his direction. The hand hit him with horrible force—as if he'd run full tilt into the iron bars of a cage. He flew back into a tangle of roses and was slammed against a side wall. The breath whooshed out of him and he found he just couldn't move.

He was aware of Peck crouching behind the sundial, still blasting away, and next saw the sundial and Peck both taken up in a single grasp, heard stone crunching, and saw something bloody being discarded to one side. Then Captain Ron was there with his machete, and the Skinner became more wary, as it dodged Ron's attempts to lop off its limbs. Suddenly it darted forward in a blur of motion. There was a clang and a whickering sound as the machete spun through the air, then another clang as it bounced off the wall to Janer's right. This second sound seemed to return the life to Janer's limbs, and he started to haul himself out of a tangle of roses, swearing as thorns snagged the skin of his face.

As Janer recovered the carbine and sighted it on the Skinner's head, he saw it looming over Captain Ron as if relishing the prospect of tearing him apart. Ron just stood there with his arms folded, his legs braced, and a placid look on his face. This made the Skinner hesitate. Janer stepped forward, then promptly fell flat on his face—briars had become looped around his ankles. As he struggled to right himself and draw a bead on the creature again, he saw Ambel sneaking in behind.

The Skinner drew back one hand clenched into a fist, but Ron merely grinned at it. As Ambel drove his sprine-poisoned knife into the calf of the Skinner's leg, Janer opened fire again.

The scream it made was deafening: an amalgam of a human scream of agony and the squealing of a pig going to slaughter, but with its volume stepped up five-fold. Janer winced at the hideous sound, but kept firing at the Skinner's head. As it screamed, it lashed back with its foot and hurled

Ambel ten metres through the air behind it. It then struck out at Ron, slamming him so hard into a wall that the Captain nearly went through it, rubble falling about him. Still screaming, it took two loping steps towards Janer, who thought he was done for then. His laser burnt away skin, but seemed to have no other effect on this monster.

The Skinner ignored him as it hurtled past, scrambling over the six-metre wall behind him.

'What the hell was that?' said Keech.

'Hell's 'bout right,' muttered Roach.

'What do you mean?' Keech asked.

Roach glanced at Boris, and shrugged. 'Ain't like nothin' I've heard before,' he said, then promptly sat down to inspect his charred boots. After searching the pockets of his ragged coat, he found a length of fishing line, which he used to bind one loose sole back into place. Keech watched Roach impatiently as the crewman finished this task, then stood to test his weight on the makeshift repair.

'Are you quite ready now?' Keech demanded.

'Ready as I can be. Had me arm busted and me legs fried, so I ain't gonna be hurrying anywhere,' Roach grumbled.

Keech stared at him, unable to find a reply, then turned and set off through the dingle again. Roach and Boris exchanged a look, then slowly moved after him. A few paces farther on, Roach gestured at the SM Boris was cradling like a baby.

'Why don't you get rid of that thing?' he asked.

'It saved our lives,' said Boris.

Roach snorted. 'It'll slow you down,' he said with a sneaky grin.

They both glanced ahead at Keech, and began to walk just a little slower.

'Yeah, definitely slow me down,' said Boris, then grunted in surprise.

The SM had abruptly become the weight of something made of paper. He held it out on the flat of his hand and looked askance at Roach.

Roach shook his head. 'Didn't say we was in any hurry.'

Boris grinned weakly, tucking the SM under his arm, and together the two crewmen dawdled after Keech.

'Signal detected. Transmitting,' said SM5.

Sniper slammed himself into the sea as the only effective method of high-speed braking. As he went in, his course cut like a white icicle under the waves, until he had slowed enough to turn and explode from the surface again. In seconds he was accelerating towards SM5's last location—only the drone was gone. All that showed on radar was a dispersing signal.

'It got him,' said SM1 angrily, as it came hammering in from the west.

'No kidding,' said Sniper. He now routed the radar signals through a clean-up program and detected the Prador drone a couple of kilometres from where SM5 had been, and moving away.

'I can see you,' he sent.

The Prador drone swerved in a 'u' and came hammering back towards him.

'That you behind me, Two?' Sniper asked conversationally.

'Sure is,' replied Two.

'Good, I want you to veer off and go drop a cluster of mines *here*.' Sniper sent co-ordinates. 'Seems these arseholes always miss the upswing.' Behind Sniper, Two shot away, chuckling over the ether.

'One, you put a laser on it, and keep it on it,' Sniper instructed.

'Won't touch that armour,' SM1 pointed out.

'I know it won't, but it'll have to keep on juggling its sensors. It won't lose me, but it may well miss something smaller.' Sniper turned so he was hurtling sideways and, reaching precisely where he wanted, spat two missiles into the sea.

'Warden, how much code did you get?' he asked as he observed the missiles torpedoing away on their pre-programmed course.

'I could do with more, Sniper,' said the Warden. 'Why— are you getting bored?'

With the Prador drone hurtling towards him behind its two rapidly accelerating missiles, Sniper swore then slammed down into the sea. He was fifty metres down when one of the Prador's missiles detonated on the surface spearing white lines after him with its shrapnel. The second missile followed him down. He released some chaff, then a couple of mines, before abruptly changing direction. There were explosions behind, then a huge splash to his right. The Prador drone was coming straight after him, vapour and bubbles exploding from armour that had been heated by SM1's laser.

'Over here, arsehole!' Sniper sent.

'You are dead,' the Prador sent back.

'Ooh, now I'm all frightened.'

Sniper instantly changed course and shot up to the surface at forty-five degrees. The Prador went straight back for the surface, knowing it could come on Sniper quicker through the air. With its sensors confused and misreading, it saw only at the last moment the mines Two had dropped there. Emerging from the sea in a swarm of explosions the Prador shuddered into the air, seemed merely to shrug to itself, then accelerated towards Sniper again. Sniper turned on it and fired his antiphoton weapon. Violet fire ignited on the disk of a projected screen.

'OK, so you're tougher than I thought,' sent Sniper.

The Prador slowed, its screen still out in front of it.

'You're looking forward to this, ain't you?' Sniper sent, bouncing his signal off the sea.

'I am,' returned the Prador, 'and now it will end.'

Below the Prador, two white fumaroles speared up from the sea. The first missile was powerful enough to blow a bar of plasma through its armour. The second missile went in through the same hole and gutted it. The distorted shell, which was all that now remained of this Prador drone, arced into the sea. Still burning inside, it planed for a moment on superheated steam, then sank.

'Stupid,' said Sniper as he tracked the glow into the depths.

* * *

The screams were terrible, and Erlin was glad to hear them recede into the distance. If the Skinner had come her way, she was not sure what she could have done, other than die.

'Do you suppose that's it, then?' she said. 'Do you think they've poisoned it?'

'You'd know as well as me,' said Anne.

Erlin shook her head and concentrated on the task in hand.

Pland finished knocking a length of peartrunk wood into the ground nearby on which Erlin suspended the drip she had prepared, then turned on its plastic tap. Next, she pressed another tranquillizing drug patch against Forlam's upper arm. The recumbent crewman was completely out of it, and that's just how she wanted him to stay—for the present. She pressed a thumb to his bottom jaw and pulled it down. Forlam's tongue had turned into the feeding mouth of a leech, but at present it lay flaccid behind his teeth. Erlin inspected the back of her hand and the hole where a neat circle of flesh had been excised. Forlam's tongue had done that to her when she tried to look in his mouth earlier, while he was conscious. He'd been most apologetic afterwards.

'Needs lots of Dome food,' suggested Pland, staring off in the direction the other four had gone.

'I know that,' said Erlin, 'but right now we haven't got any—just a few supplements.'

'There's plenty on the *Treader*,' said Anne. 'Maybe I ought to sneak back and fetch some.'

Erlin glanced at Forlam, then back at her.

'He certainly needs some Dome food. Could you manage it without getting yourself killed?'

Anne gave her a pitying look, then stood up.

'I'll run,' she said, and turned to go.

Just then, three figures stepped into sight. All three wore black crabskin armour. All three were armed.

'Shit,' said Pland, and reached for the laser at his belt.

His hand touched the grip just as there came a sound as of a hammer striking an apple, and he flew backwards, landing on his back and skidding along the ground. Wisps of smoke rose from his chest. He just had time to lift his head and blink at his attackers, then a dull explosion turned his torso into an expanding ball of fire. In an explosion of torn flesh and blood, his head flew one direction and his arms and legs in various others.

'Nobody move!' yelled the figure which had fired.

Anne moved to draw her automatic and Erlin quickly grabbed her arm.

'Don't!' she warned. 'Your bullets won't get through that armour.'

Anne seemed about to ignore her and Erlin knew that she could not restrain her. Anne stared round at the steaming remains of her fellow crewman, and for a moment wore a puzzled expression. Erlin had seen this look before; because death was such an uncommon occurrence among them, Hoopers found it a very difficult concept to accept. Slowly the expression of puzzlement turned to one of resigned anger.

Anne returned her attention to the approaching three, slowly moving her hand away from her weapon. 'I hope I don't regret this,' she said.

'So do I,' said Erlin.

The foremost of the three removed her helmet, and looked from Anne to Erlin with a deranged expression.

Here is something horrible, was Erlin's immediate thought.

'What have you done to my Jay?' the woman asked.

So, this is Rebecca Frisk, concluded Erlin. Superficially she appeared an attractive young woman, but that this was merely a veneer over something old and ugly was also evident. Erlin kept silent.

Frisk turned from them and gazed at the Hoophold, smiling wistfully.

'You'll walk ahead of us,' she instructed. 'Try anything and you know what will happen to you.' She gestured to Pland's remains.

'What about him?' asked Erlin, gesturing at the unconscious Forlam, then instantly regretting that when one of the Batians turned his weapon on the prostrate crewman.

Frisk held up her hand. 'No, I don't think so,' she said. Gesturing with her laser for Anne and Erlin to move aside, she approached then squatted down beside Forlam. With one finger she pulled down his jaw to peer inside his mouth. She gave a small laugh and rocked back on her heels. 'We'll leave him here,' she continued, then abruptly yanked the drip from his arm and cast it aside.

Anne went rigid.

'The weapon—throw it on the ground,' ordered Svan, levelling the snout of her weapon at Anne's middle. Anne hesitated for only a moment, then undid her belt and dropped it to the earth. Svan now turned to Erlin, who wondered what she might want of her. The mercenary's hand snaked out at Erlin's belt, and she glanced down to see her QC laser being removed. *How alert am I?* she wondered. She'd been wearing the thing for so long, she'd forgotten its purpose.

'Step back, both of you,' said Svan, and the two captives did as directed.

Svan walked over to the belt, and stooped to withdraw the holstered automatic. She inspected it for a second, and then gave a bark of laughter before tossing it aside. The QC laser she tucked into her own belt.

'Get moving.' She pointed, as she stood up again.

Erlin and Anne turned and headed down the slope.

The Warden observed that the warning Windcheater had delivered earlier had been heeded, then concentrated its attention on another area of ocean. Even from one of the orbital eyes it had been possible to track the occasional flares of energy. It had to admit Sniper knew his business. Even with 'attitude', the enforcer drones remained pretty ineffectual in this situation. They were constructed for local police actions involving human terrorists, so could only cope with the kind of weaponry such groups normally possessed. They should still, though, have outclassed the antiquated war drone, just as the Prador war drones, with their heavy armour, outclassed them. But every time Sniper had come up trumps. The Warden suspected that Sniper had been constantly upgrading himself over the centuries that had passed since the war. Back then the old drone had certainly not possessed ballistic programs of such accuracy, nor did he own an antiphoton weapon. Even so, those Prador drones, with their armour and weaponry, should still technically have been superior. The Warden supposed Sniper's victories indicated that it wasn't the size of a weapon that counted, but how and when it was used. Each of Sniper's victories was like that of a medieval pike man bringing down a mounted knight in full armour.

'Signal detected. Transmitting,' piped up SM1.

The Warden soaked up the signal and hoped that there would be enough information this time before the fighting recommenced. It carefully studied the quaternary code as it came in, then loaded it into the same program as the rest.

'That's it,' concluded SM1.

'Where is it?' Sniper queried, as he hurtled towards the war drone.

'No sign of any Prador war drone,' said SM1, managing to sound utterly casual.

'You know what this means?' said Sniper to the Warden.

'Enlighten me.'

'It means that the Prador that's down there can't afford to lose any more of its drones, so has told them to head for cover rather than fight.'

'Yes, so it would seem.'

The Warden was distracted now. That last two-second sequence had been enough for decoding. 'Sniper, I have enough. You may withdraw,' it sent.

'Withdraw?' Sniper asked.

'Yes, that's what I said. I see no reason to have any more of my SMs destroyed.'

'Whatever you say,' said Sniper, shutting off with a crackle of static that sounded suspiciously like a raspberry. The Warden did not pursue this thought.

'SM Eleven, initiate and upload to com relay shell,' it sent to the satellite orbiting between itself and the planet. Two seconds later the satellite opened and spat yet another coffin-shape out into atmosphere. The Warden observed it for a moment, before concentrating a whole quarter of its processing power on the five seconds of coded transmission it now possessed. There was no point seeking to obtain any more, since if these five seconds couldn't be cracked then the rest certainly couldn't. After two seconds, the Warden ascertained that the code was based on random number generation from the quantum decay of a mixture of three rare isotopes. *A real bastard*, it thought. The Prador had never bothered much with building AIs, as they considered their own minds to be the pinnacle of excellence. This was unfortunate for them, as it deprived them of the knowledge that there was no such thing as a 'random number'.

17

Emitting low-frequency screams, the heirodont thrashed about as the giant leech drove its mouthparts into it. One thrash of its tail had the whelk shell tumbling over into the abyss, like a disconnected diving bell. The pain for the heirodont was horrific, as the leech reamed from its body a tonne of flesh and blubber, and even chunks of the flat black bone that comprised its skeleton. In comparison the rider prill, which came scuttling in anticipation down the leech's long slimy body, were only a minor irritation as they spread out from the predator's head to slice off for themselves portions of skin and blubber, then squat feasting with their little red eyes zipping constantly around their carapaces.

Vrell shifted uneasily, scraping his back legs on the deck. The adolescent Prador was feeling a strange sort of tension in his back end, under the ribbed plate that covered his rear stomach. He was also beginning to entertain thoughts about how unfair it was that he might soon die. Grinding his mandibles, he shook himself then brought his scope up to one of his eyes. There was no sign of any ships, but the relayed transmission from one of his father's remote probes had already shown that the Convocation fleet had halted ten kilometres away. Vrell glanced at the relevant screen: all the

sails had folded themselves up and there was still no movement there. The adolescent Prador turned his attention to the
blank at the instrument console below the set of screens

'Are we still being watched?' Vrell asked.

The blank reached up and touched one of the screens.
Four black dots slid across a white background, Prador
glyphs flickering and changing beside each one.

'AG signatures still present above us,' said the blank.

Vrell turned in agitation, his sharp legs further tearing up
the already splintered deck. Speaker, her one hand gripping
what remained of the port rail, turned her head towards the
adolescent. 'Father,' Vrell said towards her. 'The Captains
have been warned off. This is evident. They are not within
the blast radius. Perhaps we should abort.'

'You wish to abort, Vrell?' said Speaker.

'It is hard, father. I wish to complete my mission.'

'Vrell, you will complete your mission. There are twenty
ships out there now. When that figure reaches twenty-one, as
I am sure it will, then this ship will go out to join them.'

'The blast radius will then not include the island,' said
Vrell, flicking a look towards the Old Captain at the helm.
The man was scratching at the back of his neck again. Vrell
was very unsure about this, as he couldn't remember having
seen any of his father's blanks do that. He did remember
how the Captain had fought when the back of his neck had
been opened for the insertion of the spider thrall, and how
still he had become once it had connected. He was not so
still now.

'Correct,' said Speaker. 'Which is why you will go ashore.'

'Ashore?' Vrell flicked his attention back to Speaker.

'Yes, detonation of the device will be initiated by this
unit. You will take three other of my units to the shore with
you, and complete your mission there,' said Speaker.

On the cabin-deck, Drum continued to scratch at the back
of his neck. When the Prador clattered itself around to face
the shore, he paused, then really dug in with his fingers. Finally he managed to get the leverage he wanted, and he had
to repress a gasp of relief as the irritant started to come out
like a particularly hideous splinter. When the grey cylinder

of the thrall unit thudded to the deck, waving its legs just like a dislodged spider, Drum shifted his boot to one side and crushed the thing under one heavy hobnailed sole—then kicked it under the side rail into the sea. He had turned back into position and wiped his face of expression by the time Vrell could peer up at him again.

'When should I set out?' the Prador adolescent asked Speaker.

'Vrell, you will leave immediately.'

The three blanks sitting waiting by the forecabin wall abruptly rose to their feet. Vrell studied them for a long moment before turning his back towards them and squatting. He felt a weird twisting in his back end as they clambered on to his shell and took a firm hold on the rim.

Speaker snapped her attention up to Drum. 'Hard to port and full speed,' she said.

'I hear and obey,' said Drum, and spun the helm.

Speaker regarded him intently. Drum still kept his face free of expression as he opened up the throttle and the ship surged towards the distant Convocation fleet. Speaker turned back to Vrell. '*Now*, I said.'

Vrell moved to the place where he had torn the rail away while boarding, and launched himself over the side. He hit the water with a huge splash, and one of the blanks lost his grip, clawed at slick shell, and fell into the sea. Vrell observed the blank kicking at the water as he tried to recover a grip. The blank went under, came to the surface again. Grabbing the man with one claw, Vrell hauled him up and back on to the carapace. The man slid down again, but finally managed to cling on, but with his legs trailing in the sea. In the water around his legs, there started frantic movement, but his face registered no expression.

Vrell turned and sculled for the shore, and in doing so experienced a strange surge of emotion. He felt glad he was no longer on the ship. Twenty metres further away, sudden red fire flung Vrell's shadow across the sea. He turned for a moment to see smoke gusting from the ship's deck, needled through with bars of laser light. He turned for the shore again and sculled faster, an exhilarated but guilty feeling shuddering through his body. Perhaps if he didn't look, he would have no reason to go back.

Something flashed in the sky, and a projector mounted at the prow of the ship began to hum. Further laser strikes were abruptly shielded from the smouldering deck timbers. Drum tilted his head slightly and saw lights flickering above, and fast-moving shapes blackly silhouetted against the sky. That machine on the prow had to be a flat-shield projector. He lowered his gaze and observed the blank at the console tapping in instructions. The missile turret at the stern of the ship swivelled and began to cough out missiles from a spinning carousel. White fire lit the sky, and behind it flashed lines of red incandescence.

Speaker, who had been staring upwards, brought her attention down to Drum again for a moment, then across to the blank seated at the console. That blank was punching out further instructions. Speaker turned, as if jerked round, and walked over to the aft hatch. She lifted it and started to climb down. Drum grinned and pulled back on the throttle. When it didn't move, he swore and put on more pressure—but the metal handle snapped off in his hand. He cast the handle aside, then seized hold of the rest of the control and tore it from its optic cable. The ship still did not slow.

'Bugger,' said Drum.

At this, the blank on the deck below him abruptly turned from the screen and picked up the weapon propped against the console. Drum swore again, and ducked as purple fire lit the air, and both the front rail and helm exploded into splinters. Lying on the cabindeck, by what remained of the rail, Drum peered over the edge to see the blank stand up and begin moving back towards him. He had few options: diving over the side, which would lead to a slower and more painful death than that the weapon would provide—or he'd have to try for said weapon. He edged back, in readiness to fling himself down on the approaching blank, but then the back corner of the forecabin exploded and the deck he was on sagged, suddenly sliding him toward the main deck. He halted himself by bringing his feet down what remained of the helm's column.

'A full coring would have been a much more efficient option,' said the blank, aiming the weapon casually from his waist. Drum realized that it did not matter how casually the weapon was aimed, as even an indirect hit would kill him.

'You really think you can get away from here, Prador!' Drum yelled. 'The Warden'll tear you apart!'

'That will not be your concern,' said the blank.

There were three distinct cracks followed by a low snarl. A steel staple went skittering across the smouldering deck, then something long and pink, ending in a head full of charcoaled teeth, swung out from the mast. The blank had time only to look up at a black silhouette against the burning sky. The sail bit down hard and shook. The blank's body fell to the deck and the sail raised itself up and spat the head into the sea.

'Good job!' Drum yelled, sliding down the sagging roof and leaping on to the main deck.

The sail blew disgustedly through its lips, as if it didn't like the taste of what it had just bitten off. As Drum stepped forward, it glared at him then lunged. Drum dropped down with his forearms across his face—then gradually parted them when he realized he wasn't about to lose his head too. The sail had halted with its snout half a metre from his face. Exposing its charred teeth, it snarled at him, then tried to speak.

'Whas my names?' it hissed, the stub of the tongue Shib had removed waving obscenely in the back of its mouth.

'Anything you like,' said Drum.

'Goods,' said the sail. 'You wisl caulss me Winscasher.' The sail turned away from him and sniffed the air. 'Thiss ships nots neesd me.'

Drum edged past the creature and took up the weapon the blank had dropped. He inspected the controls then glanced to the aft hatch. He looked then at the turret still spitting out bursts of missiles, the shield projector swivelling to intercept incoming fire, then he gazed far out to sea. At this rate, it would not take very long at all to close in on the Convocation fleet.

'Sorry, old boy,' he said, and pointed the weapon at the deck.

As soon as he reached the beach Vrell shrugged the blanks from his back and inspected the scrapes made on his carapace by the questing mouths of leeches. None of them had been able to get through his armour. Vrell then turned his attention to the three blanks. One of them was lying on the sand.

'Why is this unit not standing?' Vrell asked, and received no reply. His father's attention had to be concentrated elsewhere at that moment. Vrell tried not to study too closely the surge of gladness he felt at that. Deliberately not looking out to sea he concentrated his attention on the fallen blank instead, and soon ascertained the reason for the human's difficulties: the flesh had been stripped away from the lower half of his body.

'Follow,' said Vrell to the other two and led them into the dingle. Had the Prador adolescent looked behind just once, he would have seen the flashes of purple fire from the *Ahab*, and seen the ship foundering. The blank he left behind still kept trying to stand up, under the instruction of his thrall unit. Instead, his fleshless legs collapsed under him every time.

Through the eyes of its four enforcer drones the Warden watched as they tried to get past the shield projector on the *Ahab*. The images it received were hazed with smoke, flashbacks, and the explosions of the missiles that the screen intercepted.

'APW fire!' shouted SM7.

'Not at us, you idiot,' SM12 replied. 'Eight and Nine, I want you to go in low over the sea, from the rear. You may get a window opened near that missile launcher. Use railguns to try to put a hole in the hull.'

'Moving in,' replied the two SMs, and soon the Warden had a clear view of them hammering in over the sea. Something cut a huge shadow above them for a moment.

'That's the sail,' said SM8, tilting in midair. The Warden froze the image it received, and would have smiled had it the ability. It flicked back to Eight as the SM opened up with its rail-gun.

For one second the stern of the ship was exploding into splinters, then a flat-shield cut between, and before this the sea turned white with repelled fire. The two SMs cut up into the sky.

'It's listing!' shouted Nine happily.

'That wasn't you, Nine. See if you can now get underneath the ship,' said Twelve.

The two drones arced around in the sky, then hit the sea. The Warden received sonar and ultrasound images of leeches fleeing the area like squid, then an image of the bottom of the ship like an open lantern. Its timbers were splintered and broken, and fires were burning inside.

'You may stand down for now,' said the Warden. 'If the ship does not go down, soon, then hit it again.'

'What about the Prador that went ashore?' asked Twelve.

'Leave it,' said the Warden. 'I don't think it will be going very far. Also, SM Eleven will be with you very soon, in the com relay shell, and I want you take make sure it is unharmed.'

With that, the AI cut contact and returned its full attention to those five seconds of Prador code. Already it had separated thrall code from carrier signal. The thrall code definitely had five distinct threads, which meant the adult Prador somewhere under the sea was linked to two blanks still on the ship as well as the three accompanying the adolescent Prador.

'SM Eleven,' the Warden sent. 'Here is the carrier signal. Trace and connect.'

Eleven, still decelerating into atmosphere, opened out its wings and extruded instrument pods and signal dishes. It was utterly without weaponry, its domain solely being that of communication and information.

'Tracing underspace signal. Connected and decoded. Tunnelling link establishing . . . established,' said Eleven.

'Stand ready,' said the Warden as it applied the full quarter of the processing power it was using to the carrier signal code alone. The signal separated into two strands almost immediately: *send* and *return*.

'SM Eleven, here is your decoder program.' It took a full second for the Warden to transmit the program. 'Now, I want you to boost the return signal one hundred per cent. If it looks to be fading into shut-off, I want you to increase power and maintain at that level.'

'Initiating,' said SM11.

Ebulan crashed against the wall of his chamber, then over-corrected with AG and slammed against the ceiling. He sent the shutoff code; the return signal started to fade, but then quickly reinstated. The signal wouldn't stop coming in, and was far too powerful: one blank decapitated yet still broadcasting, one burnt and drowning, and another with the flesh stripped from half his body. Ebulan had never known such pain. He tried to tear the control interface boxes from his body, and the stumps where once he'd had legs shifted and quivered. He could do nothing for himself. In panic, he sent a signal that summoned his ten remaining blanks. He had to get these boxes off himself *now*.

The human blanks entered the chamber, moving unsteadily under the impetus of Ebulan's erratic control. Under his instruction, two of the blanks came forward bearing shell cutters. He had one of them set to work on the box that controlled the blank abandoned on the beach, which was still trying vainly to stand. The shell cutter penetrated too deep and Ebulan jerked forward, pushing the blank holding it up against the wall and pinching him in half with the scalloped rim of his shell.

No pain. The return signal, from the blank he had just cut in half, immediately shut off. Ebulan backed away from the two quivering halves of what had once, centuries ago, been a human being. It had to be something affecting the return signal from *outside*, not a fault in the control boxes. . . . No, no that was impossible: the codes were quite simply unbreakable. Ebulan dispelled that aberrant thought and concentrated on controlling a second blank. This one carefully sliced down between control boxes and Ebulan's shell, severing the filament links into the Prador's nervous system. When, at one point, the blank cut deep, Ebulan bore this comparatively small pain without reaction and began, in his opinion, to think more clearly.

Ebulan stopped the blank when it came to the fifth box, and ground his mandibles as he bore the continuing pain from that box. All things in their time and place. He concentrated all his attention through that same box: seared skin in salt water . . . the continuous sensation of drowning as the body filled with virus fibres adapted to extracting oxygen from water . . . the hits of leeches coming in through the burn holes in the hull and the hatch . . . Ebulan elicited some movement from Speaker by having her open her one remaining eye. *Too dark*. He had her turn herself in the water-filled hold, sculling with her one remaining arm. It took a nightmare time for the display lights from the motor to come into view. He had her pull herself towards it, to grab the cowling and, bracing herself against the side of the ship, tear the cowling away to expose the blinking detonator. Leaving a delayed instruction in her thrall unit, he withdrew from her, then had the blank holding the shell cutter remove her control box too. Now to deal with the source of his pain.

Traitors. There were traitors on board his spaceship. Not the blanks, of course, as they could no more betray him than could one of the ship's engines. He turned in midair to observe the nine remaining blanks, then instructed them to return to their stations. One after another, they filed from the chamber and the doors slid shut behind them. Through their eyes, he saw that everything ouside appeared to be as it should. Ebulan bubbled and hissed.

At any other time Vrell would have had to be his prime suspect. But Vrell was not here now, and it would have been foolish for the adolescent to initiate an attack of which he could not take advantage. And Vrell was not that stupid. In fact, Ebulan had only recently put off killing the adolescent, for despite his imminent translation into adulthood Vrell had always proved very efficient and useful. Perhaps, though, the attack had indeed been planned by Vrell—and was carried out prematurely by the adolescent's accomplices.

'Second-children, come to me,' said Ebulan to the air. Lights flickered in the stone-effect surface of the wall to tell him his summons had been acknowledged. After noting this, he moved over to one side of the chamber to study a cluster of hexagonal wall screens, all of them showing only white haze. He disconnected one of his control boxes to link through. As he did so, two of the screens lit up displaying scenes across atolls and open sea.

'War drones,' he ordered, 'head for the island. Attack all my enemies. Do not cease till you destroy them all.'

'We will kill the old drone,' one of them promised.

'As you will, but you will not return.'

A message began coming back, but Ebulan disconnected. The screens began to white-out, but he kept his attention fixed on them as the chamber's sliding doors reopened and numerous hard sharp legs clattered on the flooring. As the doors shut, he slowly turned.

'Second-children,' he greeted the four adolescent Prador arrayed on the opposite side of the room—then he turned slightly towards the doors. There came two loud clumps as their locking systems engaged.

'Father, what do you want of us?' asked one of the second-children, slightly larger than the rest.

Ebulan's AG hummed as he tilted and slid forwards rapidly. The four of them scattered, but he pinioned two of them against the wall. They both let out a siren wail as he rammed his huge carapace into them. One after the other, their shells collapsed with a dull liquid thud, their wailing died off in hissing gurgles. Ebulan now levelled and backed off, with pieces of broken shell and ichor clinging to his scalloped rim. He slowly turned to the other two, who were scrabbling desperately at the door.

'There is no escape for traitors,' he said.

'We did nothing! It wasn't us!' the two screamed together.

Ebulan slid towards them. He'd catch one of them in his mandibles this time. It had been a while since he had tasted juvenile flesh.

* * *

The blank with fleshless legs tried standing yet again, and fell over yet again. A shadow passed over him, but he was oblivious to it as he tried to rise for perhaps the fiftieth time. As the shadow passed over him a second time, he was jerked into the air with a snapping crunch. This time he collapsed to the sand minus his head, and did not try to get up again.

After it had crunched a couple of times more and spat out a mess of bone, flesh, and thrall unit, the sail dropped the Captain on the beach.

'Thanks!' Drum yelled as the sail's wings took it booming off over the island. Turning his attention to the hideously mutilated corpse on the sand, he aimed the weapon he had brought, and fired at it once. Violet fire flashed with a sucking boom, and Drum staggered back. When his vision cleared, he found that all that remained of the blank were scattered fragments of burning flesh, and a quickly dispersing cloud of oily smoke. Thoughtfully he adjusted a slide control on the side of his weapon then turned to look out to sea.

The *Cohorn* was completely gone. The ship he had sailed on for a hundred and fifty years, and owned for a hundred of those, was now a wreck at the bottom of the sea, and soon, he knew from all he'd overheard, it would be less even than that.

'Payback time,' he muttered, and, as if in reply to this threat, a giant flashbulb went off under the sea and the beach shifted.

'Shit,' said Drum, as before him the water began to bulge. Then the bulb went off again, and for a few seconds the sea turned red as far as the horizon. He turned and ran into the dingle.

Their trail ahead was easy to follow, as inevitably the Prador had flattened foliage as it progressed. Drum leapt a broken tree and kept moving as fast as he could. From behind him now came a deep rumbling, and he felt further tremors. Leeches fell from the trees and he snatched them off as he ran on. Ahead of him, the dingle began to thin and he was relieved to see the ground sloping upwards. The tremors now settled to a deep and continuous vibration. Drum emerged from under the trees just as an explosive wind struck. It hurled him on his face in spherule grass, while it blasted leaves and branches and even leeches past him. The force of the wind even slid him further along the ground.

As it began to ease off, he stood again and ran up the slope, slipping and sliding on the broken grass. As he reached the brow of the hill, the wave hit.

The flood climbed the beach and flattened the dingle. To one side Drum saw a ship flung inland that he instantly recognized as the *Treader*. He wasn't high enough for safety, yet there was nowhere to run now but down the other side. A two-metre-deep torrent of seawater caught him halfway down the far slope and tumbled him the rest of the way. For a moment, he was tempted to release hold of his weapon and swim for it. Instead, he curled himself in a ball around it, and let the flood take him.

'What the hell was that?' said Janer. 'This a volcanic island?'

Peck managed just a bubbling sound, his broken bones moving about under his skin. The Captains, Ambel and Ron, both watched as the lights faded from the sky, then Ambel made another attempt at relocating Ron's dislocated shoulder. It finally slid into place with a muted thud.

'I don't know,' replied Ron, wincing and rubbing at his injured joint. 'But we got problems enough of our own.' He went over to his machete and gingerly picked it up. Inspecting its sprine-coated edge, he nodded with satisfaction.

'What about you?' Ambel asked Peck loudly, as if talking to someone hard of hearing.

In his bed of foliage Peck tried to nod in response, then stopped immediately when the bones in his neck crunched. He sat upright and reached to straighten his jawbone while Janer tried not to turn the other way. There was something really macabre about watching someone with so many broken bones still move about. After he'd finished prodding his numerous fractures, Peck used his shotgun as a crutch to pull himself to his feet. Both his arms and one leg had not been broken: that was the best that could be said for his injuries.

'Good lad,' said Ambel, patting him carefully on the shoulder.

Peck tried nodding again, and pointed back the way they had come.

'We'll be back when we've seen the bugger dead,' promised Ambel. 'I'll bring you a souvenir.'

'We're going after it?' asked Janer.

'Too right,' said Ron.

'But it's been poisoned with sprine,' said Janer.

'Didn't seem in a hurry to die though, did it?' said Ambel.

Ambel and Ron headed for the entrance to the garden. Janer looked at Peck, who waved at him to follow them. At the entrance, he glanced back and saw Peck begin his limping progress back out of the Hoophold. Beyond the garden, Ambel took the lead, and Janer wondered what to make of that. Did the Old Captain remember something of his own time here?

Shortly, the three came round to the other side of the wall over which the Skinner had scrambled. From there, its further course was only too obvious. It had ripped right through another wall into a courtyard, on the other side of which was a high tunnel leading straight into the thick dingle. By Janer's estimation, they were now on the opposite side of the Hoophold to where they had entered. He followed Ambel and Ron through the tunnel to where the Skinner had opened a path of destruction through the dingle itself.

'Should be easy enough to follow him now,' said Ambel.

Ron gave him a look, but reserved comment as they moved on in.

Vrell watched the flood subsiding in the dingle, then shifted his attention in the opposite direction. The island was large but that did not matter. Vrell had all the time he needed to track down the four of them: Frisk, Balem, Ron and Hoop. No one would be coming to rescue them, now that the Old Captains were all dead. Vrell began to contemplate his dismal future. If he did not get killed during this hunt, then he must kill himself so as not to become a danger to his father. This seemed his only option, though at that moment Vrell was beginning to wonder why his father could not come and rescue him. Having been separate from the normal domination of his father's pheromones for some days, Vrell was even beginning to have thoughts he had never entertained before, and to brood somewhat more about the fairness of things. He also could not help thinking about his harem mothers, and that too elicited some strange feelings. On top of everything else, his back pair of legs felt loose. Perhaps it was these upsets to his equilibrium that made Vrell less observant.

The blank did not scream. The only sounds made were a huffing expulsion of air and then an oily crackling as he staggered, burning, back towards the dingle. Vrell crashed away through foliage to seek cover, and looking back realized that the other blank had not moved. It was clear that his father had not yet resumed contact, so he himself must give verbal instructions to the idiot thrall unit.

'Take cover and return fire,' Vrell grated.

As the blank turned at last to leap into the dingle, the beam of antiphotons struck him in the back. The two burning halves of him were all that reached cover.

'We're gonna have a barbecue, Prador!' yelled Drum.

Immediately to Vrell's left, a peartrunk tree exploded into burning slivers. Using his manipulatory hands Vrell drew four different weapons simultaneously. As he backed deeper into the dingle he felt the weirdly pleasurable sensation of one of his back legs breaking off. He aimed one of the weapons, depressed a trigger, and swept the weapon back and forth. Explosions tore apart the dingle below, and the sound of needle shrapnel hitting trees became a drawn-out high-pitched shriek. Trees and branches fell all around. Vrell next opened up with a heavy QC laser that sent flashes of red shooting through the ruined trees and set fires burning everywhere.

'Missed!' shouted Drum. 'But I won't.'

The antiphoton burst struck Vrell's side and tipped him over. One of his main claws burst open, spraying steaming flesh all about. He lost two hands and the weapons they held—one of them the shrapnel rail-gun. Vrell uttered a shrieking gobbling sound and backed away at high speed from the searing heat. The antiphoton blast had burnt out two of his eyes and cracked his carapace. At that moment his remaining back leg dropped off and he abruptly made the transition from adolescent to adult. With this sudden transformation came a new set of imperatives: the first of them survival.

On his four remaining, though unsteady legs, Vrell turned and ran.

Because of the ground's vibration, Keech had steadied himself against a tree, but wished he hadn't when a leech the size of his arm dropped on his head and coiled round his neck. He reached up and caught hold of its front end just as its questing mouth tried to take his ear off. Wrenching it away in disgust he hurled the leech to the ground then, knocking down the setting on his APW, he fired at the foul creature. The leech disappeared as the ground erupted in a purple blaze that threw up a wall of debris and hurled all three men backwards. The sound of the explosion echoed through the dingle.

'It's stopped,' observed Keech, flinging a smouldering branch from across his chest, and standing up.

'What?' said Boris, sitting up and gazing about with a slightly stunned expression. After a moment, he located the SM and rested his hand on it.

'The shaking, the ground's stopped shaking,' explained Keech.

'Yeah,' said Roach. 'And didn't you say something earlier about that damn gun's settings being screwed?'

Keech flashed him a look of annoyance then turned to Boris. 'You OK?'

Boris pulled a sliver of wood from his shoulder, then nodded. He stooped and picked up SM13 and carefully brushed ash out of the ribbed pattern of the machine's casing. At that moment light flashed in the sky, then the sky darkened. Clouds like bruises swirled overhead, then were dragged into lines.

'Some kind of explosion—probably Prador weapons,' Keech observed as he moved on.

He'd gone perhaps ten paces when the same pig-like

shriek they had heard earlier came from ahead of him, accompanied by the sound of something crashing through the dingle.

'It's all happenin' now,' muttered Roach, as he and Boris came up behind Keech.

Tracking the noisy progress of whatever it was out there, Keech then moved on again.

Shortly they came to the path recently broken through the dingle. Here peartrunk trees had been pushed aside and discarded branches crushed flat. Keech glanced both ways along it, then turned to the others.

'What is that?' he asked flatly.

Roach just could not prevent himself looking sneaky, while Boris stared at the ground like a guilty schoolboy.

Keech went on, 'It's the Skinner, isn't it?'

Boris mumbled something.

'What?' Keech snapped.

'The Skinner,' Boris explained. 'Reckon it found its body, then someone else found it.'

'Hoop? . . . They're killing Hoop?'

'I reckon.'

Keech glared at the both of them, then turned into the path heading in the direction from which those squeals had come. Boris plodded after him without comment. Roach looked rebellious for a moment, then sighed and followed as well. They walked with more caution now, because of leeches in the crushed foliage, but even more because of what they were following. Ahead of them, they heard that squealing yet again, and all three of them halted. Keech stared at the settings on his weapon for a moment. He was just about to continue along the path, when Roach caught his shoulder.

'Someone comin',' the crewman warned.

Keech gestured off to one side, and the three of them quickly moved into the shade of a tilted peartrunk tree. Three other people soon appeared on the track behind them.

'That you I see sneaking about in there, Roach?' said Captain Ron.

'It weren't my fault,' said Roach.

Keech stood up and stepped into the open. Janer momentarily followed him with the raised snout of his laser, then guiltily lowered it.

'Seen any Skinners hereabouts?' asked Ron.

Keech looked at him sharply.

'Can't miss him,' continued Ron. 'Big blue fella even uglier than Roach, and thoroughly pissed off. He went this way.'

Keech glanced farther up the track they had been following. He gave a grim smile. 'Let's go,' he said.

Sniper scanned the atolls lying far to the right of him, and tried once again to get a signal through.

'Hey, Warden! What the hell are you doing?'

This time—the first time in many minutes—the Warden replied. 'What I am doing, Sniper, is decoding a Prador thrall-controller-code, and I would be thankful if there were no more interruptions.'

'What about us?' Sniper asked.

'Head for the island, and take over there from Twelve. This is not yet over,' the Warden replied, then disconnected.

'You hear that? We've got to go and take over from Twelve,' spat Sniper, who always started to get a little tetchy when he didn't have anything convenient to blow up.

'Wonderful,' said Two, who was developing a definite sarcastic mien.

'Right on,' said One, who was still a bit wobbly since receiving the Prador rail-gun hits.

Six never even got a chance to reply, as an explosion knocked it tumbling off course, then a second missile blew it into red-hot scrap.

'Scatter!'

One enforcer drone shot into the sky and two planed out to the left. Sniper went right, heading for the atolls. On his cleaned-up radar return, he got nothing for a moment, then the two Prador war drones shot up out of the sea and, ignoring the two enforcers, both came after him.

'Great,' Sniper muttered, then sent to them, 'Why don't you go play hopscotch on a black hole?'

The Prador replied with two missiles each.

'Touchy,' Sniper sent—abruptly changing direction and leaving a cloud of chaff behind him. The missiles went through the chaff, swung round, and zeroed in on him again. Sniper shot up higher and released a cluster of little parachute mines. These mines perfectly intersected the course of the missiles as they changed direction. Two of the missiles blew and one went tumbling off course, corrected, then shot back towards the explosion of the others. It, too, detonated shortly after.

'Mmm, heat-seeking.'

Sniper arced over and accelerated towards the atolls, with the remaining missile closing in. He went low to the surface and headed straight in for one of the atolls. The missile meanwhile drew closer and closer. At the last moment, Sniper shut off his fusion engine and dropped straight down into the sea. The missile went over him and, with its sensors confused by the sudden disappearance of the heat source it was pursuing, did not correct in time and slammed straight into the atoll.

Submerged in the shallow water, close to the atoll's narrow beach, Sniper raised his antennae and scanned. The two Prador drones were still heading right for where he had gone in.

'Right, how you gonna get out of this one, big shot?' Sniper muttered to himself. Still in the water he hurriedly altered programs and fed them into his smart missiles. That Prador missile that had tumbled away had given him a bit of an idea. As the Prador drones drew closer, he shot up into the air, paused for half a second, then fired off four missiles. One missile hit a screen and exploded, one exploded under rail-gun fire, the remaining two simply tumbled away—and the Prador came hammering on in. Sniper accelerated for the atoll, then was knocked sideways as rail-gun was trained on him. He felt his plates buckling and a couple of his legs fell away. Turning in midair, he opened up with his APW—a short burst only as there was little power left in the laminar batteries. One of the Prador swerved out of the way, but the other continued in for the kill.

Sniper accelerated straight towards it. 'Well I'll take you with me, fucker!' he sent.

The Prador extended its screen in front, but a second after, Sniper's two missiles—which had now corrected from their tumble—hit it from behind. It still came on, its armour distorted, its screen out, and its engine powering intermittently. Sniper hit it with his APW, then swooped over the top of it as it hurtled towards the sea, a burnt-out shell.

'You gotta watch that upswing!' Sniper sent, but had no time to feel satisfaction when another two missiles swung abruptly up from the sea towards him. Again he changed course, curving down towards the atolls. The second Prador came hurtling towards him just above the waves. Sniper aimed himself at one of the atolls, firing off another three missiles. The atoll erupted in a fountain of broken coral, just prior to him flying straight into it. He shot out of the other side of this, trailing dust clouds and leaving two explosions behind him, then turned back towards the approaching Prador. As he fired his APW, violet fire hazed the air between them, terminating on a disk like a white-hot coin—the Prador's projected shield. The disk went out, and the fire extinguished shortly after. Both drones fired missiles and opened up with their rail-guns. Two of Sniper's missiles blew in between, but a third took a curve and came at the Prador from the side. After the explosion, Sniper had the satisfaction of seeing the drone lurch through the air, with a split opened in its armour—then the missile he had overlooked came up underneath him and exploded.

'Oh bollocks,' groaned the war drone, as he tumbled through the air. His APW was out, and though he still had missiles to launch, they could not get past the molten metal blocking his launch tubes—the same mess that had also scrapped his rail-gun. It was all academic really, as he had little chance of staying airborne for any length of time, with his AG gone as well. Intermittently he spotted the Prador war drone ahead of him. At least it seemed to be having as much trouble as he was. One last chance? Sniper fired his fusion engine at a precisely timed instant, opened out what remained of his legs, and slammed himself into the other drone. Immediately the Prador accelerated and rolled, trying to shake him off.

'Y'know,' said Sniper. 'when the going gets tough . . . '
And with that he plunged his heavy claw through the split in
the Prador's armour. Its only reply to him was a thin screaming over the ether as it fell towards one of the atolls below.

'Sniper . . . Sniper?' the Warden sent—and didn't even get
back a return signature. 'SMs One and Two, what happened?'

There was an equivocal humming over the ether before a
response came through.

'Sniper had a run-in with two Prador war drones. We can't
find him,' explained Two.

'Yeah, he sure stuffed 'em,' added One.

'But it seems they stuffed him also,' Two then pointed out
and, so saying, transmitted a replay of what it had captured
and recorded of Sniper's last moments.

Stubborn to the end, thought the Warden. In such a crisis
Sniper could have linked through and transmitted himself,
all of himself. But Sniper had preferred to remain individual,
had not wanted to be subsumed. And so, the Warden
thought, he is gone in heroic battle. What a waste, and what
a disappointment—the Warden had been quite attracted to
the idea of *changing* Sniper.

'One and Two, join your brother drones off the Skinner's
Island,' instructed the Warden, and then linked through to
Twelve. 'Twelve, I want you down in that trench, searching
for this Prador vessel. We still don't know quite what we are
up against.'

'On my way,' sent Twelve.

There were no probes in the area, so Ebulan despatched the
nearest one of them available. This same probe—built in the
shape of a small Prador, with thrusters shell-welded
underneath—burst from the sargassum where it had been
squatting and rocketed up into the sky, then went hypersonic
for twenty seconds before shutting down its thrusters and
coasting to the edge of the tsunami. To Ebulan it returned an
image of the fleet of ships riding the swells behind the initial
huge wave, their sails belled to bursting. Maybe one or two
of them had been sunk, but no more—the CTD concealed

inside the *Ahab* had not been close enough to cause any real damage. The probe then transmitted back the information that objects were now approaching it at hypersonic speeds. This transmission was abruptly curtailed as the probe became an incandescent cloud of metal vapour.

Ebulan crashed around his chamber, in increasing anger, and it was some time before he could think clearly again. Vrell would soon be in the process of making the change, so would be useless to him now. The pheromones that kept a fully limbed Prador in a state of adolescence until the father of the family died were not present where the adolescent now was, and because the 'change' had been suppressed in it for so long, Vrell would make the transformation to adulthood very quickly.

The blanks out there might still be of some use if he dared reconnect their control boxes, but he did not. He did not want again to risk feeling the pain from their bodies. They never felt it as, though having nervous systems, they had no brains to understand the signals from them—he was the one with the brain. Their thrall units were the nearest things they possessed to intelligence, and those devices merely translated verbal orders to action, or acted as the interface between the blank's nervous system and its controlling Prador mind.

No blanks, no Vrell, and no second-children either. Perhaps the war drones, then? Ebulan spun round and slid up to his array of screens. He used the control box of the blank he had cut in half earlier to try to link through. The whited-out screens threw up nothing but static. The drones had to be all dead?

It was painful to Ebulan to admit to himself that he no longer had any control over this situation, and therefore it might be time to pull out. The thought of doing so left an unpleasant taste in his mouth—like too-fresh human meat— and was just as upsetting to his digestion. What other options were there? He considered the armament carried by his ship. A brief flight and a sweep or two by the particle beams, perhaps a CTD for the island itself, and all who had any direct knowledge of his involvement in the coring trade would become so much airborne ash. All the forms of information storage that the humans so valued were as nothing to the Prador. Only living witnesses counted to them. Ebulan then pondered the consequences of such actions.

The Warden would certainly attack . . . but was that such a problem? The Warden, though it controlled formidable devices, could not move away from the moon. Its SMs, though they could destroy Ebulan's war drones—something Ebulan still could not quite get to grips with, as he'd assumed there were only enforcer drones here—stood no chance of getting through this war craft's armour, nor of surviving assault by its weapons. How formidable exactly were the weapons the Warden controlled? And would they prove so effective with a planet in between? Also, though there would still be living witnesses to his proposed actions, all they would truly witness would be anonymous attack by a Prador destroyer. No one had yet seen Ebulan himself, as they had in the old days when he came here each Spatterjay year to collect his cargo of cored humans.

The more Ebulan thought about it, the more attractive the case for attacking seemed. It started hormones and juices surging in him that had not flowed for the last thousand years—as they had once done in that time when he still possessed all his legs and a scattering of arms. That Prador medical science had long established such feelings as the first signs of senility, he did not even stop to consider.

18

Managing to turn itself far enough round to get hold of the leech with its mandibles, the heirodont brought mounds of slimy flesh up to its mouth and bit down. This, though, was still not enough to prevent the leech feeding. The prill now fleeing from the body of the heirodont, signified that the leech was about to detach, which it did, leaving in its victim's side a huge

*round hole that might have been neat but for the broken bone
and ballooning out of ripped organs. Too weak now to maintain its own hold on the leech, the heirodont released it, and
dropped into the depths, trailing a new cloud of ichor and
chyme. Down it went, its body compressing, and the outflow of
vital fluids slowly decreasing, but not sufficiently to prevent a
drop in pressure in its brain. Recovering consciousness only
when it hit the bottom, it found itself surrounded by a mob of
the giant whelks upon which it normally fed, they having come
to investigate the emptied shell of one of their comrades. Its
low-frequency screams then echoed through the depths as this
mob squared away what they felt were certain . . . inequities.*

Erlin was wondering how much longer she, and Anne, had to
live. Shortly Frisk and her pet Batians would start to consider them a hindrance rather than useful hostages. As soon
as that time came there would be no hesitation to kill them.
The Batians would do it with workmanlike precision. It was
what they were employed for, after all. Frisk, however,
would do it with great enjoyment, and probably as slowly
and painfully as possible. Erlin had enough judgement of
people to recognize a raving psychopath.

'Halt here,' ordered Svan.

As she and Anne stopped in centre of the courtyard, Erlin
could see the crew-woman working her wrists against the
cable-cuffs securing her hands behind her back. She thought
to warn her of the futility of trying to break woven ceraplast,
but changed her mind—she did not know, after all, how old
Anne was—and instead looked away to survey her surroundings.

It was impossible for Erlin not to think about what had once
happened here: the horror of it all. A thousand years ago, Jay
Hoop and his crew of pirates had landed on this island to establish a permanent cache of arms and loot. At one time or another, all of them had been bitten by the leeches and to their
surprise subsequently discovered that they did not grow old
and die, but while growing older, were becoming stronger and
more resistant to injury. With the confidence this imparted, for

centuries they had terrorized the quadrant, using this planet—named Spatterjay, after Jay Hoop's nickname—as their base. Then had come the Prador, and the war, and . . .

A distant horrid shrieking distracted Erlin from her rumination. She looked around and saw Frisk move over to one side of the courtyard, and then pace along it.

'We'll go this way,' she gestured to a door in the wall. 'I'll lead.' She pointed at Erlin and Anne, 'You two follow me.'

The two captives crossed the courtyard and began to trail Frisk through the warren of dank corridors, past rooms scattered with such objects as could survive seven centuries of rot and decay. On the floors lay items of ceramal and glass, silicon and artificial gemstone. Remaining from personal units, comps, and the many other devices carried by the citizens of the Polity seven hundred years ago, were the practically indestructible chips—the metals and plastic long having corroded and decayed to dust. There were also ornaments and storage crystals, visors from soldier's helmets, diverse items of ceramal armour. Erlin was thoroughly aware that these objects were things once carried by Hoop's captives—all things that during the war became of least value to Hoop and his crew. They had wanted the persons who wore them.

Frisk led them further through the Hold till they reached a high tunnel on the other side. Beyond the tunnel mouth, the dingle was crushed and flattened.

'Svan, go check for tracks,' called Frisk.

Svan trotted past them, sped through the tunnel, and began to examine the soft ground beyond. Frisk looked back at her two prisoners and grinned.

What figure had Keech once quoted? Ten million. *Ten million* humans cored here during the Prador-Human war. And *this* woman had been one of the murderers. Erlin now knew what Keech had meant when he had predicted Frisk would no longer have the face by which he had known her. The thought of it sickened her.

'They did come through here, but there's some sort of animal footprint as well,' called out Svan.

With a smirk Frisk followed her into the tunnel. Anne and Erlin remained where they were, until Shib barked at them to get moving too. Through the tunnel and out into the dingle, Svan walked ahead and Frisk shifted to one side. Erlin reflected about how she herself had come here to learn from Ambel how to live—but now it seemed she had in fact come here to die. She turned suddenly when she heard a horrible high-pitched scream behind her.

The mercenary, Shib, had made the mistake of brushing against a tree. He was now wearing a leech like a feather boa, and seemed unable to overcome his disgust enough to grab it and throw it away. The creature flowed round his neck, and drove its mouth in against his cheek. Even now the mercenary could not react.

Svan ran past Erlin and grabbed at the leech. With a yank, she tore it from his face and flung it to the ground. Shib still stood there, keening, a circle of flesh missing from his cheek, his teeth now exposed underneath. Svan backhanded him across the other side of his face, once, twice, knocking him to the ground. The keening suddenly stopped.

'Get up.'

Shib slowly rose to his feet: shame, fear and madness fighting for predominance in his expression.

'Keep moving you two,' said Svan, heading back to lead the way. Erlin thought her insane to leave this humiliated man at her back. When Shib drew his hand laser she assumed he was going to burn a hole through Svan's back. Instead, he incinerated the leech, and reholstered the laser.

'Get a move on,' he snarled at her.

SM12's cockle shell body was of an extremely rugged construction: its outer shells formed of centimetre-thick foamed steel, and its internal components braced in a ceramal-composite lattice, but even so it knew that the pressure a kilometre down would collapse it as easily as a snail in a vice, if it did not prepare. Floating on the surface, Twelve folded away its single laser, then using an internal system pumped crash foam at high pressure into all its internal cavities. Next with its shells slightly open, it turned off its AG and sank like the lump of metal it was.

Five hundred metres down Twelve observed with interest

one of the herbivorous deep-water heirodonts cruising past, the leeches on its body turned to strands by the pressure. The creature resembled a truncated whale, its face, however, just a wall of feeding sieves; its body short and roped with muscle, studded with round fins, and terminating in a wide vertically presented tail. It suddenly dived when it was past the SM and, as it went rapidly down, the leeches clinging to its skin began to break away. A little relief it would find in the depths, before having to return upwards to feed and be fed upon.

Twelve followed it down, the drone's crash foam collapsing into a thick hard layer around its internal components. The substance offered some protection, but the SM knew that some parts of itself would inevitably get damaged. Essential components, however, would be fine, being constructed on the whole of hard silicon composites and foamed ceramal.

Seven hundred metres down, and the SM's self-diagnostic program told it that a reflective cylinder in its laser had cracked. Twelve had expected this to happen, as there was no way of injecting crash foam, or even admitting seawater, into the cavity within the cylinder—and to do so would have screwed the optical perfection of the system anyway. The rate of its descent was also slowing in proportion as the density of the water increased. The drone dared not reverse its AG to pull itself down faster, as that would be too easily detected. Shortly it passed the heirodont, which was now thinner than it had been above, the water having compressed it too. The creature's eyes glimmered from their pits as it turned and sculled hesitantly towards Twelve, but the drone was well past it before it could decide if this strange looking object was animal or vegetable.

Now it was getting colder, and dark enough to necessitate Twelve switching from visual to low-intensity sonar, changing the emitted signal at random so that nothing constant could be detected. The Prador vessel lurking down here somewhere would be sure to have some kind of detection equipment out. A thousand metres down, and the lip of the trench finally came into sight. But Twelve did not bother to alter its course as it hit solid rock and, in a spray of silt, bounced over the edge. Using water jets, it corrected its tumble and studied the cliff face it was falling past. Down here, in weedy crevices, were whelks as big as houses riding on spreads of flat white tentacles; odd, diamond-shaped jelly-fish adhered to clear surfaces, giving some expanses of rock the appearance of one great scaled beast; and long blue glisters hunting bulbous boxies that might easily be mistaken for soap bubbles. All very interesting, but all recorded and on file up on Coram. Twelve focused its attention downward, as the bottom of the trench floated up to meet it. It bounced in a cloud of silt and razor-thin shell fragments, then with great care extended the range of its sonic scans.

Nothing—nothing within range at least—but there was still plenty of the trench to search for it was many kilometres long. Twelve chose one direction at random, and with a blast of water propelled itself that way. Even before it properly got going, it noticed that one very regularly shaped boulder to its right was returning an odd signal. It risked a change in frequency and got an immediate result: the boulder was *hollow*. It had found the Prador ship already! But, no, that couldn't be right: this object was much too small to contain an adult Prador. With care, Twelve moved in closer and closer to it then settled to rest on the bottom. A feeling almost like frustration came over it when it realized that nearly half of its scanning signals were now coming back to it with the same odd reverberation as had come from the unknown object. With chagrin, it admitted to itself that the pressure must have damaged its sonar. Unless . . .

In its cortex, SM12 mapped the shape of the boulder and compared it to images of Prador ships it had kept stored in a history file. This object was a flattened ovoid with one end seemingly sheared off. It therefore did not match the shape of any of the ships in Twelve's file. However, it did match *part* of one. Twelve shot up from the bottom as it realized what it had found was a weapons turret, and that what it had just been resting on was not the bottom of the trench. Jetting higher, it scanned right across what it had landed upon.

'Fuck,' said SM12, who—unlike Thirteen and Sniper—was not normally given to profanity.

* * *

The flood had turned the ground into a soft morass, and made it easy to dig himself into. Vrell remained utterly motionless as the mad human yelled and stomped about.

'Come out, come out wherever you are!' Drum yelled.

Antiphoton fire suddenly incinerated a tree only a few metres to Vrell's right, dropping burning cinders on the ground all around the eye he had folded upwards from his visual turret. He slowly turned that eye and observed the human drawing closer, as he inspected the muddy ground.

'Fucking Prador,' growled Drum.

Vrell assumed this anger must be directed at him personally because he had been the one who had installed the thrall unit in this particular human. Didn't this Drum understand that Vrell was only obeying orders? Vrell watched the human's antics some more, while slowly sinking his eye deeper into the concealing mud. Soon the human would be right on top of him. What would he do then? A few hours ago, he would have leapt out of this muddy hide and blasted away with his weapons, but now . . . what if he missed? The human could kill him. Vrell felt terrified. Deep inside himself, he felt a certainty that violence was meant for others. His own task now involved frequent use of the complicated organ exposed by the shedding of his two back legs—the organ he now squatted protectively over.

The human came forward, till he stood right at the edge of the morass. He first tested it with his foot then put weight on that foot. Vrell remained utterly motionless as the foot trod down on his carapace. He observed Drum scratching his head, then slowly revolved his muddy eye as Drum walked right across the Prador's back and off on to the boggy ground beyond. Once the Captain was out of sight Vrell shifted slightly, and again considered making his escape. On the other hand, Drum had not detected him here. Vrell decided to stay buried for a while longer.

Captain Sprage stood on the main deck of the *Vengeance*, his thumbs tucked into his thick leather belt and his pipe tucked into the corner of his mouth. He seemed oblivious to the bucking of his ship as it rode the swell, but stood there firmly, almost as if his feet were nailed to the deck. He observed that the waves were decreasing now, and the main danger was past. Surprisingly, there had not been that much danger. Yes, that first immense wave had sunk the *Bogus* and the *Rull*, but captains Jester and Orlando had survived their dunking in the sea, along with all of their two crews. The irony was that the undersea explosion causing the wave had also affected just about every sea creature in the area. Sprage pulled his pipe from his mouth and studied the leeches and glisters floating on the surface. He had counted fifteen different varieties of whelk, and noted that the underwater shock had broken open prill and that many were floating dead on the surface. He even noted some forms of life he'd never seen before: deep-bottom dwellers that had swollen into grotesque giant shapes on ascending to the surface. None of these creatures showed signs of recovering.

'How come none of 'em are reviving?' he asked generally.

Windcheater lifted his head from the deck and peered over the side. Sprage took a furtive glance at the creature's metal aug and wondered if that was the reason for the sail's need to interfere with the status quo. On the other hand it had probably been bolshy long before, else why would it have acquired an aug in the first place? After a long hard look overboard, Windcheater swung his head round and up to the deck.

'The hyper-shock has caused major cellular disruption. The EM burst killed between eighty to ninety-five per cent of the viral fibres. The combination of these two has taken each life-system beyond chance of recovery,' said the sail with extremely uncharacteristic precision.

'What about us, then?' asked Sprage, scratching at his sideburns.

From where she was leaning on the rail, Tay turned and glanced towards the sail as Windcheater's eyes crossed. Tay said, 'You ran that last one through a weapons-site learning program. I suggest you try the Warden for your next answer.'

Windcheater uncrossed his eyes, tilted his head for a moment, and then parroted, 'The hyper-shock only affected creatures in the water, and the EM burst was considerably damped by the dense wood of your ship's hulls. The Warden estimates that the any of the EM burst that did get through will have killed less than ten per cent of the viral fibres in your bodies.'

'Beneficial, then,' said Sprage, putting his pipe back in his mouth with a solid click.

'Signal from the *Pumice*!' yelled Lember from the nest.

Sprage took the small metal cylinder that Tay had given him, out of his pocket, and held it above the tobacco packed into his pipe. After a couple of flickers of red light, the tobacco began glowing again, and Sprage thankfully sucked in a good lungful of smoke. As he let it trail back out of his nostrils, he decided he had a lot to thank Polity technology for, not least being able to light up his pipe on a windy deck.

'Relayed signal!' shouted Lember. 'They want to know if it's time to go in!'

Sprage extracted his pipe. 'Tell 'em yes. We'll moor for the night and land in the morning. No point blundering about in the dark on Skinner's Island. That'd be unhealthy.'

When Twelve shot screaming from the sea, the Warden picked up the gist of what it was saying, and reacted immediately. A high-speed analysis of its files provided some basis on which to make its suppositions. The AI was now eighty-seven per cent certain that the Prador aboard the war craft was the old Prador called Ebulan. Ebulan had been Hoop's main Prador contact during the war, and at the forefront of some of its more risky campaigns. Confirmation then: Ebulan was here to cover his tracks. Any other Prador would have remained in the safety of the Kingdoms, and sent agents here instead to accomplish its ends. That Ebulan had come here himself was indicative of—to put it succinctly—which way he might now jump. Maybe Ebulan might not go so far as to directly involve his own ship but, that ship being a Prador light destroyer, the Warden was taking no chances.

'Priority message: Gate for all incoming visitors is now closed. More instructions to follow.'

The Warden observed the effect of this announcement in

the main concourse and in the arrivals lounges. People immediately began consulting their personal comps. In the first minute, the Warden counted two hundred enquiries directed through the consoles on Coram base. It fielded these with the same message, then directed its attention towards the code-breaker programmes it was running. No closer to cracking it yet, and that code was the easiest way through the skin of the Prador vessel should it eventually show itself. The Warden gave yet another command.

In the lounges and concourses, humans and altered humans observed—through the chainglass panoramic windows—weapons turrets cracking through the ice and sulphurous crusts, and rising into view. These turrets were black and grey and vaguely resembled the feeding heads of giant water worms. Some people nodded their heads and related to newcomers how this was the second time this had happened since they had been here. Children pointed out the various protrusions from the turrets, and identified them as antiphoton cannons, particle beam projectors, racks of smart missiles, near-c rail-guns, and so on. Concerned parents remarked that there must be a deal of meteor activity occurring in this system and wondered why they had not been warned.

EXIT GATE IS NOW OPEN-PORT TO LOCAL SYSTEMS.

As soon as this message came up on the board, a silence descended in the base. Those very few ancients who were old enough to remember the Prador war, or even more recent conflicts, immediately headed for the runcible gate to get through before a panic started. Many of them remembered open-port evacuations of stations and moons near space battles. A few of them remembered what had subsequently happened to some of those stations and moons.

The Warden let things ride for a while as, after its first message, the exit gate had begun working to full capacity. It directed its attention planet-ward, to its submind on the Polity base.

'Full lock down and defences,' it instructed the submind.

'Shit about to hit?' asked the mind.

'Most likely,' conceded the Warden.

All around the Polity base, shield projectors began rising

out of the sea. Huge automatic clamps closed over the three
shuttles grounded there, and the platforms they were located
on began to sink into the sea. Aircabs took off en masse
from the jetties, as the base slowly drew in those jetties like
a starfish pulling in its arms. The aircabs went at full tilt to
the Domes on the nearby island, dropping in through the
tops of them, then the Dome hatches irised shut. At the same
time as these were closing, Polity citizens were rushing back
into the Domes from the Hooper towns they had been visit-
ing outside. Not all of them made it unfortunately, as the armoured doors rolled shut and left many terrified citizens
outside with the bemused Hoopers. These Hoopers became
even more bemused when turrets, much like those recently
exposed on Coram, started rising out of the earth of their
own island.

'Attention all Polity citizens,' the Warden announced. 'A
Prador light destroyer has been detected in-system, with
hostile intent. Proceed in an orderly manner to the gate.'

After this announcement, the Warden allowed information access to the hundreds of enquiries pouring in. Polity
citizens learnt that 'open-port' meant they'd be thrown out
through the gate as fast as was possible, to be fielded by
those runcibles anywhere else that could handle the load. So
they'd all arrive . . . somewhere. The Warden noted, with a
small but pleasurable surprise, that there was no obvious
panic. Its pleasure was tempered when it counted how many
questions coming through concerned the Prador, and how
many Polity citizens were learning for the first time about a
war that had ended more than seven centuries ago.

The terrain became increasingly rocky as they laboured up the
slope, and the vegetation had changed to accommodate this.
Here the peartrunk trees were squat and gnarled and tangled
with the same vine-like growths that coated the boulders and
slabs of rock jutting up through the soil. Janer walked a couple
of paces behind Keech, the carbine resting across his shoulder. In the half-light, he noticed Keech grimace and probe his
wrist, then clench his hand into a fist, then open it again.

Also studying Keech, a pace or two to one side of Janer,

Captain Ron asked, 'When you went after her ship, what happened?'

'I hit some powerful defences, which nearly brought me down.' Keech gestured with his thumb towards Boris and Roach. 'On the way out I saw your ship burning and picked up these two on my way back.'

Ron stared at Roach.

'It wasn't my fault,' protested Roach.

'I know that,' said Ron, since he and Ambel had already had a long talk with Boris and ascertained most of the facts. He gestured to the probe Boris still carried and said to Keech, 'What I'd like to know is what's happening now.'

'The Warden will be, let's say, playing close attention to events down here,' explained Keech. 'Spatterjay might be officially Out-Polity, but it still comes under Polity protection. There was that much agreement between you lot and the Polity at least.'

'What's out there, then?' asked Ambel, pointing seawards.

Keech gave Ambel a long look, then said, 'Where there's Prador adolescents there's a Prador adult around too. In the absence of an adult, one of their adolescents becomes one very quickly. Prador adults are pretty careful about their own safety, so if there's one anywhere here it'll be heavily armed.'

'Spzzckt light destroyer,' SM13 chipped in.

They all stared at the drone Boris was carrying.

Keech continued, 'A ship like that in hiding somewhere and Prador agents running around all over the place—that isn't something the Warden would tolerate.'

'But is it something the Warden can do anything about?' asked Ambel.

Keech gazed at him again, and it was obvious to Janer the kind of thoughts that were going through the monitor's mind.

'I don't know,' replied Keech.

They trudged on a little further, until Ron suddenly halted, staring at the ground.

'I reckon it's circling back on itself. But if we go on any further in this light, we'll lose the trail,' he warned.

Janer sighed and slipped his backpack from his shoulders.

Ambel gestured to a protected spot below a single huge slab jutting up diagonally from the ground. The six of them made their way over and sat in its dark shadow. Shortly, Ambel opened his bag and passed around dried strips of rhinoworm. Janer chewed on a length of it while pulling what remained of his heat sheet out of his pack. Roach began tugging lengths of dead vine from a nearby rock, and made a pile of them, then Boris ignited the heap with a quick burst from the laser he carried. He then looked to Captain Ron and tossed the laser over to him. The Captain caught it and pocketed it in one swift motion.

'There'll have to be payment for Goss,' said Ron.

Boris nodded as he squatted by the campfire, and began poking it with a stick.

Drum stumbled on through darkness, aware that he needed rest but knowing that, if he stopped for it, there would be no one to watch his back and that he'd wake up to find the leeches sucking on his face. He was tired, but most of all he was hungry. The injuries he had received from both Frisk and the Prador were well healed now, but they had drained his resources to the limit. He needed food to top up his strength, but particularly he needed Dome food to prevent him from going 'native'. He considered stopping to light a fire, but decided against this. Warmth would only make him sleepy and would do nothing to keep the leeches away.

As he proceeded, Drum could hear the sounds of heirodonts feeding nearby, and their wails as leeches fed on them. This caught his attention for a while, but soon his head began to slump and he walked an increasingly wavering path through the endless dingle. Some unconscious instinct still kept him away from the trunks of trees, a touch on which could bring leeches raining down on his head. That same instinct did not however prevent his walking slap-bang into a metal post.

He stepped back and swore, then reached out and ran his hand over the corroded metal facing him. *Slave post*. Immediately he knew where he was and gained new hope of finding a place free of any concentration of leeches—a place where he could rest. He moved further through the remaining dingle as it gradually thinned and the light of Coram could reach the ground.

'Who's that bugger?' spoke a voice to one side of him.

'Whoisss? Wooisss?' said a voice not entirely human.

'That you Peck?' asked Drum of one of the shapes visible nearby.

'Tis.'

'Who's that with you?'

'Forlam,' said Peck. 'He's a bit buggered,' he explained.

When it was fully dark, Vrell finally summoned the nerve to pull himself from his muddy hideaway. This at first proved difficult because the mud had meanwhile dried into a hard crust over the top of him. When he eventually broke free, much of this crust still stuck to his carapace; a weight more difficult to carry now he was reduced to being quadrupedal.

With his extra burden, Vrell moved slowly down towards shore, anxious to make as little noise as possible. Even this proved difficult, since Prador were not by nature adapted for travelling through thick dingle; their home world consisted of shallow seas, wide and level tidal areas, and extensive saltpans. However carefully he moved, Vrell kept knocking over trees as he progressed, thus getting so many leeches swarming on him that every so often he had to stop to tip them off. The worst of it was that he was no longer invulnerable to the creatures. The sensitive burned flesh of his burst claw was open to their attack, as was the raw area on his side where his shell had been charred to powder. Every time he wrenched an eager leech from his wounds, he hissed like a steam kettle and cursed all humans.

Half the night, it took Vrell to reach the shore, and finally squatting on the beach there, he gazed out at the glowing lanterns of the ships moored in the cove. For a while he felt confusion, then he understood and lowered himself dejectedly to the sand. Of course: Drum. Somehow the Captain had foiled his father's plan, which meant that he, Vrell, had also failed. Father would depart now and find some other means to accomplish his ends.

Vrell unfolded one of his remaining arms and gazed at the device held in his complex hand comprised of fingers and hooks. With the blanks all around him directly linked to his father, there had been, up till now, no need for this. But he had brought it along anyway, in the eventuality of all the blanks being killed. It was a communicator that linked him with his father's destroyer. He could call now and speak. He could call now and ask his father for instructions. With a sinking depression, he lowered the communicator. He already knew what those instructions would be: something along the lines of, 'Return inland, kill and die.' This was not what Vrell wanted to hear. Instead of using the communicator, he slid himself down the beach into the sea to soak off the weight of mud on his back.

With the cool water soothing his wounds and the mud slewing from him, Vrell carefully studied his surroundings, noticing all the dead sea creatures floating on the surface. Seeing such a preponderance of dead leeches raised his spirits a little, till he began to think more positively. He had done all he could, and only failed because the odds were insurmountable. Perhaps his father would make the small diversion necessary to pick him up, before quitting the planet. Perhaps Vrell could get out to the destroyer and be taken aboard?

He again checked his communicator, switching to one of its many facilities. The beacon setting sent his location out to the destroyer, just as it revealed the location of the destroyer to him. It was still sitting out there at the bottom of its trench. Vrell heaved himself ashore and pulled the medpack from his underside. A few shell patches should be enough to keep any more leeches out of his wounds if he were forced to swim the huge expanse of intervening sea. He fervently hoped that would not be necessary.

As Vrell softened his shell patches and spread them with glue, he was aware that he was only delaying things. But then, the better he made himself feel, the more persuasive he could be with his father. He took his time affixing the patches, drying them afterwards with the blower from the medpack. When he had finished, and neatly stowed away the medpack, he noticed with some surprise that the sky was getting lighter. It suddenly occurred to him how visible he would soon become to the ships out in the cove. He backed up the beach into the cover of dingle, and again took out his communicator.

'Father?'

There was a long pause before he received a reply.

'Vrell, my son, you are an adult now,' said Ebulan. 'Have you completed your mission upon the island?'

'I . . . I encountered more resistance than expected,' said Vrell. As a Pradar very new to adulthood, it did not yet occur to him to lie openly—only to bend the truth a little.

'You failed, then,' said Ebulan.

'The fault is not entirely mine. Captain Drum came ashore—'

'No matter,' Ebulan interrupted. 'I will be taking care of this matter myself, now.'

'You'll be coming here?' Vrell asked, with renewed hope.

'I will come.'

'And you will pick me up?'

The grating, bubbling sound that issued from the communicator was the Pradar equivalent of a laugh—something Vrell had rarely heard. He held the communicator away from his body, and gave it the full attention of all his remaining eyes.

'Vrell, you are now an adult male, and as such you are no longer of any use to me. You are more of a hindrance and a threat. So when I reach your location and shower it with CTDs to kill off the Old Captains, your death will be an added bonus.'

'But, father—'

Ebulan cut off, and Vrell stared at the communicator for a long moment before his survival instinct belatedly kicked in. He stood up and made ready to charge down the beach to the sea. But the sight of twenty rowing boats heading for the shore had him drop back on to his belly like a falling dinner plate. He watched the men step ashore, as he slowly backed through the dingle, wondering if the ground back there was still soft enough somewhere to dig.

* * *

Using his heavy claw and few remaining legs, Sniper crawled over to the Prador war drone, clambered up on to it, and peered into the wide crack through which he had gutted it. The drone's central core was now a mash of Prador brain tissue, insulation material, and optic nerve linkages. In the bottom of its armoured shell lay pooled the amniot in which the brain had been flash frozen. The drone was undoubtedly dead, but, Sniper noted with interest, many of its systems were not too badly damaged. Reaching inside with his precision claw, Sniper took hold of one of the optic linkages and pulled it up for closer inspection. The interface was a straightforward electrochemical job he had come across many times during the long-distant war. Often damaged himself, while far from a Polity facility, he had scavenged Prador technology to repair himself. Circumstances were not quite the same this time, but he didn't want to just sit here stranded on this atoll, waiting for one of the Warden's SMs to eventually find him.

Sniper pushed back from the Prador's shell and, with an internal order, dropped his lower head plate. The plate stuck part way, buckled and partially welded in place by spatters of molten metal from his missing legs, so he grasped it with his heavy claw, and tore it away to expose his solid-state insides. Reaching inside the Prador shell again, he pulled out a mass of optic linkages, and one at a time plugged them into an interface he'd had installed inside himself seven centuries ago. After ten minutes of swapping optic cables, and sorting the machine code return signals, a high-pitched whine was emitted from inside the Prador shell, and it lifted itself a few centimetres from the atoll before clunking back down again.

'Bollocks,' said Sniper, and this time relayed the internal order that opened the lower plates of his body, to expose the densely packed machinery of his life.

Later, a recessed nozzle on the side of the Prador shell briefly spat a fusion flame that nearly rolled the shell itself over on top of the old war drone. With his head now nearly inside his dead enemy, Sniper hardly noticed, as he worked away, discarding pieces of twisted metal and burnt components, and replacing them with pieces removed from himself.

* * *

'Wake up,' said the mercenary, Shib.

Erlin sat up quickly, half expecting a boot in her side. Anne was already up, squatting impassively by the ashes of the fire, wrists still twisting against her cuffs, eyes fixed on the weapons the Batians carried.

'I need to urinate,' said Erlin firmly.

Shib looked down at her. 'Well then do so.' The mercenary's voice sounded watery and distorted by the hole in his cheek and the dressing covering one side of his face. Of them all, thought Erlin, he seemed to be coming off the worst. At some point, he'd lost a couple of fingers as well, she had noticed. She stood and looked about for something to squat behind: a tree or a rock. As she started towards the nearest tree, Shib jammed his weapon in her stomach.

'I said "do so". I didn't say you could go anywhere,' he said.

Erlin stared at him, then turned away. It was obvious that he was frightened and that his fear was making him vicious. She'd have to hold it. She'd be damned if she'd pee with him watching.

'Come on, get them moving!' yelled Frisk, trotting back into the campsite.

Shib jabbed both the prisoners in the back in turn, and they started to follow Frisk through a stand of peartrunk trees. Luckily no leeches fell. Beyond the trees, Svan waited with her weapon on her shoulder.

'It looks easier further up,' observed the female mercenary. 'Fewer trees and less crap on the ground. Once we get up there, we should get a clear view all around.'

'Let's go, then,' said Frisk, with a slightly crazy expression.

So Svan led the way, Frisk immediately following her, while Shib did his jabbing trick with the barrel of his weapon. Erlin thought gloomily that it was enough they were going to die—was it necessary to continually humiliate them as well?

They emerged out of thick dingle into a different terrain that was rocky and netted with vines. The peartrunks and

other strange varieties of tree had the looser concentration
here of a deciduous woodland. Leeches lying across their
branches had the same hue and colour as their cousins nearer
the shore. Putrephallus weeds grew singly, and the occasional
lung bird spooked into flight was smaller and coloured like
mouldy bread. As she walked Erlin brooded, and decided not
to suffer any further indignity. She had come here seeking
reasons to continue living—to discover how Ambel had
achieved it. She had come here understanding that life on its
own was not enough. She'd be damned if she'd give up everything else just for life itself. Anyway, she had an intimation
that this increasingly frightened mercenary could be manipulated. She stopped abruptly and glared at Shib.

'I'm going over there—to urinate behind those rocks.'
She indicated a cluster of vine-covered boulders. 'You can
kill me if you must. I leave that up to you.'

She turned on her heel and strode towards the boulders.
She had expected to feel fear, but felt only a curious free-
dom. Shib himself said nothing, and Erlin was aware that the
others had halted to stare at her.

Once out of view, Erlin struggled to loosen the catch on
the side of her trousers. It would be too embarrassing to call
for assistance. Stretching round until she felt she was going
to sprain her shoulder, her cuffed hands finally managed to
locate the catch. After blissful relief, struggling to get her
trousers back up again she found she now could not fasten
the catch. Dammit, she'd just go back and ask Anne to do it.

As Erlin walked from behind the boulders, she noticed the
group had closed up, with Anne on her knees and the others
standing over her. Erlin approached and stood before them
waiting for some reprimand. Frisk just stared at her for a
long while, then slowly drew the laser from her belt. Erlin
noted a look exchanged by the two mercenaries.

'You're Hooper,' Frisk said, 'you have the virus.'

Erlin nodded.

Frisk went on: 'I've decided I need only one hostage now.
What I'm going to do next is laser you from the feet up. It'll
take a couple of hours, but I'll enjoy every minute.'

Just then, everything happened at once. Anne shot to her

feet, crashing right into Frisk, knocking the laser from her hand but throwing them both off-balance. A huge shadow fell across Erlin and the two mercenaries stepped back— Svan looking wary but prepared, Shib with blank horror on his mutilated face. Something nearby let out a hissing snarl, in a vast exhalation.

Recovering her own balance Frisk tripped Anne, then kicked her hard in the side of the head when she tried to rise again. Then Frisk looked up.

'Jay, darling,' she cooed.

Erlin wondered just how hollow had been her sense of en-nui with life. Here she was with her hands tied behind her back; the people in front of her wanted to kill her—and she had a damned good idea of what was standing behind her. She had never before felt so vulnerable and so mortal. Then she heard a friendly, familiar voice.

'Erlin, get down!' Ambel bellowed at her.

Erlin flew face-down on the earth just as Ambel's blunder-buss boomed.

19

The tonne of fresh heirodont flesh had contained sufficient protein to initiate certain changes in the leech's body, for its huge size was such that prey from which it could extract such massive plugs were now rare. An organ that had been growing inside it for some time, now ruptured the membrane connecting it to the creature's stomach, and began producing a differ-ent bile. Thus this leech began to transform into one that could feed upon whole animals rather than parts thereof. Now cruising along the surface it felt the urge to take on an entire prey. Unfortunately it came upon a suitable candidate—the molly carp gorged on turbul-inflated glister—before the transformation inside itself was complete. Its mouthparts

*opened out wider and wider as it instinctively swallowed its
victim whole. The carp, suddenly finding itself inside a creature it often preyed on, though reluctantly, began to gnaw its
way out—the leech's bile not having developed sufficient
sprine in it yet to kill.*

Janer saved the charge in his laser carbine for more opportune shots. Ambel's barrel full of stones and rusty nails sent
the Skinner stumbling, and Ron's measured shots were
burning the skin from its face. But the weapon the Batian
was using on the monster was the most effective of all. The
screaming man kept backing away from it in terror, the explosive shells he fired repeatedly taking lumps out of the
Skinner's diseased-looking body.

'Back it up. Back it up,' yelled Keech, the snout of his
APW flicking from the Skinner to Frisk, then back again.
Janer knew that with the setting randomized, as Keech had
explained earlier, the monitor could not risk taking a shot
with Erlin and Anne so close to his targets.

Abruptly the male mercenary turned and ran. The other
one, the woman, stayed by Frisk's side, abruptly opening up
on the slab behind which Ambel and Ron were crouching.
Shells exploded against the rock, flaking off large chunks of
it and showering them both with hot splinters.

Janer drew a bead on the Batian woman and let the autosight pick her up. He pulled the trigger and saw her flung
back, her crabskin armour flaming and smoking. She rolled
away and, still clutching her weapon, scrabbled for cover.

Frisk snatched up the laser she had dropped earlier,
pointed it straight at Anne's head, and pulled the trigger,
then pulled it again and again, raging as nothing happened.
Janer swung his carbine towards her, but the auto-sight kept
tracking back to the fallen mercenary. So he fired on manual
and set a tree behind Frisk to smoking. Frisk threw her useless weapon on the ground, then turned and ran. Janer let the
sight slip back to the female mercenary, but she had now
made it to cover.

'Clear shot,' said Keech distinctly.

Janer assumed he meant on Frisk. He did not.

A purple flash lit the air as the Skinner was knocked flat. It howled in fury.

Just then, Ron leapt from behind the rock slab with his machete raised.

'We'll finish it!' he bawled, charging towards the fallen monster. Janer tried another shot at Frisk as she dodged through the trees, missed, then swore and looked around. Boris and Roach had vanished, though he hadn't seen them go. Keech suddenly rose and leapt out of hiding. The monitor fired once into the woods and a muted purple flash showered burning leaves some distance behind the escaping Frisk. Then he turned and looked over towards the Skinner. Ambel came running to stand at his side.

'You'll kill it,' he said flatly. As Ambel nodded, Keech went on, 'Then Frisk is mine.'

The monitor set off at a trot down the slope taken by Frisk.

Ambel went after Ron, who had nearly reached the fallen Skinner. Janer followed.

It had all become just too much. The work offered by Svan had seemed attractive enough at the time: a month at most spent on a low-tech world where apparently Sable Keech had arrived, without backup. It had been described to him as a job combining protection of the client, who would meet them there, with the burning of a few natives, and which would culminate with the hit on Keech, for which they would apparently receive a bonus on top of their usual daily rate. However, from that first moment of incredible luck, stepping out in the shuttle and seeing Keech right before them, it had all started to go terribly wrong.

First Nolan being blown away by a dead man, then a rhinoworm trying to bite their dinghy in half and deposit them in a leech-infested sea, then that screw-up on Tay's island, then the journey in the Prador spacecraft with those monstrous stinking creatures all around, then—after finding a suitable ship—the swim through the sea with leeches grating at his armour and other things trying to drag him down. He hadn't believed the stories about Hoopers, until he'd seen how hard they really were to kill, until he'd seen what happened to the hardest and most professional of his comrades, until he'd seen Dime die . . . There had been no relief after that. He'd relaxed his guard for just a moment and lost two fingers to a thing out of an ancient cartoon. Then the prill . . . Tors screaming . . .

Shib ran blindly. He didn't know where he was going. He just wanted to be anywhere that *thing* back there wasn't. The sails, the prill and the frog whelks were bad, and the leeches worse still. His insides folded with shame at how he'd reacted, but there had been nothing else. He'd just been unable to move. Even the pain of that leech grinding into his face hadn't unlocked his paralysis of fear. Now . . . now that thing . . .

When it stepped out of the trees behind the black woman, Shib had questioned his own sanity. There were horrible things on many worlds, and he had seen many of them, but this thing was beyond all that. It was something out of fairy tales and hell. It was *evil*. He had felt that instantly. With this thing there could *only* be pain and horror. Yet this thing had once been a man. He'd waited desperately for the order to fire on it, waited for Svan herself to open up on the thing, longed to see it obliterated.

'Jay, darling.'

That had been enough and Shib had cracked. *No way. Just no way. I'm gonna kill the bogeyman.* Only it didn't die. The shells he fired made holes in its diseased-looking body, but it just howled and looked even more pissed off. He felt shame again that he was running. But at least that thing was behind him now.

And, as he ran, Shib slowly began to regain control of his fear. As he slowed down and glanced back, he heard the sounds of a firefight. Perhaps if he circled round and attacked those newcomers from behind . . . No. Svan wouldn't be convinced. She knew he had run and would kill him for it. There was no give in her when it came to things like that. Gasping, Shib came to a halt. There had to be some other way off this island—off this planet. Perhaps if he directly contacted the Warden, he might get picked up, turn over evidence and testimony . . .

Movement to the right. In one motion, Shib dropped, turned, and fired. His shot cut between the trees and the shell exploded out of sight. He backed up, realized with sudden horror that he was standing underneath a leech-infested peartrunk, then he turned and ran on.

Again: sounds. He was sure he heard running feet, human feet. Was it Svan come to deliver the Batian punishment for his desertion? Perhaps it was one of those others and he could cut a deal. Maybe there was an easier way out of here?

'Shib, isn't it?' spoke a voice to his right. Shib stopped, dropped to one knee and brought his weapon up. This time, if anyone showed, he wouldn't miss. But no sign—no sign of anyone.

'You know, Shib,' said the voice, this time further to one side. 'Goss was three hundred and twenty-two years old, and she sure knew how to make a man happy.'

'I reckon he ain't interested in that,' said another voice behind Shib. Shib turned and fired, then ducked and ran, expecting fire to be returned. He released one other shot in the direction of the first voice, abruptly changed course, saw perfect cover between two boulders and ducked into it.

'He's a nervy one, ain't he, Boris?' said the damnable second voice. It was close now.

'Sprzzte phobe,' said something else.

Shib glanced to either side. He could feel fear rising in him again. He shouldn't have stopped here. He should have kept on running. Hoopers. Hoopers everywhere.

'You all right down there?' asked Roach, leaning over the rock.

Shib fired at him, but he was already gone.

'Over here.'

Shib glanced to one side, where a Hooper with a long walrus moustache had now stepped into view. He was unarmed, but oddly held the burnt-out SM that Shib distinctly remembered throwing into the sea. Then the mercenary recognized this Hooper—and also the one he had seen just before. This

one had gone into the sea, and the other they had left tied to
the mast of a burning ship. They had survived, *but not for
much longer*. Shib swung the snout of his weapon round as
the Hooper tossed the SM towards him.

'Here, catch,' the Hooper said.

'Sprzzzt,' said the SM, and abruptly accelerated. It
slammed into Shib's stomach, and his shot went wild and
blew a crater in the ground before him. He tried to bring his
weapon to bear again, couldn't get his breath. Then the other
Hooper was beside him and he had time only to see the
man's grin before a fist like a lump of rock came speeding
towards his face.

Ron reached the Skinner just as Keech disappeared at speed
into the dingle. The monster had been struck repeatedly:
there were burns all over it, cavities where the male mercenary's shells had hit, and yellow blotchy patches that had
festered. From it arose a stench as from an abattoir drain. Its
right leg had turned entirely yellow, and seemed almost
falling apart. That must be due to the sprine, Janer reckoned.
Yet, injured and dying as it was, the monster managed to
heave itself upright as Ron hammered towards it. The Old
Captain yelled and swung his machete. A hand like a huge
spider spun free, hit the ground, then hopped along for a
couple of metres before flipping on to its back with its fingers wriggling in the air. The stump of the Skinner's wrist
hit Ron in the chest, then came on like a hydraulic ram and
slammed him flat on his back. The machete cartwheeled
through the air and stabbed into the ground a couple of metres away.

Janer fired and a sheet of skin slid smoking from the Skinner's back. Hissing loudly, it grabbed Ron with its other
hand, lifted him and bit down on him, as if he were a sand-
wich. Ron bellowed. Janer started firing at the monster's
legs, then ceased when Ambel got in his way—going to retrieve the machete. The Skinner spun round, discarding Ron
like a fast food meal not to its taste, and now Ambel and the
creature confronted each other: Gosk Balem and his old
master, Hoop.

The Skinner hissed at Ambel, and crouched. Ambel advanced with the machete gripped two-handed and inclined to one side. Perhaps something of survival instinct kicked in then, as the monster backed off. Abruptly it turned and, with long unsteady strides, it ran. Ambel reached Ron just ahead of Janer.

Captain Ron lay with one side crushed and ripped open. As Ambel crouched by him, he reached up and caught hold of his fellow captain's hand. Hearing movement behind, Janer glanced round to see Erlin and Anne approaching, leaning against each other for support.

'Get these off me,' said Erlin, holding out her wrists. 'I can help him.'

Janer looked at the braided cuffs, and then inspected the charge meter on his carbine. He gave an apologetic shake of his head before returning his attention to the two captains.

'It has to die,' Ron insisted. 'It has to die finally and completely.'

'It will,' promised Ambel. He glanced round at Erlin, then, freeing himself from Ron's grip, he stood and stepped up to her. Almost casually, he clasped the material of the cuffs between her wrists and pulled. There was a hollow thud as they broke and he moved on to free Anne next. Erlin immediately went to Ron and inspected his torn side.

'Nothing much wrong,' muttered Ron, then, looking up at Ambel, 'What are *you* waiting for?'

Ambel turned to Anne. 'Get everyone to cover. Boris and Roach should be back soon. When they arrive, go find Peck and Forlam. Wherever they are, wait there with them,' he said. Then he turned to Janer and indicated the laser carbine. 'You come with me.'

Janer gave a terse nod then followed the Captain into the dingle.

Svan halted at the edge of a wide clearing, resting her weapon on the ground, then quickly unclipped the section of hot armour on her side. Underneath, her clothing was charred and it crumbled when she touched it. However, the burn on her skin wasn't as bad as she had expected. She took a spray from the medpack on her belt to deaden the pain, coating it with synthiskin. The armour section felt hard and brittle, but she clipped it back into place anyway. What now, she wondered; what the hell do I do now?

She stood and took a drink from her water bottle, before moving on through the dingle. Her satlink position finder rendered her the information that she was located on one of the Segre Islands, and showed her as a little dot near the centre of that island. Beyond telling her that, it was useless to her and she had little clue as to where she was and where she must go next. She'd lost sight of Frisk almost immediately, and cursed herself for letting the woman continue to carry a laser with its power pack disconnected. Frisk had been their only chance to get away, and now she was on the run, unarmed, with a half-crazed monitor with an APW in pursuit. Svan did not rate Frisk's chances very highly. So what must she now do? She had no idea which direction the madwoman had taken, just as she had no idea where Shib had gone. Though in his case she did not really want to know: if she ever saw him again he was dead.

Svan decided to keep moving, her best option seeming to head downhill towards the coast. Her first priority was to get off this island, and then off this damned planet with all its weird people and weirder animals. She moved fast, aware of sounds in the dingle around her, and determined to survive. After an hour, she heard the first screams, and recognized them as Shib's. She would not have bothered changing direction to help him, but the screams came from straight ahead of her, where the dingle thickened.

Svan was heading into deeper shade, where the trees were tall and debris lay thick on the ground heaped in thick drifts spotted with orange fungi. She noticed the tracks of some kind of large animal and some of the tall stalk-trunks had clearly been gnawed on. Animals didn't worry her, but the cause of those screams did. Eventually, Svan saw a white shape hanging in a peartrunk tree ahead of her, and immediately knew what it was.

Shib had stopped screaming by the time she reached him,

though he was groaning and gasping, occasionally weeping. Someone had suspended him naked by his feet from the branches of a peartrunk tree. Runnels of blood crisscrossed his body, and below him crawled the sated leeches that had fed and dropped away. Attached to him there were four still feeding. His feet had been totally stripped, but from his ankles downward the bloody holes cut into him grew increasingly disperse. He'd lost so much blood and flesh yet he still remained conscious. Svan wondered if those who had done this to him had known that suspending someone upside-down prevented them from fainting and that, with his strength, Shib would probably lose half his flesh before he died. She watched as a leech fell from him, setting him into a slow turn. He looked at her with his remaining eye.

'Svan,' he whispered.

There was such pleading in the single word that Svan aimed her weapon at his head for a long moment, then slowly swung it away. Another leech was already making its questing way down his leg, and Shib started gasping again. She knew, from long experience in such matters, that in a moment he would start screaming again. If she intervened and stopped his screams, that would forewarn anyone ahead of her presence, so, without further acknowledgement, she walked away.

Shib's renewed torment soon echoed through the dingle. Svan paused for just a moment before moving determinedly on. The next scream sent her into a trot, then a run, convinced that she wasn't running from him and what was happening to him: she had to move fast, just get out of here. Suddenly, ahead of her, she spotted three figures. They turned as she approached, one of them raising Shib's weapon.

In one smooth motion, Svan dropped to her knees and aimed.

'Drop it! Now!' she shouted.

The one called Roach tossed the weapon to the ground while Svan stared at him in disbelief, trying to comprehend how the hell he'd got here. Keeping all three of them in her sights, she stood and slowly advanced. The other one, with

the moustache, she also recognized from the ship Frisk had
torched. The third one, who was leaning on a stick and
didn't look so good, she did not recognize.

'You,' she gestured at him. 'Who are you?'

'Bugger you,' was his only reply.

Svan considered wasting him right there, but she desperately needed to get off this island, and for that she needed
help. She moved closer. Suddenly the ground erupted in
front of her on a purple flash. As the blast flung her back, she
felt her grip on consciousness slipping, and fought it. Burning debris rained down while she rolled and tried to stand.
The flat of a hand slapped her back to the ground and her
weapon was tugged from her grasp as easily as from a child.
After a moment she was hauled to her feet and suspended in
front of the bulky shape of Drum.

'Where is she?' demanded Drum, then flung her to the
ground again. In her struggle to sit upright, Svan backed into
someone else. Hearing a hiss, she turned and gaped in horror
at the man right behind her.

'Giss a kiss, girlsy,' said Forlam, waving his leech tongue
at her.

Frisk was just ahead of him, yet managing to stay frustrat-
ingly out of reach. Keech tried firing his APW, but it
dropped into cutting mode and spat out a purple bar only a
metre from its snout. As she dodged behind a stand of putrephallus, his second shot went on full power and blew up a
wall of burning vegetation. Lung birds dropped squawking
and burning from the sky.

'Frisk!' bellowed Keech as he ran on after the swiftly retreating silhouette. Glancing down at the displays on his
APW he saw that the remaining charge was very low, but
couldn't even be sure if that reading was accurate. Best to
save his shots, so he ran even harder. It felt good. It felt good
to run and to feel anger. With surprise he realized he hadn't
enjoyed himself so much for . . . seven hundred years.

Ahead, the ground began to drop away again. Keech realized he had passed the highest point of the island and that
from now on, on the way down, the dingle would begin to

thicken again. He couldn't afford to let her get there. He just could not let her get away. The prospect of chasing her around this entire sector for the next couple of centuries filled him with total dismay. It had to end now! *Today.*

Suddenly he spotted her clear ahead of him, and couldn't resist firing. The APW emitted a stuttering pulse, a sure sign of it reaching the end of its charge. But he dared not stop to change canisters now. He might lose her. He could lose her at any moment. He saw her glance back. She must be well aware what that disperse emission from an APW signified.

'You'll have to do better than that, Keech!' she shouted.

He fired yet again, damning himself as he did so, but unable to do otherwise. This time there was light, but no fire, no damage.

Suddenly Frisk was running towards him, screaming, her face twisted with hate. He continued to aim his APW at her, its trigger depressed. Spurts of fire started her clothing smouldering, but the weapon put out nothing effective. He dropped it to pull out his pulse-gun. His first shot slammed into her left biceps, gouging a chunk of muscle and spraying fragments behind. His second shot caved in her stomach and bowed her almost double, but did not slow her. There was no third shot, for by then she had slammed into him like a collapsing wall.

Keech went down with Frisk on top of him, the pulse-gun spinning away. She hammered a fist into his face—once, twice. He felt his cheekbone break, and aug contacts discharging under his skin. Then she was off him, and hauling him to his feet. She was *strong*, strong as an Old Captain. Keech found himself airborne, then lost all his breath as he slammed into a tree trunk. Leeches started falling about him.

'This body,' croaked Frisk, 'is all old Hooper.' She pressed down on the mess he had made of her arm, then made a horrible groaning sound. As she slowly paced towards him, Keech was struggling to recover his breath and to beat away leeches that were oozing towards him. He'd need a lot more than his slowly returning heavy-worlder strength to defeat her.

'I should have done this myself long ago. I should never

have left it to hired killers,' she sneered. 'First I think I'll
tear your arms off.'

Keech began breathing slowly and evenly. He recalled she
had always been a talker, had always loved going into detail
about how she was going to kill her victim. That anticipation
was a large part of the pleasure for her. She came to loom
over him, then bent and grabbed the front of his overall to
haul him to his feet. In one quick motion, he brought both
his hands to her throat and, as he closed them with all his
strength, she laughed in his face.

'I know it's not enough,' he said. 'You may kill me now,
but the machine that is me will keep working after I am
dead. So go ahead and tear my arms off.'

Slow realization dawned on her as he initiated the cybermotors in his fingers and completely relinquished his mental
control of them.

His fingers began to close on her hard Hooper neck.

Even with its wavering unbalanced gait, the Skinner easily
stayed ahead of them. They only gained on it when it fell, or
when it needed to shove its way through thickening dingle,
but wherever there was open ground it quickly pulled ahead
again. Ambel just kept going at the same dogged pace,
though Janer was beginning to find the chase exhausting. He
had reached the stage where he felt he must soon quit, when
the Skinner began to stumble and show signs of slowing.

'Now we have you, my lad,' growled Ambel.

The Skinner suddenly fell forwards in a rocky open space,
sprawled out like something dead washed up by the tide.
They quickly moved in and, with grim purpose, Ambel approached it holding his machete to his side. Janer stood back
and watched with morbid fascination as the machete whis-
tled down.

Thunk. A diseased leg jerked away. On the backstroke, he
took off the Skinner's remaining hand. Janer stared at the
head: the hate-filled black eyes and gaping mouth. There
was no sign on it of the yellow that denoted sprine poisoning, and it had nearly detached itself from the body.

'Ambel!' he yelled in warning, then began firing.

Ambel turned and hurled his machete. It struck rocks with a ringing clash that sent sparks skittering into the air. Janer set those same rocks smoking as he pressed the trigger down and kept on firing. Thumping between the rocks like a pig escaping the slaughterman, the head moved too quickly into cover though. They ran to the spot where it had disappeared, and stared down at a dark hole cut deep into the ground. Janer crouched forward, pushed the snout of his carbine into the cavity, and pulled back on the trigger. Nothing at all happened. He stepped away and peered at the carbine's display. Empty.

'Bugger,' said Ambel.

They continued to gaze into the hole, and Janer even thought he caught the glint of eyes looking back out.

'We could bury it in there,' Janer suggested.

Ambel shook his head. 'It'd only dig its way out again. Just one thing for it.' With the power of a machine he stooped, gripped rock, and broke it away from the edge of the hole, then reached down for more. There was a tenacity in the Captain Janer found a little difficult to comprehend.

'Why wasn't the sprine killing the head too?' he asked.

'Had never fully connected itself. I wounded the body,' said Ambel, still relentlessly pulling away rock. Janer watched him a while longer, then removed his own backpack, extracting from it the hexagonal box. He couldn't help feeling a certain inevitability about this moment.

'I have a way we can kill it,' he said. 'All I need is a crystal of sprine.'

'*At last,*' breathed the Hive mind.

Ebulan reached out with rigid control, and Pilot touched and manipulated the various complex controls to start AG and warm the thrusters. Through another blank, the Prador put the weapons console online and checked the loads. All readings were optimum. The rear nacelles contained a hundred and forty-four missiles fitted with CTDs, as well as cluster and planar explosives. There were four defence lasers and

two giga-joule particle beams. Even the old rail-guns were
in perfect order, and had carousels full of ceramo-carbide
missiles that could be fired at half the speed of light.

Meanwhile other blanks were running on the slave programs loaded into their thrall units, maintaining the ship, or
standing ready to replace Pilot or the blank seated at the
weapons console, all ready and equipped with hull patches
and fire retardants, should the ship be hit.

The Prador destroyer rose out of the trench spilling an ac-
cumulation of silt and broken shell from its upper surfaces.
It rose past heirodonts pausing in the depths for one brief
respite in their painful lives, till finally it came up underneath an island of sargassum. As it rose it hauled up tonnes
of seaweed with it, so that leeches and prill cascaded about it
in organic rain. For a short while the hull matched the colour
and texture of the floating mass of seaweed, then a line of
fire traversed the ship, from its sensor arrays to its rear
thrusters. Weed exploded from the armoured hull and fell
flaming into the sea. Clouds of superheated steam were
blasted away, then recondensed in an expanding cloud as the
destroyer began to move. As it tilted, the sea below it flattened, then three evenly spaced thrusters blasted ribbed blue
flames, and with a crash the destroyer accelerated into the
sky.

Pilot moved a hand across the weapons console and
slapped in a launch-and-seek program. A rear nacelle
opened and three lines of fire sped away. Ebulan viewed
them for just a moment then turned his attention to the de-
tectors ranged before his own eyes and the eyes of his
blanks. It hardly mattered if those departing missiles found
their target; they were merely diversionary.

The Warden observed the path of the three missiles for a mi-
crosecond then sent a warning to the Dome.

'Acknowledged,' said the submind there, with a heavy
emphasis. The Warden probed a little and discovered that
the submind had been on to the missiles from the moment
they were launched so had already been tracking them for at
least a whole second. It ignored the mind's sarcasm and,

with that part of itself not tied up in trying to crack Prador code, it turned its attention elsewhere.

'Twelve, take the SMs out from the island, to attack the Prador ship,' it sent.

'Yeah, let's kick us some ass!' returned one of them.

Two observed, 'I note you say "attack" not "destroy". You realize we'll be lucky even to slow it down?'

'If you can realize that then the Warden certainly can,' said Twelve patiently.

The Warden watched the seven drones accelerate out from the island and fall into an arrow formation. It prepared itself to upload all the subminds, should—at the moment of their physical destruction—they even have time to transmit themselves. Through their eyes it watched the Prador destroyer come into view and with a little further probing, learnt that the enforcer drones were ready and willing for the fight, and that SM12, though ready to do what it could, felt certain it was about to become a metallic smear on the ocean surface.

'We go in like this,' explained Twelve, sending them details of an attack formation selected from its library. One, Two and Seven slid to the fore and spread to the three points of a triangle. The remaining drones spread to the corners of a square. Both shapes began revolving.

'And the purpose of this?' enquired Two.

'We'll present a dispersed and more difficult target,' said Twelve. 'We also have a better chance of firing past shield projectors, and intercepting lasers and rail-gun fusillades.'

'In your arse,' said a voice.

'Who the . . . ?' began Twelve, but by then they were already on the Prador ship.

The drone formation slid over the destroyer like a tube. Lasers heated their casings on this pass, and they only managed half a second of fire. Their missiles needled down at the golden armour, most of them blasting against projected fields so that for half a second the destroyer was surrounded by coins of fire. Some missiles did get through to blow concentric ripples of flame around the hull of the ship. But where they struck, they left only glowing spots on its armour, and those spots quickly faded.

'Loop round,' said Twelve. 'We'll go in from the side this time.'

'Yeah, and with that you'll achieve what?'

'Prador war drone approaching from the east!' yelled Seven.

'It *was* a Prador war drone, but now it's me.'

'Sniper, is that you?' asked Twelve.

'Isn't that what I just said?' replied Sniper.

The old war drone had now become an amalgam of dented Prador drone with a headless aluminium crayfish attached to its surface and linked to the inside, through the split, via a fountain of optic cables.

Sniper went on, 'Dispersed and more difficult target, my arse. That Prador is playing with you. While it appears that you might be doing some damage, it knows there's less chance of anything else being sent against it. Otherwise you'd all be scrap by now.'

'What would *you* suggest?' asked Twelve.

'I don't suggest. I'm telling you that a dispersed attack is going to do nothing to affect that armour. You need to go in randomly and concentrate on just one point. Go for something vulnerable: a sensor array or a thruster. Now do it!'

Twelve bowed to Sniper's experience, and the formation broke as it hurtled back in towards the ship, the drones weaving all over the sky as lasers tried to pick up on them almost with a casual indifference.

'Seven to Ten, concentrate everything you have on that port thruster,' sent Sniper. 'One and Two, once they hit it, you hit the port laser with your rail-guns. Twelve, you've only got a geological laser—so why the hell are you here?'

'As a distraction?' Twelve suggested.

'Yeah, if you like,' said Sniper.

'Where are *you* going?' Twelve asked, noticing that Sniper was receding into the sky.

'Don't worry about me. I'll be back before you know it. Or, rather, back before our friend in that ship knows it.'

The SMs shot in over the destroyer and their missiles spread like a cloud of gnats around it. Everything seemed random until the cloud suddenly closed on the rear of the destroyer. A constant stuttering explosion bloomed, and the casing of a thruster went incandescent. The destroyer tilted as if a giant hand had slapped its back end—but then it quickly corrected. Shortly after that, there was a flash of purple fire, and an extrusion on the front of the Prador ship suddenly blackened and cracked open. Directly on top of that a luminous green line stabbed up from the destroyer and something danced before it, flickered, and became just a line of dust in the sky.

'There went Seven,' said Two.

'Particle beam,' observed Nine—then, 'EM shells!'

Twelve flew over the top of the ship, through a wall of fire. It could do nothing: its little geological laser, had it even been working, could not have touched this Prador armour. As it passed through the fire, Twelve closed its cockle-shells and tumbled through the air, as the EM pulse knocked its AG controls out of sync. Correcting at the last moment, it noted the crash foam inside itself melting, and that the casing on its micropile was developing hairline cracks.

'Warden, take me,' it said, accelerating towards the nearest weapons blister. The particle beam flashed out so all that struck the ship was a metallic cloud of vapour.

'Sniper, what now?' asked Two, as it swerved away and watched Nine, caught in the intersecting beams of three or more lasers, trying to get away, but distorting and melting in midair.

'Keep hitting it,' instructed Sniper, his signal now echoey with distance.

With machine-gun sonic cracks, the surviving SMs turned and resumed attack.

'Where *are* you?' asked Two, as it emptied its rail-gun magazines, ahead of the last of its missiles.

There came no reply from the ancient war drone.

With a fragment of its mind, the Warden watched the battle. Much of its attention was channelled through SM11, who it had hovering geostationary over the island. Through this drone's sensors it observed Sniper taking the Prador drone shell up and out of atmosphere and, knowing just how effec-

tive Sniper's ballistics programs were, it knew what the
drone had in mind. From the Polity base, it observed shield
projectors slam two of the missiles fired at it down into the
sea. Those two missiles vanished in two explosions that
were discs of fire: straight planar explosive—a diversion.
The third missile bounced off a shield, went up, and came
back down. A smart missile, released some time before and
sent on patrol, made the decision to go get it. The two missiles collided high above the base. The ensuing explosions
continued all the way down to the shields, which heated under the load. Cluster missile, the Warden observed dispas-
sionately.

With the rest of its resources, the Warden was concentrating on its code breakers. Momentary break-through there . . .
but the sequence folded after a half a second. Through
Eleven, it had some feedback from the blank called Pilot, so
now it knew it was on the right track.

Secondary automatic systems absorbed transmitted subminds, as one after another the enforcer shells were destroyed by the Prador ship. It would handle these later, the
Warden decided, as it shunted them into storage.

All that evinced any apparent emotion in the AI was when
the Prador code finally started to come apart.

The island was now in sight and in range, but firing the CTDs
was as yet out of the question, as they'd be intercepted long
before they reached their targets. Particle beams could not be
intercepted, though. Ebulan set his blank to firing on the island and through his own viewer had the satisfaction of seeing
great swathes of dingle exploding into fire, with even rock
melting wherever the beams touched it. He gave a mental instruction for Pilot to move them in low over the Old Captain's
ships, so a CTD could be used on them. When nothing happened, he probed down the link—and just found nil response.
Pilot must have been destroyed. There must have been a hit
Ebulan was unaware of. He looked through another blank's
eyes in the control area but saw no sign any damage. Pilot
simply stepped away from his console and walked from the

area. Ebulan knew horror then: someone else was controlling his blank. He instructed yet another blank to draw her weapon and go after Pilot. But Pilot acted first. He activated the emergency door between the control area and central corridor, then drew his weapon, put it on high discharge, and with a single blast he fused the door to its frame.

Ebulan focused on the blank seated at the weapons console, and the two still here with him. He soon sent them up and running for the central corridor. The blanks inside the control area he quickly got firing on the door. But the female blank he'd made draw her weapon first, abruptly stopped firing at the door, turned to her two companions, and cut them down—before putting the snout of her weapon in her mouth and blowing her own head off.

In panic Ebulan did an emergency reinstall of the random code. But this made no difference to Pilot; while Ebulan was effecting the reinstall, the blank caught hold of the first of his companions to come in after him, slammed that one's head repeatedly against the wall, then tore out the back of his neck. Along with the flesh and bone came the spinal section of the Prador thrall unit, and the corpse slumped. Without further instruction from Ebulan, the other two blanks stood unmoving while this happened.

Suddenly the ship lurched sideways under multiple concussions. Ebulan made one of the two blanks draw his weapon and shoot Pilot through the chest. In panic, he sent the other blank back to the weapons console. There he checked the readings and saw that the attacking SMs had finally managed to blow a thruster.

An abrupt feeling of pain. Shut off. Ebulan lost contact with the blank that had just shot Pilot. He now sent the one over at the weapons console to go and look, and meanwhile transferred direct control to himself. Now he had full views outside, tracking on the attacking SMs, and could also see through his remaining blank's eyes. He fired off the defensive lasers, shifted shields and strafed the sky with particle beams.

Pilot wasn't dead—just a hole through his chest. Old

Hooper. Ebulan's blank drew his weapon, but his arm, and the hand holding the weapon, thudded to the deck.

Another attack from the SMs. Ebulan released five missiles on random trajectories to pull them off.

What? The last blank went too, collapsing into pieces. Pilot held a shell cutter, and was coming this way. *What?* Armoured doors were opening and closing back there. *How?* Something above, but now control codes were going haywire, and external vision was fading. Behind Ebulan, the shell cutter screamed as it bit into the armoured door. He spun around and stared at the door in horror, blind now to everything outside his ship.

Sniper gazed down at the planet through the Prador drone's eye pits, and all he got was an image in shades of grey. Well, he thought, if that was how they saw the universe, it was no wonder they were so unfriendly. Switching back to his remaining palp-eye he got the same image in panoramic colour, before turning that eye to the stars. Might be the last time he saw them, he thought, then berated himself for getting all slushy. Then reversing AG on his cobbled-together vehicle, he plummeted for the planet below.

'Hey, Warden, what's the SP?' he asked.

'Sniper, I see that underestimation of you has been somewhat of a fault in your enemies. Do you think you'll manage to stay on target?'

'Yeah, but I might not get there all in one piece.'

'Then,' said the Warden, 'you'll be glad to know that I've just broken the Prador control code, and the master of that ship is not having a very good time.'

'Well, if you've broken the code, that means you've got some capacity spare to receive me,' replied the war drone.

'You're prepared for subsumption then?' asked the Warden.

'Not really,' said Sniper, 'but it beats actually dying.' As he said this, he felt the underspace link with the Warden open and consolidate. This was strictly his option, and it seemed like an open pit-trap to him. 'You know,' he went on, 'a guy once called me ugly inside and out.'

'And what was your response to that?' asked the Warden.

'Cut his head off,' Sniper replied, and so saying began to hum a tune over the ether. Then the old war drone grated out the words to a song:

'There once was an ugly duckling, its feathers all tatty and brown.'

The armoured shell exceeded fifteen thousand kilometres per hour through the stratosphere. Sniper fed all power not already being sucked away by the reverse AG into the Prador shield, and by distorting its focus managed to cone it out in front. This gave him another couple of thousand kph, even with increasing air resistance. Now he also fed pure water into the fusion boosters and accelerated.

'All the other birds, in so many words, said—'

From the Prador ship, precisely in the predicted position below him, no weapons were fired, and no shields swung into place. In this last second Sniper managed to broadcast his final words, before transmitting himself.

'Quack, get out of town.'

The explosion blew plasma through the central corridor. The dead blanks lying there were picked up in the blast and turned to oily flame. The wave of fire hit the weakened door into the control area and folded it back. Instrument panels and dead blanks alike were pasted against the inner hull by the blast, and feedback knocked out generator after generator. AG motors shut off; others came on and were instantly fused by power surges. The thrusters went out, and Ebulan's ship dropped from the sky like a brick. Now direct-linked into the controls, Ebulan gave off bubbling screams as those links fed power back to him, and set two of his control boxes on fire. He slammed against the wall of his chamber, and his own AG went out. He had just regained enough control to get the shields out underneath the ship to absorb most of the shock. But projectors burnt out as the ship hurtled towards the sea, then slammed into the waves. Seawater exploded out from under the destroyer as it settled, almost gracefully at the last.

Then the water washed back. And the ship sank.

I'm alive, Ebulan thought. *I can survive this*. Just then, the door behind him gave way and Pilot reeled into the chamber wielding the shell cutter, ready to carry through the last instructions the Warden had programmed into him.

Ebulan's bubbling screams continued until water came flooding into the ship through the hole Sniper had punched through its hull.

But even that did not stop the ancient blank. Pilot continued to hack away at his Prador master until there was nothing left to see in the soupy water—and the power pack of the cutter was totally drained.

As Sniper arrived, the Warden felt an almost excited anticipation of the coming subsumption. There would be so much to upload from the ancient drone: the memories and experiences; the direct recordings of events Sniper had seen with his own palp eyes; ancient battles and scenes from worlds now metres deep in radioactive ash. Then would come the long overdue—and pleasurable—task of reprogramming that infectively abrasive personality and making Sniper into somebody a little more tolerable. The Warden put online the overlay personality programs, and the necessary search-and-destroy programs. However, its excitement began to turn to dismay when the drone's mind just kept on arriving . . . and arriving.

20

The giant leech surfaced and rolled as the molly carp tore out through its side, then dived, and with its flat tentacles dragged itself with all speed back to its atoll. The huge wound the leech had received would not have been enough to kill it, had not its bile duct continued pumping bile with increasing levels of sprine into the injury. So the leech died by poisoning itself, and as it died it sank. For some while, nothing came to feed upon the corpse, as the sprine diffusing into the sea deterred them. Once the poison had diluted enough, first to come were the boxies. In huge shoals they quickly snatched what they could, while they could. A small flock of frog whelks came next from a nearby islet, eager to feed on both boxies and leech. Then came hammer whelks sneaking up on their kin, shattering their shells with an enthusiastic racket that of course attracted turbul . . . then glisters . . . It was unfortunate that all this was still happening near the edge of the oceanic trench. Dinner-plate eyes observed the descending debris and tiny brains wondered what had attracted their fellow residents up there—so ascended to find out. And as an organic cloud again spread across the seabed, siphons, noses, antennae, and organs not easily described twitched and shivered, and nightmare mouths opened in anticipation.

Janer sat up, brushing embers from his hair. A black and red rain was falling about them, and smoke was belching up from the burning dingle below. He glanced across at Ambel who was still squatting by the Skinner's hideaway, rubbing at his eyes.

'What the hell was that?' Janer asked.

The sounds of explosions had carried across the water, and they'd gaped up at the enormous ship hurtling towards them like a floating arcology, surrounded by energy displays, fast-moving objects and actinic explosions. Then: blinding greenish light, and fires and smoke all across the island, followed by an explosion that blew a cone of fire out of the bottom of the ship. The destroyer had then slid sideways and, trailing fire slammed into the sea: a hot coal boiling into the depths.

'Prador,' muttered Ambel, blinking to clear the spots from his vision. 'Don't know what the Warden hit it with, but it was damned effective, I know that, lad.'

Janer took a shuddering breath, then raised his hand and opened it. Revealed was a single red crystal on a piece of cloth. Lucky he hadn't lost it when he'd dived for cover. He

looked round for the hexagonal box, took it up from where
he had dropped it, and moved over to join Ambel. Setting the
box on a nearby rock, he pressed a touch-plate on its side
and a small door irised open at one end of it.

'You know what this means?' he asked the Captain.

'I think I do,' said Ambel, 'perhaps more than you. Do you
think for one moment that the Warden doesn't know about
this?'

'Then why would the Warden allow it? Why allow the
Hive here at all?' Janer asked.

'Balance,' said Ambel. 'The Warden has the overview, and
knows that a *balance* needs to be struck here. You can't have
people as durable as Hoopers running around the galaxy
without at least one Achilles heel.' Ambel grimaced at the
unintended pun. 'They'd end up either destroying or being
destroyed. Power must be tempered.'

Janer said, 'Erlin says it's rumoured that the Polity is
scared of you people, so that's why it prevents further devel-
opment of this place. But she says she doesn't believe that.'

'Erlin likes to believe in goodness,' observed Ambel.

'And you?'

'I prefer to believe in what's true.'

'You get to know what's true out on your ship, do you?'
asked Janer, with a grimace. He manoeuvred his hand so the
sprine crystal slid down the cloth that was channelled between his fingers, and into the opening in the box. The hornet waiting there grabbed the crystal and pulled it inside. *Ten
million shillings*, brooded Janer. *What the hell*.

'Thinking is something you find you do with increasing
clarity as the years pass, and after a time you find there is
very little you have not thought deeply about. Truth and clarity are one,' said Ambel, seeming calm as he said this.

'I guess that makes sense.' The opening promptly irised
shut. Janer stared at it for a moment then looked up at Ambel. 'I wonder what *your* truth will be.'

The Captain had no reply for this.

Janer studied him for a moment, then nodded in response
to an internal monologue. 'The mind tells me everything is
primed,' he said. 'It'll only take a minute.'

* * *

The Skinner had little of human thought left to it. It now hated with the intensity of a human and it hungered like a leech. It had also come to understand fear, but knew it was safe here in the darkness.

Memory was a strange thing to it. Pictures and concepts occasionally connected in its hard fibrous brain, but it did not understand those connections. Its imperative was simply to eat and to grow, yet it had *recognized* some of those creatures out there.

'*Jay darling.*'

Those two words were somewhere deep inside it, and caused in it something that was like—yet unlike—hunger. The creature that had attacked it at the last, had aroused a deep fear and loathing somehow connected to another darkness and a time of long hunger. That creature had fed it, yet it had also hurt it, long before. It now wanted that creature, as it wanted all creatures. It wanted to feed on that creature, but it wanted it to be a long feeding: a long dismantling and slow feast. But it was not strong enough just now. Its other part was dead, killed by that same creature. It must get away, go deep and feed on the things there, then return strong and ready for . . . *more* feeding.

In the darkness the Skinner shifted on its spatulate legs, and licked its black tongue over its teeth. Can't get me here, it thought in its disconnected way, but I'll get you. I'll pull off your skin and chew on your bones. I'll have you wriggling in my mouth, and I'll have you scream like a unit for coring . . . Unit for coring? The Skinner was puzzled for a moment. It didn't quite understand those . . . words. Where had they come from?

'Hey, Spatterjay Hoop! We've got a present for you!'

It was the creature accompanying the pain giver: the one that had burnt the Skinner with red sunlight. The Skinner concentrated its black glare on the circle of light far above it. The circle was blotted out for a moment, and then there came a sound. It was a buzzing humming vibration. Again the Skinner was puzzled, until it found a connection, deep, so deep. From that connection rose an atavistic fear, and it backed deeper into the crevice in which it had wedged itself, again licking its tongue over its teeth. Something hard landed on its tongue, and it lifted that something up before its eyes and tried to focus on it with what little light was available. It could just make out something many-legged, a thorax, and a body like a severed thumb, painted with lines in luminous paint.

Then came the pain.

The Skinner tried to howl—but the rudimentary lungs it had grown did not yet have the capacity. It snapped its tongue back into its mouth and tried to worm even deeper into its crevice. The second sting was on its snout. It shot out of the protective crevice, and ran towards the light. The buzzing again. Another sting on its wing-ear. It could feel the dying pain spreading from all those areas. Its tongue felt flaccid, with a putrid taste. It scrabbled to get closer to the light, points of agony spreading out all over it.

It was in the light! The creature—

Ambel stepped back, pulled from his belt the cloth he had earlier loaned to Janer, and wiped clean the blade of his machete. The Skinner's head lay on the ground in two neat halves. Those halves moved still, but they were dying from the sprine injected by a hornet's sting. The queen hornet flew out of the hole in the ground, circled for a moment, then landed on Janer's shoulder. Janer turned his head to look at it, and suddenly felt a terrible tightness in his stomach. *Good grief, what have I done?*

For a moment he thought he had gone blind but, after a time, vision began to return. He gazed up from where he lay on his side, and saw that a trench had been burnt into the slope above him and that the lips of that trench were of glowing magma.

Coherent thought did not return to him until minutes after his vision returned. And his first thought was: *I hurt.* His second thought was: *Why am I alive?* He'd closed his hands on her neck and she'd reached for his neck. Her grip had closed like a shear and he'd known she was going to tear his head off. Then had come that light as bright as the sun, and the explosions, and the fire. Particle beam—almost certainly from the Prador ship. The ship had to be gone now, else this entire island would be nothing but magma.

Keech sat up and surveyed his surroundings. Frisk lay on the ground before him, her neck twisted and crushed, her windpipe torn out. He gazed down at his hands: they were locked into fists, and there were fragments of flesh caught between his fingers. He sent an instruction to the cybermotors in his fingers, and slowly his hands opened and, as they did so, he wished he'd kept them closed. For they felt as if they been worked over with a hammer.

'Near tore her head off, you did.'

Keech slowly turned, feeling as if someone had hit him in his face with a spade. And as for his neck . . . An Old Captain he did not recognize sat on a nearby rock. On a lesser rock sat Boris, with the seahorse SM upright next to him, poised on its tail and with topaz light intermittently returning to its burnt-out eye. Roach and Peck were perched on two other rocks. Keech studied this tableau for a moment, before dropping his gaze to Forlam rested against the rock below them, his arms and legs firmly bound. The crewman had his lips sucked in, as if fighting to keep his mouth closed, and a particularly demented expression. Keech managed to raise a quizzical eyebrow.

'He's getting a bit dangerous,' the Captain explained. 'We need to get Dome food into him quickly, before he picks up too many nasty feeding habits. Need some of it meself, too.'

Yes, thought Keech, the Captain was gaunt, and had the same definite bluish tinge and slightly crazy look as he had previously seen in Olian Tay—though obviously his condition was nowhere near as advanced as Forlam's. He wondered what had happened here. Forlam, he noticed, was now staring guiltily down at his feet, but his leech tongue was now darting in and out of his mouth regardless. Keech stopped himself from shrugging—it would hurt too much— and just let it go. He didn't really want to know about Forlam's feeding habits; he was not sure how much more knowledge of Hoopers he could stand. He reached up, felt at the vertebrae of his neck, and hoped none of them was broken. Then he wondered how much it mattered anyway, as he himself was a Hooper now. He'd gone from someone dead to being someone so determinedly alive that a broken neck was probably something quite minor to him. And, so thinking, he stared across at Rebecca Frisk. He realized that the two shots he had managed to hit her with had probably been enough to save his own life. With her torn arm, she could not have been able to get a *proper* grip on his neck.

The Captain stood and walked over to him. He reached out a hand and helped Keech to stand.

'I'm Drum,' he said. 'I just wanted you to see her.'

Keech looked at him questioningly.

Drum gestured to Frisk, and Keech returned his attention there. Now he could see that her eyes were open, and her mouth was moving slowly. How long, he wondered, would it take her body to repair itself. How long until she stood again and killed again—and spread horror again.

'She's got a Hooper body,' said Drum. 'And we don't want any more Skinners running around.' Keech watched him as he put his weapon up to his shoulder. The monitor recognized it as being of Prador design, but designed for humans—for their blanks.

'I know you can't speak at the moment, Rebecca,' said Drum. 'I also know just how badly this is going to hurt you. I'll try to be quick, though . . . well, actually that's a lie. I'm going to do this as slowly as possible.'

Drum dropped the setting on his APW, and took aim at Rebecca Frisk.

'No, don't!' someone yelled.

Keech watched the Old Captain lower the APW, then look about himself in bewilderment.

'What's that?' asked Boris, pointing.

Keech glanced up at the small metallic object hovering above them. He was about to explain to them that it was a holocorder, when Olian Tay and Captain Sprage stepped into view. Tay was holding a screen in her hand, and had an avid look on her face.

'You seem remarkably well,' she said to Keech.

'I've felt better,' said Keech, ignoring the irony. But, even as he said it, he knew that was wrong. Despite how much he hurt, he felt wonderful—never better. Tay now turned to Drum. 'I don't want you to destroy her, Drum. She's too valuable to be destroyed,' she insisted.

Drum stared at her with a mulish expression and raised his weapon again.

'You know, Drum,' said Sprage, nodding to Frisk. 'She's caused a lot people a lot of hurt. Maybe it'd be a good idea if she had some time to think about that.'

Drum's expression did not change, until Sprage pointed with the stem of his pipe back down the slope. Now coming into view were two crewmen carrying a metallic coffin suspended from poles. Drum looked momentarily puzzled, then a slow grin spread across his face.

'How much time?' he asked, still grinning.

'About as long as Grenant, I should think,' said Sprage, glancing at Olian Tay for confirmation.

Tay said, 'A few thousand years of waking in those coffins, before they've no mind left to speak of. I want them both to last a little while.'

While Drum laughed, Keech just looked on in confusion, until Olian Tay's plans were explained to him. He then watched with grim satisfaction as the coffin was opened and the now slowly recovering Rebecca Frisk was laid inside. At one time he had felt that no amount of suffering could be enough punishment for one of The Eight. Now he was not quite so sure.

Captain Ron was on his feet by the time they returned, and he held up his fist in victory salute when he saw what Ambel was carrying.

'Grendel is dead,' said Ambel briefly.

Ron, the only one of them who understood the obscure reference, said, 'Do you think there's a mother as well, then?'

'I hope you'll explain that,' said Erlin in mock anger.

Janer started paying attention then. He'd missed the earlier exchange, so deep was he in conversation with the Hive mind: making arrangements for his ten million shillings. He watched Ambel walk up to Captain Ron. Ambel was carrying the two halves of the Skinner's head tied with the same length of string, and hung over his shoulder like a pair of huge grotesque shoes. He made to give them to Ron.

'Best you keep it with you. It'll look good,' said Ron, then he pointed down the slope, past the scarred rock and burning vegetation, to where the dingle had escaped being flattened. As Janer gazed in that direction too, he saw figures emerging from under the trees. There were many of them, and all clearly Hoopers.

'The Convocation,' said Ambel, looking very directly at Erlin. He unhooked the sprine parcel from his belt and tossed it to her. 'Remember what I said,' he reminded her.

Janer wondered at that. Surely there would be no problems for Ambel now. Surely he had proven himself beyond doubt? He raised his image intensifier and focused it downwards at those approaching. Keech was walking with Captain Drum and another Captain who was smoking a pipe—something Janer had never before seen in his life. Others walked there as well, and Janer could easily tell which ones were the Old Captains. There was an assurance about them, a certainty.

Sprage, as Janer later learnt him to be called, was the first to test the crust on the cooling magma and cross over, so was consequently the first to reach them.

'You got his parole?' Sprage asked Ron.

'Yes,' said Ron.

Sprage nodded and drew on his pipe. With fascination, Janer watched the smoke trickling out of his nose.

'We'll decide it here then,' said Sprage, then pointed at the two halves of the Skinner's head. 'But first we'll have us a fire and be well rid of him.' Only after he had said these things did he look Ambel directly in the eye.

'*You* named me Ambel, so you must have known,' Ambel said.

'I knew who you were,' agreed Sprage.

'You did?' Ambel asked.

'Oh yes, I did—as I do now. You're the same Gosk Balem we threw in the sea, the same one who burned Hoopers,' replied Sprage.

* * *

With the last intermittent faults ironed out of its AG unit,
Thirteen rose into the air and surveyed its surroundings.
There were nearly two hundred people gathered on the face
of the hill. Twenty-three of them were Old Captains—
including Drum, Ron, and Ambel. All of them worked together to drag together fallen trees and build a suitably
dramatic pyre on which to hurl the remains of the Skinner. It
did not take much discussion for them to decide who would
enjoy this moment, and it was Keech, using the laser he had
retrieved from Janer, who ignited the pyre. As afternoon slid
into evening, all stood in contemplative silence and watched
the Skinner finally shrivel and burn away. There were no unexpected movements, no sudden resurrections, and there
would be none.

It its memory, Thirteen drew a line underneath this moment, then tried for the nth time to get a signal somewhere,
to someone.

'Warden? Warden? Twelve, do you hear me? What's going on out there? Sniper? Sniper?'

Again there came nothing over the ether but an empty
hiss. Something catastrophic must have happened, for even
the Coram server was dragging its heels, and Thirteen could
get little of relevance out of it.

The SM at the planetary base was the only one with anything to offer. 'The Boss broke contact when that ship blew.
He was fooling with Prador control codes, so maybe he got
some feedback.'

Thirteen acknowledged this possibility, but doubted it
very much. Deciding it could do nothing else until contacted, the little drone decided to continue observing and
recording the events here. Seeing Sprage and Ambel standing somewhat apart from the rest, as the fire burnt lower, the
drone dropped into the trees behind them and moved in
close. The two captains were silent for a long while until, after filling his pipe and getting it going, Sprage said, 'Decision goes against you, and it'll be the fire. No one'll want
you coming back again.'

'Then I must be convincing,' said Ambel. 'Why did you

say I am Gosk Balem? I have no memory of him. There's nothing of him left.'

Sprage said, 'The house may be gutted, even its inner walls and floors and ceilings torn out—but the house still stands.'

'Very wise, and I'll burn for that,' said Ambel bitterly.

'That's something to be decided,' said a voice out of the twilight. Captain Ron walked up to stand to one side of Ambel, then continued, 'Time for you to tell it all again.'

Thirteen watched as the Captains and crews coverged out of the twilight, their flickering shadows cast about by the flames. There was no formality here, and no requirement for it. Most of the Captains were gathered together, so this constituted a Convocation. Anything decided by these captains, while they were together, would be written in stone. Thirteen rose higher and swung out to get a better view of proceedings, and immediately found that it was being accompanied through the air. That Olian Tay's holocorder dogged its flight should have come as no surprise at all.

Janer sat on a log with the queen hornet on one shoulder, and with interest watched the gathering. He liked Ambel and certainly didn't want to see him burned alive, but if the decision went against the Captain, what could Janer do? He glanced at Erlin, who was watching events with something approaching terror in her expression. Janer noted that she had acquired one of the Batians' weapons, and he wondered if she intended anything rash. If she did, he felt he must intervene—though he was not sure to what end. He turned to Boris and Roach, sitting on the log beside him.

'What happened to the two mercenaries?' he whispered.

'They both got eaten by leeches . . . sort of,' Boris whispered back.

Behind them a crewman, who could have been Goss's twin, shushed them to silence. Ambel had begun telling his tale in a flat emotionless voice. Janer knew how effective that telling could be, but he'd heard it before and was getting bored now.

'Where will you establish the first nest?' he whispered.

'*The hole into which the Skinner fled seems a viable proposition,*' replied the mind.

'You don't sound wholly convinced.'

'*Until two hours ago I was. I have since spoken with an augmented sail called Windcheater, who has offered me a place on the rock where the sails roost. Windcheater has an agenda, I believe,*' said the mind.

'World domination? Humans go home?'

'*No, Windcheater wants humans and everyone in here. He wants the Polity in. He wants the Hive minds in. He would like the Prador here, if he could get them. He has augmented his innate intelligence and is absorbing knowledge at an astonishing rate. I well understand this, as he has been starved of these things for many thousands of years.*'

'Thousands?'

'*A tentative estimate. The sails themselves don't really know. They don't die very often.*'

'One moment,' said Janer. He turned to Boris, 'What happened to that adolescent Prador?'

'Still looking for it. Reckon it went into the sea,' Boris replied, and was again shushed from behind. Janer noted that Ambel had not quite reached the end of his story, so returned to his conversation with the mind.

'Still no answers to the question, why does he particularly want your nests on his rock?' Janer probed.

'*Windcheater wants us all here because, the more Polity entities there are here, the more opportunities there'll be for him and his kind. Specifically, I think he wants us on his rock so he can charge rent.*'

'And what form would the rent take?' asked Janer.

'*Quite simply money—with which he can buy augmentations for all of his kind. AI linkups, high-tech tooling . . . all the trappings of technology. As Windcheater so appositely put it to me, "Spend a thousand years sitting on a rock having conversations that consist mainly of comments on how windy it is, and you'll have a true appreciation of library computers, walls, and solar heating." I somehow suspect that in the near future Hoopers will have to learn to handle fabric sails and rigging themselves on their ships.*'

'Forgetting that, are you prepared to pay the rent? You could just as easily establish a nest here.'

'The rock has its attractions. For one it is not easily accessible to Hoopers.'

'You consider them a danger?'

'I cannot say. How will they react when they discover that creatures with stings that inject sprine are about to colonize here?'

'I guess it'd be worth your while to take a few precautions,' agreed Janer.

Ambel had just finished his story, and now the Captains were asking him questions. What did he remember? Did he now consider himself free of guilt? Did he think there should be a statute of limitations on multiple murder? Would he be prepared to undergo an AI-directed mind probe? Ambel seemed to give the right answers to all these questions, then at the last, a question was flung at Captain Sprage.

'Why did you insist he is the same Gosk Balem we flung in the sea?' asked Captain Ron.

Sprage stood up and drew deeply on his pipe. The tobacco's glow was reflected in his eyes so they glimmered like embers.

'He's the man. Memories are gone but the framework is still there. He has the morals, the understanding and the empathy that were Gosk Balem's. Put in the same position as he was put a thousand years ago, and likely he would do exactly the same things again,' said Sprage.

'You're saying he'd still throw Hoopers in the furnace?' a Captain asked, eyeing Sprage doubtfully.

'He threw just the brains and spinal columns of Hoopers into the furnace. The rest of the bodies were sold to the Prador, like empty cups to be filled with metal and Prador thoughts.'

'Very poetic, Sprage. We all know about coring,' growled someone in the darkness.

Sprage went on, 'Gosk Balem was an ECS soldier who was captured by Hoop and his crew. They brought him here to be cored like the rest of their captives, but as he was ECS, and so obviously horrified by what they were doing here,

Hoop decided to keep him alive in order to extend his suffering. They forced a slave collar on him, then put him to work at the furnace, burning the physical remains of coring. He had no idea then that those remains were still living and, even had he known, would he have chosen not to burn them? Would any of you?'

Silence met this question, so Sprage continued: 'The Hoopers that were cored were too recently infected with the virus to have survived long in that ganglionic form. Those that weren't eaten by leeches would have died or slowly transformed into leeches themselves. He never burned anything that still had a chance at life. He worked for Hoop because he made the choice of survival.'

'Yeah,' said Boris. 'But he didn't have the slave collar on all the time.'

'Survival again,' said Sprage. 'Hoop removed his collar so as to further extend his torment. He could try to flee into the wilds, but it was unlikely he would have succeeded. Hoop really wanted him to try. Instead, he stayed and he continued feeding remains into the furnaces. And do you know why? Because while he was there, he might find the chance to act against Hoop.'

'How do you know all this, Sprage?' asked Ron.

Sprage took a short penknife from his pocket and scraped round in the bowl of his pipe. After knocking out the pipe's dottle on the palm of his hand, he immediately began to refill it.

'I know because I saw him doing something then that I only came to understand a few years after we caught him and threw him in the sea. The furnaces were powered by an old fusion reactor Hoop had removed from one of his landing craft. I still had my collar on then, while the virus established itself in me. I was three weeks, a month perhaps, from being cored. It was at that time I saw him carry a piece of reactor shielding and drop it in the moat.'

Abruptly Keech was on his feet, having been squatting by the flames. 'He what?' said the monitor.

'The war was ending and the Prador retreating,' said Sprage, ignoring Keech. 'There'd been little chance of rescue during the war, but as it ended there was hope.' He turned to address Keech. 'You came here then. It was you who broke the program controlling the slave collars, and helped free those who remained. But how did you know where to come?'

Keech stared at Ambel, who was looking increasingly puzzled.

'We knew from which part of the *sector* the coring trade was operating, but we didn't know which sun or which planet. We swept that area searching for some kind of trace, some sign of spacecraft, orbital stations, field tech—we used all available methods to pick on high-tech usage.'

'What finally brought you here, then?' asked Sprage.

'The distinctive signal from a fusion reactor. Normally you will never pick up on it, but this reactor was completely unshielded,' said Keech.

'Bugger,' said Boris, still sitting beside Janer. He was not alone in his exclamation. There was a sudden surge of talk, till Sprage held up his hands.

'I called him Ambel when I found him. I'd recognized him right away. I didn't throw him back and I didn't tell anyone because they might have voted to throw him back. I let him find his own life, and always hoped no one would ever know. He's Gosk Balem all right. He's the one who, over a period of years, stripped the inner casing from the fusion reactor so it would act as a beacon for ECS. He's the reason every one of us old slaves is still alive. We shouldn't have thrown him to the leeches in the first place. We had too much hate back then and we did wrong. Let's not compound that error now.'

With a click, Sprage placed his pipe back in his mouth and then relit it. A roar of talk erupted again, while Keech walked up to Ambel and stood before him. A silence descended and the Hoopers watched. They knew how for centuries this monitor had hunted down and killed off members of Hoop's former crew.

Keech held out his hand to Ambel, and Ambel solemnly shook it. Boris stood and walked over to his Captain. Other members of Ambel's crew then emerged out of the darkness. Then Old Captains, and other crews. Hoopers were shaking

Ambel's hand, pounding him on his back. They were shaking each other's hands and pounding each other's backs.

Janer looked over at Erlin and saw that she was crying. The Convocation had clearly made its decision about Ambel.

'*Touching*,' said the Hive mind. Janer glared at the queen hornet on his shoulder, then stood and himself went to shake Ambel's hand. Feeling a slight lump in his throat, he didn't really want to listen to the mind's cold analysis. Ambel was grinning as Janer approached. His usual calm had been fractured by . . . *happiness*.

'Congratulations, Captain,' said Janer.

He took Janer's hand and shook it.

'What now, lad? You'll stay around a while?' asked Ambel, still shaking Janer's hand.

'I think so,' said Janer.

'Good lad,' said Ambel, slapping him on the shoulder with his free hand. The Captain then turned to Erlin and carefully took her in his arms.

Janer kept the grin on his face as he backed out of the crowd of jubilant Hoopers and went back to sit on his log. He tried to figure out if what Ambel had just done was deliberate. He glanced down at his shoulder and the mess on it that had once been the mind's colonizing queen. From the Hive link came a buzzing scream, as of a circular saw going into hardwood. Janer grimaced and pulled the link out of his ear, to drop it into his pocket. The transfer had already been made and he now had ten million shillings in a private account. The future looked good.

Thirteen decided that nothing more of any moment was going to happen near the fire, so it rose up over the trees and floated down the slope of the island to the beach. Here it settled to scan something else, so that its record of events here might be more complete. An accurate description might be 'for morbid curiosity', but Thirteen did not allow itself to think like that.

The coffin had been placed in one of the rowing boats beached here, ready to be returned to Sprage's ship. Thirteen hovered above it, and tapped the palm lock with its tail, but to no effect. The drone then projected a complex lasered image at the lock, then tapped it again, thus opening the viewing window. These particular actions it would edit from its final record, before allowing that record to go out on general release. It wouldn't do for the Warden to know that one of its SMs had had been buying and uploading black software normally employed by the less salubrious members of society.

Through the window, the drone observed Rebecca Frisk thrashing her head from side to side and rolling her eyes. Every time her mouth passed underneath the panel, her breath frosted the chain-glass. Touching the surface of the coffin with its tail to detect the vibrations, Thirteen surmised that the woman was screaming. *Amazing* how much energy she had. The drone tapped once on the glass with its tail, and Frisk stopped her thrashing to stare at it bug-eyed. She started to shout, to beg, her eyes filled with tears. The drone linked to the Coram server, trying to find a lip-reading program, but had no time to download the sluggish spurts of information before huge movement in the dingle at the head of the beach distracted it.

Thirteen shot high into the air, watching as the Prador came out on to the beach and, after counting legs, made an understandable mistake. It was the adult! Somehow, the Prador in the spacecraft had survived and come ashore!

'Warden! Warden! The Prador is here!' the drone screamed over the ether.

This time there was an immediate response. 'Lemme see,' someone said, and a huge threatening presence linked through Thirteen, and gazed through the little drone's eyes.

The humans were all still up the hill now involved in some sort of celebration. Earlier, parties of them had come down to fetch barrels of alcohol and various seafoods, but at last all movement was confined to the hill. Even the ships had been abandoned on this night of celebration and had he wanted to the Prador could easily have taken one. These primitive wooden ships were not what he was aiming for, though.

As Vrell held his communicator up before his eyes, he bubbled with satisfaction. The beacon was now operating and, even with the distortion through the water, he saw that his father's ship was less than a kilometre away from the island. All he had to do was swim out to it and get inside. No problem there. He knew all the access codes, just as he knew that the ship carried spare AG units and generators. It would take him a long time to make repairs, possibly years, but he could always get himself some help if the surgical facility was still operational. He knew that Ebulan had always carried a stock of spare thrall units.

Vrell moved on to where the rowing boats were beached, and in one of them detected movement. Strapped to the woodwork of one of these boats was a large metallic container, and through its luminous window Vrell saw that inside it was Ebulan's tool, Rebecca Frisk. For a moment, he considered taking her with him, and installing a thrall unit, but quickly rejected that idea. He did not want to leave any clue that he was still alive. He edged on past the boat and into the sea, and began swimming.

Ten metres from the shore he submerged to pass underneath the ships. Leeches, coming from the other side of the island to repopulate the irradiated water, grated at his armour and fell away. A glister attacked him, but he cut it in half with his working claw. Ten metres beyond the ships, he surfaced and kept going, occasionally emitting bubbling coughs of pleasure. He would repair the ship and take it out of this human-infested system, so fast the Warden would not even have time to react. Once back home, he would assume Ebulan's position, and then perhaps concentrate his attention on some of the females Ebulan had kept at his undersea residence. The future looked good. Nothing could stop Vrell now.

Behind Vrell, the oil-dark waters swirled as they were cloven by a steep head that left a deep trough behind. The molly carp had gorged on dead leeches, but its recent upsets and that odd intestinal complaint had left it feeling a void in its stomach—one that it just had to fill. Also, the tickling stinging sensation that had started in its head only minutes earlier only ceased as it turned in this direction—but it was glad to have been led here. The creature ahead of it left a very intriguing taste in the water; something like that of a glister but without the slightly rancid tang.

With its stomach rumbling the molly carp decided to investigate.

On Coram, all the humans were now gone, and only maintenance robots independent of the Warden continued with their tasks. Outside the base the weapons turrets had sunk back out of sight, and the cracked crust of sulphur and ice had dropped back into place to begin the healing of scars. Deep in the centre of the complex, the physical container of what was essentially the Warden appeared no different from how it had always appeared. However, inside, things were very different indeed.

'An easy mistake to make, but that's not the one called Ebulan, not the one from the ship. It's only just become an adult, and it won't live long enough to enjoy the experience,' Sniper informed Thirteen. 'That molly carp's jaws even dented my armour so they should have no trouble with Prador shell.'

'Where is the Warden?' asked Thirteen, from the planet below.

'Dunno,' said Sniper, withdrawing.

Finding his position in a recently vacated silicon vastness the mind of the war drone asked of his surroundings, 'Is this subsumption, then? I don't feel any different.'

From behind a wall of paradox and short circuits in that vastness, the Warden replied, 'You know, Sniper, underestimation has been somewhat of a fault in your friends as well.'

'Waddaya mean by that?'

'I mean that, no, this is not subsumption, Sniper . . . for I had no wish to be subsumed by you.'

Sniper connected to the many links now available to him and inspected his vast surroundings through a thousand eyes, and he grinned . . . somehow.